Dead of Night

*Also by Randy Wayne White
in Large Print:*

Everglades
Tampa Burn
Twelve Mile Limit

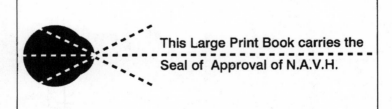

This Large Print Book carries the
Seal of Approval of N.A.V.H.

Dead of Night

Randy Wayne White

Thorndike Press • Waterville, Maine

Published in 2005 by arrangement with G. P. Putnam's Sons, a division of Penguin Group (USA) Inc.

Thorndike Press® Large Print Mystery.

The tree indicium is a trademark of Thorndike Press.

The text of this Large Print edition is unabridged. Other aspects of the book may vary from the original edition.

Set in 16 pt. Plantin by Al Chase.

Printed in the United States on permanent paper.

Library of Congress Cataloging-in-Publication Data

White, Randy Wayne.
    Dead of night / by Randy Wayne White.
       p. cm. — (Thorndike Press large print mystery)
    ISBN 0-7862-7845-5 (lg. print : hc : alk. paper)
    1. Ecoterrorism — Fiction.   2. Revenge — Fiction.
    3. Large type books.   I. Title.   II. Thorndike Press large print mystery series.
    PS3573.H47473D43 2005b
    813'.54—dc22   2005012553

This book is for my daughter,

Kate,

a dear and gifted young lady.

National Association for Visually Handicapped
-------------------------- *serving the partially seeing*

As the Founder/CEO of NAVH, the only national health agency solely devoted to those who, although not totally blind, have an eye disease which could lead to serious visual impairment, I am pleased to recognize Thorndike Press★ as one of the leading publishers in the large print field.

Founded in 1954 in San Francisco to prepare large print textbooks for partially seeing children, NAVH became the pioneer and standard setting agency in the preparation of large type.

Today, those publishers who meet our standards carry the prestigious "Seal of Approval" indicating high quality large print. We are delighted that Thorndike Press is one of the publishers whose titles meet these standards. We are also pleased to recognize the significant contribution Thorndike Press is making in this important and growing field.

Lorraine H. Marchi, L.H.D.
Founder/CEO
NAVH

★ Thorndike Press encompasses the following imprints: Thorndike, Wheeler, Walker and Large Print Press.

author's note

On Friday the thirteenth, August, in the year this book was written, the eye of a category 4 hurricane made landfall on Pine Island, west coast of Florida, and the storm's northeasterly tornado wall savaged the village of Pineland, where I've lived for many years.

It was as if a five-hundred-pound bomb exploded overhead. My 1920s Cracker house, built on an Indian mound overlooking the bay, had to be gutted because of water damage. My guesthouse was crushed, the houses of neighbors leveled, and acres of old tropical growth were flattened, including avocados, poinciana, key limes, and also three gumbo-limbo trees that were several hundred years old.

The irony that, five years earlier, I'd written about Marion Ford climbing an Indian mound to escape a category 4 hurricane with the same name (Charles) did not mitigate the difficulties that followed.

It was a month before I got water, six weeks before my power was restored, and, as far as I know, my phone at Pineland still doesn't work. I don't know because, three months later, I am still homeless, as are several neighbors.

Here is what I've learned: A hurricane is just bad weather, unless you are touched by the eye. But if you are in the path of that tornado phalanx, your life is forever changed.

I am happy to report that a disaster of Charley's magnitude mobilizes a lot more good people than the few who became profiteers. Many dozens offered me help, even their homes. I will forever be in their debt.

I am especially grateful to Jill Beckstead and Dean Beckstead, and the staff at Palm Island Resort, Cape Haze, Florida, a barrier island hideaway south of Sarasota and north of Fort Myers. Palm Island is a Florida classic: miles of beach, classy Gulf Coast architecture, few automobiles, swimming pools long enough for laps, and a fine restaurant, Rum Bay, where much of this book was written. During many busy lunches, the staff kindly tiptoed around me as I typed away. Chef Khoum, Jennifer Graham, Phyllis Muller, Walt Mintel, Dave Comello, Campi Campese, Capt. Blackie, Jay Hodges, Liam Crowley, and others very supportive.

Other places where people went out of

their way to provide me a place to write include Doc Ford's Sanibel Rum Bar and Grille, Sanibel Island, Matt Asen's Sanibel Grill, the staff of Pine Island Library, the staff of Holmes Beach Library, Sharkey's Steak on Bradenton Beach, the staff of Sanibel Library, and people associated with the *Queen Mary 2*, especially Ms. Mary Thomas, Sara Andersson, Jennifer Schaper, Laura Penfold, and Capt. Ronald Warwick's brilliant staff.

Others who were generous beyond the expectations of friendship include Sandra McNally, Gary and Donna Terwilliger, Mrs. Iris Tanner, Tom and Sally Petcoff, Capt. Steve Stanley, George and Michelle Riggs, Craig and Renee Johnson, Kevin and Nadine Lollar, Moe Mollen, Dr. Brian and Kristan Hummel, Capt. Craig Skaar, Bill Gutek and his Nokomis pals, the Wells family of Cabbage Key and Pineland, Bill Spaceman Lee, Diana, Ginny Amsler, Allan W. Eckert, and Jennifer Holloway. Wendy Webb — a gifted singer and songwriter — provided much needed musical relief, and Erin Edwards, and the band AMERICA, gave me an emotional lift when it was much needed.

This book demanded extensive research in several fields, and I am grateful to the experts who took the time to advise me. I'd like to thank Animal Planet's Jeff Corwin, a man who is as decent and funny off camera as he is on. Dr. Thaddeus Kostrubala, a brilliant psychopharmacologist, has once again provided behavioral profiles on some truly nasty fictional characters. Dr. James H. Peck, fellow Davenport Central (Iowa) graduate, has compiled exhaustive notes on all the Ford novels, and is due much thanks.

Also providing valuable aid or information were Dr. Kim Hull of Mote Marine, Dr. Bob Vincent, and Dr. Alan Rowan, both with the Florida Department of Health.

These people all provided valuable guidance and/or information. All errors, exaggerations, omissions, or fictionalizations are entirely the fault, and the responsibility, of the author.

Finally, the islands of Sanibel and Captiva sustained damage from the storm, but they not only survived, they are thriving, and open for business. As always, they are real places, faithfully described, but used fictitiously in this novel. The same is true of certain businesses, marinas, bars, and other places frequented by Doc Ford, Tomlinson, and pals.

Finally, I would like to thank my sons, Lee and Rogan White, for, once again, helping me finish a book.

Reptiles are abhorrent because of their cold body, pale color, cartilaginous skeleton, filthy skin, fierce aspect, calculating eye, offensive smell, harsh voice, squalid habitation, and terrible venom; wherefore their creator has not exerted his powers to make many of them.

— Carolus Linnaeus, 1758

Thou shalt not fear the terror of night;
nor the arrow that flieth by day;
nor the pestilence that walketh in
　darkness;
nor the destruction that wasteth at
　noonday.
A thousand may fall at thy side,
and ten thousand at thy right hand;
but it shall not come nigh thee.

— Psalm 91:5–7

1

serpiente

Solaris thought of her as "Snake Woman" because the first time she asked to see him, he thought she'd pointed at a crate just arrived from South Africa that contained leathery eggs and baby snakes.

He'd said, "Of course. You are the buyer, I am the seller. It is your right."

He wasn't the seller. Solaris was nineteen years old, lived with his family in Vinales, west of Cuba, eight people crowded into a shack near the village baseball diamond and communal fields where he'd plowed behind oxen until the Chinaman hired him as labor for his smuggling operation.

The Russian, whose name was Dasha, was blond, tall. Good teeth and skinny hips like women he'd seen in American magazines. Still aiming her finger at him, she'd smiled. "No. It's you I want to see. We're alone, aren't we?"

She'd come into the barn where the

Chinaman had organized the unloading of seventeen crates of African reptiles, parasites, spiders, and South American fish recently delivered in an old Soviet freight helicopter, a Kamov. It was a barn for drying tobacco. It smelled peppery and sour. Good, like the inside of a whiskey keg. Dusty light leaked through the wooden siding and roofing shingles. The interior seemed brighter when she pulled the door closed and slid the wooden bolt.

Yes. They were alone.

"My . . . *private* thing?" Was she joking?

"When you take your shirt off, your skin looks like it's stretched tight over cables. Every muscle vertical or horizontal. So I'm curious about the whole package. Don't be shy." Looking up into his eyes, she reached and cupped him in her fingers. Still holding him, she backed Solaris into shadows against the wooden wall, the pepper smell stronger now, staring into his face, her expression different: He was a toy, his reactions amusing.

"Is there a zipper?"

"No. Just my belt. I didn't expect —"

"Untie your belt. Or I could use my knife. It's only rope. Would you like that?"

Solaris fumbled with the knot, his fingers shaking as the woman pulled his pants down

14

over his hips, then to the floor, pausing to slowly retrace the curvature of his buttocks with the tips of her fingers.

"Step out of them."

She moved away as he kicked off his pants. Stood there like an artist, her pale eyes inspecting, vacuuming in color, angles, texture.

"Nice. So smooth."

Solaris was aroused, but he also felt ridiculous. Could this really be happening?

Now the woman was unbuttoning her blouse as she returned to him. He'd never seen skin so white.

He held his hands out to embrace her.

"*Stop.* Just stand there. Don't do anything."

He let his arms drop to his sides. "But if we are to make love, then you must let me —" Solaris stopped, not sure how to continue. The only woman he'd ever been with was a prostitute on the beach at Veradero, and that had lasted only a few minutes. How did a man go about making love, particularly with an older woman who was so certain of herself and aggressive?

The Russian saved him, barking, "This has nothing to do with love. I want to have fun after a shitty day. For *my* pleasure. Just stand there and keep your mouth closed."

15

Like all Russians, she spoke Spanish as if she had a bad cold and was coughing.

"Don't try to touch me again. Unless I give you permission."

He nodded. Stood upright, shaking, not wanting to ruin it.

Her voice was dense and sleepy once again. "He has eyes. The way he follows my body. What does he remind you of?"

A picture came into Solaris's mind of a man wearing a turban, sitting before a woven basket, playing a flute. A cobra followed the movement of the flute, head swaying.

Culebra.

Another reason he thought of her as the Snake Woman.

Serpiente.

The way she was holding him, fingers gripped, steering him into the shadows as if he had wheels, Solaris realized something that he would later find unsettling. He'd been born with this weakness. Maybe all men were.

A man with his built-in leash.

They'd been coming to Vinales, western Cuba, for the past sixteen months, arriving in a Volvo limo, or by small helicopter, dropping over rock towers into the valley beneath mountains where coffee grew green in summer, white when bushes bloomed.

There were two, Dasha, the blond Russian, with an older American man who had money, no mistaking it. It was an attitude, the way the man's eyes blurred, empty as a camera lens, indifferent to breathing things that were tiny, peasants who would die in silence.

Dr. Desmond Stokes.

Rich Americans, they never had to open their mouths. As a boy, Solaris had pushed an ice cart around the docks of Marina Hemingway west of Havana. He knew.

They came every other month, sometimes more, the two of them alone, or with an associate. Usually a gigantic Russian with black hair that grew out of his ears like a wolf. Aleski was the wolf's name.

Once, they'd brought a nervous little man with glasses who carried a microscope in a case. A biologist of some type. He'd jumped at unexpected sounds. Began to cry when they told him he had to fly in the helicopter again.

Solaris had never seen an adult man cry. Disgusting. Even so, the woman treated the little man like he was important. Spent time off alone, whispering.

Usually, though, Dasha was with Dr.

Stokes. He allowed her to leave his side only when he talked privately with the Chinaman. Business. Money. Powerful chiefs cutting a deal.

Actually, the Chinaman was Vietnamese, Bat-tuy Nguyen. A fat man who wore bright scarves, gold jewelry, who'd learned the exotic animal trade from someone named Keng Wong. This was before Wong got extradited from Mexico to the U.S., and was sentenced to twenty-five years.

"The best known rare animal dealer in the world," Nguyen told Solaris. It was part of the sales pitch when the Chinaman recruited Solaris and his uncle, who was in charge of the village landing strip.

Same with the article about Wong in *El Mundo*, part of which read: ". . . reptiles rate third as the world's most lucrative commodity to smuggle, after firearms and drugs. According to U.N. officials, the trade is worth about $10 billion internationally. It is further evidence that capitalism must destroy natural resources to fuel its own growth. . . ."

The article was written months before the Bearded One died. Before world crime syndicates rushed into the political vacuum to stake out territory.

Cubans no longer cared about politics,

only dollars. And survival.

"If you work hard, learn how the business works, maybe you'll one day be as rich as the great Keng Wong!" the Chinaman told him and his uncle.

His cynical uncle had replied, "If the *Chino* is so great, why is he in a Yankee prison?" but they accepted jobs anyway.

Nguyen did a surprising business, using the village as his rendezvous place and warehouse. He imported strange creatures, illegal products from all over the world. Not drugs, though. Too risky. Better wealthy collectors than desperate addicts.

The clients were from the U.S., sometimes Europe or Colombia.

Once, Solaris said to the Chinaman, "What kind of people buy this shit?"

Nguyen told him, "We sell to a few scientists who can't get permits, men looking for cures for cancer, high blood pressure, whatever. Discover a drug that works, you're rich forever. Like Dr. Stokes, when he lost his license and got run out of the U.S. That's how I started with him. Just snakes at first, now everything."

Otherwise, the Chinaman said, most of their clients were people so protected by their wealth that they enjoyed toying with danger.

"It's why I know we'll make money. Something that's illegal and dangerous — it's a way of showing off. One of the scorpions in that cage?" He'd pointed at scorpions with robotic tails as thick as the fat man's thumb. "They cost us twenty cents, U.S. A penny if we hatch them from eggs, which we've been doing. Calcutta funeral scorpions — poisonous, but not as dangerous as people think. Because of the name, we can charge two or three hundred dollars a pair. Where else can collectors buy them?"

Speaking of "us" and "we" as if Solaris and his uncle were getting part of the profit instead of the wrinkled dollar bills the fat man stuffed into their hands at the end of the day.

"Komodo dragons? They kill a man by biting his stomach open, eating his guts. The rarest of rare. In Indonesia, we buy a dozen Komodo eggs for twenty dollars, ship them like gold for a thousand. If only three hatch? There's a group of ranchers in Texas who buy all the Komodos I can deliver at fifty thousand cash, no questions as long as their veterinarian okays the animal.

"Man-children. They wear loincloths, carry torches at night, hunt the lizards with spears. Probably paint their faces and scream at the moon. Play caveman, then go home and enter their wives from behind. Who knows? They tell me dragon tail tastes like eagle squab."

African mambas, the Chinaman said, were the most dangerous snakes on earth. They moved over the ground faster than a racehorse; grew more than five meters long. Australian death vipers were a better example, because of the name. For an adult female death viper, he could get five, ten thousand. If the female was gravid — "they're live-bearers," he explained — twice that.

"Both are listed among the ten most venomous snakes in the world," he said. "It's like a sports title. Deadly, so valuable. Understand what I'm telling you?"

Solaris was in charge of maintaining storage barns, procuring feed, keeping track of inventory. Also, he was big enough to scare anyone thinking about robbing the place.

The morning Snake Woman lured him into the barn for the first time, he'd copied the Chinaman's writing onto a clipboard.

Sold to Dr. Desmond Stokes:
25 dozen African mamba eggs & hatchlings

10 death adders, 6 gravid females
25 pint containers of thick-tailed
   scorpion eggs & hatchlings
50-liter drum/parasites, West Africa
50-liter drum/mosquito larvae, Brazil
50-liter drum/sewage, East Africa
14 laboratory rats test-positive,
   cholera, Johannesburg

Cholera? *Madre de Jesus*. The things they ordered were always like that. Weird. Dangerous. Dirty.

What sort of research was that strange man doing? This was not like the pet store toys other clients wanted.

But God, the blond Russian, what a body. Solaris would think of her at night, his four younger brothers asleep in the same room, and try not to tremble.

The Chinaman wasn't dumb. He caught on quick about what the two of them were doing alone in the tobacco barn.

"She'll be the death of you," the fat man said one afternoon, not laughing.

Solaris took it as a joke. "But that woman loves me so much, what a way to go!"

But the fat man was right.

2

Aside from a strange, shy message on an answering machine, the first words I heard Jobe Applebee speak were: "Please, don't hit me again. My brain . . . you don't understand. I *can't.*"

The way he said it, "I can't," sounded touchingly childlike. This thirty-some-year-old man wasn't begging. He was apologizing. Telling the blond woman who was beating him that he wanted to cooperate. He simply didn't know how.

Only a minute or two before, I'd been standing on the porch of Applebee's secluded island home on Lake Toho, Central Florida, in citrus, cattle, bass boat, and Disney country. I'd stood there feeling out of place, a little silly, looking up at all the dark gables and darker windows of the man's solitary three-story. I would have guessed the place was empty but for a golf cart umbilicaled to a charger next to the porch.

Golf carts are standard transportation in Florida's island communities. Drive them to the boat dock when leaving, drive them home upon return. The cart meant that Applebee probably was inside.

I didn't know the man. Had never met him. I was there because I'd made a reluctant promise to his sister, a friend.

It was a promise I already regretted.

As I stood there trying to decide what to do, I grunted and I sighed, made the silly, adolescent sounds that a person utters when he's about to continue some damn, silly task he doesn't want to continue. I certainly did *not* want to do this, but, as Applebee's sister pointed out, I am an ever-dependable pushover. I am Marion D. Ford, the amiable marine biologist, bookworm nerd, collector of sea creatures, and "wouldn't hurt a flea, cheery sunset cohort who can't say no to a pal."

My friend's words.

Finally, I stepped onto Applebee's porch, went to the door.

There wasn't a bell, so I leaned to knock . . . then stopped, knuckles poised, head tilted, listening to an unexpected sound. Stood for long seconds straining to identify an indistinct moaning. It was a noise that someone in pain might make. Or someone frightened. Or someone trying to pull a very bad joke.

This was no joke. The moaning was coming from the rear of the house.

Quietly, I tested the doorknob. Locked.

I waited, ears focused . . . heard it again: Someone in pain.

Hurrying now, I swung over the porch railing, and jogged to the rear of the house. That's when I heard Applebee's frightened, apologetic voice; heard him in person for the first time: "Please, don't hit me again. My brain . . . you don't understand. I *can't*."

Heard the words during a lull in the music that was being played loud, probably to cover the man's pleading, and then his scream: "Stop, *please*. I can't stand this!"

In bizarre contrast was the music, a Disney tune that even I recognized. Something about it being a small world after all.

The sound of a grown man begging detonates all the primitive caveman alarms. Terror has a distinctive pitch. We hear it through the base of the skull, not the auditory canal, and it's interpreted as an electric prickle down the spine.

I waited until the music resumed, then began to move toward a set of French doors from which Applebee's voice drifted. As I did, I fished a cellular phone out of my pocket, dialed 911. To the woman who answered, I whispered, "There's a man being assaulted on an island, south of Orlando. Night's Landing . . . no . . . *Nightshade* Landing. House number thirty-nine; owner's name is Applebee. Dr. Jobe Applebee. Get a police boat or a chopper out here A-S-A-P. I'm going to try and help."

I listened long enough to make certain she understood, then shoved the phone into my pocket.

There was a smaller porch at the rear entrance. I stepped up onto the deck, and pressed my face to the double glass doors. Through a space in the curtains, I saw the little man I knew to be Applebee — recognizable because he's the fraternal twin of the sister who'd asked me to check on him.

Even with Applebee's bloodied face, the likeness was unmistakable.

He was sitting on a chair in the dimly lighted space, dressed like an underpaid junior college professor: charcoal slacks, white shirt with a collar stiff enough to hold a clip-on tie. He was barefooted, which gave the peculiar impression that he was unclothed.

Men like Jobe Applebee do not go around

without socks and shoes.

On his right ankle was a sloppy surgical dressing of gauze and tape. Maybe that's why he was shoeless. He had a minor injury. It seemed a further indignity that the bandage was visible.

He had his face buried in his hands, rocking rhythmically even though the chair wasn't a rocker. Nose and lips were bleeding, glasses askew. He had angular features, more feminine than his sister. His body was frail, as if his bone scaffolding were made of balsa wood.

Two people stood over him. One, a man, was behind the chair, his hands on Applebee's shoulders, steadying him, while the other, a woman, crouched in front, a leather belt doubled in her right hand. That moronic song had begun to play yet again — *It's a small world!* — but I was close enough to hear the woman say in clumsy English, "Why you make us do this thing to you? You think I like hitting your face, idiot? Tell us what we want to know. Then we stop. We all be friends afterward."

I watched as the woman used the belt to slap Jobe's face sideways. It made an ugly, bullwhip *th-WHACK* against flesh.

She was Eastern European, probably Russian. Her accent was as telling as the high Slavic cheeks and forehead, the short chin, the high nasal bridge. She was tall — over six feet. Lean, athletic, flat chested with skinny ballerina hips, long sprinter's legs, and short ballerina blond hair.

The man was her opposite. He was oxlike, with curly, shoulder-length black hair, and dense body pelt showing on arms, the backs of his hands, and neck. His face had similar Slavic characteristics.

He wore the sort of workman's pants you find in chain outlets, and an equally cheap T-shirt, breast pocket squared by a box of cigarettes. The woman, though, dressed like she had money: pleated boating slacks and a baggy, silken blouse that gave her a traditional peasant look.

I'd seen the style when I was in Moscow.

Conclusion: Two immigrants from the former Soviet Union. Suspicion: Russians who slip into the U.S. illegally are often black marketers. They bring their talents with them. Crime is what they know best.

So maybe I was witnessing a robbery, or a crime-for-hire.

Ancillary impression: The woman enjoyed her role as abusive interrogator. She was the sort of person, typically male, who should be boxed up and studied like a bug.

This all went through my mind as

subtext. I was more concerned with whatever weapons they might be carrying. Charging in, getting shot, wasn't going to help anyone. I do dumb things on a regular basis, but seldom intentionally.

I held my glasses to my face as I touched my right eye to the door's window. If they were armed, it wasn't obvious. No telltale bulge of pocket, or pant cuff.

I was still watching as the woman used the belt on the little man again. Slapped him hard, then hit his face again.

Yeah . . . she *liked* it.

After that, I wasn't thinking anymore. Just reacting.

I took three long steps backward, then charged the door, shoulder down.

Even though we'd never met, the guy I was attempting to rescue seemed worth rescuing. Jobe Applebee, Ph.D., was the twin brother of my old friend Dr. Frieda Applebee Matthews, both considered by peers to be among Florida's finest field biologists.

Frieda is an authority on Caribbean sea mammals. The manatee, a hippo-sized, fluke-tailed estuarine mammal, is her specialty. You seldom read a newspaper story on the animal in which she is not quoted, or a scientific paper on the species in which her work is not referenced.

Brother Jobe was a hydrobiologist, an expert on the flow of nutrient pollution through karstic systems: how water makes its way through regions of porous limestone, plus the impact once the contaminants have spread.

Freshwater was his main interest, but I'd read some of his papers relating to salt water as well. He'd done work with deep-ocean blowholes and freshwater springs found a hundred miles out at sea. His data suggested that karsts channel ways to transport the same poisons you'd expect to find in garbage dumps of industrial towns.

Really excellent stuff. Painstaking and professional, but also brilliant in the same quirky, left-field way my old hipster pal, Tomlinson, is brilliant. Tomlinson, the unrepentant social revolutionary, drug fancier, and Zen Buddhist monk who might say something like, "Jogging is a masochistic form of bulimia, only in the active tense," then give you a perfectly logical explanation for why the statement's justified.

Applebee had the same weird gift. In a couple of his papers, he started with premises that seemed unlikely at first pass, but then he backed the data with a series of unexpected proofs, all from oddball angles (anomalies in his field, at least) to reach what I considered to be virtuoso conclusions. The way he stacked figures and minutiae suggested a penchant for the obsessive — not a bad thing for a scientist.

Numbers. The man loved numbers.

People who'd worked with him said that he was as introverted as his sister Frieda was outgoing. She lived in Tallahassee, the state capital, and was at ease drinking cocktails with lobbyists and upper-echelon bureaucrats. As a researcher and environmental consultant, her work required that kind of interaction, but she also enjoyed it.

Her brother, the lady told me, never socialized.

My friend Frieda lives with a much-loved husband and young son. Brother Jobe had lived alone his entire adult life, much of it on an island in a lake south of Orlando. As far as she knew, the only time he went out was to buy necessities, or to do fieldwork.

She'd written me that in an e-mail the week before, then added, "He'll at least answer the phone, though. But he hasn't for the last three days. I'm worried about him. I wouldn't ask, but you said you were driving to Vero Beach to go surfing, which means, coming and going across the state, his house isn't that far out of your way. Plus, you're trailering your boat. You'd have access. I know it's a pain in the butt but would you mind stopping and checking on Jobe?"

I'd made the mistake of mentioning that I was supposed to meet Tomlinson at Sebastian Inlet, north of Vero Beach, to try my hand at surfing. The Atlantic has bigger, more dependable waves than Florida's Gulf Coast. But just in case a nor'easter wasn't blowing, I was also bringing my twenty-one-foot skiff so we could poke around the Indian River Aquatic Preserve, an interesting estuary separated from open sea by a strand of barrier islands.

"Skiff" is another word for a fast, shallow water boat with low freeboard.

So, yes, it was true that a detour to see her brother would not take me far off course. The woman was familiar enough with my habits to know that I avoid driving interstate highways. Hate the damn things. So the route from my little stilt house, Dinkin's Bay, Sanibel Island, on the Gulf Coast, to the much busier Atlantic Coast would wind me through Florida's agricultural, theme-parked, and water-rich interior. It would take me within a few miles of the lake, and the tiny island development where her brother lived.

I didn't like the idea of interceding in someone's personal business, and wasn't comfortable imposing on a reclusive man I'd never met. Friends — true friends — show up when there's trouble, or work to be done, and stay long after everyone else is leaving or has left. Friends are also obligated to intercede if the situation warrants. But I wasn't the man's friend.

So I put her off, saying I'd think about it — my cowardly way of declining.

When Tomlinson called an hour or so later, though, he told me I was behaving like a thoughtless jerk.

Actually, he told me I was trying to avoid my "own preordained karma concerning a man you are destined to meet," but his tone communicated what he really felt.

"Jobe Applebee is Frieda's brother?" he added, surprised and impressed. "I've never met him, but I saw a diorama he built. It was featured at a rally in Coconut Grove a few months back. Mind-blowing. Incredible."

Most people think of dioramas as three-dimensional models of events like famous battles, but they're also used for settings like the interlinkings of natural habitats: a mangrove forest, a saw grass prairie.

When I asked, he told me the rally had been hosted by something called the Albedo

Society. "A very sporty group of souls who believe the earth is a single organism that regulates her own well-being. The name has something to do with the earth's color when it's healthy, seen from outer space."

There were a couple thousand people, he said. Speeches, a unity march to the nuclear power plant, and lots and lots of get naked and go swimming types.

I wondered why Applebee, a respected hydrobiologist, would join something like that. If he had.

The diorama was incredible, according to Tomlinson, a work of art: underground river systems, South Florida bionetworks.

"The guy who created it had his shit together. A couple of us asked around, wanted to say howdy, but I guess he doesn't make the public appearance scene. Doc, if you don't stop and check on the man, I *will*. At least call his sister back and get a few more details."

Tomlinson seldom pressures.

I called.

Frieda told me that building dioramas was one of her brother's recent passions.

"Obsessions," she said. "That's more accurate. It's his nature, so anything less than museum quality wouldn't be acceptable."

34

I'd told her Tomlinson's reaction.

She knew the story, although she'd yet to see his newest work. He'd been contracted to create a data model of South Florida's subterranean aquifers, then convert the data into charts. "Aqua-geology." Her word.

"Who's the contractor? Tomlinson mentioned a group called the 'Albedo Society.'" At first, I couldn't picture an introverted scientist hanging out with Tomlinson types, but maybe it was a good thing. Healthy for both.

"Actually, I think it was one of the big sugar companies. Tropicane? I'll ask him. Or you can ask him when you meet. Either way, Jobe wouldn't care who hired him. He lives for his work."

What Applebee created far exceeded specifications. Instead of charts, he built a three-dimensional model. A diorama so detailed, Frieda said, that it was more like a satellite photo — if satellites could photograph what's beneath the ground.

A friend had told her about it, not her brother. He seldom shared personal information, even with her. She didn't know why.

There was a lot she didn't know about her brother, she said. For instance: Why hadn't

35

he returned her calls?

Using my shoulder to hold a phone to my ear, I listened to her say, "It's just him alone in that great big house. I'd contact his neighbors if I had some names, but I don't. And asking the police to stop by, well . . . that would scare him. It'd be way too much emotional trauma for someone like Jobe."

Her inflection left the statement open-ended, maybe inviting questions, maybe not. Applebee was a brilliant recluse. She was hinting that he also had some emotional instabilities.

But then she added, "You two might hit it off, professionally. The only friend Jobe has is his laboratory. You're both goofy that way. And you've both obsessed with water, with what goes on among those three tricky atoms. Plus, he's a fan. Did you know?"

I said, "Huh? I've got a fan?"

"*Fans,* sweetie. My brother's read your papers; a lot of us have. And Jobe's kind of a star himself. Nobody knows more about groundwater, and how it flows. If you two kooks put your collective heads together, all your knowledge about the environment, it could be a damn good connection for this screwed-up state of ours."

That sealed it. In a subtle way, Frieda had withdrawn her request that I go on a snooping mission, and transformed it into an elevated meeting between two biologists. A professional courtesy call.

"You're driving across the state Saturday?"

I told her no, I was driving over tomorrow — Friday — coming back Sunday.

"Excellent. Then you will be able to stop and say hello . . ."

I had no out. We both knew it, which is why she was laughing when I replied, "Why is it I feel like I've just been leveraged by a master?"

The lady had a nice laugh; lots of joy, with a hint of the devil. "It's because you haven't spent enough time in Tallahassee to recognize a master. Florida has an annual budget that's creeping close to seventy billion. Bigger than lots of sovereign nations. Centralize that kind of power in a small town, and that's where you're going to find the real manipulators. Compared to some of the sharks here, I'm just a toothless dogfish."

I found a notepad. "I guess this is where I write directions. You knew I'd say yes, so you've already figured out the best route for me to take. Correct?"

The woman thought that was hilarious. "Damn tootin', sweetie. You'd make an awful woman, 'cause you just don't know how to say no. Either that, or a very, very popular one."

When I finished talking with Frieda, I let my eyes move around the lab, taking refuge in its orderliness. My lab's one of two houses built over water on pilings, beneath a communal tin roof. I'd chosen the largest of the two as a workplace. A lucky call. The lab's where I spend most of my time, and where visitors prefer to gather if it's too hot, or rainy on the deck outside.

I prefer functional to fancy. Not everyone does. A disapproving lady visitor once told me the place was a cross between Tom Sawyer's raft and a castaway's tree house. She pretended not to be offended when I thanked her.

Some people are lucky enough to find their life's love. I've found my life's home in this drafty, salt-glazed wooden vessel — which is another rare kind of luck. It's a good place for a biologist who makes his living collecting and selling marine specimens, but who also enjoys socializing with fellow islanders with a beer or two at sunset.

I like approaching the building by boat, seeing the horizontal banding of clapboard exterior balanced on stork-legged pilings, the tin roof pitched like the bow of an Indonesian junk, all framed by deck railings.

The place also possesses a distinctive olfactory mix — which is something else not everyone appreciates. It's a fusion of ozone from aquarium aerators, graphite from precision instruments, chemical reagents, and formalin all mixed with odors that sift through the wooden floor: the smell of barnacles, creosote, and salt water.

On the walls are shelves of books, lab instruments, paintings and pictures tacked at eye level so I can look at them if I want, chemicals in jars, and rows of tanks that hold fish, crabs, shrimp, bivalves, and mollusks — including one goat-eyed octopus that now watched me, its focus as intense as my own.

Octopi are the geniuses of their phylum. I was the entity that delivered a crab into its tank daily. To this animal, I was food. If it were larger, or if I were smaller, it would have stalked, dispatched, and eaten me with equal relish.

I stood alone for a few moments in the middle of the room, and let my attention settle on a 250-gallon aquarium into which I'd released five newly born bull sharks; genus: *Carcharhinus,* species: *leucas.* My son, Laken, visiting from Central America, had helped me build the thing, rig the filters and aerators, so the water inside was Gulf Stream clear. The finger-sized sharks were active, always moving. They seemed to be acclimating just fine.

I've had a long-standing interest in bull sharks; spent a lifetime traveling the same jungle rivers and remote sea places they inhabit. I find their ability to prevail in dissimilar environments fascinating. They roam tropic waters worldwide, commonly forage hundreds of miles up rivers, and can thrive in freshwater lakes.

Because the species is identified by various names — Zambezi River shark, the Lake Nicaragua shark — it's not widely known that it's responsible for more serious attacks on humans than great whites.

In popular literature, bull sharks are often described as "ferocious," which is misleading because the word implies emotion. *Efficient* — that's more accurate, and the way I prefer to think of them.

I'd discovered these five pups while doing a necropsy on a two-hundred-pound female one of the guides brought in. Finding living young inside a shark isn't uncommon. But three of these fish were uncommon, which is why I'd rigged this big tank. Like the mother, three of the five had visible spinal deformities. It was probably a genetic defect, though it might have been caused by waterborne contaminants. Whatever the source, the deformity was unusual in the cartilaginous fishes. A first, in my experience.

The big female had found a way to survive. Would her young?

On a table near the aquarium was a leather-bound daybook in which I'd been keeping lab notes, a things-to-do list, a few personal observations on people and events. It was novel-sized, with SHIP'S LOG embossed on the cover. A salty touch, but a tad theatrical. It was a present from my son, so I used it.

That morning, as had become habit, I opened the log and noted date, tides, and moon phase, before writing:

5 immature specimens, C. *leucas*, 18 cm long +/-. 3 exhibit obvious spinal deformities rarely reported in sharks or rays, but common in bony fishes. I've found only two cases of deformed elasmobranchs, both bull sharks, both collected in Florida waters (Eugenie Clark, 1964; Mote Marine Laboratory). Deformities include: scoliosis (lateral spinal curvature), lordosis (axial spinal

curvature), and kyphosis (humpback curves). . . .

I also made some personal notes. Wrote more than usual, referencing Lake, my girlfriend Dewey Nye, and Tomlinson. No one is entirely the person he or she appears to be. We all inhabit a more solitary dimension in which we deal with our secret aspirations and fears; frailties seldom suspected even by those closest.

It's true for me. I didn't realize to what extent until I began keeping daily notes. Writing allowed me to fret or inspect on a private level, so I now carried the journal even when I traveled.

It wasn't long before I transitioned back from personal matters to the more interesting subject of sharks:

No field observations on immature sharks with skeletal abnormalities have been published. Does deformity = handicap? Am I wrong to suspect lineage between these fish, and the abnormal bull sharks collected by Dr. Clark several decades ago?

I was excited about the project. Which is why I was proportionately pissed off at myself for saying yes to Frieda. Did I really want to go off and leave the sharks, leave my work, to look for some oddball biologist who lived on an island in the middle of the state?

No, I didn't. Hell no. Didn't want to leave Sanibel. The longer I live where I live, the more I dislike being away. Hate missing a good sunset. Hate missing the 5:00 a.m. silence of a fresh tropical morning.

But the woman had me.

Before I'd received her first Internet message, I'd even already formulated a plausible excuse for not making the surfing trip. But now I was committed.

Tomlinson and I are close enough that it would have been okay to bail. He'd have understood. But I didn't know Frieda well enough to disappoint her.

3

LOG
10 Dec. Friday
Low tide: 10:21 a.m.; Tortuga's wind 15 knots. Night jasmine, and owls during talk with Laken about paternal genetics.

He's interested for a reason. . . .

Checklist: 1. Cat food @ Bailey's. 2. Reserve hotel, Vero Bch. 3. Learn to say no, dumbass.
— MDF

LOG
11 Dec. Saturday
(Driftwood Motel, Sebastian Inlet)

. . . too clumsy for surfing, shins all bruised. Tomlinson's weird pals driving me nuts & worried about my sharks. Home tomorrow. Prefer windsurfing.
— MDF

So it was on a blue bright Atlantic Coast

Sunday, just before sunset, the twelfth of December, and only slightly more than twelve days before Christmas, when I detoured to check on Frieda's brother. I'd left Tomlinson with his gaggle of new surfer pals, old doper buddies and adoring Zen students, dropped off the crappy rental at Ron Jon's Surf Shop in Cocoa Beach, and drove my truck inland.

I could have stopped at Applebee's home two days earlier, on my way to Sebastian Inlet, but procrastination is a powerful copilot when it comes to unpleasant duties. I wanted to put this one off as long as I could.

Later, my conscience would play the inevitable game of "What if . . ."

What if I *had* stopped by the man's home on Friday instead of Sunday night? What if I hadn't interrupted the two people who were interrogating and beating him? Would he have lived? Or would he have died? And what would have happened then?

I had Frieda's directions on a square of paper stuck to the truck's dashboard, so I knew he lived on a lake twenty-some miles south of Orlando, and slightly southeast of Kissimmee, on a little unincorporated island I'd never heard of, Nightshade Landing, Bartram County.

Nightshade grew wild on the island,

Frieda told me. The bushes were something to see come spring, all those white blooms. Even so, locals had shortened the name to Night's Landing. Typical. Boat access only, she said, which is why the place had never really flourished — even though real estate values had soared because of Orlando's theme park boom.

"Night's Landing is about a hundred acres, but the population can't be more than a few dozen people. In the early nineteen hundreds, some New York developer tried to create his own little Cape Cod. But he so sufficiently pissed off the local power structure that they refused to build the bridge he was counting on. Plus, most of the properties have title problems. It's tough to sell or resell what you can't prove you own. Which is why he never finished the project."

She'd added, "I think the island's a little creepy. A few sand roads, all Victorian houses. Some abandoned. Lots of gables, turrets, towers, and New England porches. The kind of architecture that a New Yorker would think of as classy. The island's perfect for Jobe, though. It's the sort of place that people don't go to live. They go there to disappear. Or hide."

The scrap of paper also contained her brother's phone number. On my way to

Kissimmee, I used my cell phone. Tried three times. Got nothing but his short, shy phone message: "I am not available. Try again. Or leave your name, number and the first four digits of your birth date, zeros included."

Birth date, zeros included?

Weird. Did that suggest an interest in astrology? It didn't mesh with what I knew about the man — nor any responsible scientist I've ever known.

Another unusual thing was that he spoke with the careful, halting diction that I've come to associate with people who have speech impediments, or drunks who are trying their best to convince police that they are not drunk.

I'd read his papers.

The man wasn't a drunk.

When I got to Kissimmee, I dialed and listened to his recorder for a fourth time. Wrestled with the decision to launch my boat and go bang on his door, or buy time by having dinner. Maybe he was outside taking a long walk, or just getting back from a research trip, or maybe working in his lab.

If I could get him to answer the phone and confirm that he was fine, my obligation to Frieda would be fulfilled.

Never in my life did I ever think I'd own a cellular phone. Now I seemed tied to the damn thing.

I drove along Kissimmee's oak-lined and Christmas-bespangled main boulevard, Broadway, finally found a triple-big parking space for my truck and boat trailer in the heart of downtown next to Shore's Men's Wear and Joanne's Diner. A gas station attendant had told me the diner served good country-fried steak, collards, and iced tea. Florida's restaurant fare proves that the state has become the Midwest's southernmost possession. I wasn't going to miss a chance for some authentic Southern cooking.

But Joanne's was closed for some reason on this early Sunday eve, so I roamed around town to get the kinks out of my legs, and to give Dr. Jobe more time to materialize. I looked at plastic snowmen and candy cane decorations. I tried to decipher inscriptions on a stonework called "THE MONUMENT OF STATES." Stood beneath a streetlight and watched an Amtrak passenger train *clickety-clack* its way through downtown, bells ringing, red lights flashing, on its way to somewhere far, far north of the horizon.

It was a little after 6:30 p.m. three days

past the dark of the moon; the sort of black night that invests city parks, benches, and trees with a glistening, winter incandescence. The air had a hint of cool; tasted of snow.

Half an hour later, I was sitting at the bar of the Kissimmee Steak House out on Bronson Monument Road, eating an unexpectedly fine piece of beef while the affable bartender told me about the local fishing woes. The city sits on the northern shore of nineteen-thousand-acre Lake Tohopekaliga — called "Lake Toho," locally. It's one of a hundred or so lakes that comprise the freshwater headwaters for the Everglades system.

As Tomlinson is quick to point out, one of the earth's few unique ecosystems — Florida's River of Grass — actually begins on the outskirts of Orlando. "The *real* Magic Kingdom," he often adds.

But things weren't going too well for anglers on Lake Toho, the bartender told me.

"Last year, the state wildlife people decided the lake needed what they call a 'drawdown.' It's like an artificial drought to lower the water level so exotic plants and stuff that's not supposed to be there can die and be hauled out. But the state people emptied so much water into the Kissimmee

River and Lake Okeechobee, that local marinas — Richardson's Fish Camp, Skinny Al's, some others — you couldn't use the boat ramps. The canals was just mud. I haven't been out fishing for nearly a year! They're letting the water level come up now, and fishing's supposed to be great once they're done. But we'll see."

Some perverse part of me was heartened by low water and difficult boat ramps. If I couldn't launch my skiff, then I couldn't check on Frieda's brother, could I?

But at Big Toho Marina, not far from downtown, I was told there was plenty of water, and I'd have no trouble at all floating a boat.

So at a little after 8 p.m. on a winter Sunday night, I launched among docks where a bunch of bass boats were moored — fast, low freeboard craft that, to me, always look as if they were designed by people who should be building customized vans for a living. The boats seemed gaudy, with their carpeted Corvette appointments, vinyl swivel seats, and fiberglass glitter. In comparison, my twenty-one-foot Maverick flats skiff appeared as functionally staid as a knife blade; an outlander without makeup, or ribbons.

I idled alone out into the darkness, running lights shining.

I didn't have a chart, but had been told that Night's Landing was only a mile or so from shore. Not hard to find — even on a black night.

It wasn't.

Nor was it difficult for me to locate the island's communal docks. The narrow channel wasn't far from the steady car traffic and lights of the road it paralleled, and only a few hundred yards or so from an area buoyed off for competitive waterskiing — or so a big, white wedge of floating ski ramp suggested.

I idled down the channel, into a marina basin where a sign next to several empty slips, a pontoon boat, and an overpowered bass boat, warned: RESIDENTS ONLY, ALL OTHERS PROSECUTED. THIS MEANS YOU!

Friendly place.

The lone bass boat was a twenty-footer; well maintained, but the person who'd moored the thing had left the huge Yamaha outboard in the water — not something watermen do when securing a boat. An aluminum motor casing in electrically charged water creates electrolysis, and it's also a platform for barnacles or mussels.

It was a lapse that only an experienced,

anal-retentive boater would notice.

Someone like me.

It took a quarter hour of wandering poorly marked sand trails before I was standing on the porch of Applebee's secluded three-story home. I stood there looking up at all the dark windows and darker turrets, fuming because I was here and not halfway home by now. If it wasn't for the damn golf cart plugged to its charger, I'd have concluded he was gone. No use trying.

Now, instead, I raised my fist to knock . . . and then stopped when I heard the indistinct moaning of a man in pain.

Seconds later, I was standing at the glass doors of the back entrance, peering in between the curtains. I could see that it was Frieda's twin brother, the gifted, reclusive biologist, face bloodied, expression terrified.

It was Applebee, my colleague who built amazing dioramas, the expert on the interlinks of water.

A man worth rescuing.

The back doors were locked. But French doors are notoriously poor security risks, and these imploded on their dead bolt when I took two short sprint steps, and crashed my shoulder into the midframe, just above the brass handle.

I had a lot of adrenaline, sufficient weight, and momentum when I hit. The doors were flimsier than I'd anticipated, which is why they barely slowed me, and I went stumbling, clawing, falling into the room . . . and continued to stumble across the floor, out of control, trailing splintered wood, shattered glass, plus the door's lace curtain, which had somehow gotten tangled over my head, covering my face like a shroud.

Because of the curtain, I couldn't see. But I could hear a man and woman scream Russian words of surprise just before I collided with someone — no telling who — then hit something else hard but moveable. A chair?

Whatever it was cut the legs out from under me. I somersaulted forward, my right shoulder down, and used the momentum to roll immediately back to my feet just as a good CPO had taught us to tumble and roll long ago. One thing the CPO hadn't taught us to do, though, was to use that fluid energy to vault ourselves face-first into a stucco wall. Which is what I did.

Poor judgment became dark comedy.

I hit the wall squarely. Felt an ether-like explosion inside my head, and saw a starburst of expanding colors. The next thing I knew, I was sitting up groggily, pulling a damp and scarlet-stained curtain off my head, wondering who in the room was bleeding.

Me. I was the one bleeding. It had to be me because the Russians had bolted, leaving Jobe and me alone. The little man was in the corner, balled up in a fetal position, still rocking, face showing his own blood.

I sat there for a moment, listening to him whisper in mantric rhythm: "Leave me alone. . . . Please leave me alone. . . . Leave me alone, alone, alone, please. . . ."

The Russians didn't have much of a head start — I could hear the dissipating racket of limbs crashing. Before I started after them, though, I wanted to make sure Applebee was okay. I got to my feet, wiped my hands on my fishing shorts, and knelt beside him. I touched him on the shoulder, before saying, "It's okay, Jobe. They're gone. You're safe. Jobe? Dr. Applebee?"

The man didn't respond. He seemed deaf; his eyes glazed, catatonic. He continued to chant, "Leave me alone, please leave me alone. . . ."

I spoke louder; gave his shoulder a quick shake. That got a reaction. The little man screamed, and began to flap his hands. "No more! Please no more. I can't . . . I can't. . . . I'm sorry, I *can't*."

Kept yelling until I took my hand away.

Once again, I was struck by the childlike quality of his voice. Once again, I got the impression that this distinguished scientist wasn't begging. He was apologizing for an inability to cope.

I tried a final time to get a response. Nothing.

Applebee was frozen by pathology; hysteria that would not tolerate outside stimuli. He wasn't capable of communication. Not now, not with me.

I stood, took my cell phone from my pocket, and slid it next to him, after a moment of indecision. "The police have this number, so answer if it rings. My name's Ford, I'm your sister's friend. Tell the cops. I'm going after them, the people who were beating you."

The frail man was balled up like an embryo, eyes glassy with terror.

I jogged off through the broken doorway.

4

The woman looked like a sprinter because she was. An athlete. She had that kind of freaky quickness. I was still a hundred yards or so away from the communal docks, running as hard as she was, when I heard an outboard engine start.

Her ox-sized accomplice wasn't as fast. Him, I almost caught. He was jumping aboard when I came sliding around the storage shack that separated the golf cart path from the marina basin.

They were in the bass boat, the one with the oversized engine — left in the water for a reason, I now realized.

The woman was at the wheel, already gunning away. I went charging down the dock, thinking that if I timed it right I might be able to vault myself aboard, yank the key from the ignition, and then escape by tumbling into the water before they had a chance to beat the crap out of me.

Leaving them stranded on a small island would be as good as catching them. Just hide out until the cops showed.

But the woman knew how to drive fast, too. She was no stranger to water and boats. Clear of a mooring piling, she rammed the throttle forward. The stern-heavy skiff lifted like a rocket before leveling onto plane, already moving fast through the basin toward the channel. The g-force catapulted Oxman backward onto the stern deck, and he came close to rolling off into the water. He screamed something in Russian — I have no idea what. It was a scream of fear, not anger. Maybe he didn't know how to swim.

I grabbed my skiff's lines and jumped behind the wheel. I wanted to follow them closely enough to find out what marina or dock they were using as a land base. No confrontations, no problems. Their boat had a high performance engine, but so did mine — a recently mounted 250-horsepower Mercury Optimax that I kept shielded from law enforcement types with a black engine cowling that claimed less horsepower.

I'm not a speed freak. I'd yet to push this engine beyond the modest threshold of forty miles an hour, my favorite cruising speed. But those of us who know how fast bad, random things can happen at sea tend to build in little safety hedges. If I ever get caught on the fast edge of a really bad storm, or in a tight and nasty situation, an extra twenty-five horses might make all the difference — or so I tell myself.

I used the additional horsepower now, throttling into the bass boat's expanding wake. There was no moon, but the trail was easy to follow in the winter starlight because of the froth of overoxygenated water stirred by their propeller. I watched my speedometer, illuminated in red, move from forty to fifty and then fifty-five — and I still had a couple of inches of throttle left.

Fifty-five in a boat feels dangerous, especially at night. Sixty seems crazy. I held her steady.

The speed created a wind stream that made my cheeks flutter, eyes teary. I leaned forward, hands tight on the wheel, concentrating on the black water ahead. The closer I got to the bass boat, the narrower its wake would appear . . . and it had already narrowed a lot in a short time.

Most boats with high-powered outboards also have what's called a "dead man's switch" near the helm. Mine is next to the ignition, attached to a coiled red wire that clips to the belt. Fall out of the boat, the engine shuts off automatically. Because I don't relish the idea of trying to outswim an empty boat that is making fast circles around me, coming ever closer, I always use the switch.

I reached now and clipped the wire in place.

I was gaining on them.

I spotted the bass boat just a minute or so later. Saw the metallic glitter of fiberglass and chrome, saw two people silhouetted by the lights of the busy highway that was ahead and off to our left.

It was the road that paralleled the channel, not far from the waterskiing area I'd noted earlier. I'd marked it mentally because the unlighted buoys and the floating ski jump made it a dangerous place at night.

The Russian woman was steering for it.

When I was thirty yards or so off their stern, I backed the throttle, matching my speed to theirs. We ran that way briefly before they turned and sprinted ahead. I'd been spotted.

Which was okay. I was just playing good citizen; a bird dog for the police.

I caught the boat a second time, and maintained the same safe distance astern. As I did, I fished the little handheld VHF marine radio out of its holder beneath the console, pressed the squawk button, declared that this was an emergency transmission, and did any law enforcement agency copy? Within a few seconds, a woman's voice came back, saying, "This is Port Canaveral Coast Guard. What's your emergency?"

I told the woman I'd interrupted two people assaulting a man on Night's Landing, Lake Toho, and that they were now escaping by boat. I gave her Jobe's name, his address, and told her that he needed medical attention. I was careful not to use police jargon such as "perpetrators" and "victim." It's something solid citizens don't do, so the usage makes law enforcement types suspicious.

We were inside the ski area now. With my peripheral vision, I'd already seen a couple of plastic, pumpkin-sized buoys flash by. Hit one of the ropes or chains that were attached, and the Russians were in for one hell of a jolt. The same was true for me.

Holding the radio to my ear, I listened to the lady Coasty say, "Our duty officer strongly recommends that you break off pursuit. I say again, end your pursuit. We are notifying the Bartram County Sheriff's Department. Let them handle it. We can't allow you to put yourself in personal danger."

I pushed the transmit button. "Recommendation noted. No danger, no plans to confront. I'm just following. And they don't seem to be carrying any —"

I was about to say "weapons" when I was interrupted by a loud *th-WHACK,* and the hull of my skiff jolted as if someone had just slammed it with a sledgehammer. For a confusing moment, I thought I'd hit one of the ski buoys. But then the hull shuddered again — *th-WHACK* — and I knew that I was taking fire. Someone in the bass boat was shooting.

I told the lady, "Out for now," and dropped the radio as I turned the boat sharply to the right, then back to the left, then to starboard again, making myself a more difficult target.

I'm not a fool, nor am I particularly brave. When someone is shooting, and you can't return fire, the wise course is to run. That's exactly what I was trying to do. I was scrambling like hell on an arc that would turn me in the opposite direction. The Coast Guard was right: Let law enforcement handle it.

So I was squatting low in my swivel seat, head ducked, eyes barely above the steering wheel, making my zigzag return to Night's

Landing, when I again heard the piercing sound of lead hitting fiberglass and felt the skiff jolt. Simultaneously, I felt a burning sensation on my right ear.

I touched the side of my head. Felt something warm, slick. More blood. My nose was still swelling and leaking after my collision with the wall . . .

Bastards.

They had no reason to continue firing. I'd broken off pursuit, yet they were still plinking away. Their behavior wasn't just violent, it was senseless. And vicious.

It scared me. *They* scared me.

Throwing the wheel to port, then starboard, I continued to run. A moment later, though, I felt a sudden percussion of air above my head; a shock wave vacuum that I associate with a bullet passing close to the auditory canal. They were *still* firing at me.

That did it. The combination of fear and anger — the two are often associated — did something to me, caused an emotional overload felt as a physical chill; a sensation not unlike being dosed with a shot of liquid hydrogen. Cold fury — maybe the term comes from that.

Furious. I certainly was. So mad I behaved irrationally. I turned my skiff toward the white hedge of wake created by the bass boat, then slammed the throttle forward.

Or maybe it *was* a credible reaction. A military maxim came into my mind: *When defeat is certain, the only practical course is to charge the bastards and attack with all assets.*

Reasonable or not, I took the offensive. If I was going to die by their hand, I wasn't going to die running.

I backed the throttle slightly when my skiff began to push sixty-five; then slowed again when I saw the first ski buoy sweep past. I stayed low, using the front of my boat like a gun sight, aiming it directly at the black vacancy that marked the terminus of the bass boat's expanding white wake.

They would be there in the blackness.

We would soon meet.

Once again, I spotted their boat in the panning car lights of the adjacent road. I closed within forty yards before they saw me. Maybe they thought they'd scared me off, or hit me with one of their wild rounds.

I saw their vessel fishtail, and recover — a measure of their surprise.

I wasn't done, nor were they.

Off to my left, two abrupt geysers of water kicked spray onto the deck. Shooting again as they tried to accelerate away.

Ahead and to my left, I could see the

vague outline of the ski ramp. Did they see it?

Yes . . . but only at the last second. I was close enough to watch them veer sharply, ramp to their right, then swerve back on course. They would soon pass directly in front of the ramp, with me only a few yards behind, if I continued at my current speed. But our intersecting angles, I realized, gave me an unusual attack option.

A ski ramp at an intersecting angle . . .

It was an option too crazy, too lunatic risky to deserve rational consideration. But I wasn't rational, so I didn't pause to think about it. I just did it. Let it happen, watched it play out as if from a higher aspect, making up the moves as I went.

I touched the dead man's switch to make certain it was still attached to the ignition and my belt. I removed my glasses and jammed them securely into the baggy front pocket of my fishing shorts. Then I pointed my skiff at the base of the ski ramp where the ramp's incline entered the water. As I did, I used the throttle switch to tilt my engine upward, moving the angle of the spinning propeller toward the sky. Gradually, instead of pushing the hull only forward the propeller's thrust was also pushing the back of my boat lower in the water while raising the bow.

I had plenty of speed. With my hand fixed on the throttle, I gauged the bass boat's speed and angle, trying to time it just right. I continued to steer toward the ramp, determined to hit the thing dead center.

Spend time around Florida's waterways and you'll acquire all kinds of useless information that may become useful if you live long enough. I'd seen boats go over ramps at boat shows, which was maybe where I'd learned that the standard competitive ski ramp is several boat widths wide and five or six feet high. The ramps have a gentle, engineered pitch that can vault a skier, or boat, a couple hundred feet through the air.

But what was the optimum safe speed? That figure was buried in my brain somewhere. Had I heard that boats towing ski jumpers travel at forty miles an hour? Or was it fifty?

I couldn't remember. A troubling lapse.

To compensate, every few seconds I glanced at the speedometer, aware that if I hit the ramp too fast I might not have time to bail out before my skiff nose-dived back into the water. Watched the needle read 50 . . . 45 . . . 48 . . . 45 . . . figures varying with my indecision as the ramp grew huge before me . . . the bass boat out there in front now

65

. . . maybe going faster than I thought.

I'm going to miss them, damn it. . . .

Which is why I panicked, burying the throttle forward as I hit the ramp bow-high. It added a final rocket thrust of acceleration that sent me careening toward outer space — stars bright up there — as the deck beneath me listed wildly to starboard, accompanied by a terrible screeching of fiberglass on fiberglass.

I was on the ramp for only a couple of seconds, but it seemed longer . . . and suddenly my boat straightened itself as we went airborne. I was floating, weightless, holding the steering wheel, fighting to steady myself like some novice astronaut experiencing zero gravity for the first time.

Intense concentration can add to the illusion that things are happening in slow motion. From high over the water, I turned my head to look. I could see that the bass boat was directly beneath me — a circumstance I hadn't anticipated. If I bailed, and landed on their boat instead of in the water, the impact would probably kill me.

Slow motion or not, I knew I had very little time to react. Yet, I now had to wait a scary, tilting instant longer before throwing myself out of my skiff.

The sense of weightlessness continued as

I shoved myself away from the steering wheel and floated out into the dark and spinning stratum that partitioned sky from water. . . .

5

In the instant before I plunged through the lake's surface, I could see my skiff above the bass boat, falling toward it in a ponderous arc. It looked as if I'd timed the intersection perfectly.

In the silence of that micromoment, I heard a woman scream. Or maybe it was the man: a shrill, atavistic sound so energized by fear that it was without gender.

They saw my boat, too. They knew they were about to be crushed.

Then gravity slammed me earthward.

My body had been traveling over the water at more than forty miles an hour. Add another twenty-five miles an hour to that, because, if you jump from a plane, that's the approximate speed attained during the first second or two of free fall. Mitigate the impact slightly because of the trajectory created by the combined forces of gravity, air drag, and velocity. But it was still one hell of a collision when I hit the lake's surface. I skipped over the water like a rag doll, and then was augured deep into blackness.

I've jumped into dark water many times. Jumped from fast boats, helicopters, and parachuted from planes. But there is only one other time when I'd experienced a water landing as violent — and that was not so long ago on the headwaters of the Amazon.

I tried to swing my legs beneath me but hit hard on my left side, shoulder first. I knew enough to have arms and elbows pulled in tight against my body, chin firmly on chest, both hands shielding my testicles. Hit any other way, arms can be ripped from their sockets, teeth shattered, necks broken.

I didn't fight it as momentum took me deep underwater. I was aware of burning cold — Central Florida had had a frost or two this December. Was also aware of changing pressure. I let drag slow me before lifting my head upward, hands and arms out, sculling to end my descent. Then I began a slow swim toward the surface, exhaling bubbles as I went.

Surfacing seemed to take a long, long time.

Finally, I was breathing air again; warm, rich air that floated in layers atop the cold lake; my vision blurry because of water and my bad eyesight. Still, I could see sufficiently well to be, at once, disappointed and also relieved.

I expected carnage, the aftermath of a boat collision. I didn't relish such a sight, but the Russians had invited attack.

But there was no carnage. Nor had they returned to kill me. Instead, all that awaited was the reassuring silhouette of my own skiff floating upright, engine off, not far away.

No sign of the bass boat. For a moment, I considered the possibility that I had hit it and their vessel had already sunk, the two passengers with it.

No. It would not have gone down so quickly.

I searched the distance until I recognized a fuzzy, flickering image caught in the light of the nearby highway: the Russians' boat disappearing fast, already more than a hundred yards away, still heading south. Somehow, the woman had managed to avoid the unavoidable. Impressive. But why hadn't they come back to finish the job?

I began to swim, thinking about it. Could the shock of what I'd done scared them into running? They'd managed to scare me into flight. Maybe I'd returned the volley.

I decided that I would discuss it with Tomlinson in a day or two, when we were both back on Sanibel.

I couldn't get the engine started . . .

I figured it was because of damage caused by the ski ramp. Or maybe a stray bullet had pierced the motor's cowling. But then I realized I'd forgotten to insert the dead man's switch into the little slot next to the ignition. Stupid.

The big engine fired, burbling its Harley rumble as if this night were nothing out of the ordinary.

The skiff seemed okay. A swivel seat was gone, steering wheel bent. That's all the damage I noticed — until I flicked the bilge switch. A fire hose stream of water began to jettison from the boat's starboard side. It pumped water for five or six long minutes as I idled toward Night's Landing.

The hull was damaged. I was taking on water, maybe sinking. Finally, when the pump's rhythmic whine told me the hull was empty, I jumped onto plane, steering fast toward the island. I'd stop and make certain Jobe Applebee was being cared for, then bust ass back to Dinkin's Bay.

As I steered, I did some rough calculations. Felony investigations tend to be lengthy. But with a little push, if I kept it simple, didn't tell the local cops that I'd been shot at — a biggie — I might make it home before midnight.

Wrong.

I tied up at the same slip. Just to be safe, I flipped the bilge switch again. More water inside.

The hull had taken a beating, was maybe too badly damaged to be repaired. The prospect irritated me. Some people — sailors most often — say they feel affection for their vessels. They can become very sentimental, particularly after a few rums.

I don't share the feelings. I've never felt anything close to emotion for the many boats I've owned. Yet, the thought of having to switch from this skiff to another was upsetting. I valued it as a tool. I trusted it. I knew how to make the thing perform. It'd kept me afloat through lots of bad weather, and at least a couple of tough encounters. If I believed in luck, I would have considered this skiff particularly lucky.

Watching water jetting from hull, I realized there was something else I'd have to deal with: The automatic bilge switch was broken. I'd have to get that fixed, too.

Leaky boats sink. I couldn't risk leaving

the thing unattended for long. Which is one reason that I headed off for Applebee's home at a jog. A more pressing reason was that there were no law enforcement boats here. No sirens or blue lights flashing in the distance.

So maybe EMTs had come by chopper. Possible. But it was also possible that the local water response teams hadn't had time to scramble. I'd called 911 around 9 p.m. According to my watch, it was now a little after ten. The idea of that terrified little man alone for more than an hour set off the guilt response. Dread, too.

When Applebee's house came into view, I stopped running, reassured by what I saw. Standing near the front door was a woman in official-looking blue coveralls, a walkie-talkie on her belt, plus a noisy, static-loud police scanner.

I took the porch steps two at a time. "How's Dr. Applebee doing? Have you already transported him to a hospital?"

I could see that the questions confused her. I thought, *Uh-oh,* moved past her, and tried the door. Still locked.

Shit.

"He's not in there alone, is he? He *has* been transported to the hospital? Lady, please tell me someone's checked on him."

"Who's been transported where?"

"Applebee."

I looked at her for the first time. She wasn't a woman; she was a kid. Sixteen, maybe eighteen. Pudgy, buttery face, multiple earrings, Cinderella bangs, hair cut boyishly short. But she sounded infuriatingly officious as she replied, "Mister, I have no idea if he's alone or not, but I can't let you go inside to check. The sheriff's department dispatcher told me I'm in charge of this location until they're ten-twenty. Which means until they arrive. She told me to wait on the porch and not let anyone inside. Especially civilians. That means you."

I was not in the mood; and was already crossing the porch, headed for the rear entrance. "Are you a cop? You're not old enough to be a cop."

"I'm old enough. But, no, not officially, anyway."

"Part of some kind of Girl Scouts program or something? I don't understand why you're here."

She didn't catch the mild sarcasm. "I'm the constable of this island. Of this unincorporated village, I mean. The sheriff's department contacts me when there's trouble, but this time I was home listening to the scanner. Now, if you'll —"

I'd vaulted the porch railing, and was walking fast. Now the girl was trotting after me, calling, "Hey, hold it, mister. Mister? You're not going into that house. I'm warning you right now, I'll arrest you."

"Arrest me? On what charges, for Christ's sake? How long have you been a constable, anyway?"

I was almost to the back of the house; I could see light angling through broken French doors. The light was bluish where it touched shadows, yellow on palms with their pineapple-ribbed trunks.

"Since the election in November."

I turned and looked at her for a moment before saying patiently, "A *month* ago? So maybe inexperience explains why you're acting like a jerk. Look, Dr. Applebee was in bad shape when I left him. He needs medical attention. So go right ahead and arrest me — but later. Not now. For now, just stay out of my way."

That inane song was still playing, coming from the open room.

"It's a small world, a small world . . ."

Following me through the broken doorframe, the girl had to speak louder because of the music. "Okay, sir, you give me no choice. You have the right to —"

We stopped. Applebee was no longer in the corner where I'd left him balled up like a child. There was a visible spattering of blood on the floor; more on the overturned chair. My cellular phone was gone.

I leaned over the record player and used the edge of my boat key to lift the tonearm off a revolving 45 rpm record. The record was made of glossy cardboard, like something from inside a cereal box. It had to be old.

In the new silence, I headed for a hallway as she found her voice again. "Damn it, you've got to stop or I'll . . . Oh my God!"

I'd already stopped. Stopped twice. First to pick up my phone, which was lying near the door. Then I halted more abruptly in the hall at a small, walk-in utility closet, louvered doors pushed open wide. From the closet emanated a subtle stink that took me several beats to identify, even though I've smelled it too many times.

I knew what was inside the closet without looking.

I stood there feeling a gauzy sense of unreality as, behind me, the girl said it again: "Oh dear God!" Then she made a snorting noise, followed by a low hissing wail that was mostly air. It was the shadow scream we experience in dreams. The dream where we open our mouths to cry out but there's no sound.

I spun and threw my arms around her, trying to shield her vision by holding her close. Then I steered her away. She was shivering, the earliest stage of shock.

Jobe Applebee, the preeminent field biologist, was in the closet. He was hanging from a galvanized crossbar. There was a section of nylon rope tied to the bar, and also knotted around his neck.

The bar wasn't high enough to hold him off the floor, so he was squatting, bulging eyes wide, arms dangling. It was as if he'd been in the process of seating himself in a chair only to be pulled up short like a running dog startled by the limits of his leash.

The girl was crying now; crying and babbling: "Oh, this can't be happening . . . he's dead. Is he really dead? I *knew* him, since I was a little girl. But that's not Mr. Applebee. It can't be him. He doesn't look anything like him."

True. I'd seen Jobe only briefly, but the combination of strangulation and gravity had transformed him. His head was now oversized on a shrunken body, his skin the color of potter's clay, black hands engorged, lips blue, dark eyes protruding.

The most striking change was the facial

expression. The man had been much tormented. Not now. But before leading the girl outside I took another look to confirm I wasn't imagining it.

No.

Applebee's eyes had a glazed, dreamy look, as if he were enjoying himself. His pale lips were contracted into a slight smile. It was the mild, secure smile that you see on the faces of children as they retreat into the arms of a parent. It's the smile that forms when they realize they're safe from all harm.

Applebee had retreated to some far, safe place; vanished somewhere inside himself. If the man's expression mirrored his last, fading sensibilities, then he'd experienced something that pleased him, but also surprised him a little. Maybe it was peace . . . or just an absence of turmoil, which is another form of liberation.

Later, when I made the dreaded call to Frieda, that's the way I would describe her dead brother: peaceful.

I talked with her after first speaking confidentially to her husband, telling him what had happened, seeking his advice and permission. I said to Frieda that Jobe looked as if he'd died peacefully; set free in a way that couldn't have been painful.

I evaded details, and tried my best to comfort her.

But the girl was right. Jobe Applebee looked nothing like the person she said she'd known since childhood. Nothing at all like the terrified man I'd left alone to die.

6

Whenever Solaris asked Dasha where she lived — "Maybe I can visit you one day!" — she would shrink him with a withering look and reply: "I live on the islands. That's all you need to know, because it's all you can understand."

Dr. Desmond Stokes and his staff lived on two islands in the southern Bahamas, part of the Ragged Island and Cays chain near Cuba. A couple hundred acres each, shores separated by a passage so narrow that tidal current roared between the islands like rapids down a river.

The main island had buildings, staff housing, a small, modern manufacturing facility that converted blocks of coral, cut from reefs, into holistic calcium tablets. The island was manicured, planted with citrus, avocado, and bananas.

On the second island, there was an air-strip, storage facilities, a few huts, a small lab equipped for extracting and preserving reptile poisons, a crane for stacking blocks of coral. Mostly, the second island was jungle. Wild things lived there. Wild things were kept for research. People on neighboring islands who practiced Obeah, a complicated religion similar to voodoo, wore special charms to protect them from the evil they believed existed there.

The first time Dasha saw Dr. Stokes's islands was on the laptop screen of his personal assistant, Mr. Luther T. Earl. A tall, dried-up, Lincoln-looking man who wore bow ties and smelled of lavender, big white teeth when he smiled, skin the color of a black pearl. That's what he claimed, anyway.

"Earl the Pearl," he told her. "You can call me that, if you like."

This was long before she found out Earl the Pearl was also Dr. Stokes's organizational brains, and his front man.

Mr. Earl told Dasha they were actively recruiting someone "with unusual qualities" to take charge of security at his boss's retreat in the Bahamas. There might be some personal work involved, too.

The woman had a pretty good idea what that meant, or they wouldn't be recruiting staff at an executive security trade show at

81

the Bellagio Hotel, Vegas. A couple thousand *Soldier of Fortune* types — fakes, gun freaks, and skinheads — paying money to attend lectures on how to survive the coming revolution, the ghetto monsters, and watching firepower demonstrations, rocking to the latest weaponry, out there in the desert, when they weren't getting shit-faced on cheap booze.

Mr. Earl had rented a three-bedroom suite. Interviewed forty-seven candidates, he told Dasha later, but only three made it far enough to see pictures of the rich man's tropical estate. The manufacturing plant was smaller than she'd expected, neon lighting inside, where employees wore masks and plastic gloves. They turned raw coral and seashells into vitamin pills that cured all kinds of diseases.

"We have thirteen employees, ferried in and out every day," Mr. Earl said, "Dr. Stokes has a personal staff of three, counting me. If I find a top security person, we can hire more people. Your call."

Dasha barely heard, she was so focused on what she was seeing. They were digital photos set to music; scenes from two green islands rimmed with sand beneath vodka-clear water that darkened incrementally as the bottom dropped away, jade green, forest green, turquoise, then purple, showing that the islands were actually mountain peaks, anchored solid and alone in a blue tropic ocean.

Golden beach and rain forest. *Heat.* Jesus. No wonder Dasha had to wait so long for an interview. She sat there in a hotel suite with a dozen tough-guy strangers, some wearing their black berets and camo, others dressed the way they imagined secret agent types would dress — black sport coats, black shades — all applying for the same job, but none wanting it more than Dasha.

Jungle waterfalls. A jungle river, steam rising . . .

Dasha had grown up outside Chernovo near the Volga River, which flowed south toward the Chechen border when the stinking ditch wasn't frozen. She was one of five children born to a single mother who couldn't afford to buy coal in a slum so cold that, between October and May, Dasha learned to identify neighbors by their eyes and whatever bit of nose their scarves left unprotected. Months went by, she saw only bits and pieces of her own body. Never naked all at once.

Sitting in the Vegas hotel room, seeing photos of the island — palm trees, coral mesas beneath blue water, sun-bright sand

— she thought to herself, *I'd kill to get this job.*

Turned out, that was part of the deal.

Dasha, the ideal choice.

Of the couple thousand *Soldier of Fortune* types strutting around Vegas, she saw two, maybe three, people who had the look. Who'd been places; done some jobs. If you served in the military on the Chechen border, you learned to know the real ones at a glance. Operators. The others did their Hollywood hero impersonations. "When I shoot a man, he stays shot," she heard some guy say one night, sitting, drinking martinis with Aleski at the pool bar.

They'd looked at each other and rolled their eyes. Aleski said loud enough for the whole room to hear, *"Raspizdyay kolhoznii! Pizdoon!"*

Stupid redneck! Fucking liar!

They both laughed and laughed.

They'd worked as interrogation specialists, Russian military. Dasha had also been recruited and trained by national intelligency, the FSB, or Federalnaya Sluzhba Bezopasnosti. Made some money on the side feeding information to Chechen separatists before Dasha got sick of the gray winters, the gray architecture, the gray pasty faces of Russian men, and said fuck it. She was out of there.

Aleski was her operative partner. Played good cop to her badass cop, which wasn't an act. He'd never put a move on her, never asked for anything, but was always there. Sexually, he had some kinks — the man liked being watched. Otherwise, Aleski was like a stray dog that followed the first person who walked by and didn't try to kick him.

After Mr. Earl showed her the photos, he told Dasha about the unique security problems of owning isolated islands that, legally, were part of the Bahamas, but also had to interact with government con men from Cuba, only thirty miles away. The dried-up man asked how she'd handle certain situations.

"Create redundant cells to protect water, fuel, and mobility," she told him. "Those are the necessities. All security problems can be reduced to those three things."

"What about food supply? Water's important, but people got to eat, too."

Dasha replied, "Food *is* fuel. Water, fuel, and mobility — see how I compartmentalize them? If I make sure they're secure, your islands will be secure."

The man said, "Cool. Very cool." His smile read: *Impressive.*

Mr. Earl the Pearl had a big brain behind that great big smile. The questions, she noticed, became more carefully couched.

"If your employer asked you to break the law, would you?"

A standard setup. Only an amateur would fall for it.

"No."

"What if you were in a place where there was no law?"

"Is there such a place?"

"This is hypothetical."

Dasha thought, *Clever.* Said, "In such a place, I would consider my employer the maker of laws."

"You would carry out any order?"

"Reasonable orders. The man's paying my salary."

"Even murder? You wouldn't kill a person if you were told to do it."

Dasha had looked into Mr. Earl's mean, judgmental eyes and nodded imperceptibly. Barely moved her head, in case this was a different sort of setup and she was being videoed. Waited for several seconds, sure the man knew her meaning, before saying, "Murder's never legal."

She got the job.

When unimportant people — people such as the young Cuban — asked where she lived, Dasha always said the same thing: "On the islands."

A private place inside her was smiling. *Where it's warm.*

In the first months, before Dasha asked to see his body, Solaris thought of her as the Snow Witch, and Dr. Stokes as Mr. Sweet. Everything about her was pale and distant — icy. Solaris, who'd only seen snow in photographs, liked the word. It fit.

Witch: A woman who could make magic.

Dr. Stokes had translucent skin like rice paper, or refined sugar. He wore white gloves, and a paper device over his mouth and nose because the man was afraid of germs — or so said the Snow Witch.

Months later, when he knew her better, the two of them naked in the tobacco barn, Solaris said what he felt the first time he'd heard about it. "The man's afraid of germs, but he buys the kind of nasty shit he does? Sewage? Water with invisible bugs? He's crazy. He looks like what the Santeria people call 'the Walking Dead.' "

The Cuban was imagining the man in zombie-white makeup, with pointed teeth and ears, like a bat. Not so different from the way he actually looked.

Dasha replied, "He's afraid of anything

unhealthy. An uneducated boy like you has never seen diseases under a microscope. He has. If he knew I'd touched your *yieldak,* had your sweat on my skin and didn't wash? He'd never let me in the car."

The Chinaman had already told Solaris why the man ordered such strange things. Research.

Maybe true; maybe the Chinaman was making it up.

He'd also told him the doctor had invented vitamin pills and become rich. Made good investments, owned many businesses even though he was *socioalista* at heart. Loved the old Cuba during the days of the Bearded One, which had something to do with him buying sugarcane acreage in the Everglades, west of Miami, a city Solaris dreamed of visiting.

"Probably because of the trouble he had in Florida, he hates the U.S. government," the Chinaman said. "That's why I pretend to give him a discount."

Why did the Yankees bother growing cane? Cuba had once produced enough to sweeten the world, yet the arrogant imperialists had nearly strangled the island to death.

The Chinaman didn't say that. One of the old villagers had told him. Gave him a speech. Solaris wasn't interested.

So it was "Senorita Bruja Naver," and "Dr. Dulce," until the woman asked to see his body in the dim light of a tobacco barn that smelled of sour pepper, like a whiskey keg. Now she was "Senorita Serpiente."

On her next visit, Dasha allowed him to touch her breasts. Part of the reward system. The third trip, she behaved as if he were invisible until she stepped into the building and bolted the door. Then, step-by-step, she instructed him on how he could please her.

Her body was different than the prostitutes he'd been with. Different than women described by older men in the village — all they talked about were sex and baseball. Solaris felt very strange when he did what she asked him to do, yet it was impossible to refuse her.

As their helicopter lifted over the mountains, he'd gargled with rum, hacked, and spit into the sand. But he still loved the thought of her body, the way her pale skin burned beneath his hands.

During a recent visit, she'd held up a rubber balloon shaped like a plantain.

"If he learns how to control himself," she told him, "waits until I'm ready, I'll let him

89

use this one day. But don't expect it every time."

Solaris had tried to hold back. God he'd tried. He'd thought about baseball, then about old women stirring beans, even imagined dogs farting. Nothing could dull the voltage of her fingers on his skin.

She was livid. Went looking for a towel and didn't come back.

His last performance, a month ago, was worse. When he bragged to his friends in the village about what the blond Russian did to him in the tobacco barn, they'd spit and whistled in scorn. Called him a crazy liar. To prove himself, he'd borrowed a camera from an old man who'd once been the village Party captain. Solaris had wedged the camera into the barn rafters, lens pointed downward, a long piece of fishing line tied to the shutter release.

Just being in the barn, the way it smelled, imagining being with her, made it difficult to breathe.

Their small helicopter landed five days later.

When Solaris was naked, and she had her bra off, he tried to position her in a way so that her face and body would be visible to the camera, all the while feeling blindly for the fishing line that his stupid fingers could not locate.

"What are you doing?"

"Doing?"

"Yes, *doing?*"

"Trying to find a more comfortable position against this wall."

"No, I meant him. What's wrong with *him?*"

"Wrong?"

"Are you blind? Idiot!"

Solaris looked. *"Oh."* The pressure of making a photograph had affected him in a way that imagining old women stirring beans, and farting dogs, could not. "I think . . . he's learning control."

The woman slapped his flaccid member, then slapped it again. "If this is what he calls control, I have no use for him. Or you."

There was something vicious in her voice, a deeper pitch as if there were an angry man hidden inside.

Solaris had called after her, "Maybe he wants to listen to your lips, not your hands —"

Too late. She was dressing, already on her way.

The last time Solaris looked into Snake Woman's face was in the final minutes of his life, hearing the man-voice inside her, seeing the revulsion that she felt for him — for *men* — as his eyesight and his hearing faded, recognizing both and wondering why those frightening qualities hadn't alerted him before.

It was a couple of weeks before Christmas, dry season, when coffee bushes were blooming white as snow on hillsides above the village baseball diamond, near the vegetable fields where he'd once plowed behind oxen.

The streets of Vinales were decorated with ribbons and candles that were lit each night. They hadn't celebrated the holiday while the Bearded One lived, so the decorations seemed more colorful because they were unfamiliar.

This trip, three of them arrived in the helicopter. Dasha, dressed in black blouse and slacks; Mr. Sweet; plus the lardish-looking Russian man who sometimes accompanied them, black hair growing on the backs of his hands, and out of his ears like a wolf.

Mr. Sweet slid into the back of the waiting Volvo, never said a word, as usual, adjusting the paper mask on his face, not touching the door handles even though he wore gloves, his eyes sweeping the area but nothing registering.

He'd speak with the Chinaman, no one else.

The big Russian gave Solaris the familiar stare — contemptuous, aggressive. Solaris returned it: *If you had the chance, cabrone, you wouldn't risk it.*

Didn't matter. When Dasha wagged her finger at Solaris, inviting him to follow her into the barn, he was so grateful that his voice broke when he said to her, "After the last time, I thought you were so disappointed in me that you would never —"

"Shut your mouth, fool. If your body wasn't attached to a brain, we'd get along much better."

Even with her bad Spanish, the woman could joke with him. That's the way Solaris took it: *This is how close we've become.*

There was something different in her manner. She was rushed, a critical woman more critical than usual. And the hairy Russian shadowed her movements, but from a distance, his attention swiveling from Dasha to the Chinaman who was now sitting in the backseat of the limo with Mr. Sweet.

There was an energy in the air, volatile.

More than once, he heard the name Applebee mentioned — the disgusting little man who'd cried like a baby because he had to ride in the helicopter.

"I would spit on such a man!" Solaris had

once bragged to Dasha. "Why bring such a person to Cuba? What use could he be?"

He was testing. Wanted to see how she reacted. He could picture the blond woman and Applebee off by themselves, whispering. The Chinaman had told him Applebee was there to confirm there were tiny creatures in the South African crates the doctor was buying, and also to test the local water supply.

The woman didn't discuss business with Solaris, so she surprised him, replying, "He's going to make me rich; that's his use. He's finding a cure for a parasite. A sort of worm."

"What kind of worm?"

"The kind of worm people will pay anything to get rid of."

That peculiar little guy with a microscope. It was impossible for Solaris to compete. "A man who cries isn't a man. He's worthless!"

"Worthless?" The woman's tone was cutting — yes, her way of joking, he decided. "You'd be an expert on that."

Later, as he died, Solaris realized he'd misread more than just her sense of humor.

Never saw it coming.

7

By 11:30, I'd finished giving my edited statement to detectives. During the interview I told them that, because I'd left my cell phone with Applebee, I'd checked the log. The last two numbers dialed were unfamiliar. They'd been made while I was chasing the bad guys.

"It was either Applebee or whoever killed him."

The cops were not pleased that I'd retrieved the phone. They said I'd maybe screwed up any chance of fingerprints. They copied the numbers, letting me see they were pissed off.

So maybe that's the reason they told me I couldn't leave: a mild punishment.

At twenty minutes before midnight, and with nothing else to do, I took aside an investigator from the Bartram County Medical Examiner's Office to ask if she'd come to any conclusions about Jobe's death. I'd assumed murder, but realized there was another possibility.

The investigator, whose ironic name was Rona Graves, replied, "Are you a relative? A close friend?"

"No. His sister's a friend. I'd never met him."

"Are you wondering suicide or murder? It's really impossible to say right now. Too soon. Too much to sort out."

We were standing outside, Applebee's porch light casting tree shadows on sand, stars beyond the tree canopy, the two of us separated from a handful of curious neighbors by yellow crime scene tape. Ms. Graves, in jeans and a blue blouse with rolled-up sleeves, was an interesting-looking woman, with her Appalachian face, Latina cocoa skin, wild black surfer-boy hair cropped short. She had all the professional mannerisms, didn't have to think about it: the voice, the wording, body language that served as a barrier. She'd been in the business for a while. But she could also wrinkle her nose to show you how hard she was thinking, or brush an elbow. Ways of letting you know there was a human in there.

She was wrinkling her nose now, tapping thoughtfully on a clipboard. "I probably shouldn't discuss this any more than that.

We're all going to have to wait for the autopsy."

I nodded and looked toward the house — silhouettes of busy cops — then down a sand trail that led to more dilapidated houses. This island was prime for one of the big developers to move in, get the title problems resolved, then start all over demanding really big bucks.

It would happen.

"This could be a really nice place."

I said, "Lots of waterfront, good trees. Yeah." Startled we'd shifted to a similar pattern of thought.

"When the nightshade blooms here, it's like snowdrifts. All those white blooms. But you've got to be careful, especially with kids. The berries are poisonous. We've done several of those cases."

"I didn't know."

"Two died."

She was still tapping on the clipboard. I got the impression she was marking time, just like me. Her preliminary examination was done. Now she was waiting for detectives to finish so she could bag the body and be on her way.

"Do you have any nonrelated questions, Dr. Ford?"

"Just Ford. Or Marion."

"Okay. Ford. Anything else I can do for you?"

There *was* something else on my mind. I was concerned about the young constable.

I said, "The teenage girl who was here, the one the EMTs treated for shock? Her name's Melinda Voigt. Local girl. She's never been through anything like this. I think she's going to need some help."

"I haven't met Melinda, but I know who she is. What kind of help?"

"Maybe a couple of visits with your shrink buddy. Better yet, the kind of help where someone with some authority — like you — tells the girl a small lie. A lie of kindness. I think someone needs to get the girl off alone and tell her that Applebee was dead before she arrived here."

"She feels responsible?"

"The girl was on his porch when I arrived. She hadn't gone in. She refused to let me in. After we found the body, she started wondering if maybe she could have saved him. If she hadn't waited. Behaved a little more human and a little less hard-ass."

"She played the role, huh? The big boss in charge."

"That's right."

"I'm not surprised. The cops tell me she's a pompous ass. Even before she got elected constable, they say she was a pompous ass. Do you know what the vote was? Four to three. Only seven island voters. She'd cooked up the constable idea herself. A title, some power. I hear she comes from big money."

"Acting like a pompous ass is one of the stages most of us go through, isn't it, Ms. Graves?"

"I'm not so sure. Are you including yourself?"

"Sure. I've got lots of experience. Not just the pompous ass stage, either. On a regular basis, I invent all kinds of ways to behave like an ass. Thoughtless ass. Clumsy ass. Dumb ass. Myopic ass. Name one."

She was grinning as I added, "The kind of guilt Melinda's starting to feel could become permanent. The kind too heavy even for us experienced asses to deal with. She told me she's only twenty. A small lie of kindness might help."

Graves thought about it for a moment, letting me see that her professional side was uneasy with the idea, before she said, "From what I was told, Applebee was still alive at a little after nine when you telephoned 911. Slightly more than an hour later, you called to say that he was dead. What time did the girl arrive on scene?"

"Nine-forty. That's what Melinda told me. I showed up about twenty minutes later."

The woman was shaking her head. "The window's too small. We can't pinpoint the time of death that closely."

"I've read there's a way by measuring the body's core temperature —"

"Yes, I've already done that, but not with any . . ." She paused to organize her explanation. "Let me put it this way. After somatic death — that's when the body as a whole stops functioning — a corpse's core temperature can remain normal for one, even two, hours afterward, depending on conditions. Then it drops by one to one and a half degrees per hour. That's what you're talking about. I did my preliminary examination at eleven-thirty. Applebee's temp was thirty-five Celsius, which is only two degrees below norm. See what I mean?"

Intentionally ignoring the point, I said, "Then he *could* have died half an hour or so before the girl came on scene. What a relief if Melinda heard that. It might spare her one hell of a lot of emotional turmoil down the road."

Ms. Graves began to chuckle, her tone saying, *Okay, you win.*

I said, "It's a good cause."

"You've never met the girl before, Ford?"

"Nope. But she needs help."

"Are you always so persuasive? If the motivation wasn't so noble, I might be offended. Instead, I might let you persuade me to have a cup of coffee after we're done. There're a couple of all-night places near Kissimmee. But we can't stay long. I've got an early call."

I said, "I'd like that. I really would. But there's another detective coming to talk with me, and it's already close to midnight."

The woman was nodding, looking at me, stroking her brown cheek, amused. She waited for a while, letting me see that she knew something I didn't, before asking, "Why can't men just come out and say that they're already involved with a woman? Is it because they want to leave their options open? Or is it because they're embarrassed?"

"Embarrassed?"

"Embarrassed to be in love."

"It's that obvious?"

"Not until I asked you out for coffee. That expression on your face. Talk about panic. For a second, I thought you might run away and hide."

"For the record, Ms. Graves, the answer

would have been yes. Under different circumstances."

"Rona."

"Rona."

It was true. I've met enough decent, interesting women over the years to wish that we lived lives proportionate in number to the number of strangers we'd like to get to know better.

The woman gave me a fraternal pat on the shoulder. "You really *are* a persuasive one. The professor type, but with charm. I'll speak with the girl. You're right. It could be a good and healthy thing for me to do. If Her Highness the constable reads the official report, though — well, there's no way to control that."

My cell phone began to ring as I thanked her. Watched her walk across the lawn toward Applebee's brightly lighted house.

With the phone to my ear, from across eleven hundred miles of America, I listened to my old workout pal, my lover, and the expectant mother of our unborn child say, "Ford, what bullshit excuse do you have this time? Have I told you lately what a gigantic pain in the ass you are? If I haven't, let me say it again just to be sure you've pulled your head out of your butt long enough to listen."

I waited until she'd repeated herself before I replied with affection, "Hello to you, too, dear Dewey Nye. You expect to kiss an infant with that sailor's mouth of yours?"

"You'd give a week's pay to get a wet one from me."

"More."

"Really. Then I may start charging."

She could. Dewey is a very kissable woman: Blond, fit, five-ten, and a 160 pounds or so of raging, self-reliant pregnant female. She was once ranked among the top-ten tennis players in the world, and plays mostly golf now, beach volleyball, and some racquetball. Still competitive and out-spoken. It's hard to tell from her locker-room vocabulary, but she's also intuitive and sometimes overly sensitive.

"How much would you pay?"

It was fun talking with her. Nice not to be locked inside my own brain, launching from a ski ramp over and over, seeing Applebee in the closet, so I played along. "Money is so awkward between friends. I was thinking more of a barter system. You scratch my back, I'll scratch yours. So to speak."

"Oh sure. Take it out in trade. Trouble is, it's tough to remember what you look like. I see you so seldom. Or even hear from you."

I thought, *Uh-oh*. She wasn't playing anymore.

"I'm serious, Doc. I got a bellyful of baby, and I can't carry the load alone."

"Dewey, I tried to call twice this morning, got that damn recorder. And my evening has been — unbelievable."

"Bite me, Thoreau. So what's your excuse? It's ten o'clock in farm country, which is beddie-bye time, sport, for those of us ladies who happen to be knocked up."

She was calling from the little farm she'd inherited outside Davenport, Iowa. It's a house and barn on two hundred acres where the Mississippi River flows west, then turns sharply southward toward Missouri. Cornfields, rolling hills, white two-story houses, red barns, hickory and oak, narrow gravel roads. Because she was pregnant, Dewey had decided the family farm was the right place to be.

"A good luck sorta deal," she explained it. "Something I can feel, but can't explain."

It was one of those instinctual judgments that I'm incapable of understanding, so take pains not to contest. Why risk offending someone you care about?

So I'd been commuting to Iowa when my schedule, and my lab work allowed — not often enough, obviously. Flying back and forth between the west coast of Florida and Quad City International Airport, Moline, Illinois, at least once a month. When I wasn't visiting, I telephoned often, and always, always just before bed.

I apologized again, adding, "Trust me, you'll understand when I explain. Not now, though, Dew. Tomorrow, if that's okay."

She didn't want to let it go, but at least sounded playful again. "Tomorrow, huh? Why don't you let me guess? You probably had those Coke bottle glasses of yours glued to some test tube. Or maybe you discovered some kind of insect that's new to science. If that's what it is, I hope the thing crawls out of the jar and bites you on the ass. Or on something that's a lot more delicate."

The woman cracked herself up. She was making her familiar chortling noise, as I replied, "Nope, Dewey, I keep that particular item reserved for you. Only you."

"You'd better, Thoreau. If you don't, I'll . . . I'd get you blind drunk one night, then tattoo my name on that pecker of yours. 'Dewey Aubrey Nye' " — she spoke louder to prevent me from interrupting — "the whole thing. Middle name and all. That way, when you're in some freezing locker room all shrunken up, or just before you started boinking some new chick, she'd look and see DAN. My initials in capital letters. Get it? She'd be like, 'Hey, get this fruit loop away from me!' Like some sweetie boy had branded you. Your own special butt buddy named Danny Boy!"

Dewey has lived as a gay woman, so maybe that's why she uses language she wouldn't tolerate from outsiders. Not that she seems to worry about offending. You never know what she's going to say or do next. It's one of the reasons I like her. The only predictable thing about Dewey Nye is that she always does the unexpected. Each and every day, she reinvents herself in some small way — a new quirk, a favorite new word, an unexpected interest. Every morning, she opens the door to a secret little carnival that is going on inside her head and chooses a different ride to try, a new attraction to investigate, or flavor to taste.

If you're among the lucky few, she'll sometimes invite you to travel along.

Over the years, she's invited me into that private place several times . . . but then always *un*invited me later. Usually for good reason.

This time, though, we seemed to be sticking. Maybe because there was more at stake.

Trying to sound stern, I said into the phone, "Jesus, that's a tired old joke. I'm not even going to reply until you stop making that awful hooting noise. It's disgusting."

"Awww-hoo-hoo-hoo. I can just *see* it! Your pecker with a guy's name on it. Three letters in red, blue . . . no, *lavender* — and all it says is DAN unless I'm around, get you in bed, and make the thing angry. Then it'll say my whole freakin' name. *Some* of it, anyway. Ohhhh . . . Awww . . . Oh, my poor ribs."

"Stop," I said. "You're making me wince. Don't babies sleep inside the womb? At least try to pretend you're normal."

Baby.

Live your entire life alone, it's a scary word. We'd both given it a lot of thought. The subject was not without fresh scars.

The previous spring, Dewey discovered that she was pregnant. It was unplanned; a surprise to us both. But that didn't make it any easier when she miscarried near the end of the first trimester.

Only a few weeks before she lost the baby, a blind ex-carney and fortune-teller named Baxter had told me something bad was about to happen to a child of mine. I'd shrugged it off until I got Dewey's hysterical call. It gave even a skeptic like me pause.

He'd also told me that I would soon end the life of a friend.

Unsettling. If I believed in such things.

So, in June, I visited the lady in Iowa where we talked it over. Discussed all the pros and cons, all the many obligations, responsibilities, the amount of time, money, and dedication that were necessary.

When we both felt certain, we gave it another try. Dewey's the one who insisted that the smart thing to do in any business partnership is hash out the details of dissolution before starting. We did that, too, even though I secretly believed it trivialized the commitment — but I was also secretly relieved. Each had the right, we agreed, to end the partnership, but parental rights, and financial obligations, remained.

In September, we found out that she was pregnant again. So I'd been commuting when I could. Lately, I'd also been working my butt off so that I could get away and spend the holidays with her as promised.

Still chortling, though not nearly so hard, she reminded me of that promise now.

"But you can't use this tattoo gambit as some lame excuse for not showing up for Christmas. You *will* be here a week from now? Sunday, the nineteenth."

As I replied, "I've already got my flight booked," I was also watching Rona Graves, the medical investigator. Watched, puzzled, as she rushed out onto Applebee's porch, then trotted down the steps. She was in a hurry, but also in distress, judging from her jerky, uncertain movements.

Graves was searching for someone, head scanning, as Dewey told me, "Tomlinson's welcome, too. But no dope smoking on my property. In fact, now that I think about it, I'm not sure Iowa's ready for someone as weird as Scarecrow. It's so freakin' cold here tonight, they'd stick him in a padded cell if he went out wearing one of his sarongs, and no underwear."

Scarecrow — a pet name for one of her favorite people. She still credits him for healing her after she'd been badly injured. A spiritual intervention. Another instinctual conviction beyond my understanding.

I was about to say something when I noticed that Graves was waving at me, calling, "Ford? Dr. Ford! Get in here quick. Hurry, *please.*"

Her turn to panic.

I told Dewey, "Hey, something's come up. Gotta run. Call you later."

Before I hit the terminate button, I heard

her say quickly, "Make sure you do, Thoreau, because there's somethin' important we need to discuss. Guess who called me, who wants to visit —"

I told her, "I will. I *will*," already walking fast toward the house.

8

Graves was waiting on the porch, holding the door open. She used her hand to urge me along. Beside her was a uniformed deputy, a huge guy. He shifted from one foot to another, hands on his gun belt, an indicator of stress.

So I hurried, ran up the steps, asking, "What's wrong? Is it Melinda?," because that was the only possibility that entered my mind. Because I'd shown an interest, maybe Graves felt I deserved to be informed.

That vanished when the woman said in a rush, "You're a biologist, you said. My God, I've never seen anything like this in my life. It's just awful. So maybe you can figure out what's happening, what's going on inside."

"Inside where? The house?"

"No. *Him.* Dr. *Applebee.* Maybe you can identify whatever it is that's . . . Jesus, I can't even describe it."

The deputy said in a sheepish, Southern voice, "Miz Graves, I'm sorry, but I can't go back in there. I think I'll be sick if I go back in that room. If it's okay with you, I'd rather stay out here where the air's fresh."

Graves dismissed him with a nod of her head, still speaking to me. "Do you mind taking a look? You're not going to like it. But it's closer to your field than mine."

I was thinking, *What the hell's going on?* as I followed after her, Graves hurrying, taking long steps. "The body's in the room where you broke through the door. We were getting ready to cart him out when one of the deputies noticed that . . . when we noticed those . . ."

In her hand she carried a couple of odor-reduction masks. They consisted of elastic ear loops connected to a gauze rectangle. She turned and shoved one toward me. "You'll want this."

I've seen some nasty things. Witnessed scenes so appalling that an attempt to communicate detail would reenergize the event and give the thing life again. Those images are best sealed away, never reviewed in memory, or conversation. Invite the monster to return, you may end up living with the monster. It's just my way of dealing with it.

What I saw in Applebee's house ranks among the worst. I took one look and knew I'd never burden anyone with the details. *Ever.*

The two detectives who'd questioned me earlier would've agreed. They were in the yard just outside the broken French doors, each hunched over in the shadows, hands braced on thighs like exhausted runners. One was sucking in great gulps of air. The other was coughing into the bushes.

Beside me, talking through her mask, Graves said, "All the shitty stuff I've seen in this business, you'd think I'd be ready for anything. Do you have any ideas? What the hell are they? And how'd they get inside him?"

I said, "I'm not sure. Give me a second."

Applebee's corpse lay on a collapsible gurney in the middle of the room. He was naked. The body bag beneath him had yet to be zipped. I took a couple of steps closer to the gurney, moving as if I were approaching a ledge . . . or something that might strike out and bite. Not looking at her, I said to Graves, "Do you have rubber gloves my size?"

She said, "Jesus Christ, you're not going to touch one of those things, are you?"

"Maybe. I think they're harmless — to

touch, anyway. I need a closer look."

I held out my right hand, eyes fixed on the body, until I felt her place surgical gloves into my palm.

"I think I know what they are. I've seen something similar, anyway. It was in Africa." I paused for a second. "What happened to the bandage on his ankle? It's gone now."

"I took it off during my preliminary examination."

I was pulling on a glove. "Then that explains it."

The bandage had been taped over a dime-sized hole in the dead man's ankle. The wound was black, gangrenous looking. Protruding from the hole was the head of something that was alive, active.

I moved closer as I snapped on the second glove. Took a few more thoughtful seconds to confirm that what I was seeing appeared to be the scolex, or head, and the anterior segment of a long, white parasite. Its prostomium — the tip — was knobbed. Its ventral underbelly was flat. The dorsal was ridged and segmented.

A worm.

One of several parasitic worms — a dozen or more — sprouting from the man's body.

Their movement, in chorus, gave the corpse an appearance of macabre, auguring animation. It was one of those nasty scenes that memory etches with acid, which is why I narrowed my focus from the general to the specific.

Visually, the parasite exiting from the ankle was the least repellent, and so I concentrated on it.

The thing was pencil lead–sized in diameter. The section that had already breached the hole was more than a foot long. Another two feet still lay beneath an elevated mound of blistered skin. I watched for a while, noting details that would not be shared. The parasite writhed and undulated like a baby snake fighting its way out of an egg casing.

The observation was fitting. Applebee's body was serving as an egg casing. He'd been a vessel; host to a feeding, breathing, subcommunity of parasites.

Now that the host was dead, members of the community were fleeing. They were abandoning this cooling vessel.

Every few minutes, the woman asked did I know what they were, what the hell they could be?

Some people burn adrenal excesses by talking. She chattered away before asking again: "You really think you've seen these things before?"

I was standing with my hands on the base of the gurney, leaning over Applebee. I was so focused, it took me a second to realize she was waiting for an answer.

"There's a parasite I've seen in . . . West Africa, the poorest areas — Ethiopia, Nigeria. Maybe other parts of the tropics, too, but I'm not sure. They're called guinea worms. People get infested by drinking water that contains little tiny water fleas. They're actually copepods — barely visible — that have fed on the parasite during its larval stage. Copepods are little crustaceans related to crayfish. All they do is eat and reproduce. They're worldwide. Ponds, ditches, even standing water in old tires. You need a microscope to see them, so you wouldn't know they were in a cup of water."

Graves looked at the body, then looked away. "Those things come from water fleas?"

"No. Inside the fleas, the guinea larvae develop teeth. Once they get inside a person's stomach, they eat through the intestinal wall. When they've mated, ready to release larvae, the females move through the body's soft tissues, and finally break through the skin looking for freshwater."

Graves said, "My *God.*"

"Uh-huh, an unattractive life cycle. In Africa, I saw street people who were infected. The common treatment isn't pretty. I'll spare you."

When the investigator pressed for details, however, I told her what I'd seen, finishing, "The worms can be three or four feet long, so it's the only way to prevent them from breaking off beneath the skin. Which could cause infection, maybe death."

"Ohhh, awful," sorry now that she'd asked. She pointed. "But how do they know which areas of the body are soft enough . . . ? Do you see the one that's . . . that's . . . ?"

I looked; turned away. "I see. I don't know how they navigate. It's an interesting example of specialized adaptation."

"Sickening's a better word. These things aren't found in the United States, are they? They can't be. I'd *know* about something that nasty."

"Guinea worms aren't indigenous to North America. I'm almost as sure that they aren't found in this hemisphere. They aren't *supposed* to be here, anyway. These are exotics. Not native to Florida."

I added, "Exotic plants and animals thrive here. It's the heat; all the water. Or maybe these are just similar in appearance to guinea worms; not the same species. But I think they are."

I stood, glanced around the room. One of the detectives had recovered. He was standing, his back to us. I wanted a pan of water — not to drink, but to see how the parasite reacted to water. I decided to find the kitchen myself. Rona Graves followed, relieved to be out of the room.

As we walked, she said, "Please tell me that we can't be infected by contact with the body. God, I don't think I could handle the thought of having —"

"No, don't worry. You have to ingest contaminated water. I might be able to show you why in a second."

"They're from Africa? Do you know if Applebee had traveled to Africa? Maybe that's where he was infected."

"I'll ask his sister, because you're right: It's important to nail down the source. If Applebee picked them up locally, if he wasn't studying the things for research, this county's got a serious problem. Maybe the entire state's got a problem."

"How serious?"

Instead of telling her, I took a chance and demonstrated; did it to convince myself of something that I already believed was true. Witness an emaciated street child using a

Popsicle stick to spool a guinea worm and you'll never forget what the parasite looks like, how it behaves, nor what you've later read about it.

In the kitchen, I'd filled a glass bowl with water. Now, back in the room, I placed the bowl on the gurney next to Applebee's ankle. After several seconds, the parasite's senses began vectoring, its bristled scolex twisting, searching. After a few more seconds, it leaned toward the bowl, arching like a caterpillar. Then it stretched until it could insert its head into the water.

Instantly, from its mouth, the parasite began to emit a milky current that bloomed slowly, slowly, murking the bowl.

"You're seeing why it could be a serious problem. Males die after fertilization, so these are all gravid females. The milky substance is a stream of larvae. Each female releases tens of thousands.

"Imagine them dumping many millions of larvae into a lake or river. The copepods I mentioned feed on them, and the worm begins to develop. Then you or I come along, swallow or inhale a few drops of the water. Our bodies become part of the parasite's life cycle."

The woman made a shuddering noise. "Did Dr. Applebee know — do *victims*

119

know — what they have inside them?"

"I'll do more research when I get home, but I think it's asymptomatic. Maybe a low-grade fever toward the end, but that's all until the parasite begins to exit."

Sounding woozy, the woman said, "Ohhhh, that's *revolting*. I've got to get out of here." She turned and walked toward the hallway door. "What about the deceased? Is it safe for us to bag and transport?"

I told her I thought it was, but suggested she contact the Centers for Disease Control in Atlanta right away.

"They need to get a team down here and start collecting samples. It takes the female parasite a year or so inside the host to reach sexual maturity. If Applebee was infected locally, then they've had at least twelve months to spread."

The Everglades watershed begins just below Orlando as a series of lakes known as the Kissimmee Chain. Lake Toho was one of the largest lakes in the system. I didn't tell her that the entire southern part of the state might already be infested because of the natural, slow flow of water.

No one was more aware of the Everglades' complicated interlinkings than Jobe Applebee.

Something else I chose not to impose on

Rona Graves was a request for plastic specimen bags. I wanted to harvest samples of the parasite so I could have a look under the microscope when I got back to Sanibel.

The medical investigator didn't seem up to that.

9

LOG
(Kissimmee motel)
13 Dec. Monday
Cold front dissipating, gray jet stream clouds. Damaged my boat. Nose, shoulder, ribs ache. Dreamed of parasites, then old familiar nightmare. Awoke w/sweats.

Spoke w/Dewey 3 times this morn. Still pissed off, irritable, eager to get off phone.

List: 1. Meet Frieda, search Applebee's house. 2. Call Laken, check on sharks. 3. Xmas presents.

Frieda Matthews told me the family seldom disclosed the truth about Jobe, he'd done so well professionally.

There was a reason he was different.

"When we first found out, I guess we were ashamed. By the time we knew there was no

122

reason to be ashamed, he'd already made it on his own. So it didn't seem to matter."

Her brother had been born with Asperger's syndrome. She said it had nearly destroyed him as a child, but then defined him as an adult. He was one of those uncommon people who found success through his handicap.

Asperger's is a form of autism; a neurological disorder that causes developmental problems.

"Aspey people, like Jobe, have a unique view of the world because their neuron pathways develop differently. They approach problems from unexpected angles because their brains are uniquely wired. It's like there are two different software platforms for human beings. For every thousand IBMs like us, there are two autistic Macs."

It was a little before noon on Monday, the thirteenth day of December, the morning after I'd found Applebee's body. A gusty north wind was pushing gray stratus clouds toward Key West. The void was filled with Canadian chill, dropping the temperature into the mid-fifties. Because she'd been unable to sleep after hearing about her brother's death, Frieda had left her son and husband in Tallahassee, pointed the family

SUV toward Kissimmee, and called me on the way. Would I wait there for her?

I didn't want to spend another night away from Sanibel. But how do you say no to a twin whose sibling has just died?

I got a room at a place outside Kissimmee called Caribbean Villas — but only after first having a late-night bottle of wine with Rona, the much-shaken medical investigator.

"I usually don't guzzle my wine like this," she'd told me more than once. "But after witnessing something like that — *my God.*"

I replied, "I'll believe it about you if you'll believe it about me. Then maybe we can rationalize a second bottle."

Now Frieda and I were in my leaky skiff, idling away from the marina, headed for Night's Landing. I wore a red Gore-Tex squall jacket zipped tight. I would have worn gloves if I'd had them — water intensifies cold. I was taking my time, going slow. A sheriff's detective said he wanted to meet us at the house and go through Applebee's personal effects, maybe find something that would tell them why two foreigners had been interrogating the man. Also how and why he had died.

I'd told Frieda about the Russians, but not about their interrogation techniques.

Also told her about the two late calls made from my cell phone.

While on our second bottle of wine, Rona and I had redialed the numbers. At that late hour, we'd expected to get recordings, and did.

One was the voice of a woman who said I'd reached the environmental engineering office of Tropicane Sugar. The second was a digitized message that said I'd reached the Florida offices of Environmental Protection and Oversight Conservancy, a nonprofit group, and that I should try again during regular business hours.

Neither gave the option of leaving a message.

I knew a little about them both. Tropicane was one of Florida's largest producers of cane sugar. It was a privately owned, megadollar corporation, from what I'd read. It employed hundreds of people, maybe thousands. A major economic and political player.

Frieda said it might have been Tropicane that had commissioned one of her brother's dioramas. He'd done work for both organizations.

The Environmental Conservancy, or EPOC, was a watchdog organization. It kept a low profile in the way of the Nature

Conservancy, and the Natural Resources Defense Council. It was well financed, politically conservative. It favored lawsuits over headlines, unlike more controversial nonprofits, such as Greenpeace, PETA, and the Earth Liberation Front.

It was a more thoughtful group that preferred to work in the background. That was my impression, anyway.

Frieda surprised me, saying, years back, she'd been introduced to EPOC's founder, but the meeting had had nothing to do with environmental issues.

"At the time," she said, "he was still a practicing research physician. Dr. Desmond Stokes. A real doctor, but he had a more holistic approach to medicine. I wanted to get pregnant, but was worried because I had an autistic twin. The genetics were risky."

Stokes had published a study that suggested that high doses of vitamins during pregnancy, combined with a diet of organic whole foods, reduced the risk of autoimmune disorders in infants. Stokes was working on the premise that autism had an autoimmune link. His research suggested neurotoxin pollutants in the environment were contributing factors.

"Heavy metals," she said. "The sort of

stuff you and I find all the time in water samples. Mercury's the most dangerous during pregnancy. It's everywhere — vegetables, fish, even some infant vaccines. People don't realize. So I went to one of Stokes's lectures. Impressive. But a very neurotic guy. What's the phobia when a person's afraid of germs?"

I said, "I don't know, there's a whole list. Germ-a-phobic?"

That got me a smile. "Whatever it's called, he told the audience his parents were doctors who'd specialized in infectious diseases and parasitology, and they'd given it to him — the phobia. Like he was kidding, but I think he was serious. He was explaining why he wouldn't be shaking hands, hanging out later. I signed up for what he called a 'dietary protocol,' which meant buying his designer line of vitamins."

Even I recognized the brand when she said it.

She added in a wry tone, "A year or so later, I read that the state took away his medical license because of a new procedure he was trying, sheep placenta injections. Something like that. You don't remember?"

I told her I'd been working out of the country during that time. There was an entire Florida decade missing from my memory banks.

"It was ugly. Tabloid stuff, which I followed because I felt like I'd been taken in by a quack. He moved his whole operation to the Bahamas. The vitamin company's huge, and Dr. Stokes is now so rich that he doesn't have to worry about strangers and their germs. Founding EPOC was maybe a PR move, but it's also a way he can fire back at the U.S. government with lawsuits. The 'Angry Expatriate.' He's been called that."

"Did your brother know Dr. Stokes? The autism could've gotten them together."

"Possible, maybe probably — now that I know he had some contact with EPOC. Jobe was big on vitamins."

"What about Tropicane? Any friends there? Someone who might be hanging around the office that late, waiting for his call?"

The woman shook her head: No. Said that Jobe being Jobe, he didn't have personal relationships, especially with employers. He contacted clients at their office, never at home.

"But why would he call both offices that late, when he was in trouble?"

She said, "A clock meant nothing to him.

Maybe someone was supposed to answer. I don't know."

Finally, I mentioned the guinea worms, told her that I'd found the parasite in his house, nothing more, and asked if Jobe had ever been to Africa. Could he have been doing research?

If the animal's life cycle included water, she said, he *might* be studying guinea worms. But, no, he wouldn't leave the country, and definitely not for Africa. He hated travel.

"A year or so ago, he surprised me by going to Cuba for some kind of meeting. When I asked about it, all he said was, 'Never again.' That's how much he despised travel."

Disturbing, but I didn't react. The woman had enough to deal with.

Frieda is a lean, handsome woman who usually dresses more like a fishing guide than a respected scientist — pleated shorts, lots of pockets, baggy shirt — but on this chilly morning she wore business slacks and a suit jacket in mourning black. Her face was gaunt from lack of sleep, her brown hair dull as winter leaves. I was there for moral support, which consisted of providing a shoulder to cry on — she'd already done that a couple of times — and an attentive ear. Let her talk away some of the pain.

Talking about her brother's disorder was part of the process. Perhaps because the subject had once been a source of shame.

As I listened, I also allowed my attention to shift to the bilge switch, periodically, and the amount of water leaking into my boat. I'd loaded it on the trailer the previous night and found a radiating crack near the starboard chine. I suspected this would be the last time I'd be aboard.

I flicked the bilge switch now, then accelerated onto a slow plane, as Frieda continued talking. "Asperger's is a milder form of autism. Some call it 'high functioning' autism. Growing up, kids with Asperger's lack basic social skills most of us are born with. They tend to focus their interest on objects, not people.

"Jobe had a tough time learning to talk. He didn't like being around people, and he was obsessed with orderliness. He . . . well, here's an example. He always counted his Cheerios, and separated M&M's by color. His toys had to be arranged *exactly* the way he wanted. If anything screwed up our daily routine, he'd run around flapping his hands and crying. He wasn't a brat. Emotionally, he was just incapable of handling disorder.

"Things in the external world — noise, certain smells, harsh light — it affects autistics differently. Seeing the color orange, for example — neon orange? — it made Jobe wince. Hearing several people speaking at the same time drove him nuts. He loved the sound of trains, though; the rhythm — but only from a certain distance. Amtrak goes through Kissimmee, the perfect distance, and one of the reasons he chose Night's Landing. That, plus it's close to Disney World."

"He did environmental work for Disney?"

"Some. But that's not what I meant. Jobe was uncomfortable in public places. Disney World was the exception. You've been, of course."

"No. Never."

"*Really?* Well, my brother had a love-hate relationship with the place. Disney is the most orderly place on earth. Every venue is predictable and tidy. No surprises, no clutter. Jobe liked that. On the other hand, he hated what the theme park industry has done to Central Florida."

Even so, she said, her brother went often, always, by himself.

"Otherwise, autistics tend to retreat into their own internal world. A place where they can fixate in peace. With Jobe, it was water and numbers. He was hooked on both. Did you try to call him on the phone?"

"Yeah. His message was strange — leave your four-digit birthday, zeros included. Like it had something to do with astrology. I didn't expect that."

"No, not astrology. My brother couldn't remember names — they were *words*. But he never forgot a birth date. That's how he cataloged people. Phone numbers weren't good enough. Phone numbers change. That would have been upsetting. He even referred to family members by number. Our father was '10-7.' October seventh. Our mother was '3-2.' March second. He called me '6-6-4,' because I was born a few minutes before him on June sixth. See how it works?"

I started to say, "I thought autism was a form of mental . . ." but caught myself.

Frieda patted my knee. "You were about to say 'retardation.' It's okay. Most people think autistics are also retarded. About half *are*. IQs less than seventy. But some of those are savants. They don't have the intellectual capacity to use a calculator, but they can look at a pile of toothpicks and tell you the exact number. Remember the film, *Rain Man*? That's Jobe.

"Aspies are like alien beings who aren't

programmed to understand normal social behavior. They can't decode body language, or sense the feelings of others. Even motives. *Especially* motives. If I told my brother that I wanted him to rob a bank as part of an experiment, he wouldn't see it as sinister. It was an experiment, so that would make it okay."

She added, "It makes them vulnerable. Early on, they learn to understand that they're easy targets for cons and practical jokes. So Jobe preferred his own little world. No one was allowed in. Not even me, his twin. I learned never, ever, to push, because it doesn't pay to piss off an Aspie."

In my mind, I could hear the man's voice crying over and over, *I can't*, as if apologizing for being unable to cooperate.

Frieda said, "When we were kids, the doctors didn't bother testing him — this was thirty years ago, remember. He didn't talk, wouldn't interact, so he was labeled retarded. Autism wasn't recognized as a neurological disorder until we were middle school age."

But when Jobe was five, she told me, he stopped at a table where his mother was doing a complicated jigsaw puzzle. He studied it for a few minutes, then began to lock pieces together. Never paused, not one misjudgment. In twenty minutes, he'd finished a puzzle that would have taken an adult a week.

"Our mom was so darn happy; running around, laughing. Her so-called mentally retarded son had just demonstrated that he was actually very gifted."

Further testing proved that the boy had an extraordinary gift for mathematics. He could multiply long columns of numbers instantly and factor cube roots in seconds. Jobe's family was elated.

The elation, Frieda said, didn't last.

Because of his behavioral problems, his tantrums and refusal to interact with people, doctors decided that if the boy wasn't mentally retarded, then he must be mentally ill. At age six, Jobe was diagnosed as schizophrenic and social-phobic, with a severe anxiety disorder.

I'd turned my skiff into the island's channel, slowing for the boat basin ahead, as Frieda added, "It was considered a dangerous combination. Particularly dangerous for me, his sister. I needed to be protected, they said. Jobe had never hurt me, but the potential was there. So doctors insisted that my parents have him institutionalized. He spent the next four years in an asylum, being medicated and treated

just like the rest of the crazies."

But, when she was eleven, Frieda said, their father read a news item about Asperger's. He contacted one of the country's few experts and had his son reevaluated.

Frieda leaned her shoulder against mine, squeezed my arm tight, pained by guilt. I shifted the engine into neutral and let the boat drift, giving her time to finish.

"Doc, I don't know how he endured that place. I was terrified the few times I visited. The screaming, crying, people in straitjackets sitting around muttering. It even smelled of something dark . . . chaotic. There's that word again. We'd sent my brother into the thing that terrified him most. Chaos.

"Jobe told me there was only one place to hide. The asylum had a wading pool. There couldn't have been more than six inches of water in the thing. But it was deep enough to cover Jobe's ears if he laid on his back. He spent hours there lying in water, eyes closed. It was his only refuge."

"*Water,*" I said, sharing the significance.

"Yes. That's why, last night, on the phone, when you described him as having a look of peace on his face, like he'd been set free — it meant so much. My dear, sweet,

135

misunderstood twin had suffered . . ."

She couldn't finish. I turned so she could bury her face in my chest again.

Inside the late Jobe Applebee's home, sheriff's detective Jimmy Heller said, as if finding it difficult to believe, "The deceased was your twin. But you've never seen the upstairs?"

Her eyes dry, and more businesslike now, Frieda replied, "Nope. My brother was a private person. Geniuses can be idiosyncratic."

I stood beside her at the stairs, admiring how she normalized her brother's behavior by elevating it.

When we'd arrived, there were two detectives, not one. The second detective was the one with the digital camera and recorder. But he'd been called away, leaving us alone with Heller. So this meeting was more informal. Heller was a squat little man, plaid sport jacket, Bronx accent, smelled of cigars. He had the look of racetracks and bookies, not inland Florida. It caused the man's questions to have a prying quality.

The question about the upstairs wasn't out of order. An iron gate had been installed on hinges at the third step, locked with a padlock. We couldn't find a key, so we'd have to climb over to search the rest of the house.

The detective pointed at the gate now. "Did you find *this* unusual? How many people you know got a lock on their stairs?"

"My brother despised conflict. The downstairs was available to visitors. The upstairs, though, was his. The gate was his way of not having to explain."

Heller said, "Mind if we go up, have a look?" Said it in a way that let us know he didn't need permission.

Frieda was taking off her suit jacket. "It seems like an intrusion. Even with . . . even with him gone. But I guess we have to."

Yes, we had to.

We'd spent an hour going through the downstairs. As we did, the detective told us that the boat used by the duo I'd described as Russian had been found abandoned in the south part of the lake near a road called Pleasant Hill Boulevard.

It'd been stolen, and was being checked for fingerprints.

Heller added, "If we didn't find any useful prints here — after the mess they made? — I doubt if they were dumb enough to leave them on a hot boat."

They'd torn the house apart. Files ransacked; cabinets and bookshelves overturned. They'd smashed the hard drive to Applebee's desktop computer, then poured some kind of syrup into it.

They'd been looking for *something*.

In Jobe's office, next to the study, Frieda compared the various power cords, kicked around the rubble, before deciding his laptop computer was missing.

"It was a Mac," she told us. "A PowerBook. Silver."

The Russians hadn't been carrying a laptop when they ran.

Heller said, "His computer's missing. That could be important. I don't suppose you know how he backed up his information?"

Disks, minidrives, floppies. There were none among the wreckage.

"No, he never backed up anything. His memory was so good" — Frieda tapped the side of her head — "he kept everything up here."

Heller said, "Which maybe could make it more valuable. Depending — see what I'm saying?" He looked around the room, as if the computer might materialize. "Where you suppose it disappeared to?"

The woman told him, "Maybe somewhere else in the house."

10

Detective Heller climbed over the stair railing. Frieda began to follow, but I touched my hand to her shoulder.

I wanted to go next.

I didn't know what we'd find, and I wanted to be in a position to shield the lady if something nasty was waiting up there.

What we found, though, was the opposite of nasty. It was a lesson about the strange little man whom I was beginning to admire.

Florida was up there. The delicate peninsular oddity that European discoverers called the "Flowered Land." It was the state as if seen from a space capsule, reproduced as a diorama. Maybe the same intricate, three-dimensional model that Tomlinson had seen at that save-the-planet rally.

My pal was right. An exceptional work.

"How beautiful," Frieda whispered, all three of us staring. "So this is what he did up here all alone."

I said, "This kind of precision . . . meticulous. I've never seen anything like it."

"Thank God, they didn't do too much damage."

The Russians had been here. Cabinets were opened, contents scattered. Dust streaks showed they'd moved the diorama, maybe to look under it. Not easily done. The thing was huge. Dominated the upstairs.

Jobe had knocked out all but load-bearing walls. The room was raw-beamed, high-ceilinged, open as a warehouse. It was a big space that echoed. Later, I would pace it: approximately twenty-five yards by twenty yards. The diorama took up most of it.

He'd painted the floor a vivid, Gulf Stream blue to represent water. Then he'd constructed a scaled-to-size likeness of the state, shore to shore, from the Panhandle to Key West, all in interlocking sections. I paced this, too: seventy feet long, not counting the scimitar chain that represented the Florida Keys. At the middle, near the Lake Okeechobee area, the model was a little over twenty-five feet wide.

This was a museum-quality replica work built of wood, wire, paint, clay, natural stone, sand, and earth.

Peninsular Florida is about four hundred

miles long and a hundred fifty miles wide. I did the rough calculations in my head. Approximately two inches equaled one mile. It gave Applebee room to include unexpected surface features.

At first glance, the detail was remarkable. It got better. There was a pan-sized magnifying glass mounted on a nearby trolley. I switched on the light, lowered the convex lens, then stared awhile before giving a low, soft whistle. "You need to look through this."

Tomlinson was right. This was art. The magnifying glass changed the aspect from a satellite view to what you might see flying over in a Cessna. What seemed to be beaded mosaics were actually micro-sized communities, bricked downtowns, shopping centers. Cars were half the size of a rice grain, yet so exacting that Applebee must have used surgical instruments. Diminutive wire trees — cypress, mangroves, gumbo-limbos, and oaks — the river systems, sinkholes, lakes, pine uplands, cities, military bases, train lines, baseball stadiums, and strands of royal palms were meticulous. This might have been a miniature world, populated by a miniature race.

Some landmarks were larger than scale. Near Orlando, he'd built a tourism icon disproportionately big: the Disney World castle, spires, and flags in place. Had Frieda not explained her brother's love-hate feelings, it would've seemed absurd.

The castle dominated the region — maybe a symbol of perfect order in the little man's orderly and private world.

Or maybe a symbol of something he detested.

The model could have been created only by someone with a hydrologist's eye for the interlinking of water. The man knew the fragility of a biota that was floored with porous limestone, dependent on moving water.

Kneeling, I said to Frieda, "Look underneath. It has layers, like a wedding cake. Everything built on tracks, so it can be viewed in sections. There's a pump system, too."

Heller helped me slide away a portion of the top. The region's substrata lay exposed.

Florida sits on a skeleton of prehistoric sea creatures and corals, karsts topography. It's a honeycomb of caves, underground rivers, and permeable limestone. The diorama showed sections of the state's three main aquifers. The depths were labeled incrementally from one hundred feet to three thousand feet.

I'd read about the complicated interlinks; here they were easily seen. Every water source served as a conduit to another. Drop a gallon of red dye into a sinkhole near Cross Creek, or Gainesville, and a red bloom might reappear days later, and several hundred miles away, in some inland lake near Miami. Or Florida Bay off Key Largo. Or Marathon — the dye jettisoned from the inner earth by subterranean current.

Applebee's creation was a three-dimensional schematic. Plastic tubing replaced rock corridors. Aquifers were walled with Plexiglas. He'd elevated everything off the floor to hide the complicated pump system beneath.

I found the switch, and the pumps were soon making a pleasant, burbling hum as water circulated throughout the model, re-creating flow patterns below and above the ground, including the slow, pan-flat drainage of water from lakes of the Kissimmee Chain into the Everglades.

That caused me to think of exotic parasites.

"How long you think it'd take a man to build something like this? A couple years?" Heller was impressed, but his tone was also saying, *A nut case, man. A kook.*

Frieda said, "My brother? When he got into something — a project, an experiment — nothing else existed. He'd stay up forty-eight hours working nonstop. Seventy-two hours — whatever it took. But even for him, lots and lots of hours."

I said, "This needs to be preserved. Maybe Gainesville, the Florida Museum of Natural History. They have good people there."

The woman was nodding. "Or the Smithsonian."

She was standing in what would have been the Gulf of Mexico, at the Florida Panhandle, near Tallahassee. I realized that I, too, had drifted automatically toward my home. I was standing above Sanibel and Captiva islands, still using the magnifying glass, charmed by the micro-sized docks of Dinkin's Marina, and the pinhead-sized stilt house that represented my home.

Like certain salmonidae, humans tend to gravitate to the place of their origin.

Applebee hadn't included all the marinas in Florida — impossible — but he'd included my little island, larger than scale.

I was touched. I remembered Frieda saying that he'd read my papers. He was a fan. It could have been the sort of flattery that we all indulge in from time to time. But the man had included my home in his intricate vision of Florida, so maybe it was true.

The woman stooped, touched her finger

to a watery area southwest of Tallahassee. "Unbelievable. Doc, you've been to Apalachicola?"

"My favorite oysters."

She was staring at the tip of her finger, then held it out to me. "Miniature oyster bars. Real shell flakes. He probably had to use a surgical microscope."

I told her, "That's what I was thinking."

We both glanced around. No microscopes. No lab, no tools. No work station, either.

"The house has a third floor and an attic," she said.

Detective Heller said, "Mind if we take a look?"

Jobe's workshop and lab were up there, and the Russians had made another mess. Piles of wreckage, everything scattered. There were broken microscopes, files, computer discs, plus vials, test tubes, cabinets, and aquaria all smashed or ransacked. Same with shelves that had been filled with power tools, jeweler's tools, chemicals, and hundreds of bottles of hobbyist oil paint, glue, books, manuals — all left torn, broken, or leaking on the floor.

The little man had been working on a second diorama. It was Central Florida, from Orlando to the lower fringe of the Everglades. The Disney Castle was waist-high, a couple of yards wide. A theme park complex was built around it, including lakes, islands, restaurants, buses, parking lots, and miniature paddle wheel boats.

The Russians had been rougher on this model. They'd busted open the castle, all of the larger buildings. The destruction seemed more of a violation because, through the broken roofs, we could see that the interiors were as detailed as the exteriors. Each and every room was painted, appointed, furnished.

"This guy — your brother — he really got into this stuff."

The detective's tone said again — a kook — but also that it was kind of cool.

"I've got a bunch of nieces and nephews, so I've been to Disney World more times than I wanted. The inside of these buildings, your brother has them nailed perfect. Like he shrunk them down itty-bitty."

He was moving from venue to miniature venue, inspecting. Looking into drawers, under piles of wreckage. Doing a thorough search of his own — my read.

"No offense, lady, but why'd he screw around, waste his time on something like this?"

I interrupted. "Whoever made this mess didn't think it was a waste of time. Why so much damage? They didn't have to tear the place apart." I said it tactfully, hoping he'd correctly interpreted the mayhem in this room. It had a frantic quality. Whatever they were after, finding it was important enough to risk prison — even for murder. The object was valuable . . . or incriminating.

Why else pour syrup into a computer? Break so much valuable equipment?

Heller didn't seem interested. He continued poking around — a bloodhound sniffing. That was the impression. Or maybe he had that low-key city guy in the sticks style: Sounding dumb was a way to play it smart.

"Look'a there," he said, pointing at tiny green boats on a miniature lagoon. "I've *been* on that ride. My sister's kid, it's her favorite."

Frieda was staring across the room at something. "That's the Magic Kingdom. It used to be his favorite; dioramas there, too, so maybe that's where Jobe got interested. Each diorama represents a different country."

She began walking away. "Earlier today, I told Doc that my brother hated to travel. I guess he did all his traveling at the Magic Kingdom."

When she told us the name of the ride, that inane music came back into my head.

What had grabbed Frieda's attention were dozens of pencil sketches tacked to the wall. Several were rough studies of what, at first, I took to be faceless, noseless sketches of Mickey Mouse viewed from many angles. The sketches had a geometric quality, as if someone had taught a machine to use a pencil.

They were unsigned.

The adjoining wall was papered with computer-generated images. Charts of South Florida, arrows to illustrate water flow vectors. Graphs representing outflow from Lake Okeechobee, month by month. Cross-sectional water tables showing elevations of bedrock or sand. Diagrams on grid paper, labeled, "The Effects of Altered Hydrology on Sugar Retention Areas."

Incongruously, there were also the likenesses of two easily identified singers, and also a female actress — her brother's favorite entertainers, Frieda said.

A woman, too. Several of her. Attractive in a feral way, high cheeks, pointed chin. Blond? Couldn't tell. I wondered if it could be the woman who'd been beating him, but decided it was unlikely. There was warmth in the woman's expression.

Applebee showing a glimpse of his human side.

Frieda was there, too; a child with a handsome face and pigtails. Beside her was Jobe — a self-portrait created by what looked to be thousands of dot-sized zeros.

Or were they?

Sniffling, trying to hold back tears, the woman said, "When we were kids, he couldn't color between the lines. It embarrassed the heck out of him. I'm surprised he ever picked up a pencil again."

She was studying the likeness of a large man, thick glasses atop his head, leaning over a microscope. It took me a moment to realize that it was me.

"This is from a photograph I sent him. Do you remember when I took it? You were visiting the lab in Tallahassee. Jobe always asked how your work was going. I sent him a photo just in case you two ever met."

I found it more than peculiar. The woman sensed my uneasiness, explaining, "It's like with the singers and the actress. He was a fan. Plus, who knows, maybe he saw you as a normal version of himself. Two guys obsessed with water, but you were the sociable version. We all live vicariously through others at times, don't we?"

I told her, yes, most of us do.

I'd been studying the tiny zeros; decided they weren't zeros after all.

"Take a closer look," I told her. "What do you see?"

She looked for a moment, then turned. "They're not dots like I thought. It's that damn cartoon mouse again. Reduced, then computer-generated thousands of times. Round face, two round ears on top. So childlike."

Heller said, "Like a kid, yeah. A thing for Disney." His tone created more distance, saying, Weirdo. "If you find out anything about that missing computer? You call me pronto. Okay?"

I was studying the facsimile of my own face. The pupil of my right eye was darkened by hundreds of the micro-sized symbols. An oval absence of symbols created a glint in my left eye.

Heller was right. Weird.

But, an hour later, as Frieda and I sat over lunch at a Kissimmee restaurant, I interrupted myself in midsentence. Snapped my fingers, saying, "Hey . . . wait a minute. Those idiotic Mickey sketches. I just realized something. We're wrong. They're not images. They're symbols."

I asked the waitress for pencil and paper, then slid into Frieda's side of the booth.

"I feel like a dope not thinking of this," as I drew a large circle in the middle of the paper. Atop the circle, I drew two smaller circles, like ears.

She looked at it for a moment. "Sorry, pal. Maybe I'm too upset for my brain to work. What I see is that cartoon mouse again."

"Nope. You told me your brother had a love-hate relationship with Disney. Which is why I don't think it's the mouse. Watch."

On the largest circle, I wrote: "O–2."

On each of the smaller circles, I wrote: "H+1."

I touched the pencil to each. "Pretend you're looking through some futuristic electron microscope. The mouse's face is a single, large-charged oxygen atom. Its ears are positively charged hydrogen atoms, each tilted at an angle. The degree of the angle is a little over a hundred degrees. I remember that from high school biology.

"It's this shape — the cartoon shape — that causes one end of the molecule to be negative, the other positive. If the atoms were arranged to look like anything but

Mickey Mouse, the molecule couldn't adhere to its fellow molecules. Which means it couldn't take fluid form. If the atoms weren't arranged precisely as they are, there'd be no life on Earth."

The woman was puzzled for a moment, but then a smile came to her face. "I can see it now. *Water.* It's the atomic model for water."

"I should've realized it right off."

"Yes! That's why Jobe used it over and over. It's not that damn mouse, it's a water molecule. Should we call Heller and tell him?"

I wasn't impressed by the man. Nor was she. On the drive into town, Frieda had told me there was something about the guy that made her uneasy.

"No, don't call him. I met the county medical investigator. I'll let her know."

Frieda said it again, grinning. *"Water."*

I felt good. Pleased because the Mickey Mouse fascination had seemed inane.

I liked Applebee again.

"You called it his refuge. That's what he was sketching: a mathematically correct likeness of water. With me, it's bull sharks and tarpon. I do the same thing. If I sit down and doodle, they're what I draw."

The woman was pleased, reflective, as she

said, "He was such a dear, private person, my brother. What kind of people would hurt someone like him?"

The image of the Russian woman, belt in hand, came into my head. I heard the belt snap against flesh. Heard the quality of her voice: She liked it, causing pain.

I shrugged. "No telling."

But I was thinking: *People who are abnormal. Someone dangerous.*

11

serpiente

The nineteen-year-old Cuban followed the woman into the tobacco barn, and his abdomen fluttered when he heard the door shut. He'd been trying to think of ways to please her, rehearsing the words he'd say.

Solaris said them now. "I have a present for you. It's in the village. Very rare — the carving of a monkey in jade. Small." Solaris touched thumb to his index finger to give her an idea, smiling to show they shared a secret. "I found the jade as a boy. It's my present to you."

Dasha was unbuttoning her blouse and said nothing.

He noticed that there was a bruise on her cheek and a knot on her forehead. Recent injuries. "Someone has hurt you, beautiful lady. Tell me who and I will kill him with my hands. I'll do anything you ask!"

That got her attention. "A boat fell out of the sky and almost crushed me. I guess you're as dumb as a boat, so maybe you could find a way to kill one."

"A flying boat from the sky?"

"Don't ask."

Mother Mary, what did he have to do to impress this woman? He continued with the speech he'd practiced.

"I've been thinking about something . . . Dasha. Our business — the Chinaman's business? — we've been doing very well. You are my favorite client, but not our *only* client. I'm a young man, but I am thinking of using my money to buy property. It's legal in Cuba now. And taking a wife . . . of marrying. I have to be honest — I miss you when you are away from our valley. You are always in my mind."

Christ, the look she gave him — like he was a bug, but an entertaining bug.

"You missed me. *Charming.*"

As a child, Solaris had fallen off one of the local rock towers, ten meters or so to the ground. The way the woman was reacting, it was the same helpless sensation: no way to stop the momentum of his fall, everything happening in slow motion.

"You are not so old that we can't have children. Can you imagine the babies we'd produce if you'd allow me?"

Her expression said, Are you insane?

The Cuban managed to laugh despite the chill he felt. "We could grow old and rich together. Make children who would take care of us, and we'd sneak back to this barn to make love and remember old times. I would make a very good life for you here. The village grows the best vegetables in Cuba, and the sea is nearby for fish."

The woman spoke to herself in English. "Us have children together? Me and a Cuban mongrel. What are you, part Portuguese, Spanish, some Pole? A little African and Czech in there, too? Bits and pieces of trash left over from the Cold War. I look in your eyes, I see wood fires and an outhouse. I'd rather mate with an animal."

Solaris stared at her blankly. "I don't understand English."

Her eyes became amused. "I'm so flattered by your offer. The two of us married, living in a hut with bawling children. I can stand in the river and scrub clothes with the other fat women while you get drunk in town on pine rum with your worthless comrades. Then you'll stumble home and make another baby in me."

The man held his hands out to her, palms up, choked by emotion. "*Yes*. We will do all that. It will be wonderful."

His chest began to heave, as he thought,

Have I ever been so happy?, when he heard *POP-POP-POP*, three muted percussions outside, like a hammer denting tin. He and the woman both turned to look.

"A car backfiring," she snapped, her tone telling him, *Ignore it.*

Moments later, the barn door swung open, light swinging across their faces. She hadn't bolted the door — a first.

"Dasha?"

"Da!"

The hairy Russian stood silhouetted in the doorway, blue sky and mountains behind, hillsides frosted with white coffee blooms. Solaris used his hands to cover himself as the man and woman exchanged guttural words. Dasha was asking questions, he was answering.

Before he left, though, the big man pointed a finger at Solaris, and yelled something that sounded like, *"Nu vse, tebe pizda!,"* then slammed the door behind him.

"What did he say?"

The woman was hunting around in her bag.

"Aleski? Oh . . . he's probably a little jealous. He told me to go ahead and have fun anyway."

Solaris felt certain that's not what the man had said.

The Cuban watched Dasha take a jar from her bag, and unscrew the lid — maybe there was an oil inside. But, no. He watched as, very carefully, she removed a plantain-shaped balloon like the one she'd shown him before.

"Remember this? I think it's time. After all, if we're to marry . . ." Her tone was teasing.

"Really? You want me to — ? Of course!" Solaris rushed to take the condom before she changed her mind. Took it in both hands, rolling it down over himself.

"I've never used one of these. It feels so strange."

"Does it?" She was smiling.

Solaris was touching the end of the condom — something was inside the elongated tip; something moving. "What is this thing I feel — ?"

The blonde watched intensely, using her tongue to wet her lips. She leaned and retrieved a second container as she saw the man's eyes widen in confusion . . . then fear. Watched his hands slap at the condom as his face contorted with unexpected pain.

"AHHHH! It's biting me!"

She jumped back as he tore off the condom and threw it. Stood and looked at the latex undulating on the dirt floor like a worm in a casing until a miniature scorpion charged out, purple-black, pincers up, tail ready to strike again. Aggressive, even though it was only a week old.

"A scorpion? Did you put it in there?" The way he asked it, Solaris was begging her to say that she didn't.

"Of course not." She was opening a sealed Tupperware container. Inside was a leather pouch. She slid the container next to Solaris. "There's salve inside the bag. It's something I always carry. It'll make the pain go away."

He grabbed the leather pouch, hurrying. Inserted his fingers to force the drawstring open, then screamed again, hurling the bag away. "Jesus Christ, what are you doing to me?"

Dasha kept track of where the pouch landed. Had to. She watched a yellow-and-red-banded snake emerge, longer than her index finger, and as round.

It was a day-old Australian death adder. That morning, a gravid female had dropped seventeen young. They'd been importing the things for more than a year, and Dasha had come to admire the way these snakes, even newly hatched, behaved as if they were old. It was the way they moved: slow, deliberate — animals that interpreted the behavior of other animals before acting.

She'd slid into her sandals. Took two steps and crushed the scorpion. More carefully, she approached the tiny snake from the rear, then stepped on its head, twisting her foot as if it were a cigarette butt. Solaris was telling her, "Something's happening to me, Dasha. I feel very sick. You did this to me."

"No. It was accidental."

He was trying to get to his feet, but he was off balance and easy to push back to the ground. "You'll be fine. It's nothing serious. Relax, you idiot."

A lie. Death adders and Calcutta scorpions were poisonous from birth. On their first trip to West Australia, she'd seen a professional snake handler die from a death adder's bite. They were in the bush, too far to go for help. The man had sat in the shade of a tree, resigned, and told them what was going to happen before it happened.

Without antivenin, even healthy adults die.

Seeing how the snake handler's body had reacted is what had given Dasha the idea. Put the fantasy in her mind, where she played it over and over until she knew she had to find a way to live it. Coincidentally, she read about what happens to a man if he's stung in a certain place by a Calcutta scorpion. Now here it was, happening. No one around to disapprove.

Aleski would be outside dealing with the Chinaman's body.

Three shots to the head. *POP-POP-POP.*

They were done doing business in Cuba. Maybe would soon even have to flee the Bahamas, all because of Jobe Applebee.

"Are you really my friend?" the strange little biologist had once asked her.

"Yes! I'll become more than your friend if you do the things I tell you to do."

Somehow, though, the weird bastard had figured out what was going on.

Idiot!

Ruined everything. Maybe.

For now, though, Dasha would enjoy the moment, by God.

Solaris was moaning. "My eyes — everything's getting blurry. I feel so odd. Like I'm floating. Why do I hurt so bad? Was there glass in the balloon?"

"Yes. An accident. There was glass, and it cut you."

He'd already forgotten about the scorpion.

She was kneeling over her canvas purse, searching for another condom as she continued to check off the symptoms: Mental confusion. Slurred speech. Paralysis of all muscles — she could see his biceps and abdominals twitching — as his eyes turned a glassy blue.

"But him — he's still hard and strong!" Solaris was gasping, but managed a final little joke.

As she pulled his hands away to look, Dasha felt a charge she'd never experienced. Had never felt so eager, her body ready.

Total control — a feeling like that.

She placed the condom on him, like a cap, then unrolled it, stroking him, as she said, "Yes. And he will be alive and standing long after you're dead."

By the time she'd lowered herself onto him, Solaris was.

12

Sanibel and Captiva are exclusive, amiably reclusive islands with shops, shaded neighborhoods, and seaside mansions, but they're also a favorite vacation destination. Publicity about a recent hurricane had frightened off one variety of vacationer while attracting more adventurous types who were more interesting, and a lot more fun.

It'd been a busy year. Especially now. This was Christmas, near peak tourist season, so traffic was heavy even on this Monday evening as I approached the Sanibel Causeway. I crawled across the bridge in my old pick-up, ignoring the tailgaiting BMWs, Mustangs, and eager rental cars, peeved because I'd missed yet another sunset cocktail hour with the liveaboards, fishing guides, and other locals who make up the peculiar family of Dinkin's Bay Marina.

There are reasons I don't like being away

from home at sunset, some personal, most social. On the islands, sunset is ceremonial. It's the convivial, kicked-back, communal time when even strangers become a little friendlier, and the world shifts collective gears, slowing its orbit in the growing, slow dusk.

But missing sunset wasn't my biggest upset that Monday night. During the drive, I'd spent twenty minutes on the phone with Dewey. She was still irritable, quick to take offense.

To get her to talk, I had to ask questions. It's one of her gambits when she's in a certain kind of mood. Silence is a way of controlling. Her responses terse, she told me, Yes, Iowa was cold. Iowa's always cold in December. Yes, there was snow. There's always snow in winter. She'd been stacking her own firewood, shoveling her own path to the barn.

"I guess that's what I should expect, huh? Because I'm carrying a baby and living alone."

Same complaint, different conversation.

I'd replied, "Then come home. We'll live in your Captiva house. I'll take great care of you. It's warm here. Get on a plane tomorrow."

"I *am* home. Why can't I get it through

164

your thick head? I'm where I want to be, and you're where you want to be. Just admit it. Even when you're here, you're gone. I've seen that look in your eyes. Those times when you disappear and I know you're down by the river, probably thinking about fish, water, currents."

She wasn't being fair. But she also happened to be right, which made me feel like hell.

A bad beginning to a Monday night that was about to get worse.

In the mangrove gloom, sky darkening, I parked my truck outside the marina gate, shouldered my bag — several live guinea worms secured in a jar therein — and walked the wobbly boardwalk that connects my home to shore. I'm a guy of habit. The first thing I do when back from a trip is check the wooden cistern-sized fish tank on the lower deck.

Usually, I'm holding my breath as I approach the thing, expecting the worst. Pumps fail, filters clog. A decomposing soup of carefully selected marine specimens makes for an unpleasant homecoming.

But my son, Laken, had been taking care of the lab. He was on holiday from school in Central America, and enjoyed the work. So

I wasn't surprised to find that this wooden aquarium had been meticulously maintained. The sides of the tank were algae-free, the water so clear that it didn't slow my vision even in the weak yellow glow of the deck lights that I'd installed at intervals around the railing.

Everything in the tank — immature snook, tarpon, bandit-masked snappers, horseshoe crabs, spider crabs, blooming anemones, and bivalves — looked healthy and active beneath the crystal water lens.

The boy continued to impress.

Because my place is small, the living area minimal, with one bed, Laken had been bunking at the marina in the guest room of Jeth Nicholes's upstairs apartment. The lights of my laboratory were on, though. On the chance my son might still be up there hanging out at the computer, doing research on the Internet, or writing e-mails to his Latin American pals, I jogged up the steps and pushed open the lab's screen door.

Odd. He'd left the lights on, but the room was empty.

Not like him.

I stood in the doorway a moment, seeing the rows of aquaria — each glass tank lighted in blue, aerators pumping — and noted that my dissecting instruments, jars of chemicals, test tubes, and flasks were all in their place on or above the stainless steel table and sink. Saw that my microscopes were covered; that the Bunsen burner, my centrifuge, my goggles, and white laboratory smock were at the epoxy workstation as I'd left them.

Yet, something felt different.

What?

It was a sensory impression, instinctual; nothing reasonable about it. Something was amiss.

My instincts were right.

I heard a noise off to my left. It was a stealthy, creaking sound well known to me. It was the sound of a big man trying to move quietly.

Before I could whirl to look, I felt a stinging impact on my shoulders as someone grabbed me. I dropped my bag as a big man turned me . . . swung me out into the roofed breezeway that connects house and lab . . . then slammed me hard, face-first, against the outside wall.

He was a tall guy; hands with the sort of hydraulic strength that's daunting — and distressing. He'd locked his fingers around my left wrist and managed to leverage my arm up behind my back; had me pinned there in a hammerlock so painful that I was up on my tippy-toes, trying to reduce pressure on my shoulder.

With his mouth close to my ear, he whispered, "I expected it to be harder than this, Dr. Ford. The way Mr. Harrington talks about you, it's like you're some hotshot stud. I can't wait to get back to headquarters and tell him how easy it was to take you down. Consider this a test . . . and you failed, dude. He said you'd beat my butt."

The man had my face smashed so hard against the wall that I couldn't turn to look, but now I knew who he was. I recognized his voice. It was Parker Jones, the so-called executive assistant of a powerful man by the name of Hal Harrington. In practice, though, he was Harrington's bodyguard and errand boy.

Harrington needs both because he's a high-level U.S. State Department official and covert intelligence guru. What few know is that he's also part of an elite deep-cover operations team. To give members legitimate cover while operating in foreign lands, the agency provided its people with legitimate and mobile professions.

Harrington was trained as a computer software programmer, and later founded his own company. He's now listed among the wealthiest men in the country.

But he's still with the team. The head of it now.

Other members included five CPAs, a couple of attorneys, an actor, a well-known politician, some journalists, and at least three physicians.

There's a marine biologist, too. A man who's traveled the world doing research. Bull sharks, *Carcharhinus leucas* were a specialty.

Me, the much-traveled biologist.

I'd been recruited out of high school. Spent too many revolutions and wars as a covert line officer. Lots of dark nights in jungle hammocks.

Any place in the world *leucas* is found, I could be found.

But the time came when I felt I'd contributed enough. So I resigned. Moved to Sanibel. End of story.

Or so I thought.

Harrington had spent the last year trying to convince me that I was not allowed to quit. Once a member of the team, always a member.

Sending someone to rough me up, though — I never thought he'd resort to that kind of pressure.

Still on my tiptoes, face smashed flat, I listened to Parker Jones say, "I don't know what you do for Mr. Harrington, but I'm gonna tell him that, whatever it is, I can do it one hell of a lot better. So why shouldn't he pay me the extra money? Let you go off and play with your fish."

Wincing, my breath whistling, I said, "Get your hands off me. Or I will personally close your ugly fucking hole."

He hooted. "Whoo-eee . . . now, there's a nasty word I heard you never use. I heard that's not your style. Now I can tell Mr. Harrington you're starting to fall apart upstairs, too, psychologically."

I said, "I only use it on really nasty little people," as I stomped back hard, crushing my heel down on the arch of his foot. The sudden pain caused him to recoil, but he managed to keep my arm wedged between my shoulders.

It gave me enough room, though, to turn and somersault my body forward — a tumbling escape called "a Granby"; a wrestling move that a hard-assed old coach named Fries made me practice month after month until I could do it automatically. Jones maintained his grip on my wrist, but he lost his leverage on my arm.

I was already turning when I hit the deck;

came up on my feet, still pivoting, and used the heel of my right hand to slam his chin backward. Nailed him so hard that his head snapped back against the laboratory wall.

Stunned, he touched his nose, looked at the blood, and yelled, "Hey, you sonuvabitch, you're not supposed to *hit*. This isn't real; it's a fuckin' *exercise!*"

He had both his big hands up now, palms outward, but I wasn't done. I grabbed his right arm and pulled him toward me, dropping down on one knee so that he stumbled and fell, folding his body naturally over my left shoulder. A fireman's carry. My hand still controlling his arm, I stood, lifting the man's full weight on my shoulder, straining to make it seem effortless. Like picking up a child.

The guy was no child. He had to be six-five, over two-fifty.

"Hey, Ford. Stop it, man. Put me down. Goddamn it — *ouch* — that hurts!"

As I carried Jones through the breezeway, I made sure to slam his head into the wall a couple of times, accidental-like. Then, avoiding my shark pen, I continued to the railing that edges the outer deck.

"Can you swim, Jones?"

"Hell, yes, I can swi— Hey, I mean, *NO*. No, I *can't* swim. Did you hear me? *I* . . .

can . . . not . . . swim!"

I said, "Then it's about time you learn," and dumped him over the railing.

The rail is about twelve feet above the water. Jones filled the interval of his descent with a satisfying shriek. It had a falsetto quality, not unlike the sound of an adolescent girl.

When he'd surfaced, and I was sure that he could make it to shore on his own, I called to him, "When you're finished with your swim, I'll be in my lab. That's if you still want to talk. And Parker? Try not to get my deck all wet, okay?"

To Parker Jones, I said, "Don't be tricky. You don't think I know you're wired? Harrington isn't going to let some flunky talk to me unless it's recorded, just in case I get sloppy or pissed off and break one of his golden rules. So go ahead and take the thing off before you get shocked."

He was wearing expensive slacks and a blue shirt beneath a navy blue blazer with gold buttons. His blond hair had been pulled back in a ponytail. With his hair now loose and wet, clothes dripping, the man looked like some unfortunate yachtsman who'd taken a spill off the dock.

He was using a big paw to wobble his jaw

172

back and forth, testing to see if it was broken. "There was no need to hit me. I was playin' the *game,* man. The surprise takedown is part of the security business, keeps us on our toes. A fuckin' tradition. That's what Harrington told me, anyway. But maybe you missed that lesson, or it's just not hip with your tight-assed generation."

We were back in the breezeway between my house and lab; dogtrots, they were once called, for reasons I've forgotten. I'd carried my bag to the lab, placed the jar containing African parasites in a safe place, then gathered a couple of towels.

I lobbed one to him now, saying, "I think my generation must've left me off the mailing list."

"Well, you sure didn't follow the rules. Pain's okay, but you don't *break* nothin'."

"Yeah? My rules are simpler. You can say any asshole thing you want, that's okay. But put your hands on me, or hurt a friend, then someone's going to the floor. No discussion. Win or lose. It's one of my personality quirks."

"There you go, man. Playing the hard-ass again. What was I supposed to do when you smacked me? Fight back? Yeah, sure, I pop you a few times, and then Mr. Harrington would probably fire me."

He was trying to rescue his scuffed dignity by playing an old, old role: I coulda beat you if I'd wanted. But his bullying, smart-assed attitude irked me. So I tossed him another towel, but threw it a few feet over his head. Automatically, Parker thrust both hands up to catch it. As he did, I took a long step, mashed my left foot down on his right foot, then pushed him in the chest.

He couldn't backpedal, so it didn't take much of a push. His arms circling for balance, the man fell butt-hard on the deck, and the back of his head slammed the wall again. Instantly, I was kneeling beside him, my nose close to his ear.

"We don't want Harrington to fire you. So consider this your free pass, mister. Your chance to pop me. Take your best shot. Harrington will never hear about it, not from me. What your doctors tell him afterward, that's up to them."

Jones had had enough. He was waving his hands. "No, uh-uh, I'm done. Another shot to the head like that last one, I might go out permanent. I feel like I'm gonna puke."

I know what it's like to be humiliated, so I helped him to his feet, and put some warmth in my voice. "Okay, no harm done.

Now take off that wire you're wearing. We'll talk."

From the pocket of his sport coat, he removed an expensive-looking ballpoint pen and held it up. "This thing's digital; records up to six hours. Probably ruined now 'cause of the water." He handed it to me. "How'd you know?"

"Oh . . . just a wild guess. I've worked with Harrington a long time. By the way, he set you up. He knew how I'd react if you pulled some boot camp takedown routine."

Jones showed surprise. "*Why?* Like it was a test for both of us, maybe?"

I slid the digital recorder into my pocket. "It's exactly the sort of thing he'd do, suggesting you take a shot at me."

"Gezzus," Jones said, "if that's the truth, I feel kinda stupid."

I told him, "When I deal with Hal Harrington, that's the way I usually feel, too."

13

Still outside, Parker handed me an envelope made of heavy white paper. The thing had gone into the water with him. Soaked.

I told him, "You stay out here and drip-dry. I'll take a look at this and be right back."

The envelope was sealed, as our orders were always sealed, with melted wax stamped with a crest. I'd studied the elements of the crest on more than one occasion. The seal consists of a familiar Freemasons' symbol seen on the back of every U.S. dollar bill: a pyramid capped with an all-seeing eye. There's also a sword — a crusader's sword, I was once told. At the base of the pyramid are three words in Latin that, translated, read: *Forever conceal, never reveal.*

I went into the lab, used a scalpel to open the envelope, and removed a single page on which were typed three words: "Call me immediately."

Unsigned. A typical Harrington finesse.

I crumpled the letter and used a Bunsen burner to set it ablaze. The damp paper popped, sputtered. I watched until it was reduced to gray ash before carrying it to the toilet and flushing.

I couldn't use the lab phone to call him. No. I had to use a *special* phone.

I went out the screen door toward the house. Jones was waiting at the railing, looking over a dark bay that was encircled by a darker, elevated ridge of mangroves.

"You dry yet?"

"No. How you expect me to get dry so quick, man? Even the air on this island is wet."

"Welcome to Sanibel. Where do they have you based?"

"I can't tell you. I'm not supposed to."

"Near Langley, huh?"

"Yeah. Near there. It was snowing a little when I left." He'd been fussing with his jaw again, but stopped to slap at something on his neck, then his forearm. "Hey, the mosquitoes are bad out here. What kinda place has mosquitoes at Christmas? Getting bit in December, man, this just isn't right."

I said, "Deal with it. It's what you get for swimming with your clothes on. By the way, I've decided your boss is a jerk."

"Maybe so, man. I'm not gonna argue. I think my damn jaw's busted." He slapped himself on the cheek. "*Ouch.* Hey — you got any bug spray?"

I said, "Sure. Lots of it," as I opened the door and stepped into my house.

The three ceiling fans were revolving at their slowest speed, stirring the balmy winter air. The floor light between the reading chair and my old Zenith Transoceanic shortwave radio was on, and so was the light over the galley sink. I've learned to use yellow bulbs for exactly the reason Jones was outside whining. Mosquitoes have complicated eyes, but they are not sufficiently complex to recognize the color yellow. They aren't attracted to light they cannot see. Fewer bugs.

I pushed the beaded curtain aside, stepped into my bedroom, and rummaged through the desk until I found two silver keys on a ring. I got down on hands and knees, and pulled the fireproof ship's locker from beneath my bed, and opened it.

One key fits the door. The second key fits a lock to the drawer's false bottom. I opened the first door and removed a small box that contains gold coins I've collected around the world, a small sack of raw emeralds, several folders filled with documents considered important. Insurance policies; titles, stuff like that.

Once the main compartment was empty, I opened the second lock, and removed the false bottom. Beneath it were more folders, a neat stack of notebooks, five counterfeit passports, and other detritus from a covert life.

I was momentarily nonplussed when I saw that two manila envelopes were missing. Over the years, I'd grown used to seeing them when I opened the compartment. Both had been labeled in red ink. One was OPERATION PHOENIX. The other read: DIRECCION: BLANCA MANAGUA.

I'd kept the documents for years because they were my leverage against people who might try to leverage me, and a guard against potential legal problems from which no statute of limitations would ever protect me.

But not so long ago, I'd destroyed both folders. Had tossed them into a driftwood fire. At the time, it'd seemed a safe thing to do.

Now I wasn't so sure.

I still had all of my old notebooks, though. I removed them, pausing to linger over names that I'd written on the covers in precise block print. Each notebook catalyzed visual memories, some good, some bad.

A few of those memories were as unpleasant as seeing parasites spilling larvae into water. A couple, worse.

I restacked the notebooks on my bed, pausing over the familiar with the titles:

CAMBODIA/KHMER ROUGE
NICARAGUA/POLITICS/
  BASEBALL
HAVANA I. HAVANA II
SINGAPORE TO KOTA BAHARU
  (WITH 3RD GURKHAS)
THE HANNAH SMITH STORY

There were others.

I set the notebooks aside. Then a letter I hadn't read in a long time. I was tempted to open it, but didn't. It was from a colleague I'd once dated, Dr. Kathleen Rhodes, a beautiful woman who'd ended the relationship with this note.

I placed it with the notebooks.

There was a second envelope that contained a letter. It was addressed:

Tomlinson
In the event of my death

I set it aside, also.

Lying atop a black Navy watch sweater was a 9mm SIG-Sauer P-226 semiautomatic pistol, a dense black weight. Folded and tucked into the finger guard was a card that Harrington had given me not so long ago.

A name was on the card preceded by a single word: ETERNALIZE.

When "Executive action" became part of the public record, another euphemism became requisite. "Eternalize" was a good choice. Spoken or written, it could be INTERNALIZE, a typo, or something misheard.

Always give yourself an out.

Next to the pistol was a SATCOM telephone, government-issue. SATCOM is a satellite-based wireless communications network with a sophisticated scrambler system. You can speak freely.

I'd kept the thing locked in my lab, but finally stored it here because I found its distinctive bonging chime irritating. The chime was suggestive of a clock in a British drawing room at high tea — very civilized.

The stuff I'd discussed on this phone was anything but civilized.

When I touched the power button, I was relieved that it had some juice. I punched four more buttons, and, a moment later, heard Harrington say, "I knew you'd come crawling back. I hope Parker didn't have to slap you around too hard."

"A sweet guy like him? I was just telling your gorilla-sized delivery boy what a fine man you are. But he seems to think you're an asshole. Which he'll tell you himself . . . if his jaw doesn't have to be wired shut."

Harrington snorted, but was already done with small talk. "I have a couple of interesting jobs. Or have you decided to go ahead and pop your buddy?"

My buddy. The name on the card.

A great many years ago, when Tomlinson was a very different man, he'd supposedly been involved in something that had caused the death of some good people. Tomlinson had regretted it ever since — in fact, it had done a lot to make him the man he is today — but certain people had never forgotten. Harrington, for one. Who better to even the score than Tomlinson's best friend? But I had delayed — delayed, hoping that it would all blow over. With Harrington though, nothing ever blew over.

I said, "I've been thinking about that a lot lately. For a while, I thought Tomlinson was just leverage. A way to keep me on the job. You'd spare him; I'd keep working for you. But you've been pushing so hard, I'm starting to think he worries you for some reason. Something I don't know about. Is that why you want him taken out?"

"Does it matter?"

"If I had a choice, it would."

"You do. Your buddy doesn't."

"It won't be me. I'll never do it. Not a chance."

"Never say never. For now, you're being nice, buying him time. But time's going to run out, you know."

"We'll see. Now, what did you have in mind?"

I told Harrington to tell me about the assignments. I'd see if I could fit one in between having a baby, running my business, and trying to live a normal life.

Abu Sayyaf, a violent Islamic fanatic, had helped plan a train bombing in Madrid — killed a couple hundred innocent souls — and was now working on a plot to target school buses in the U.S., according to intelligence assets.

"Various agencies have people tracking the progress," Harrington said. "But they don't do the kind of work we do. Up close. Personal."

Terrorists believe they can implode the

scaffolding of a society by creating chaos. Bombing schoolkids was madness, but an effective madness if chaos was the goal.

Hal's sources had told him that Sayyaf would soon be taking a cruise, possibly out of Lauderdale. They weren't sure of the dates. Something about his European mistress having problems shaking her husband.

"What I'm thinking is, maybe you can introduce yourself to the gentleman one night while you're at sea. A quick hello. Then good-bye."

I knew what that meant. Could picture it. I had done a similar assignment years before. The complexities of International Maritime Law, and a dark, dark night, are both safe havens of a sort.

"The job's yours if you want it."

I had no qualms about intercepting a man capable of planting bombs on school buses. A couple of years back, I might've struggled with the notion. No longer. For better or worse, I've come to terms with who I am, and what I am. Darwinism describes the human condition as accurately as it explains the competitive process that is natural selection.

Harrington told me, "I've got one more. You'll find this interesting. Bioterrorism, maybe. Biosabotage, at the very least.

We've got a lead on what we think is a network. There's a small-time smuggler named Bat-tuy Nguyen who's trying to go big-time. Vietnamese, but out of Bangkok and Cuba. He's into the illegal reptile trade, importing dangerous exotics."

I was listening. Knew Harrington would save the best for last.

"Nguyen's been branching out. His people have been buying nasty stuff no normal collector wants. Fifty-gallon drums of contaminated water from malaria hotspots in Gabon and Cambodia. Shit holes of the world. Rats from a Ugandan laboratory. Bribing the staff. The rats have been infected with the plague. Bubonic, and there's another type —"

"Rats don't carry plague, their fleas do," I interrupted. "Bubonic and pneumonic. Rats carry the fleas. Jesus Christ, is he selling this stuff to people who have the technology to do something with it?"

"We don't know, it's all fresh intel. We're not even sure if the stuff is headed for the States. But something happened today that spiked our interest." From the man's confident tone — *I've got you hooked. You're back* — I knew what it was before he said it.

"Nguyen's been importing contaminated water from East Africa, too. The CIA's people thought it was the same deal. Mosquito larvae. Someone was buying. But, this afternoon, we got a report through the Centers for Disease Control saying that a certain bigshot Florida biologist had identified a weird sort of parasite near Disney World. Something called 'guinea worms.' Maybe they've spread through the water system."

He continued, "Nationwide, we have some other indicators, too. California, Arizona, some other places. Small-time bio-attacks aimed at screwing up local economies. But Disney? This one's big enough to put our little team on the job."

Yes. He had me.

I said, "I found the parasites in a corpse; a friend's brother, not in the water system. You don't want to hear about it." I was thinking about the guinea worm samples I had in my backpack. If Jones had broken the jars when he jumped me, I might have done more than dump him over the railing. Or . . . maybe putting him in the water with the parasites was the worst thing I could've done.

Salt water, but he wouldn't have understood the difference.

"Any idea who's buying the stuff?"

"No. We prioritize here. Have to, there's so much going on. The bioterror operation moved up to about twentieth on the list this afternoon."

"Then let me give you some places to start."

I told him about Jobe Applebee. Told him to have his people check out the man's business connections, any groups he was associated with. "The Albedo Society may be one," I told him. "There may be room for fringe activism there. Tropicane Sugar's another. Big money can rationalize just about anything. Also, do a search for the conspiracy theory types. People who hate the sugar industry. Or Disney."

"There are people who hate Disney?"

Harrington was being facetious. On this nation's paranoiac periphery, there are groups who believe Disney is at the core of global conspiracies that range from controlling the World Bank to building radio towers that communicate with sex-starved aliens.

Studies have been done on people who believe in conspiracies. Clinical paranoia, plus nonspecific rage, are two common components. Crazy *and* angry: a dangerous combination.

I said, "Someone else who might've been connected with Applebee is Desmond Stokes, founder of EPOC, an environmental group that contracted Applebee. Stokes is the phobic type, got rich making vitamins, but also lost his medical license, and had to move to the Bahamas. So maybe he still has a grudge.

"I'm thinking out loud here, putting together names and subjects that seem to intersect in an unlikely way: Applebee, an employer, germs, disease, an exotic parasite, water."

"The ever-logical Dr. Ford."

"I try, Hal."

"Stokes. I've heard the name. I'll have someone ship the data to you as we collect it. Doc? Let's get something clear first."

I waited.

"You're accepting the assignments?"

"This one. Yes."

"What about Abu Sayyaf, the bomber —"

"Depends on the timing. Someone needs to take care of him. We agree about that."

He seemed satisfied. "Then you're our lead tracker on this one. Work it from your end, too. When you do find Nguyen — or anyone else upper level who's involved in this kind of tradecraft —"

I said, "I know, I know. Eternalize. Your euphemism."

"Or assassinate. We can use the word. Privately. We now have four ways to officially get around Executive Order 12333. So it's legal again. I'll have the papers made out."

Harrington said that I'd be referred to as an unspecified contractor, name classified.

"Just so you know."

14

LOG
14 Dec. Tuesday
Wind NW 18 knots.
Sunset 17:38.
Manatee w/calves under dock. Wood smoke strong, curing fish at marina.
Orders received: 30 Chordates — sea horses, file fish; live barnacle clusters; 24 horseshoe crabs; 24 brittle stars & anemones mix.
Low tide — 0.9 @ noon.
Run, collect, windsurf late. Collect copepods. Mix w/*Dracunculus*.
— MDF

Early the next morning, I called Dewey. She was sleepy but civil. Sounded more like her old acerbic self.

"You keep forgetting the time difference, bonehead," she yawned. "When it's this damn cold, the roosters wait until they smell coffee before they crow. And it's gonna be another hour before I start coffee."

She had an appointment with her obstetrician that afternoon, she told me. So she was going to make the best of it while in town, and have some fun. "We're going shopping."

I nearly asked who her shopping partner was but decided not to risk this new civility.

For half an hour or so, I messed with my telescope, then walked to the marina, where I chatted with Mack as he loaded racks of fish into the smoker. When it was nearly 8 a.m., I clumped up the steps to Jeth's apartment, where I awoke my sleepy-eyed son with a smothering grizzly bear hug.

Time for our morning workout. Five days a week, we jogged Tarpon Bay Road to the beach, swam to the NO WAKE ZONE buoys a quarter mile out and back, then jogged home to the pull-up bar that I'd rigged between braces beneath the house.

Let go of the bar, you get dropped into the water. It's motivating.

We did descending sets. Ladders, they're sometimes called: fifteen pull-ups, then fourteen, then thirteen, twelve, and on down to one. A little over a hundred in all for him. I did more because I've been working at it hard the last six months, beating the body into shape. Watching the food intake. Alcohol, too, especially alcohol. Running, swimming, and I'd bought a cross-trainer bike. During our pull-up marathons, I started at twenty, finished the descending repetitions, then did as many as I could on the ascending ladder.

It was brutal, but it was paying off. I much prefer administering my pain incrementally to the sad, sustained pain of a sedentary, undisciplined life.

On our runs, the kid had had trouble keeping up during the first week or so, but that didn't last. Now I was the one who couldn't keep pace. Not when he stretched those legs of his, and pushed it. He was going to be an athlete.

Sometimes we felt like talking, so we did. Other times we concentrated on the run, comfortable in silence.

On this Tuesday morning, Lake and I ran easy eight-minute miles. I wasn't breathing too hard as we made small talk, traded marina gossip. Turning northwest along the beach, though, I risked a more serious topic. It'd been on my mind awhile.

"Last week, I was going through the garbage looking for a check I'd misplaced. No luck; still haven't found it. But I did find a receipt, U.S. Mail, for something sent overnight to a DNA lab in Texas. A paternity test place. Your name was on it."

The boy didn't turn to look at me. "Were you searching or snooping?"

I said, "I'd just dumped that turtle embryo procedure I screwed up, all those bad eggs. If the missing check had been for less than five hundred dollars, I wouldn't've bothered."

That got a slight smile. "I told you the other night I'm aware there's a chance you might not be my biological father. Mom and her chemical mood swings — I'm not holding it against her. You and I were talking about genetics. I'm curious, that's all."

"You sent in hair samples from all of us; you, me, and . . . ?"

"You, me, and Tomlinson. Um-huh. And Mom, too — I want to be thorough. You're the only one who knows about it, though."

We ran another quarter mile in silence before I added, "Back in those days, before . . . before you were born, Tomlinson and I barely knew each other. We weren't friends. And neither one of us is really sure that he . . . that he might have played a role. He has big blocks of amnesia from that time period."

Laken said, "I know. You've told me

before. I understand."

"If we'd been friends, there'd of been no chance."

"I know that, too."

"I kinda wish you hadn't gone to the trouble. Ordering the test, I mean. I don't see the point."

The boy turned then, smiling. "It's not a big deal. I'll be back in Central America when I find out, so I'll e-mail you the results, or call. Don't sweat it, Dad."

Laken had promised to help paint the bottom of Jeth's boat, so, after our workout, I left him at the marina and returned to my house alone.

I showered, changed, then sat in the lab making occasional notes on the behavior of the five little bull sharks, while also researching the complex life cycle of guinea worms.

I had more than a personal interest now. It was part of an assignment. If some group of crazies was smuggling parasites and disease vectors into the country, the operation had to be pinpointed, then disrupted. Extreme action was now one of my legal options — if the crazies existed. If I found them.

Biovandalism or -terrorism? One was expensive, the other lethal.

Bioterrorism dates back to the Middle Ages, when attackers used catapults to lob the corpses of black plague victims over castle walls. Disease is an effective weapon. Nature employs it daily. For bad guys, it's much easier to conceal and transport something like mosquito larva than ground-to-air missiles.

I wanted to learn all I could about their weapons. Understand the weaponry, understand the attackers. Where to find them, how to stop them.

I'd already had a look at a guinea worm through my old Wolfe stereo microscope, comparing it with a photo I found on the Internet. Imagine a one-eyed monster, its head covered with bristles. From that hairy head protruded two oversized scimitar teeth.

No mistaking what it was.

Tomlinson stopped by an hour or so later. He came on foot from the marina, not in his new Avon dinghy. Arrived with his salt-scraggly hair braided into Willie Nelson pigtails, wearing Birkenstocks, yellow surfer baggies, and a muscle T-shirt that read: A BOTTLE IN FRONT OF ME IS CHEAPER THAN A FRONTAL LOBOTOMY.

I was happier than usual to see him. I'd taken a break from my research, and was reading a distressing article in a scientific journal. The piece presented more proof that our ocean's shark populations are being exterminated for fins and liver. For commercial fishermen — particularly Japanese fishermen — it's a quick, space-effective process because the shark's carcass is then dumped overboard.

According to this study, the population of oceanic whitetip sharks, once among the world's most common tropical species, had declined by 99 percent since the 1950s. They were now extinct in the Gulf of Mexico.

Ninety-nine percent?

Appalling.

The study blamed overfishing, and called for tougher restrictions. Federal fisheries officials, however, responded publicly, saying that the study was flawed. Further assessment was required.

The data I'd found on guinea worms was as unsettling. I'd printed several articles on *Dracunculus medinensis.* The sheath of papers lay on the table near my reading chair.

The derivative, *Dracula,* nailed it. Associated it with a monster who roams around in darkness, living off the blood of others.

Linnaeus, founder of the world system for naming plants and animals, might have found that amusing.

The parasite was also called "the fiery serpent" because of the burning pain victims suffered. To Africa's Haile Selassie religious devotees, it was the Serpent of Israel. Apparently, any worm that generated spontaneously inside the human body was assigned divine status.

Nope, the parasites weren't supposed to be found in lakes — or in human corpses — south of Disney World. Not in the Western Hemisphere, either. Except for a few remote villages in the Rajasthan Desert of India, guinea worms were found only in Africa. The most heavily infected regions lay between the Sahara and the equator.

Subtropical and tropical climate, just like Florida.

Nigeria, Guinea, Ghana, Uganda, Ethiopia, Chad, Senegal, and Cameroon all reported thousands of cases a year, mostly in poor rural villages seldom visited by tourists.

I also discovered an article that confirmed that, once infested, there's no cure. The only treatment is to allow the worms to mature inside the human body, then deal with them as they exit. The parasite could sometimes be extracted within a few days. More often, though, the process took weeks.

During that period, the infected person suffered such agony that it was impossible to participate in normal activities. Pain continued for months. Infected African farmers couldn't tend their crops, parents couldn't care for children, victims couldn't work or attend school, and were often left with permanent crippling.

Infection didn't produce immunity. People in contaminated areas could be infected again, year after year.

A veterinarian journal suggested that some animals were also vulnerable. Dogs, horses, cows, wolves, leopards, monkeys, baboons — any mammal — could be infested.

I'd been wondering about that. Though it's not widely known, Florida is among the nation's leaders in cattle production. Central Florida is also the equestrian epicenter of a multimillion-dollar-a-year horse-breeding industry.

I remembered Harrington telling me that there were other indicators a bioterrorist group was in the States and active. Small-time regional economies were targets.

This wasn't small-time.

I didn't know how many thousands of animals were at risk. But I did know that much of the state's interior is pastureland; open range that's dotted and linked by ponds, lakes, rivers, and creeks. Natural watering holes for Brahma bulls worth ten thousand dollars a head, or a Thoroughbred stallion worth two million.

Along with a medical nightmare, there was also the potential for economic catastrophe.

As I finished reading, I couldn't help imagining worldwide headlines: PARASITIC WORMS INFEST DISNEY VISITORS.

How much would that cost the tourist industry? Billions. Add a few more from the state's agricultural losses.

So when Tomlinson came cruising in humming an old Beach Boys tune that I recognized but couldn't name, I was more than happy to take a break from the morning's research.

Tomlinson told me, "*Hola, mi compadre,* I got a present for you outside. It's gonna put the zap on that blue-collar, pain-in-the-ass work ethic of yours. So I'm like warning you up front. You're never gonna be the same again."

He stood for a moment, peeping over my shoulder at the magazine I was reading; saw printouts stacked on the table. "Hey . . . a new research project?"

I told him I'd found an exotic parasite near the headwaters of the 'Glades, but I'd give him the details later. I'd dealt with the damn things enough for one morning. I was ready to move on to more pleasant subjects.

He whistled softly as he skimmed one of the articles. "What a buzz-robber this is, man. The worm they're describing really tickles the ol' gag reflex. Not that it's any surprise to yours truly. This is the year for plague and pestilence. Some of the old hippie soothsayers, the LSD prophets, predicted it years ago. The year Mother Earth rallies her forces and fights back against the primates who are killing her. There was an article in *Rolling Stone* about it awhile back."

"*Rolling Stone?*"

"One of the anniversary issues. Had all of the old hippie predications listed. They've been making the rounds on the Internet."

I said, "Uh-huh," not paying much attention, but then realized he was serious. "Predicted what?"

"It's like the song 'Aquarius.' Remember? Only the prophecy's a downer, not an upper. The LSD prophets figured it out from the lyrics. When the moon's in the seventh house — everyone knows how it goes. And Jupiter is aligned with Mars? Well, this is the year. A planetary conjunction on the Winter Solstice, just a week from now. Seven planets in a line. They used star charts to fix the date, and now it's really happening. Back then, it was a big deal."

I said, "Oh," already losing interest. I'd been out with my telescope on and off all month, tracking the rare conjunction of planets. But it was six, not seven — unless Uranus or Neptune could be counted. And it was Venus, not Jupiter, that appeared to be cojoined with Mars.

Even so, I hit the internal mute button. I always do when someone begins talking about astrology or prophetic signs.

"We're entering a very heavy biblical phase, which I've been expecting. Read Revelations. The Seven Seals, man. It'll begin with a celestial sign — *think* about the number of planets now in a line. The scripture says the sea will become like the blood of a dead man, and a third of the fishes will die. A red tide, Doc. Understand the meaning? An algae bloom that kills fish. I bet we're in for a bad red tide very soon."

I was covering the microscope, putting

away instruments. "Nope, it's been months since I've gotten any reports about red tide. Which is unusual."

"But what about the parasite you found? It's not the only one, you know. It's been in the newspapers. All across the country, there've been demon exotics raining down out of heaven, stirring up all kind of crap."

Harrington had mentioned small-time bio-vandalism in other parts of the country. Suddenly, I was interested again. "What exotics? Raining down where?"

"That's why I read newspapers, man. One morning I'll wake up, open the *Miami Herald*, and the first sign of the Apocalypse is gonna be grinning at me from between the lines. There've been four or five articles this month — a couple paragraphs buried inside — about what they call noxious exotics turning up in different areas. Outside New Orleans, they're finding giant, poisonous toads, weighing nearly five pounds. Same type that about took over Australia."

I seldom read papers but was familiar with the amphibian. "The Central American cane toad, if that's the one you mean. They're in Delta country? That could be a mess because it's an ideal habitat. Just a few, or significant numbers?"

"Enough to poison a bunch of Cajuns

who tried to fry up the legs; ate them with red beans and gumbo. Kept right on eating until their nervous systems shut down. And they breed like bunnies. Toads, not the Cajuns — though that may be true, too. Significant numbers, and in a bunch of parishes."

I was thinking I'd ask Harrington to provide more details as Tomlinson said, "Another exotic I read about — this was just last week — they had to close a big lake near Houston 'cause some swimmers got various appendages eaten off — piranhas. Those little South American fish with great big teeth. They got their first taste of gringo."

Before I could ask, he answered, "There's a thriving population, according to the story. Like, maybe hundreds of the little darlings, if the first samples are accurate. But mostly immature, so the kimchi hadn't hit the fan as far as tourist swimmers entering the food chain."

I said, "That many fish, they had to be introduced intentionally. We find piranha in Florida occasionally, but pet store numbers, fish that get dumped from an aquarium because the kids are tired of them. But hundreds? It takes a special kind of nasty to do something like that."

Tomlinson shrugged his bony shoulders,

then told me he'd also read about exotic snakes — cobras; a couple of other poisonous African species — that had been found loose in Minneapolis, the Mall of the Americas, crawling around clothing stores, Ben & Jerry's, a CD supermarket.

No one was bitten, but a couple of shoppers were trampled in the panic. And also about a hatch of what are commonly called "seventeen-year locusts" in some rural Southern California county. Cicadas, Tomlinson knew them to be. Their numbers, he said, were so enormous that they clogged village drains, caused cars to overheat.

"This was more than a year ago. They aren't supposed to be in California, and the hatch timings are off," he added. "*Rolling Stone* said that the old LSD prophets had predicted it. A very far-out story."

I said softly, "African snakes in Minnesota, African parasites in Florida," thinking about it.

"You're wondering if it's some kind of organized deal?"

"Yeah, I am. But I also know there are a couple hundred exotic plant and animal species introduced into this country annually. Usually accidentally. So it's more likely coincidence."

"Not according to *Rolling Stone.*"

"Ah. The final word on bio-anomalies and biblical prophecy."

Tomlinson flipped his hands outward, a gesture that dismissed the sarcasm. "I don't *believe* in coincidence, man. Related events, phenomenon, everyone involved — *us* — there's linkage. A purpose."

I said slowly, "Well . . . the timing's interesting."

"Are piranha found in Africa?"

"No, only South America. And cicadas? They're in the northeastern United States, I think. Maybe Africa. I'm not sure. I don't know much about them."

Tomlinson said, "Females bite little slits in tree branches, then deposit thousands of eggs. Eggs hatch, the nymphs fall to the ground, and burrow deep. Seventeen years later, they hatch in mass. Clouds of flying grasshopper-looking things; a million to an acre. And you're right, they don't belong in Southern California. It's a mystery how they got there."

"Where in Southern California?"

"San Bernardino County. A couple little towns, Ludlow and Amboy, got the worst of it. I remember their names because, years back, there was a very cool commune near Amboy where I crashed for a month or two.

Called themselves the Rainbow Amish. A very far-out tribe of herbalists."

I knew the area, too. Near the Mojave Desert, and home to the massive Marine Air Ground Task Force Training base.

"You don't think there's a chance they migrated, got caught in a big wind?"

He said no, entomologists didn't think that was likely. They believed the insects had been imported. Intentionally or unintentionally, they didn't know.

I asked, "Then the LSD prophets are guilty. Maybe your commune friends, too. Maybe *you* — your memory's so spotty. Make a prediction, then set it up to happen. Truck branches filled with eggs across the country. Political activism in a time capsule."

"I don't know, Doc. I think even I would remember smuggling bugs." He mulled it over for a moment. "There could be a connection. Not with me — the toads, the piranha, all the exotics. The *Stone* runs a story about the LSD prophets, which is read by a bunch of wannabe ecowarriors. It gets them stoked. Mother Earth fighting back. They love the idea, so they start doing the copycat gig. Releasing noxious exotics."

Tomlinson took a slow breath, sighed, then sighed again. It pained him that his counterculture brethren may have behaved badly.

"How long ago did the story appear?"

"Maybe a year. More — could be. It's not the sort of magazine where you fixate on dates."

"Shortly after the locusts start hatching in California?"

"Yep. 'Is Aquarius Dawning?' That sort of piece."

"There's no room on your boat, so I know you don't save magazines. If you have time, could you check the Sanibel Library?"

"Sure, dude. Get you acquainted with my fellow Lysergic Rangers. I can see you have a powerful interest."

Rising out of my chair, I said, *"Dude?"*

He was chuckling, mood lightened. "I've spent the last four days hanging out with East Coast surfers. So, yeah, dude. You shoulda stuck around. The language, their tribal customs — bonfire beer bashes and sexual debauchery — I've been adopted. I'm still shredding on the whole gnarly scene. Which reminds me: You need to come look at your present."

Following him across the room, I said, "Gnarly?," as he pushed open the screen door and stepped into the breezeway.

15

With a Barnum & Bailey sweep of his hand, Tomlinson directed my attention to what stood leaning against the railing. "What do you think? You ever seen anything like it?"

I slid past him and gazed at the most beautiful surfboard I've ever seen.

It was a custom long board. Had to be over nine feet. No . . . closer to ten. It was built with an outside skin that was a mosaic of alternating wooden strips — red, onyx, and white — all sealed beneath a protective coating of acrylic. On the nose of the board was an airbrush painting of one of the mackerel sharks: a great white. On the tail was an impressionistic American flag.

Tomlinson asked, "Is this thing exceedingly bitchin', or what? At Vero Beach, when you had trouble catching waves, you should have blamed that shitty rental board instead of yourself. Just like you to take the heat."

I cupped my hands around the rails, taking pleasure in the board's convex lines and its symmetry. It had a ceramic gloss, like sculptured porcelain, and a biconical shape would not have been out of place if spiked into a bluff on Easter Island. The shape was totemic. It was suggestive of ancient stone idols, blood sacrifices.

I lifted the board — amazingly light.

"Your surfing chariot. Like it?"

I said, "It's gorgeous. Really . . . *beautiful*. What I like most is that it's not new, right? It's been refinished. Completely redone."

"My friend, you have a superb eye for artistry. This is one of the classic old Vector boards, shaped by fellow hipster Dave Hamilton on Melbourne Beach. The inlaid woods are from South America and Africa — caoba, rose, and mahogany. Otherwise, it's nearly ten feet of full balsa, but chambered for buoyancy. Dave told me he'd built this one with an extra tail rocker, three stringers, and a long panel vee to facilitate rail-to-rail turns — plus, the thinner rails will make it easier for you to keep an edge in the face of a wave. Perfect for a guy your size."

I said, "I have no idea what you're talking about. It is pretty, though. For someone to put so much time into it, I don't doubt it rides fine."

I was noting the *O* near the nose, just beneath the shark. There was the brand name, *Vector,* imposed upon a line drawing of a globe. The globe was crosshatched with lines of latitude and longitude. Still admiring the surfboard, I added, "But I can't accept something like this. It's so nice, I'd be afraid to take it near the water."

"Dude, it's a present. You've gotta accept it. And she's built to ride, not hang on the wall."

"Why a present? This thing had to cost a mint. What's the occasion?"

Tomlinson gave a regal wave of dismissal: Don't be crass by mentioning the cost. "You have a birthday coming up, young man."

"No . . . Actually, it's way past."

"So I forgot."

"No, you didn't forget. You don't recall the party? The night the fishing guides went skinny-dipping and scared off that group of nice tourist ladies? You gave me a little bag of marijuana. What you *did* forget is that I don't smoke, ever."

Tomlinson had an index finger pressed to his lips, thinking about it. Then he began to nod. "Ahhh, yes. It's all coming back. A lid of Maui Wowie, the world's sweetest, mellowest headbanger kef from Hawaii. I presented you with the classic self-serving birthday surprise. Something that the recipient can't use but the giver loves. I was trying to spare a potential host — you — from disappointing me, the potential visitor. Just in case I happened to stop by and was in the mood for a little pick-me-up.

"Say" — Tomlinson was looking over my shoulder, through the doorway — "I don't suppose you have a little bit of that herbal Kahuna goody left? Your birthday treat? It's going on noon, and I wouldn't mind a couple of medicinal hits. Just a little something to get me through a meeting I have coming up. It's with your sister, The Iron Butterfly. That woman has really been busting my Tater Tots lately."

He meant my cousin, Ransom Gatrell. She'd been raised in the Bahamas, but was now living in a little Cracker house just across the bay on Woodring Point. She's a sharp, tenacious woman who'd been staying very busy these days running the burgeoning enterprises of Tomlinson, the reluctant business tycoon.

He'd become an unwilling capitalist. Thanks to her.

I told him, "Nope. I dumped the marijuana. Threw it out, minus the plastic bag. Sea turtles eat the things."

Groaning, Tomlinson's body spasmed as if he'd been stabbed in the belly. "You threw out an entire lid of Maui Wowie? *Maui Wowie?* Oh dear, dear heaven . . . the waste . . . the *inhumanity.* And I came *this* close to splitting half a key with you! There really ought to be a law."

"There is a law. Has to do with drug trafficking. Which is why I dumped the stuff." I touched my finger to the board's surface again. "There's no occasion, no birthday. So what's the real reason you bought this?"

He shrugged and sniffed as if he had no idea what I was talking about.

"You had your crazy dream again, didn't you? The nightmare. The last few months, if you do something unusually thoughtful, it's because you've had the dream. I keep telling you, it's not necessary."

"It's my money, Marion. I can do what I want with my money. Just my way of thanking you."

I said, "It *was* the dream."

"How can you be so sure? You won't let me tell you details."

"Because I don't want to hear the details."

He referred to it as his Death Dream —

capital *D*s, because of the dramatic way he said it. That's all I needed to know.

"You'd go off on one of your talking jags. Rattle and prattle on and on about the hidden meaning. No thanks."

"I don't rattle, and I almost never prattle," he said. "I take exception to that. It's true that I'm prone to expound. But never rattle. If it wasn't for the dream, I'd of never made that miserable decision to go into business with your sister."

"I'm aware of that."

"If I wasn't sure I was going to die, I wouldn't have fallen for her trap."

"*Ransom's* trap."

"You know damn well she conned me. Got me to agree to try and make lots and lots of money. Live like some fat-ass Daddy Warbucks, then blow it on crap that's useless but establishes social status."

"I'm aware you decided to change your lifestyle."

I was expecting him to tell me, once again, that I appeared in the dream. I was the man who used what he described as "a staple gun–looking thing" to shoot him in the heart.

Another reason I didn't want to hear details.

Tomlinson and I have a convoluted history that goes way, way back. Years ago, before we'd met, a government agency accumulated evidence that a group of underground activists had committed murder. Members of the group were declared a clear and present danger to national security. Agents were sent to track them down.

As Harrington put it, "Our team can do what others can't."

I've never admitted that I was the agent sent to hunt him, but Tomlinson has hinted that he knows.

It was no surprise I'd appeared in his death dream. He'd been making weird offerings ever since.

I turned toward the house. Swung open the door as he said, "I want to share the wealth, because I have the feeling it's going to come true. I'm going to die within a few months."

I looked at him, shaking my head. "No, you're not."

"You seem so sure."

"I am."

There was subtext in Tomlinson's inflections. Mine, too.

"Guilt is a patient sword, man. It's gotta happen."

"Maybe. But not this year, not the next. Besides" — I paused to look at the board again — "I don't think you're guilty. I haven't for a long time. When the time's right, we'll find out for sure."

When he started to protest, I interrupted. "*Tomlinson?* Thanks for the surfboard."

"Pretty cool, huh?"

"Yep. Very gnarly."

"Doc?" I stared at him, hoping my pained expression would tell him I was done with it. "The only friend you don't take good care of is yourself, and the only friend I think you're capable of hurting. I want you to know I'm aware of that."

"People can consider themselves as friends?"

"Lots do. And you should."

I remembered a blind carney telling me I'd one day take the life of a friend. Suicide? An unlikely new interpretation.

"Thanks. I think."

The house phone began to ring. I let the door slam behind me, went inside, and checked caller ID.

It was Frieda Matthews on her cell phone.

I listened to Frieda say, "I'm still in Kissimmee, but Bob called a few minutes ago. Guess what a UPS truck just delivered to our house?"

Bob was her husband.

"Something from your brother?"

"His laptop computer. The one missing from his home. In the note, Jobe said to keep the computer until he asked for it back. That's all. 'Dear 6-6-4, please keep my computer.' "

I waited a couple of seconds. "No mention of why he sent it?"

"No. I had Bob open the laptop and take a look, but our seven-year-old son knows more about computers than my dear, nonconformist hubby. He even refuses to get cable TV."

I said, "There's another reason why I like the guy."

"Uh-huh. But he did find a folder on the desktop labeled Tropicane Sugar — slash — EPOC. As in Environmental Protection and Oversight Conservancy. Both names on the same folder."

Same organizations Jobe had called the night he died.

"Exactly. I walked Bob through how to use a mouse to double-click on an icon. There was only one document that he could open and read. It was a copy of a contract sent to Jobe as an Acrobat file. Tropicane and EPOC had hired him jointly to collect and test water samples over a two-year period in areas where Tropicane diverts water into the Everglades. If I remember right, diverting water to keep their fields dry is a common practice in the sugar industry."

I said, "They all do it. Fields would be flooded half the year if they didn't. But why would a big sugar company hook up with an environmental watchdog group to hire your brother? Organizations like those two, they're usually at each other's throats. Unless . . . unless the sugar company *voluntarily* invited EPOC to participate. They'd only do that if they were confident test results would be favorable."

Frieda said, "That's what I was thinking. We both know the ecobusiness. Corporate America doesn't invite independent oversight unless the news is sure to be good.

"Bob read me some of the contract details. Jobe was making decent cash. Basically, his job was to collect water from various areas, test it, then deliver the results independently to both organizations. Contractually, the data sheets were due every Monday morning.

"For better or worse," she said, "each side wanted original data. No chance of doctoring the results, or trying to hide the truth between the lines. So, yeah, Tropicane had to be darn confident that the water they're pumping into the 'Glades is clean."

I was standing, phone to my ear, near my Celestron telescope, and the desk that holds my Transoceanic shortwave radio. As I listened to Frieda, I could also hear Tomlinson in the galley, rummaging through the refrigerator and cupboards.

I get nervous when the man's alone in a kitchen. He once used mushrooms as garnish for a snapper he'd baked. I didn't know the mushrooms were psychedelic until I'd eaten nearly half the damn things. They were psilocybin " 'shrooms," as they are known, personally handpicked by him in some Central Florida cattle pasture. We happened to be down on the Florida Keys at the time. My memory still generates brief, strobing colors when I hear someone say, "Key Largo."

I interrupted Frieda, saying, "Excuse me a second, okay?," then covered the phone with my palm before calling to Tomlinson, "It's too early if you're making lunch. Unless I'm in there watching."

Slighted, Tomlinson called back, "Relax, Admiral Paranoia. What I'm *trying* to do is find some olives for my *martini*. I have one of those big beakers from the lab filled with Stoli and ice, but I need olives, man. That would seem totally, like, *normal* to most folks. But you have a way of making whatever I'm doing sound *peculiar.*"

I told him that a fresh jar of olives was in the food locker next to the fridge, then returned my attention to the lady. "How long had your brother been under contract?"

"Nearly eighteen months. He was almost done. Only six months left."

"What day did he send the laptop?"

"The UPS slip said Saturday."

The day before he died.

"Then his weekly report was due yesterday, so the report's probably still on the laptop. A portion of it, anyway. That might tell us something."

Frieda was ahead of me. "I know, I know, I had Bob open files related to the project. But he couldn't read them because there was nothing to read. No words, anyway. Only numbers. Every document. Like the computer drawings we found upstairs in my brother's house? Instead of the water symbol, page after page of numbers."

"Numbers?"

"Jobe could remember numbers. Words gave him trouble."

I thought about that for a moment, hearing the sound of ice cubes rattling in glass. "Did your husband notice if any of the numbers were larger than twenty-six? Or mention punctuation marks?"

"Twenty-six . . . ? *Oh,* you're thinking it's some kind of code. Twenty-six numbers, twenty-six letters in the alphabet. Talk about feeling dumb. I didn't ask."

We discussed other explanations. Frieda told me she'd e-mail the Tropicane-EPOC folder to me once she got her hands on the laptop, which would be soon. Her husband and son were arriving in Kissimmee tomorrow, Wednesday, for the funeral, which was to be Thursday morning.

"It's going to be a small service, Doc. Jobe didn't have friends. But do yourself a favor, do us a favor. Stay home. Get some work done. You've invested enough time and emotion. I completely understand."

Inwardly relieved, I told the lady I'd use the time to do some research on the Florida sugar industry for both of us. Refresh my memory on a few things.

I said, "You're going to want to check into the kind of work your brother was doing; who he was working with."

Her voice steely, Frieda said, "Oh, you can bet that I will."

16

LOG
14 Dec. 17:35
(addendum)

Collected copepods w/plankton net from Bailey Tract. Sample count using Wolffuegel grid: 5,000 specimens +/-. Dominant species, *Macro* Cyclops.

Separated undetermined numbers into three 1,000 ml beakers, plus 1 shallow soup bowl. Have introduced *Dracunculiasis* into beakers #1 & 2. Samples hourly.

Order 2 doz Pyrex beakers 200 ml to 1,000 ml.
— MDF

The two of us sitting beneath the helicopter shadows of the ceiling fan, Tomlinson confided, "You're right. I had the dream. I'd smoked a couple of blimpies around the fire after surfing. It was the same in every detail but for one. This time, I didn't die."

I said, "See? I told you. It's all a bunch of baloney." I was sitting on a lab stool watching the little bull sharks, pleased by their attack displays as they began to feed on the tiny, fast baitfish I'd put into the tank. Backs arched, dorsal fins down, the sharks were doing approach elliptics, then attacking.

The deformed sharks weren't as successful.

"This time when you shot me, it didn't hurt. Before, it always hurt like hell, even dreaming it —"

I stopped him with a warning look. I didn't want to hear it. "Then be happy. Believe it."

He was stressed, hyper, but starting to relax — he'd filled another 100-milliliter flask with vodka, and it was down by half. He crunched ice; used his fingers to snare olives as he replied, "Six months ago, sure, I would have been happy. I was convinced I was a goner. Which is the only reason I let that ballbreaker you call a sister turn me into the televangelist of meditation."

"Trapped you."

"Damn right she did."

"It's *her* fault that you're now getting rich by teaching nonmaterialism to the masses."

"Exactly. The American way. But *only* because I believed the dream. Now, as far as karma's concerned, I think I have seriously screwed the pooch."

I said, "I don't get it."

He was shaking his head. I'd missed something that should have been obvious.

He stood and began to pace in small, distracted circles. "All the cash Ransom's been laying on me lately! I woulda never bought the new dinghy, my Harley, the stereo system. Your *surfboard.* All my new clothes — Jesus, I just ordered two new silk suits. Plus my VW van, the Electric Kool-Aid Love Machine.

"I wouldn't have any of that stuff if I'd known the dream was bogus. Cling to earthly material possessions? No way. I'm more than just a Buddhist monk, for God's sake. I'm a fucking *boat bum.* It's against everything I stand for."

I was smiling. "Then get rid of it all. Go back to being who you really are. Ransom'll understand, and everyone at the marina will be a lot happier. We've been worried. We like the old Tomlinson better."

"Ransom won't understand. Are you kidding — tell her I quit?" He whacked himself on the forehead. "The woman's a *witch,* I tell you. She's cast a spell. I've thought and thought and there's no way out."

Ransom is my only living relative, as far as I know, and I love the lady. She's a lanky, busty, mulatto brown dynamo who wears Obeah beads braided into her hair, and sacrifices chickens, sometimes pigeons, on the full moon.

She's the closest thing Sanibel has to a voodoo priestess. Casting a spell is something she could do.

Her father was my late uncle Tucker Gatrell. She inherited his tunnel-visioned genetics, minus the craftiness he passed off as finesse.

I would trust her with my life. I hope she feels as confident in me.

Nearly a year before, we'd been sitting on Ransom's porch when Tomlinson tried to explain why he'd been in a funky mood. He didn't mention the dream, not then. He said he knew his days were numbered — "I continue to inhabit this body for strictly sentimental reasons" — and now felt obligated to explore new experiences. So far, though, he wasn't wild about the options. Maybe we could help.

"I've had this awakening," he told us. "Heaven is *happening*. They drink rum there. Even play baseball — which is the good news. The bad news is, God has me scheduled to pitch on Sunday. Or a few months down the road. So I'm in a rush. As a spiritual warrior, I'm duty bound to touch all the experiential bases before I die, like it or not."

He didn't sound as if he liked it.

Problem was, he said, not many untouched bases remained.

"I've tried damn near everything there is to eat, drink, snort, shoot, seek, try or experience, with the exception of bestiality, homosexuality, and living as a right-wing conservative dweeb." He shuddered. "What an ugly trifecta. I don't think I'm capable of taking a shot at any one of the three. My brain and my gag reflex, both have locked the gates to those particular streets . . ."

He drifted away in thought before finishing, "Bestiality, homosexuality, and dweebsville. If that's all that's left, and I *have* to choose . . ." He shuddered again. "Can you imagine me being gay? With my sex drive?"

It was Ransom who asked, "What about living as a rich man? You ever done it? That kind of change, it wouldn't be so bad."

Her Bahamian accent strung the words together as music: *Whads a'bot libbin' as'a reech mon? Daht wooden be so bod!*

Tomlinson brushed off the suggestion. Told her his family had been wealthy. He had no interest.

"I'm talking about *you*. You ever felt what it's like to make your own pile of money? To want expensive things?"

"Materialism and greed," he replied. "They're contrary to *Shiku Seigan,* my sacred Buddhist vows to live modestly, and root out blind passion. The blind passion deal — I'm not claiming to be perfect, obviously. But living like some starched suit who only thinks about money? No way."

The way he said it — his condescending tone — annoyed her. "That's the way most people live, you dumb stork. You always talking that spiritual garbage. About how you relate to your brothers and sisters around the world. But how can you feel it if you never been in their shoes?

"Most people love money. Darlin', you're *lookin'* at a girl who loves money. Work like hell tryin' to make it big, and it ain't easy. Most of us, we like to buy nice things. But not you. What you're really tellin' me is that you're too good to live like the rest of us. Sayin' money's dirty is the same as sayin' people like me are dirty. You ain't spiritual. You a *snob*."

That got to him. He sat there with lips pursed, eyes drifting, twisting a strand of bleached hair. After a moment, he spoke as if talking to himself. "Hmmm, an interesting concept. Learn to empathize with greed and materialism by experiencing it. You gotta *live* it to understand it. That's what you're saying, Rance. I never looked at it that way."

"You nothin' but a boney ol' stork of a snob," she repeated, sensing an advantage.

"Know what? You might have something. Damn it all . . . I *am* a snob. I'll say something like, 'I want to understand why people love shopping malls.' Or those big-ass, gas-guzzling cars? What's it like to touch a hundred-dollar bill and feel emotion? Work nine to five just to buy monogrammed hankies — that's a weirdy. Pay money to blow snot all over your own initials.

"I pretend to be interested in what drives materialistic people. But I'm not. Not really. I *choose* not to understand their behavior because it's beneath me." He slapped his knee. "Wow! I see it now. What an *asshole* I've been."

Ransom's expression read, There! You finally admitted it, as she said, "People out there trying to make a buck, buy a fine car, but you talk about 'em like they're fools.

Try it your own self if you want to understand. See what it's like to risk your butt startin' a business, knowin' it might fail, lose everything. On the other hand, you might make it big, too. Maybe you might like it, being rich."

"Feel what they feel. Hmmm. I *like* that." He was warming to the idea. He stood and began to pace, letting it happen in his brain. "In Buddhism, we have what are called 'the Three Precepts.' The Three Precepts of Materialism might be . . . self-indulgence, self-promotion, and . . . selfishness? Yeah. Fits. What you're suggesting, Rance, is that I might come to better understand self-*less*-ness if I experience the flip side. *Selfishness.* A very, *very* heavy approach . . ."

"No," she said, irritated, "what I'm tellin' you is to stop mopin' around, get off that dead ass of yours. Find out your own self how hard it is to build a pile of money."

Tomlinson had drifted into another world, trying it on. "Self-indulgence. Self-promotion. Selfish desire. The Three *S*s. Yes. The symbolic trinity in a nation of gold cards. *Perfect.* The dollar sign, after all, is nothing more than the letter *S* transected by vertical lines — three symbols. Get it?"

As I said, "Oh, sure. I'm right with you," my cousin told him, "Tomlinson, you a hopeless fool. I'm talking about money, and you already confused. Talking like you gonna start a new religion or somethin', not your own business."

"I already have my own religion," he answered, a little sadly. "Not through choice, either. Because of the Internet, there're people out there devoted to my writings. Thousands. Unfortunately, I was doing my own version of mandatory drug testing at the time, so I don't recall much of what I wrote. Or why I wrote it."

I watched as Ransom began to speak, then did a slow freeze as if she'd been struck by something. The woman sat in silence, pondering. Then, gradually, a shrewd glow came into her eyes — a different sort of awakening.

"You *did* start your own religion," she said softly. "That's true. It is *true*. How could my brain not thought of this idea before?"

Later, Tomlinson would say she had thought of it before. Her trap.

"We all seen the idiots come around here thinkin' you're some sort of religious guru," Ransom continued. "A spiritual man who can change water into wine, instead of what you are. Which is a donkey dick that turns rum into piss when you ain't using it to diddle. But those idiots don't know that. Fools think you're special. People *all over the world*. I seen it myself, the stuff they write to you on the computer."

Unoffended, Tomlinson said, "Yes, my students say they learn much from the little I have to teach."

My cousin replied, "Yeah, mon. But you ever thought of *chargin'* them for it?"

"Charging? You mean, *money?*"

"You want a new experience or not? If you got the balls, let me handle it. We'll both make a pile."

Sounding rattled, he said, "I don't really *want* to get rich. I was playing with the idea. On the other hand, though . . . compared to bestiality, or the other two . . ."

Ransom said, "Those are three nice options you got there. Think it over. You might look good wearin' lipstick and shit. Walkin' like your bum hurt."

Later that evening, Tomlinson told her, he didn't see any way around it. If she had some ideas about making money, go ahead and get started.

"Do it now," he said, " 'cause I don't have much time left."

Ransom was like a lion set free.

There were already Tomlinson-dedicated

Web sites — mostly in Europe and Asia, where his small, brilliant book, *One Fathom Above Sea Level*, had been widely translated and praised.

One fathom equals approximately six feet, so the title referred to a view of the world through one man's eyes.

The customer base was out there waiting, so Ransom decided to start an Internet school of meditation. From Sanibel, they could reach out to the world. In return, she hoped, money would flow in from the world.

Tomlinson was mortified. Money was the only area where he set strict guidelines: the school had to serve the public good, he said, and she couldn't charge fees of any kind. Donations could be accepted. But no pressure tactics. If his teachings improved lives, students might send a little gift in gratitude. Expect nothing more.

"This getting rich business sucks," he told me privately. "I haven't made a cent yet, and your sister already has me pissed off about the tax laws. Insurance companies? The insurance racket is nothing but organized crime with a permission slip."

As a template, Ransom copied a respected international school of Zen that offered Internet instruction. Founded by a

Korean Zen master, it had educational centers worldwide and several hundred thousand followers.

My cousin charged ahead, working seven days a week. Created a corporation. Filed forms with the IRS seeking a religious nonprofit 501(c)(3) status for the now legally chartered "Sanibel Institute of Zen Meditation & Island Karma."

"The feds should grant it, no problem. Even if they don't, we can still operate as an electronic church, and take all the donations them folks want to send us. Either way, everything will be nice and legal."

Ransom loved the acronym. SIZMIK, which she pronounced as "seismic."

"T-shirt sales alone," she said. "Think of the cash flow."

She put herself through a crash course on building Web pages, and hired one of the state's best Internet designers. They created an interactive, multipage Web site. A Miami computer bank, or collocutor, became her Web server. As a domain name, they settled on: www.KarmicTomlinson.com.

"A collocutor's nothin' but an office with computers linked to several hard drives. If one drive dies, they can hot swap a new one without shutting down, so we don't lose a thing."

The collocutor would coordinate live telecasts. Point the camera at Tomlinson and it would be sent out across the Internet. Students could interact with him in real time. Two or three live sessions a week. Everything else at the CyberZendo would be shot in advance and edited.

CyberZendo. Tomlinson's name.

Ransom did the video. She recorded Tomlinson's lectures, his sitting *zazen* demonstrations, and followed him around during a typical day — a sort of Tomlinson reality show that became popular.

She also traveled the islands recording soothing scenes of beaches, bays, swaying palms at sunset, and oceanscapes. "Meditative stuff," she called it.

Ransom worked her butt off while Tomlinson sat around brooding about his decision to get rich, and fretting about his death dream. She was often furious at him, and for good reason.

In mid-July, it happened. Ransom's Internet Zendo Village, featuring Rienzi master Tomlinson, premiered on the World Wide Web. She hosted a party at Dinkin's Bay to celebrate, though most who attended seemed confused by the occasion.

Why was there a banner over the bait tanks that read: CONGRATULATIONS

SANIBEL INSTITUTE OF ISLAND KARMA? Why was Tomlinson wearing flowing orange monk's robes instead of his trademark sarong? The video crew — *why?*

The night of the premiere, few islanders visited KarmicTomlinson.com. On the other side of the earth, though, hundreds of eager Asian admirers did. In Europe, Africa, and Indonesia, too. The spiritually minded sat at their computers and, for the first time, interacted with their esteemed teacher, the *Roshi,* whose writings they loved.

News of the link spread.

The first week, Ransom told me, the site recorded two thousand hits. By the fourth week, they were averaging that many a day, and the numbers were growing.

Donations started as a trickle. Disappointing. Ransom wanted to change the term from "donations" to "Good Karma Offerings," and pestered Tomlinson until he finally gave in.

It worked. Money orders and traveler's checks began arriving in large numbers at the post office on Tarpon Bay Road. Ransom rented a second commercial-sized box to handle the flow.

"I'd hoped for an even bigger buzz," she admitted. "I want to get rich. Wild rich. We aren't, but it's okay. Having a nice bank account will have to do."

Tomlinson, though, was distraught. By now he was too afraid of Ransom to risk a direct confrontation, so he retaliated by imploring his students *not* to send offerings.

"If the Good Samaritan wasn't rich, nobody would remember the dude. Keep your money!" he told them in his live telecasts.

Reverse psychology sometimes works when it's unintentional.

His followers sent more money, not less.

That called for another variety of celebration.

On the Monday before Thanksgiving, Ransom drove Tomlinson's venerable Volkswagen Thing into nearby Fort Myers, traded it in on a luxury van, then had it painted like one of the old hipster microbuses: flowers, peace signs, and rainbows.

For herself, she bought a Lexus LS 430, the big luxury sedan.

Over the next several months, things got stranger. Tomlinson began to change. He withdrew emotionally for a period. When he reemerged, he was the same scatterbrained, brilliant flake, but with an unexpected edge.

Something else we noticed: My old friend

began buying toys for himself. Friends, too. Spending lots of money. The only really smart thing he did was buy majority interest in a funky little restaurant near the wildlife sanctuary and rename it Dinkin's Bay Raw Bar & Deja Brew.

He stopped battling Ransom. Even tried to help her when he could.

I watched Tomlinson smack himself on the forehead again, finish his drink, then wobble toward the galley to make another. He turned toward me, exasperated. "That's the problem. I don't know if I want to go back to being my old self."

"What?"

"I kinda *like* some of the things I've bought. The dinghy's an example. It's nice not to get soaked when the bay's choppy. And the Harley. Man, what a rush to rumble down the middle of Periwinkle, cars on both sides, when traffic's backed up. *Free.*

"Then there's the clothes. Some say I look very, very hip in a white silk suit. A whole new fashion experience. And did you know Rance's going to bring out a line of sarongs? My own private label. Finest quality."

He said all this in a rush, enthusiastic, but

with a confessional undertone.

I said, "I see. That's the problem. You enjoy having money."

He looked at the floor. Nodded.

"Just like Ransom predicted."

He nodded quickly, his face blotching as if he might cry.

"Give yourself a break. You're human. It's normal to like money. She was right about that, too."

"Man, I don't like money. I *love* it," he said miserably. "Slapping down the Gold Card for anything I want? It's got me jonesing worse than a smack freak on Super Bowl Sunday. My God, Doc, I almost put earnest money on a Cape Coral condo yesterday. A place that's got *cable*. The guard wears a *uniform*. Hear what I'm saying? I'm out of control!"

Tomlinson put his palms together, then touched index fingers to his lips — usually a religious posture that now signaled the depth of his distress.

"You're right," I said. "That's going too far."

"You've got to help me. I'm thinking of buying a shock collar. Give myself a little zap every time I reach for the ol' billfold. Negative reinforcement."

"Not for you. For you, it would be recreational. How about this: I tell Ransom to keep the money, don't give you a cut."

He winced. "Cold turkey, man. I don't know. Do you think she would?"

"My cousin? You've got to be kidding."

I thought of something else. "I'm working on a job — a sort of contract deal. It has to do with the parasites I mentioned, and maybe some of the noxious exotics you told me about."

"Yeah?"

"It may be related. I could use some help. A researcher."

"Then I should find that *Rolling Stone* article for you."

I considered Harrington's reaction — he'd be furious — before I said, "That's exactly the sort of help I need. A project as important as this, it might shift your priorities. The organization can pay, but nothing like you're used to."

"A private organization, or government?"

"Government. Definitely government. But one of the lesser-known agencies."

He seemed interested. "Screw the cash. I'll do it to show goodwill — that's more valuable than cash." The old Tomlinson was still in there, talking.

I told him, "Sometimes, a lot more valuable."

17

Dr. Desmond Stokes — *Mr. Sweet.*

Dasha liked replaying the name; it gave her a warm feeling because it brought Solaris into her head.

Mr. Sweet had told Dasha, "What I've been doing is only a hobby. It's not my life's work. But the . . . *satisfaction* of the last fourteen months. Manipulating germs, disease vectors — relocating soldier-animals to help Earth retaliate. Thinning the human population of 'primasites.' I'm *contributing.* Which is why we can't allow that little retard, Applebee, to stop us."

He invented words to remind people he was a genius. Primasites were human parasites. Soldier-animals — things with stingers and teeth.

Helping Earth fight back — he had a bunch of speeches on the subject. Maybe even believed it at one time. But Dasha had been working for him long enough to know it was a lie. All the rich man cared about was scamming more money, more control. Ways to demonstrate his superiority — that's what it was about.

Revenge, too. Mostly revenge.

She'd discovered that on her own. Went through the man's files when she got the opportunity. The ones on his personal computer, the files in his office.

Head of security. Her job had its advantages.

A couple of years after Stokes had gotten out of medical school, he'd gone before a state review board and lost his license. Something to do with a therapy he'd been working on, injecting people with cells from the placentas of sheep.

Around the same time, the government shut down his fledgling vitamin company. He'd been illegally mining petrified coral somewhere around Key Largo, then processing it into calcium tablets.

Purest form of calcium. Holistic. Expensive. Buyers fell for it.

The state of Florida nailed him both times, and the feds got some licks in, too.

Revenge was a major motivator.

Power. That's what he preached to leaders of the militant Greenie Weenie groups who visited the island. Over the last year, there'd been dozens of them. From the States, Britain, France, Canada. Everywhere. They were rallying behind some idiot article in an American music magazine. Smuggling dangerous exotics across the border was the newest kind of guerrilla warfare.

Mr. Earl had sent out many thousands of copies of the article over the Internet, Dasha had also discovered, inviting Greenie Weenies to the Bahamas for help and advice.

The surest way of displacing primasites, Dr. Stokes told them, was to create panic, disrupt the local economy, then be ready with organizational funds to buy properties cheap when they came on the market. Dump a thousand piranha into lakes in Texas, Arizona, New Mexico, then sit back and wait. The West Nile virus outbreak on Cape Cod — same technique, different tools.

"The first duty of a revolutionary is to get away with it," he told them. "Abbie Hoffman."

They always applauded that line. Idiots.

"The best way to save the land is to buy from the fools who are destroying it."

The Greenie Weenies saw it as a righteous war. For Mr. Sweet, it was a way to get even.

Dasha knew. Took note of what made the rich man tick. Began researching him, putting together a secret dossier.

The only people he actually associated with? Respected? There were a handful, all billionaire power brokers. Sugarcane. A couple of Texas oil barons. A guy who ran one of the largest mining and lumber companies in the world. Private jets, private conversations, secret deals.

The idiot Greenie Weenies had no idea what Mr. Sweet was all about.

How would they? Go to the public records, do a computer search, and the name Dr. Desmond Stokes would not appear as owner of several thousand acres of agricultural property, Central Florida, or as an officer of Tropicane — even though he controlled much of the stock. Maybe a majority.

The name of his personal assistant was on the record, though. Mr. Earl. Same with a long list of companies: Off-Shore Gulf & Caribbean Petroleum, Coralway Pharmaceuticals, Ragged Isle Shipping, and others that Dasha traced to Stokes through the name of Luther T. Earl.

The man owned sugar, a couple of phosphate mines, four oil tankers his company leased to a Hong Kong–based group named

Evergreen, stock in steel mills in Sweden and Germany, a rubber plantation in Sumatra. Plus pharmaceuticals. That's where the real money was. Paid investors eight times the return per hundred thousand dollars invested.

Mr. Sweet had a bundle in the big ones. Pfizer, Great Britain Ltd, plus his own: Coralway Pharmaceuticals Ltd.

The man known publicly for manufacturing holistic vitamins and championing environmental causes was actually an international industrialist.

Dr. Desmond Stokes had discovered that the most satisfying way of looking down on people was from atop a mountain of money.

Mr. Sweet was right — screwing with the Greenie Weenies was small time. Only a hobby. But the man loved it.

Stokes's pet idea: Spread flesh-eating parasites around Disney World, into the Everglades. New strains of malaria, same delivery method. Cripple Florida's tourist industry while also devaluing massive hectares of real estate.

"We'll scare away the primasites and make more room for wildlife," he told them.

Also, more room for Mr. Sweet to slip

in and buy, buy, buy.

That's what caused Dasha to start guessing. Didn't know if Stokes wanted a bigger piece of the sugar industry, or had something else planned. The weird little nerd, Applebee, was involved somehow.

She figured that out right away.

The nerd and the rich man had a special deal going. The genius doctor helped the nerd, if the nerd did what the genius doctor told him to do.

"I'm doing research . . . procedures. In Africa, there's a parasitic worm. I'm not good with . . . with words. A cure — yes. A *cure,* that's what I'm looking for."

Applebee had said that to her more than a year ago. He was a shy little man, never made eye contact, always covered his mouth with his hands as he spoke. Hiding. That was the impression.

Find a cure . . .

A cure for an African parasite. Why bother?

Dasha had gone over and over it in her mind. Did the research, and came up with something surprising. There were prescription drugs on the market for malaria. Preventative drugs for all kinds of parasitic disease, as well as drugs that mitigated their symptoms. But for guinea worm disease?

Zero. No pharmaceutical relief available.

It was one of the few easily contracted diseases in the world for which there was no cure, or help.

Interesting.

How much money would a company make if it had a drug licensed, tested, and waiting when Florida suffered an unprecedented guinea worm epidemic? There was no profit in finding cures for diseased people in West Africa. Poor folks couldn't pay, so why bother? But visitors to Disney World?

Talk about taking revenge on Florida!

Dasha was guessing, already figuring ways to turn it to her advantage if she was right.

Brilliant.

The rich man's interest had nothing to do with saving the Everglades.

Whenever she had the opportunity, she paid special attention to Applebee. The way his skin flushed as he ducked behind his hand, she guessed he had a crush on her.

But did he care enough to double-cross Dr. Stokes?

Applebee. A sore subject for the rich man.

Standing in the doctor's office now, she listened to Desmond Stokes tell her, "Finding that computer is a *priority*. We've got to find out what he copied from my files. That's an absolute must. But there's another reason, too. Something you don't know."

Dasha tried to react with the appropriate expression: interested but confused. As if she had no idea what the man was talking about.

"What I haven't mentioned is that I commissioned Applebee to do a special study. Had to do with the guinea parasites. If we don't recover his computer, all the data he accumulated will be lost."

"What kind of study?"

"Don't worry about the specifics. You've been asking why we haven't used the crop sprayers yet? That's why. Until I see and understand the data that Applebee developed, we can't move ahead on . . . on a larger scale."

Early on, Mr. Sweet had tasked her with a problem: Find the most effective way to spread an illegal waterborne agent over a landmass.

Dasha's solution: radio-controlled helicopters, commercial-sized crop sprayers. Almost unknown in the U.S., but gaining popularity in Asia and Australia.

Mr. Sweet had been enthusiastic . . . until the trouble started with Applebee.

"Goddamn it, I want that computer. I paid for the fucking research. The results *belong* to me."

Stokes said it again: "The damn retard!"

Dasha was thinking: *The little man outsmarted you, outsmarted Aleski. Even outsmarted me. And he's the retard?*

She took a paper from her pocket, held it up. "That's why I come to you this morning, Dr. Stokes. To get permission."

It was the copy of a UPS billing receipt she'd found in Jobe Applebee's home. It was addressed to someone named Frieda Matthews, Tallahassee, and insured for two thousand dollars.

The missing computer?

Possibly, so she'd called the phone number, saying she was with UPS. Told the man who answered there was maybe a mistake, they needed to confirm the serial number.

"My wife's brother's laptop?" he asked. "It's silver-colored with an apple on it. Something called a 'PowerBook.' "

Dasha had smiled. *Idiot.*

"I don't know anything about computers, but I'm taking it with me to Kissimmee tomorrow. Maybe my wife will know how to find the serial number. Do you want to know where we're staying?"

How could anyone be so stupid?

Dasha approached Stokes's desk and placed the billing receipt in front of him so that he could read it without having to touch it.

That's what had set him off about Applebee.

After he'd ranted about it awhile, calling the little man a retard, Stokes grabbed the receipt and flung it on the floor. Immediately, he began to change gloves.

He kept white cotton gloves hidden everywhere.

"Applebee was autistic. I'm an expert on autism. Their brains aren't capable of interpreting moral subtleties. Ethics? Meaningless. He was perfect for what we wanted him to do. There was no reason for me to fear he'd sneak in and copy my computer files, then refuse to give me the results of his study."

Dasha said, "He tried to cancel your order for the drone helicopters," as if reminding him, but actually to demonstrate that she was on the rich man's side. Let her expression tell Stokes he had every right to feel betrayed. "What a shitty thing to do. Sneaky. And you were giving him special treatment."

"I acted as his physician. Created a special diet. Provided him with supplements that would purge heavy metals from his body. Coral calcium and glycosamine — products that we make right here. *Pure.* Can you imagine what I would've charged anyone else? He wanted to be normal." Stokes made a snorting noise of contempt. "As if being normal's special. Not revealing the results of his study."

"Sneaky shit fooled you."

Dasha knew he was leaving something out. Copying his files had gradually become less important than Applebee's research on guinea worms.

Find a cure.

Spread the parasites by crop duster all over South Florida and have an expensive cure waiting. Applebee had the answer.

"Stole from you, that's what the little bastard did. No way you could have known."

Stokes's expression agreed, saying, Yes, I was betrayed, but I'm used to it. "Exactly! I believed I was dealing with a man who had autism. There's no medical precedent for his behavior. I would know. Autistics can't rise above their autism. Which is why I'm now convinced that he was retarded. A savant."

Stokes slapped his desk — he had the muscularity of a corpse two months gone, so it made the sound of fingers brushing a pillow. "We've got to find the goddamn thing or I'm ruined."

Dasha told Stokes that's why she was asking permission to fly to Orlando that afternoon. Her and Aleski. They might return with a nice surprise.

As if it were unimportant to her, she added, "Mr. Earl wants permission, too. But in a separate plane. Something to do with one of your pharmaceutical companies."

She relaxed slightly when Stokes replied, "Mr. Earl can leave whenever he wants. That sly son of a bitch knows I can put him in prison. All I have to do is pick up the phone."

Dasha thought, *That explains a lot.*

She didn't add that Luther Earl could *not* leave the island any time he wanted. It wasn't the way she had the security set up.

Stokes paused; took a moment. Didn't want to sound eager. "When you say come back with something nice — do you mean Applebee's computer? I'll give you a fifty-thousand-dollar bonus if you do. And can prove he hasn't sent off copies somewhere."

"You told me Applebee never made

copies of anything. You said it was part of his —" She'd forgotten the word.

"His *syndrome*. Avoidance can be a manifestation of compulsion. Applebee refused to back up his work, as far as I *know*. But the son of a bitch copied my files, so he might have tricked me about copying his own research data, too."

Dasha said earnestly, "I'm hoping to come back with the computer. But a bonus isn't necessary. It's part of the job, and you already pay me well."

The rich man liked that. Over the months, he'd gradually come to trust her. Not in the same way he trusted Mr. Earl, but close. But that didn't mean she was off the hook.

"The whole sad episode should've never happened in the first place. *You're* head of my security. You're the one who let that little retard get away. It wasn't my fault."

Applebee was dead. That was escaping? Mr. Sweet never accepted blame. A neurotic head case.

"If I'm ruined, you people are ruined! You're like parasites. That's why you've got to protect me."

He was ranting. It would go on for a while, the fury, his paranoia peaking.

She'd gotten permission to leave. That's

251

all she cared about. You couldn't get off the island without it, not even her — and she'd made the rules.

It was the right procedural decision. A professional decision.

Dasha had tightened the island's security procedures soon after they'd finished assembling, then testing the first of four RMAX radio-controlled crop duster helicopters.

Restricted ingress and egress. She kept the chopper drones under camouflaged netting unless she, Aleski, Aleski's cousin, Broz, or one of the other Russian pilots she'd hired had them out practicing. They used laptop computer–sized remotes to make low-level passes over the ocean, spraying a watery fog that did not contain the larvae of South American mosquitoes or guinea worms — but soon would.

Beautiful little choppers, five meters long, weighed only a hundred kilograms. They carried a payload large enough to treat several hundred acres with pesticides — or any other liquid.

Dasha was proud of the choppers. Her idea.

When they'd tasked Jobe Applebee with finding the fastest way to circulate waterborne parasites through the

Everglades, he'd spent months building a precise model of the state. Something called a diorama. She should've known then that Applebee was *different.*

Mr. Sweet was still slapping at his desk. A spoiled child throwing a tantrum. "Get out of here! Come back with that computer or don't come back at all!"

Leaving the room, Dasha gave him a farewell grin. This time it said, *Fuck you until it's my turn.* . . .

18

LOG
15 Dec. Wednesday 23:30
Bay calm, western planets bright over mangroves. Lake assisted w/ *Dracunculiasis* procedure. Results unexpected. Have I stumbled onto something important . . . ?
— MDF

16 Dec. Thursday
Received email from Frieda M. and attachments from brother's computer . . .
— MDF

On Thursday afternoon, I was in the lab, squinting into a microscope and making notes, when Harrington called.

"Why don't you answer the phone?"

"What? We wouldn't be talking if I didn't —"

"The *other* phone."

I said, "Oh."

It'd taken me a moment to recognize his voice.

"I'll call in five minutes."

I'd just gotten the sea chest open when the satellite phone began its irritating *bong . . . bong . . . bong.* I rushed to hit the answer button.

"I'm in the middle of a lab procedure, Hal. Let's make this quick."

"I thought you'd be working on your new assignment. The parasites we were discussing."

I was holding the phone to my ear, already returning to the lab. I was wearing a white smock, surgical gloves, and a plastic spray shield tilted back on my head.

I said, "I am. And making some progress."

"Good. This won't take long."

He told me that Cuban sources had reported that the small-time reptile smuggler, Bat-tuy Nguyen, had been murdered two or three days ago. Him plus two of his helpers.

"Nguyen," Harrington said, "was shot in the head, execution style."

"This was in Cuba?"

"A little village in the western part. He kept a warehouse there."

"What kind of weapon?"

"I don't know."

"Had he been robbed?"

"He was one of those fat guys who loved gold jewelry. He was still wearing his rings and necklaces when they found the body."

"Then it was probably one of his clients. Or a competitor."

Harrington said, "That's what we think."

"The other two?"

"A couple of local men who worked for Nguyen. This isn't from a police report; nothing official. Just some feet we have on the ground there. So don't expect much additional information."

I listened to him tell me that Nguyen had clients worldwide, but it seemed probable that only a few were ordering virulent stuff that could be used as bioweaponry.

"Maybe just one or two organizations, or people. People who've found a way to smuggle the stuff in, then distribute it to other buyers, or give it to groups who are politically like-minded: anarchists, religious militants, the fringe group psychotics."

He said his staff had e-mailed me information regarding seven additional cases of suspected bio-sabotage. Piranhas in Houston, cane toads in Louisiana, and locusts in California were among them.

"Yours is on the list now. They've found more of your parasites near Disney World, in a couple of small lakes south of Orlando. Maybe others, they're still testing. Someone's doing it intentionally. This isn't bio-vandalism; it's terrorism. Killing Nguyen would've been a way of covering their tracks."

He told me the names of the lakes, some of the details, before adding, "Staff's also sending the transcript of a magazine article that might be related. One of our researchers found it — a very sharp piece of work on her part. She thinks the article may have motivated a few borderline kooks to slip over the edge, and start doing this sort of crap."

"The *Rolling Stone* piece?" I said.

I was pleased that he sounded astonished. "That's right. About drug cult fortune-tellers. They made predictions that seem to be coming true. How'd you know?"

I told him I had a very savvy research assistant of my own who was now at the local library, copying the article.

Harrington said, "Seventeen years ago, they predicted locusts would overrun military bases. That poisonous snakes, spiders — you name it — would all rise up and declare war against humanity. Other bizarre stuff, too: moons in alignment, hidden meanings in the lyrics of a song. Typical bullshit.

"What our researcher thinks is the druggie fortune-tellers planted the locust eggs themselves — this was near some weirdo commune. A setup. Years pass, it's all forgotten. But then the locusts hatch, and some old rock 'n' roll reporter remembers the prophecies. He writes an article —"

I finished the sentence for him: "— and inspires copycat sympathizers to get fired up. They've gone to work trying to make the rest of the predictions come true."

Harrington said, "Your researcher came up with that?" Impressed.

"I just hired him. Is that okay?"

"Hell, I'd like to hire him myself if that's the caliber of product he turns out. Whatever you're paying him, save copies of the money orders and we'll reimburse you. Just like in the old days. When you were full-time."

Without a hint of irony, I said, "Even if he needed the money, we couldn't afford him. It's more of a goodwill deal. The man has a lot of expertise when it comes to underground political movements."

Harrington said, "We can afford him, trust me. This one's been moved up a couple of notches on the list. It hasn't broken the top twenty, so I can't offer much help from staff. But we do have the funding. What else does your guy say?"

"He says we should check out the LSD prophets, find out what they're doing. He noticed that the *Rolling Stone* article only used old quotes, nothing current. Sounds to him like the prophets might have dropped out of sight for a reason."

"Really. Our woman didn't catch it." He let that hang for a moment. "Seriously. When you're finished with this project, have the guy send me his résumé."

Tempting. How would Harrington react when he found out it was Tomlinson?

A few minutes later, a man who identified himself as a special investigator, Florida Department of Health, Center for Disease Control, telephoned and told me that *Dracunculiasis* larvae had been found in two Central Florida lakes. He was aware that I'd made the first field identification of the parasite. Would I mind answering a few questions?

The investigator's name was Dr. Clark. His specialty was epidemiology, the study of the origin and spread of disease.

"Which lakes?" I asked, even though Harrington had already told me.

He said the locations weren't being released because there were only "trace numbers" of the parasite. However, the CDC was working with the Florida Department of Agriculture on a plan in the event more were found.

"That's why we're contacting independent biologists," he added. "People who think outside the box. I've been using a questionnaire for consistency."

My cynical reaction: Any agency that used the term "outside the box" would be unsettled by an original idea.

His evasiveness told me the situation was more serious than he was authorized to say.

I swung off the lab stool, got my Florida atlas, and began to page through it. *Dracunculiasis* had been found near Orlando, in Orange County's Lake Huckleberry and Lake Tibet.

It took me a moment to locate them: little bitty lakes in a region of big lakes. They were only a couple of miles outside the megaregion owned by Disney. Both appeared to be linked via various water passages with other theme parks to the east and south. SeaWorld, Universal Orlando, several smaller tourist attractions, and something called "Gatorland."

I didn't fault his department for being cautious. That headline came into my mind once again: TOURISTS INFESTED WITH EXOTIC PARASITES.

News would spread around the world within hours.

I said, "I understand that this is a delicate situation. But let's drop the shields. How can I give you my opinion if I don't have all the data?"

His silence told me that he was thinking it over, so I added, "I'm the guy who found Jobe Applebee. The medical examiner's office took photos. Did you see them?"

Clark replied, "Yes." After a few beats, he added: "I wish I hadn't."

Returning to my stool and microscope, I said, "Okay, then we both know how serious this is. What else aren't you supposed to tell me?"

The man spoke softly. Maybe he was in an office near a busy hallway. "More than a week before Dr. Applebee's death, the Centers for Disease Control, Atlanta, was informed of three cases of guinea worm infestation. Unrelated cases. Or so we believed. An adult male who lives in Seattle, a teenage girl from Ashland, Ohio, and a veterinarian from Orlando.

"We now know that the adult male and

the teenager were both in the Orlando area last December within a week or so of the other. The man's a bass fisherman; the girl spent a morning waterskiing.

"In the last few days, we've also received reports through the international health services of five more cases. People from Great Britain, western Australia, and Montford, France. We've confirmed that three of the five were in the Orlando area in late November, and early December. We're still awaiting word about the other two."

I said, *"Damn."*

"My sentiments exactly."

"The time frame's right. There's a twelve-month gestation period. But only eight cases reported?" I mulled that over before saying, "That's actually not bad news. How many millions of people hit Disney every holiday season? Statistically, it's encouraging."

Clark sighed. He sounded tired. "I hope you're right. I don't know what we're going to do if we find more. Americans aren't going to react well to the idea of being infected by a parasite like this one. Mosquitoes that carry West Nile virus, that's tolerable. But flesh-eating worms? Culturally, we can't handle that. We'll have to post public warnings. No swimming, no water contact of any kind. We'd have to shut down businesses. Marinas, farms, even tour boats."

He added, "I can't think of a faster way to spread a disease vector around the globe. Introduce it at Disney." I heard papers rattle. He was resuming his role as interviewer. "Now you know the facts, Dr. Ford. Would you mind answering our questionnaire?"

He had a written list. It was bureaucracy-think: Poll the experts, and the consensus provided an effective scapegoat for a department burdened with making a tough decision.

Clark's questions were linked to a more basic question: What is the most effective way to eradicate a species of waterborne parasite without destroying other plants and animals?

I was sitting at a table, my Leica microscope within easy reach. I told him, "The first thing I'd do is contact South Florida Water Management and tell them not to release water from Lake Okeechobee into the 'Glades. Create an artificial drought. Slow the flow of water. That might buy some time."

Clark said they'd already done that. His

questionnaire was based on a worst-case scenario: What if the parasite was already widely dispersed?

"We've been discussing two options," he said. "Introduce a fish or insect from Africa that preys naturally on guinea worm larvae. Or interrupt the parasite's life cycle by eliminating its requisite host."

I'd told him that I had a philosophical problem with importing one exotic to control another. Ecosystems take thousands of years to balance interlinkings between geography and species. The resulting milieu is not a stage for experimentation. Tinkering is a recipe for disaster that's been demonstrated too many times.

No need to pursue that line of questioning.

"Then help us choose the best way to eliminate the parasite's carrier host. Copepods, as I suspect you know."

Yes, I told him, I was familiar with copepods. In fact, on the table in front of me was a thousand-milliliter flask filled with the things.

"That's quite a coincidence," Clark said.

Looking at the flask, I replied, "Not really. I've been doing a procedure your people might find interesting."

The flask contained water that appeared

murky but was, in fact, alive; animated with the tiny crustaceans. They were silt-sized, grouped as a moving gray cloud in a Pyrex container that was shaped not unlike an alchemist's lamp.

The flask also contained guinea larvae. Which was why I was wearing surgical gloves and a face shield.

Clark said, "I have a list of pesticides. Can I read it off first?"

I was still looking at the flask. "Sure. I'll work while we talk."

I'd used a pipette to fill twin concave chambers in a glass microscope slide. One chamber contained a dozen swimming, darting copepods. The second indentation, only water.

The slide was mounted on the microscope's illuminated stage. I rotated the trinocular to medium power as Clark began to read from his list of pesticides:

"We're considering Abate, active ingredient temephos. It's an organophosphate, the same chemical group as nerve gas. Abate inhibits neural function. Even in small amounts, it's deadly to mosquito larvae and copepods — only an ounce or so per acre of water. But it also impacts aquatic invertebrates, and fish. It's currently in use in many regions of the south . . ."

"Impact." Add yet another euphemism for "kill."

As he continued reading, my attention began to blur as the magnified image of a copepod came into focus.

Hello, *Macro Cyclops*. The copepod is named for its bright and solitary red eye. Cyclops: A micromonster that feeds on other monsters.

Its body was rocket-shaped with an elegant V-tail, and a nose tipped with oversized antenna that drooped like a handlebar mustache. Its shell, or carapace, was segmented like a lobster, but translucent so that it emitted prismatic bands of color when transected by light.

This one was female. Symmetrical egg panels were attached like fins. It added to the illusion that this was a space vehicle, not one of the earth's most abundant life-forms.

Many people say they perceive the magnitude of the cosmos when they look at the stars. I see the same infinite complexities through a microscope's tube, and usually in better detail.

The Leica had superb resolution, and a rheostat-controlled halogen illumination system that transformed this tiny organism into a three-dimensional animal that moved . . . paused . . . shifted directions. It appeared no less complex, nor vital, than the largest animal that has ever walked the planet.

I rotated the trinocular to its highest power, touching the fine-focus coaxial as I listened to Dr. Clark say, ". . . the third chemical we're considering is Dylox, active ingredient trichlorfon, which is used to control insect pests on fruit trees and ornamentals . . ."

I looked up briefly, adjusting the phone between shoulder and ear. Had I missed the second pesticide on the list? Apparently.

I leaned over the microscope once again.

The copepod's translucent abdominal cavity now filled the lens, and I toyed with the focus as I listened to Clark. I was far more interested in this tiny crustacean, now magnified five hundred times. Because the animal's carapace was translucent, I could look into its stomach and see that it did not contain a *Dracunculiasis* nymph. There was no mistaking the nymph's bristling, dragon-toothed head.

There were bits of phytoplankton. There were fecal pellets in its lower gut. But, after spending an hour in water that contained guinea larvae, and, over a three-day period, this copepod had not fed on what should have been a preferred food source.

Amazing. Yes. I'd stumbled onto something important. Maybe. Predators that did not attack easy prey.

I no longer considered the behavior anomalous.

That's what I'd been doing for the last few days. Selecting copepods that refused to feed on the parasites. Each time I repeated the procedure, the percentage of nonfeeders increased.

Seeing this crustacean's empty belly pleased me. I'd seen many similar empty bellies during the course of the morning.

I shifted to low power, then used a curved probe to herd the copepod into its own personal chamber. Treated it as a hero, as I did the other nonfeeders.

After hearing Clark say, "The eighth chemical we're considering is Dimilin, a new generation of pesticides that was developed to mimic natural —" I interrupted.

"Dr. Clark? There may be a better way to deal with this. To disrupt the parasite's life cycle *without* using pesticides."

Still sounding fatigued, Clark said, "Dr. Ford, if you have a method that doesn't include poisoning every living creature in the Everglades, I will personally see that you get some type of medal. Even if I have to make it myself."

The man's field wasn't aquaculture, but he was quick and perceptive.

I told him that the life cycle of a copepod is so brief (only a week or two) that it might be possible, through selective breeding, to quickly reshape the crustacean's genetically coded behaviors.

"I think we can culture a hybrid copepod that doesn't recognize guinea worm larvae as food. If the larvae's not eaten, the parasite never matures, so it can't reproduce. From the results I've been getting, I don't think it would take us that long."

Copepods do nothing but eat and reproduce, I explained. In a week, using only a five-gallon bucket, millions of hybrids could be raised. Make it the primary function of an aquaculture facility and billions could be hatched in a month, trillions in a year. Get the Water Management people to re-create drought conditions to reduce the number of water spaces. Hybrids would soon dominate the state's native copepod population, passing their selected genetic traits into the future.

It wasn't a perfect solution. The results wouldn't be immediate. But it might reduce the parasite's numbers steadily, maybe dramatically.

"I haven't figured a quick way to disperse them through the water system," I said. "That could be a problem. Massive distribution. But this *could* work . . ."

I stopped. Felt a chill because something had just popped into my mind. I *did* know how to find the fast way to spread parasites through the state's water system. I'd known for days.

"Dr. Ford . . . ? *Ford?* Are you there?"

I said, "Yep, I'm here — although I wonder sometimes. Dr. Clark, you've been talking to an imbecile. I have information you need to write down."

I told Clark to contact the FBI immediately. Have agents check out Jobe Applebee's elaborate diorama. Get the pumps going, then use different colored dyes to trace which miniature lakes are attached to what underground conduits, and which currents are swiftest.

I added, "Tell them to start with the two lakes where you found the guinea larvae. A drop of dye in each. I hope I'm wrong. But I don't think I am. Track where that water goes. That's where you're going to find more guinea worms."

19

LOG
17 Dec. Friday, Sunset 17:39
Planets nearing conjunction
Mercury sets: 18:41 EST
Venus: 18: 52
Mars: 18:53
Jupiter: 20:32
Saturn: 21:03
Uranus: (?)
Neptune: transits 00:32
Phone interviews w/ FBI, then EPA &
Dept. of Agri. biologists. E-mailed notes
on copepod procedure to Tallahassee.
Marina Xmas party tonight.
— MDF

Friday afternoon, only two days before I was
scheduled to fly to Iowa for the holidays, I
went clattering down the wooden, water-
slick steps of my house, rushing to get aboard
the nineteen-foot Aquasport that one of the

guides had loaned me.

I'd towed my Maverick into Fort Myers Marine to have the hull inspected. A strange feeling, being boatless.

Because I was in a hurry, I was tempted to pretend I didn't hear when a woman's voice called, "Hey there, Ford! *Doc?* I was just coming to knock on your door."

I recognized the voice but couldn't place it immediately. It didn't belong to the short list of females who visit regularly. I grabbed an overhead beam to slow my momentum, turned to look, and there stood the investigator from the Bartram County Medical Examiner's Office. Despite an intense evening together, her last name returned to memory slightly in advance of her first name.

"Graves? Ms. . . . Graves? What are you doing on Sanibel?"

"The name's Rona. If I split two bottles of wine with a man, I expect him to call me by my first name. Do you have a few minutes to talk? We could get some coffee."

She was making her way along the boardwalk in the careful way of someone unsure of her footing, or unsure of the circumstances. Her facial muscles were strained — flexing, then relaxing — as if struggling to maintain a look of informal cheer.

Either that or she was dawdling. Which annoyed me. I'd just been told by a Florida Fish and Wildlife dispatcher that someone had reported seeing a big shark tangled in a net not far from Dinkin's Bay. The shark was drowning.

I started toward the boat again. "I'd like to sit and talk but I'm right in the middle of something. An emergency. I've got to take off in the boat."

"There are emergencies in the world of marine biology?"

"Nope, not usually. But this hasn't been a normal week."

From a wooden locker beneath the house, I took a nylon backpack already packed with medical kit, shark tags, and miscellaneous gear. I opened it and began to add gloves, prescription goggles, snorkel, my old and dependable Rocket fins, my equally old and dependable Randall survival knife.

"I know I should've called first. But I decided, what the hell, I've got the weekend off. I've never seen Sanibel, and you seemed like the friendly, informal type. So I . . . well, you'll understand."

I paused. There was something peculiar about her manner. "Understand what? You didn't drive three hours just to tell me the results of Jobe Applebee's autopsy, did you?

If you did, that's thoughtful. But it's not like we were close —"

"No . . . no, that's not the reason. We can talk later. How long do you think you'll be gone?"

Her insistence was an additional annoyance. I looked at my watch. It was 4:13 p.m. The dispatcher told me the report had come in around four. A shark tangled in a net is likely to die. It has no swim bladder, nothing to keep it from sinking and stalling on the bottom. Minutes count. If I found the shark quickly, and if it hadn't been too badly stressed, I might be gone an hour. If things didn't go smoothly, I wouldn't be back until long after dark.

She surprised me by saying, "Hey, how about I tag along? I'd like to see what a biologist does. I'm good around boats, I really am. I grew up waterskiing."

I wasn't wild about the idea, but I didn't want to waste additional time debating it. I told her, "Okay. But we're leaving *now*. And no guarantees about when we get back."

She seemed weirdly relieved. People used to making decisions sometimes like it when they're told what to do. "What's the problem? Dealing with emergencies is one of the things I do best."

I was already in the Aquasport, lowering

the engine as she stepped aboard. "There's a shark in trouble. It was spotted near a place called Lighthouse Point. It's only a couple of miles from here, but we've gotta fly."

"Sharks," she said, settling herself onto the bench seat beside me. "They've always scared me. They're sending you out to catch it and kill it — right?"

Locating something on water is never as easy as you hope, so I expected to have trouble finding the shark.

We didn't.

I steered the boat beneath the causeway bridge, headed for a point of land that is the island's last partition between bay and the open Gulf of Mexico. There's a lighthouse there — a maritime antique — which is why the paw of beach is named Lighthouse Point.

I'd been told the shark had been spotted nearby. Luckily, though, I noticed a cluster of four or five boats off to my right, near the channel to Sanibel Marina. They were behaving oddly. The boats jockeyed for position, leapfrogging as if fishing for moving tarpon. But this wasn't tarpon season.

To Rona I said, "Grab that stainless rail. Hang on tight," and turned sharply, not slowing until I'd closed on the pod of boats.

It was the shark. The boats were following it, each skipper vying for a better view. Understandable. It was a *very* big shark that couldn't submerge because it was tangled in a mess of ropes, plastic floats, and netting.

Beside me, Rona said, "That thing's . . . *alive?* I thought it was a small plane at first. Like maybe it'd just crashed, and these people were trying to help. But a *shark* — now I see why it's an emergency." She turned her head, searching the empty deck. "How are you gonna do this? Do you have a gun? Or maybe a harpoon, or something?"

I'd slipped in between the boats and the fish. Looking at it, I thought about my little deformed *leucas* back at the lab. This was what they were coded to become: a bull shark, fully mature. It was ten or eleven feet long, and three times the girth of my chest. Probably five or six hundred pounds.

I told Rona what she was looking at, adding, "I'm going to cut it free, not kill it. What I've got to figure out is, how?"

The shark's side fins, or pectorals, were each more than a yard long. They extended from its sides like wings. The top lobe of its tail, or caudal fin, was even longer, curved like a scythe. Tangled between the left pectoral fin and the tail was a section of gray monofilament netting.

The shark had probably gone after fish caught in the mesh. Not uncommon.

So the creature was now towing a thirty-foot shroud of rubbish — a clutter of buoyant floats and nylon that restricted its movement, and also kept it riding on the surface. The rope had cut so deeply into the caudal fin that I could see exposed cartilage. It made the tail stroke uneven, causing the creature to swim in wide, counterclockwise circles as it drifted with the incoming tide.

I was taking off my shirt, my glasses, stepping out of my rubber boots, in a hurry to get to work. "Consider yourself a lucky woman. In all the years I've dealt with bull sharks, I've only seen one other specimen this size. In fact . . ." — I considered the shark's bulk and length; the blunt head, the density of its dark eyes, before continuing — ". . . in fact, this could be the same fish. It was a year or so ago, I was windsurfing. At night. I could see its outline because the water was glowing with phosphorus. It sparkled as it swam."

It startled me, the realization. As I continued to prepare gear, I thought about it, replaying the events of that night. It was near the marina, Dinkin's Bay. I'd never seen a specimen as large before or since. Until now.

The same animal?

Possibly. No . . . *probably*.

The unexpected connection injected a new urgency, as well as irony — ironic because this shark had attacked me. Pursued and attacked my surfboard, anyway. The only person I'd told about it was Tomlinson, who, of course, assigned the incident an exaggerated importance.

He'd used a Buddhist term that I've now forgotten.

Rona watched me as I picked up goggles, gloves, and bag. Her eyes went wide. "Oh no . . . you've got to be joking. Please tell me you are not going in the water."

I said, "I'll be fine. That shark's the least of my worries. All these boats charging around, though, are *dangerous*. Were you serious when you said you knew boats? I need you to take the wheel."

"Yes . . . sure. I guess so. I grew up driving ski boats." She was studying the gauges, the throttle arm. "This is the same kind of setup?"

I was holding my fins. Should I wear them? Decided no, and dropped them on the deck.

Stepping around the console, I said, "Try

to stay between me and the other boats. Mostly, keep the engine in neutral, make them avoid you."

I slipped into the water.

The tide had put thirty yards between the shark and me. I wanted distance because I didn't want to spook the thing.

With lungs inflated to maintain buoyancy, I drifted with the current, doing a slow sidestroke, head up, watching as the shark continued to swim in a wide, slow circle. The December water was cold, and my chest spasmed adjusting to the temperature.

I'd have no trouble catching up. But what then?

We were less than a hundred yards from shore, but close enough to the channel that there was probably ten to twenty feet of water beneath us. Because the net was tangled on the shark's left side, the shark circled left, getting closer and closer to shore. Which was good. I wanted to end up in water shallow enough for me to stand.

I watched as the shark tried once again to turn into the tide. Its tail slapped the water feebly . . . strained briefly against the rope . . . then slapped the surface again, its gray body contorted, pectoral fins flapping as if made of rubber.

Pathetic. Female bull sharks drop only one to thirteen pups per birth cycle, and the mortality rate is high. Only a small percentage live the dozen or so years it takes to reach sexual maturity. By examining thinly sliced cross sections of vertebrae, a shark's age can be determined using a process similar to counting a tree's growth rings. I once did a necropsy on a bull shark that was twenty-five years old. It was nowhere near the size of this creature.

How many decades had it swum freely? In the world of sharks, size is a valid indicator of genetic ascendancy. This animal had not only survived against great odds, it had achieved a rare degree of oceangoing invulnerability. It had outsized all enemies — only now to fall victim to a bunch of plastic trash.

I waited until the shark turned, tail to me. Then I fixed my goggles in place and began to swim hard.

I caught the last section of nylon rope in my left hand, careful to match the bull shark's speed because I didn't want to add additional drag. We swam together for a time before I gradually began to kick and pull on a slightly different course, toward shore. I discovered that by applying light pressure via the rope, I could steer us toward the shallows.

I also began to work my way up the rope, closer and closer to the fish's huge, beating caudal fin.

We didn't have much time. The shark was visibly less animated. It was exhausted, and exhaustion can kill a fish just as surely as a weapon, because the muscles, saturated with lactic acid, begin to fail. The acid overload causes a domino effect of physiological imbalance in organ tissues and nervous system. Exceed a certain level of stress, and all the complicated mechanism shuts down.

So I was rushing — maybe too much.

When I was close enough to touch its tail, I nearly killed the thing inadvertently. I'd been using my survival knife to cut away sections of net. The reduction in drag, I reasoned, would reduce the energy drain. I also anticipated that it would cause a minor surge in speed.

The result was just the opposite. The floats attached to the net were keeping it afloat, so, when I cut the rope, the shark gave one last feeble tail thrust that instead of pushing it forward drove it head-heavy toward the bottom like some dead, inanimate weight.

For a moment, I stayed on the surface and

watched: watched the great shark sinking with the trajectory of a dark and cooling star.

Then I was after it, pulling myself down through the murk.

Almost immediately, I saw the tail and grabbed it. A shark's skin is covered with placoid scales, or denticles, which are similar to teeth. They're saw-edged and pointed, which is why shark skin was once commonly used as sandpaper.

The tail was abrasive, but also lifeless. I held on without difficulty as it pulled me downward. Through goggles and green water, I could see that my hand appeared tiny on the caudal lobe, and that the shark's body had turned from gray to black. The fish was too heavy for me to swim it back to the surface, and so I waited the few seconds it took for us to bump bottom. Then I went to work.

I got my feet under me, wrapped the animal in both arms, and began to walk it underwater, cross-tide, toward shore. The key to doing anything strenuous while free diving is to do it slowly. Conserve oxygen and you gain bottom time. So I took long, deliberate strides, switching my body into what I think of as conservation mode: used only the muscles required, everything else relaxed.

As my oxygen supply dwindled, I also began to play a little tune in my head, something I've always done when struggling to extend bottom time. Concentrate on the intricacies of the tune and I pay less attention to the capillary burn of lungs.

We'd hit bottom in maybe ten or fifteen feet of water. I covered enough distance toward shore that by the time I had to bounce to the surface for another gulp of air, the water wasn't more than a foot over my head.

I submerged a second time, lifted the shark into my arms again, then walked it over sand, sea grass, and shell until my eyes . . . then my nose . . . then my head breached the surface. I continued walking until I was in waist-deep water, using my knees to gently boost the animal upward whenever I lost my grip.

The backpack was still strapped over my head and shoulder. I found wire cutters, and soon had the web of net, rope, and floats cut away. I inspected the rope abrasions — they weren't too bad — and applied antibacterial cream to the wounds.

As I worked, I kept the shark's head pointed into the tide so that current swept through its gills. The shark remained motionless. Seemed near death. If I could get the respiratory system going, though, get sufficient oxygen into the bloodstream to dilute the overload of lactic acid, the animal still had a chance.

To increase the flow of water, I began to walk against the tide, slowly, slowly. I waded toward Lighthouse Point, floating five or six hundred pounds of shark along with me.

There's a row of condos near that section of shore. People were watching me from their balconies. One was a buddy of mine. He used his index finger to make a spinning motion next to his ear, then pointed at me: You're crazy.

Hard for anyone who lives at Dinkin's Bay to argue.

I walked the shark for ten minutes or so before I felt an intramuscular tremor that was not unlike a small generator trying to fire. Then the tail fin began to move . . . swung slowly and randomly, at first, then with increasing purpose and control. It fanned the current like a metronome, steady, steady, rhythmic as a heartbeat.

The fish was alive but weak. Not yet strong enough to release, or even endure the minor stress of being tagged. It would take another fifteen minutes to get sufficient oxygen into the bloodstream, but the tail thrust was increasingly powerful. Soon, I wouldn't be able to control the animal's body. Release it too soon, though, it would swim off and die.

So I tried a technique I learned years ago while working with a team of locals on the Zambezi River in Africa. Turn a big shark upside down and it will go limp in the water within twenty or thirty seconds. It's a physiological response called "tonic immobility." Keep it inverted and the fish will remain motionless for as much as half an hour.

Gently, I now rolled the bull shark onto its side, waited for it to stop struggling, then used its pectoral fin to push it over onto its back. I held it there, letting water flow through its mouth and gills — a sort of makeshift ventilator.

I got my first look at its underbelly. The most obvious indicators of a shark's sex are the absence or presence of twin penile-shaped claspers used singularly to deposit sperm. They're located just behind the pelvic fin. Because they calcify with maturity, male sharks have the equivalent of a permanent erection.

This was a male.

I also got my first close look at the great

fish's eyes. The opaque, nictitating membrane, which is a protective third eyelid, was closed like a curtain, but its eyes were visible beneath. The optic discs were yellow, the pupils black. In bright light, a shark's pupils contract to a vertical, feline slit. In darkness, they dilate, becoming a million times more sensitive to light than human eyes.

It was an hour before sunset; a bright, late afternoon. The shark's pupils looked like obsidian bands set into molten gold. The eyes were goatlike from a distance. Closer, the impression changed. A shark's retina has a prominent visual streak: a lucent horizontal band due to higher cell density in both cone and ganglion layers. Because of the streak, the eyes reminded me of a faraway nebula that I've seen many times through my telescope. The nebula is found in the belt of the constellation Orion.

That glittering streak on the optic disc, silver on gold, gave the impression that there was astronomy in the shark's eyes. Comet streaks, galactic swirls, and the black vacuum of space.

I walked it another twenty minutes before I risked turning the big fish onto its belly again. It was soon conscious, but remained docile. I paid close attention, gauging the steadiness and the strength of its caudal stroke. The respiratory system was working, flushing water through its gills. Its head swung in opposition to its tail.

I continued to walk against the tide; walked until the animal began to thrash against my grip. I held it for a few moments longer, then released it with a firm and final push toward deeper water. He swam tentatively, as if dazed, big dorsal cutting the water . . . then exploded — torpedoing off at speed, throwing a burrowing wake.

Behind me, I was surprised to hear applause coming from the boats.

I waved Rona to shore and climbed aboard.

"That was incredible," she said as I toweled off. She was bubbly, energized. "I'm so darn glad I came. I was dreading the trip . . . but to see something like that . . ."

I'd been cleaning my glasses but stopped. "Dreading what? I don't get it."

I watched her excitement drain. "Watching you save that shark, I'd almost forgotten. I wish I could forget. I wanted to wait, though, until you were done working before I told you."

What the woman had come to tell me was that my friend Dr. Frieda Matthews had been involved in a terrible accident.

20

serpiente

Talking on his motel phone, Frieda's husband, Bob, had told Dasha, "My wife's got the computer with her, but she won't be home until late this afternoon. Should I have her call FedEx? Or I can give you her cell phone number."

Jesus. The guy had the mentality of an eight-year-old. He was open to any stranger with a question.

Dasha repeated the number aloud while Aleski, sitting beside her in the white Mitsubishi SUV, wrote in his notebook.

One of Mr. Sweet's stooge vice presidents at Tropicane Sugar had already told her that Frieda Matthews had been snooping around, asking questions about her dead brother. She claimed she was going to review his work, visit some of the water sample sites personally.

"They're all remote places," the stooge VP had told her. "Not easy to find."

288

Dasha liked remote places. But she much preferred Mr. Sweet's Bahamas retreat to this isolated section of Central Florida, miles of sugarcane planted close to narrow asphalt. Black earth that smelled of chemicals; vultures perched hump-shouldered on wires above their SUV rental as they sat parked on the side of the road making phone calls.

She now dialed the Tropicane VP a second time. The man's secretary put her right through.

Dasha said to him, "I have a number for you to dial. Yes? Ask Dr. Matthews where her next stop will be, then call me with directions. Tell her we'd like to talk; share some stories about her brother."

The stooge said he'd do it. Didn't ask why, his manner making it clear he didn't want to know.

Dasha started the car and touched a button, lowering her window.

There was that chemical stink again, but it was warm at least. The woman loved heat.

They'd flown in that morning, just the two of them and their pilot, Aleski's cousin Broz. Came in one of Mr. Sweet's three private aircraft, the Piper Malibu, a seven-seater prop plane that had three seats removed because it was used mostly to carry supplies. The man's personal aircraft was a Gulfstream business jet; range: 6,000 miles, cruising speed: 550 knots. No one else was allowed to ride in the thing. Germs in a contained space? Unthinkable.

Mr. Earl would come later in the third plane, a refitted DC-3 cargo plane. It had a bed in the back, a VCR and stereo system. Nice.

The Piper was okay. Economical and fast. It covered the 187 nautical miles between Cay Sal Bank and West Palm Beach, where they cleared customs, in less than an hour.

The customs people recognized them. The "Vitamin Crew" — that's the way they were known — always puddle-jumping back and forth, hauling supplies.

Inspectors hustled them through.

From West Palm, they'd barely gotten off the ground before they were landing again at Tropicane's private airstrip between Kissimmee and Belle Glade. The rental was waiting, and now they'd been on the road less than an hour, things already falling in place.

Aleski rode in silence for a few minutes, the hectares of sugarcane reminding him of Cuba, his mind drifting, before he asked, "When we find this woman, how do you want to work it?"

Dasha said, "Remember the Greenie Weenie who started getting nosey? Maybe handle it the same way. Rent a storage garage, pay a year in advance. A place to dump this car. Maybe the body, too, depending on how it goes. Lock the doors, and fly out. Thirteen, fourteen months later, they find her. Maybe never."

"Did you bring the drug?"

He meant the stuff Dr. Stokes provided. Hypodermics and a vial of something called Versed. Ten ccs would knock a two-hundred-pound man to his knees in seconds. Keep him out for half an hour, if that's what she wanted. But the amount had to be right. Too much and he'd go into respiratory arrest.

Sometimes she wanted that, too.

Dasha told Aleski, "Yes, I have the hypodermic kit. But we don't have to use it on the woman. Not right away, if that's what you're asking."

Aleski had a deep, slow voice that fit his slow, slow intellect. But there was a little touch of excitement mixed in when they discussed Frieda Matthews. Dasha could guess why. He'd found a photo of the woman on the Internet. She wasn't bad looking, with her short hair, the smile, the outdoorsy body.

Aleski liked what he saw.

"If we have time . . . if there's no one around when we get to this storage garage, would it be possible for me . . . because I've been working so hard lately. Would it be okay for me to have a little fun? I haven't had fun for a very long time."

Oh yes, the man was excited. Dasha smiled; knew what was going to come next. "Of course, Aleski. You deserve your fun."

"You could be there. In the same room, if you wanted, Dasha. I wouldn't mind so much."

He threw it out there as if it were a new idea.

"Would you like that?"

"I wouldn't mind so much."

Always the same.

The first few times, she'd found what the man did to women interesting. Once it had even excited her, because the woman was very beautiful even though she was in her fifties. Intriguing, the way a mature woman dealt with pain and humiliation. Now, though, the thought of seeing Aleski naked made her cringe. Even so, she said, "Whatever makes you happy. You are my partner."

He grinned wickedly. "Yes, we are the best of partners! You give me such nice presents to unwrap! My little *moodozvon* pimp."

Russian profanity. It was a game they played.

Dasha said she wasn't a pimp; Aleski was a brainless bull, adding, *"Ti deegeneeraat zasranees!"* You're a degenerate asshole!

He shot back, *"Bliad! Yob tvoyu mat!"* Whore! I would like to screw your mother!

"Shliushka? Pizda na palochke? Da, pajalsta." That slut on a stick? Please do.

"Shob tebe deti v sup srali." I hope that your children shit in your soup.

They were both laughing.

"Ti menia dostal, Brat." I've had enough of you, brother.

"Ya tebia dostal, Sestra!" I've had enough of you, sister!

Sestra and Brat: pet names used fondly among members of secret Chechen guerrilla cells.

But Dasha had noticed that, lately, Aleski was treating her less like a sister and more like her keeper. Something in his manner.

Instinct.

They found a storage facility off Route 441 near Yeehaw Junction. Called the number, drove to the village, and paid the off-site attendant cash. Returned and made sure the key worked. As they were pulling away, Dasha's phone began to ring. She looked at the caller ID: the stooge from Tropicane. She listened for a moment before telling Aleski to get ready to write directions.

They had a road map. Frieda Matthews was less than twenty kilometers away.

Dasha put up her window, driving faster, as Aleski said, "Our luck has been so good, it may be possible to fly back to the island tonight."

Idiot. The woman slapped the wheel. "Don't do that! Why have you put your mouth on it? Now our luck is certain to change."

Aleski's face colored. Sick of her criticism, but not ready to show it. "I'm sorry. I was only hoping the best for you. I know you don't like spending nights at the ranch."

Tropicane maintained a housing complex for staff and guests, miles from anything, pasture all around. Mr. Earl had his own minimansion there. A man who controlled enough proxies to be majority stockholder.

"It's not that I dislike the ranch. I don't like being away from the island. You know that. So don't risk screwing our luck by being so stupid."

Aleski was eager to change the subject. "You love those islands so much, I feel you should own them one day. When the rich man dies." His tone insinuated that it could happen. All she had to do was ask.

Dasha said severely, "Don't speak of our employer in such a way. Dr. Stokes is very good to us."

There were so many ways of recording conversations, it was the smart thing to say.

"Besides, his assistant would then be in control. He's in charge of all the doctor's personal property."

Aleski said, "Mr. Earl? I like Mr. Earl. Sometimes, we drink vodka at night and talk."

Dasha was aware of that, too. But was thinking, *My islands. Yes, it could happen. Even before Mr. Sweet dies . . .*

Dr. Frieda Matthews was sitting in her green SUV, waiting for them, the small dents in the fender, the cracked taillight, and DISNEY WORLD bumper sticker telling Dasha the woman wasn't rich. That she had at least one child, but still worked for a living. She found her at the end of a dirt service road that ran beneath power lines and dead-ended at a canal, not far from State Route 60 and Canoe Creek Road.

Right where the Tropicane VP said she'd be.

Dasha wondered what the stooge would think when he read about this in the papers. Not that he'd call the cops. If Mr. Sweet had something on the guy, which he always did with his top people, there wasn't a chance. But would he feel guilty?

Dasha hoped so.

As they got out of the car, Aleski said to her in Russian, "Wonderful. She's even more beautiful than her photograph."

The woman was attractive in a handsome sort of way. Short maple-colored hair parted at the side, cargo shorts, plaid blouse. She had a sociable smile on her face, teeth very white. Also a cell phone clipped to her belt — that could cause trouble.

"She's bigger than I thought she'd be. I like that." Aleski was walking faster, bouncing along. It meant she wouldn't be as easily broken. The man couldn't wait.

"Don't do anything stupid until we get the computer. Make sure it's the right one."

"Of course. But then leave her to me. This woman, she will be fun. I can tell."

Matthews had her hand extended — nice to meet you — her smile broadening as Dasha got to the green SUV. Looked in the side window and there it was: a silver

PowerBook computer.

"Mr. Hartman called from Tropicane, vice president in charge of environmental oversight? Said you worked for him, and knew my late brother? I'd love to hear anything you have to tell me."

Fifteen minutes later, driving fast down the dirt road, all Dasha could hear was Aleski in the back of the Mitsubishi, breathing heavily and swearing because Matthews refused to cooperate. She screamed out for help only once before settling herself into endurance mode, another middle-aged woman who could be hurt but not bullied.

Dasha thought, *Interesting,* wondering if maybe she should stop and watch. She might get aroused as she had when she'd watched the beautiful woman who was in her fifties ruin it for Aleski by not showing fear.

"Get your hand off that door handle, *pizda!*"

Dasha glanced around automatically when she heard the tailgate open — they'd just bounced onto a narrow asphalt road — her hands still gripping the wheel, causing the vehicle to fishtail twice before she regained control.

"You bitch! Stop scratching me!"

In the rearview mirror, Dasha saw Matthews clawing at Aleski's face, everything happening very fast: the woman screaming; Aleski swearing, trying to subdue her. Then Aleski coughed and bellowed — a scream of pain — and Dasha watched the woman sit briefly, pounding at Aleski with her fists.

In Russian, she yelled, "Pull the door closed, you idiot, before she —"

Too late. Frieda Matthews had somehow managed to fight her way from beneath Aleski. In that moment of freedom, the woman didn't hesitate. As if lunging into a swimming pool, she rolled out of the SUV, the mirror showing it as if on a screen. Dasha saw her body drop behind the car as if in slow motion, then become instantly animated when flesh hit asphalt, a fast-forward effect, bouncing behind the vehicle like a rag doll, arms and legs flapping wildly. Watched the woman's body tumble grotesquely, gradually slowing in a boneless heap, shrinking rapidly behind them because Matthews had jumped when the vehicle was doing sixty.

Idiot. Dasha screamed at Aleski, "I knew you'd ruined our luck!"

She braked to a controlled stop, still looking at the rearview mirror.

"She's alive, Dasha. See there? She's moving." The man was on all fours, naked, hairy as a bear, looking out. "See? She's trying to stand up."

Dasha had the vehicle in reverse, accelerating. "Get your pants on, you fool. We need to find a better place. Get her up on her feet. Then we change places. You get behind the wheel. I'll take care of her, or you'll somehow manage to fuck it up again."

21

Rona Graves looked toward the shoreline, avoiding eye contact, no longer energized because we'd freed the shark. "Mrs. Matthews' husband asked me to break the news. He's a wreck, but he thought it was important for you to know."

I waited.

"She's dead."

"Dead?" Whispered the question.

For several moments, my brain refused to process the information. Rona had to be mistaken. It was Jobe Applebee who was dead, not his vibrant, brilliant sister. Rona had accidentally transposed the names.

But no. The woman confirmed it with a single nod of her head: My friend was dead.

Frieda's body had been found late yesterday evening, Rona told me, on a deserted road south of Kissimmee, the victim of a hit-and-run driver. Her car was discovered a mile or so away on a dirt service trail that dead-ended at an engineered drainage canal off what had once been the Kissimmee River. The car's hood was up, battery dead.

The fatality was still under investigation, but sheriff's investigators were theorizing that Frieda couldn't get her car started, so decided to hike four or five miles to the main road to get help. Some drunk or crazy driver had struck her from behind.

"At first, I was going to call, but decided it was a crappy way to handle it. I had a good time the night we were out. You seem like an okay guy. I figured you deserved to hear it in person from someone you know. Someone familiar with what happened."

Rona had worked the case. Her tone and facial expression told me it was unpleasant. Same with the hour she'd spent talking with Frieda's husband, Bob.

I said, "Yesterday was Thursday. Her brother's funeral was yesterday morning. She let me off the hook; said they didn't expect me to attend. And she dies a few hours later? *Unbelievable.*"

"I know."

"She had a seven-year-old son. She was crazy about him."

"Eight years old last November. Robert Junior. I'm getting to know the Applebee branch of the family one by one. Unfortunately, it's after they're dead."

I was cold and wet, beginning to shiver; needed to get home to a hot shower. I let Rona tell me the rest of it as I piloted us beneath the causeway, then steered for the power lines and mangrove point that mark the entrance to Dinkin's Bay.

According to husband Bob, Frieda had meetings early Wednesday afternoon with representatives from two of Jobe's former clients, Tropicane Sugar and EPOC, the environmental group.

The timing wasn't great. Bob and their young son had only just arrived in Kissimmee. But Frieda was eager to start backtracking her brother's work patterns, so she'd made the long drive to the sugar giant's corporate offices, just outside the city of Labelle.

Labelle is a Deep South town of moss-draped oaks, pasturelands, and river. It's west of Lake Okeechobee, west of Florida's vast cane fields.

Rona said, "Bob was so upset, I'm not clear on all the details. But the way I understand it is, her meetings went okay. The reps she met were courteous and sympathetic. They gave her a list of sites where her brother took water samples." The woman paused. "Why would she want a list?"

I thought about it a moment. "It would be a place to start."

"They also said she could take over her brother's job . . . or something that had to do with working for them. That's one of the parts I'm not clear on."

I said, "Take over his contract. He had six months left."

Wednesday night, the Matthews family had dinner at a Kissimmee restaurant, and went to bed early. The next day, shortly after her brother's funeral, Frieda took off in the family SUV, telling her husband she was going to collect water samples from a few of the sites on the list she'd been given.

Frieda told him she'd be back no later than four. At six, she still wasn't home and wasn't answering her cell phone. Bob called law enforcement.

Rona said, "Our sheriff's department, they're a good bunch. Probably because of what had happened to her brother, they didn't wait the standard period before starting a search. Deputies went from test site to test site — she'd left a copy of the list at the motel — and found her car. It was around nine when they found her body."

Rona wasn't the first responder. Investigators from the medical examiner's office seldom are. But Frieda's body hadn't yet been moved when Rona arrived.

An ugly scene. I could read it in Rona's body language, her careful inflections, and the way she emphasized what little comforting information she could offer.

"I don't think the woman knew what hit her. The vehicle was traveling fast. It was on a secondary county road — narrow asphalt without shoulders. A dredged canal on one side, cattle pasture on the other. You know the type. The speed limit's thirty-five, but there aren't any cops around, the traffic's all local, so everyone flies. The car that killed Frieda Matthews had to be going twice the speed limit."

The woman began to edit her wording. "In our business, we're taught that . . . we learn there are certain indicators regarding the . . . disposition of the deceased's body . . . the sort of *trauma*. It can suggest the speed at impact in a car-versus-pedestrian fatality."

I had a good idea what some of those indicators were, but this nice woman was trying to spare me pain by telling me that Frieda had felt none. Only a few days before, I'd tried to be similarly considerate when I'd told Frieda that her brother had died peacefully.

All lies of kindness require cooperation from the recipient. I returned Rona's kindness by moving on to a different subject.

I said, "Why would she leave her car, go looking for help when she had a cell phone?"

"I don't know. Maybe poor reception, or something. Our guys didn't find the phone. We didn't find her computer, either."

I said, "Computer?"

"Uh-huh. That was missing, too. A laptop. You'd have to visit the scene to picture what I'm saying. But the way her body ended up, she'd been knocked so far that whatever she was carrying could be anywhere along fifty yards of cattails and dredged canal.

"They had the crime scene lights on bright. The canal's loaded with gators. Lots of ruby red eyes in there after dark. Someone saw a couple of snakes, too. So our people weren't eager to wade in and search. They will, though, if my office decides it's important."

I was confused. "Her phone and computer are missing? You said her car was parked on a service trail about four or five miles from the main road. If she had to walk several miles for help, why lug a computer? She'd have left it in the car."

"One of the investigators was wondering about that, too. Her husband said it was her late brother's computer, so maybe that's the reason. She might have thought it was too valuable to leave behind."

"Her *brother's* computer?"

"That's what he told us."

I was shaking my head, not buying it. When a series of coincidences exceed the odds of probability, the events are either predestined or they are linked by design. And I don't believe in destiny.

"Then the whole business stinks. The night Jobe Applebee was assaulted, they tore his house apart looking for something, maybe the same computer. Five days later, his sister's found dead and the computer's missing. Do investigators think it was accidental?"

"Criminal Investigation Division doesn't make that call. Our office does. Our head MD or his assistant. I collect the data, then we wait for the results of the autopsy and toxicology to come back. It takes a while. We still haven't even made a ruling on how her brother died."

She shrugged, telling me it was still up in the air. "Highway Patrol won't work a traffic fatality if there's even a hint of foul play. They worked this one — which tells you something. A woman whose car won't start gets killed on a narrow road by a hit-and-run. Accidental. It happens.

"Right now, they figure some poor, scared bastard is out there, locked in his garage, trying to clean the mess off his bumper. Within the next few days, he'll either turn himself in or he'll sneak off to some body shop a few counties away and tell them he hit a deer or a bear. That's when they'll nail him."

I put my hand on her shoulder, shaking my head. "No. This is potentially a lot more serious than your law enforcement people know. A guy from the state health department called me today. They found more guinea worm parasites near Orlando. It's biological terrorism. They're brutal people — I saw them interrogating Applebee. If they wanted his computer bad enough, killing his sister, staging it to look accidental, it wouldn't be a big deal. Your people need to get the FBI in on this."

Rona said, "Know what? I agree. Too many deaths in too short a time." A moment later, she added, "Frieda's husband said she'd e-mailed you files from her brother's computer."

"That's right. I haven't opened them yet, but they're on my computer."

"If you're right about Dr. Matthews . . . Doc?" The woman was thinking about it. "You need to be on your toes."

It was nearly sunset when I backed the Aquasport into the slip beneath my house. As I tied off, Mack, the displaced Kiwi who owns the marina, yelled to remind me that this wasn't just any ordinary sunset Christmas party I was about to miss. It was a *Friday*-night party. He emphasized the word in case I'd forgotten my social obligations.

I was still dazed by the news about Frieda. Felt an inner fury that I kept hidden as I waved acknowledgment. Called back that I'd try to make it.

Among the indignities of a tragic death is that the rest of the world carries on as if tragedy does not exist. A coping mechanism, and a healthy one.

Dinkin's Bay was carrying on.

Each and every Friday, the marina hosts its Pig Roast and Beer Cotillion — acronym: PERBCOT, or P'COT, which intentionally lampoons EPCOT, as well as bewilders first-timers who expect there to be similarities.

Attendance isn't mandatory for locals, but it's considered rude not to at least make an appearance on the docks and say a quick hello to all the people having fun.

"Folks are askin' for you at the party, 'Cobber," Mack yelled. He was wearing a Cuban shirt, a plantation owner's white strawhat, and smoking a fresh cigar. Judging from the ring of keys in his hand, he'd just locked the swinging gate that marks the terminus of Tarpon Bay Road, which is publicly owned, and the beginning of the marina parking lot, which is not.

Even though I was reeling, seeing the key ring catalyzed a slight smile. Locking the gate is part of the ceremony. Once the gate is closed, the outside world is physically, and symbolically, excluded from all demonstrations of strange and potentially embarrassing behavior that are acceptable among the marina family, but probably nowhere else.

"JoAnn's wearing that slinky tangerine dress of hers none of us has seen in a while," he continued. "Since she took up kickboxing, my God, what a change. A body like hers, you don't care if a woman's in her forties, fifties, or sixties." He paused for a moment, puffing on his cigar. He seemed to notice Rona for the first time. "Your friend's welcome to come along, of course. Pretty women are always welcome at Dinkin's Bay."

Her mood had sobered while telling me about Frieda, but she masked it well. With a damsel-like flair, she replied, "Why, thank you, sir. I don't know if I'll be able to attend, but I'm honored that you'd ask."

Now ignoring me, Mack said, "You'll have a great time, there's plenty to drink, and the food's as good as it gets. Oh, but a warning: You might run into a character named Tomlinson. He almost always wears a sarong but no underwear. Don't let him scare you. He's harmless."

"I'm very sorry to hear that. One day, I'd *like* to meet a man in a sarong who wasn't harmless." Using the cheery mask to show she had a touch of vixen in her, too.

Mack liked that. "In that case, I may go ask Tomlinson if he has something soft and silky I can wear."

Rona made a purring sound."You *do* that, big fella."

22

I telephoned Fish and Wildlife and told the lady in charge that the shark was now free, and that one of the helpful amateur skippers on-scene had collected the remains of the net for disposal.

Mission accomplished. But I felt sick.

Rona had fetched her overnight bag from the car. While she used my house to freshen up, I took a warm shower beneath my outdoor cistern, changed into fresh shorts and a gray wool shirt that felt good, because the temperature was falling along with the winter sun.

Back in the lab, I leaned over the computer keyboard to make sure I could open the files Frieda had sent. No problem. There were three documents, nothing but numbers. There were spaces between some blocks and columns of numbers, and some punctuation, too.

It was a substitution cipher, but it wasn't obvious.

There was also a note from Frieda. Painful to read. It ended: "I know my brother would have wanted these files to go to you, old buddy. He admired your work so. Opposite sides of the same coin — if Jobe believed that, he made a good choice."

I didn't like the way I felt, so I turned from the computer and dialed Dewey's number. I'd already spoken with her twice that day.

No answer, so I left a message. Told her to call when she got back from Christmas shopping in the big cities of Davenport, Moline, and Bettendorf.

Hearing her voice made me feel better. We are all prone to behave as if our friends are as enduring as the stability they contribute to our uncertain lives. The death of one punches a hole in that delusion. It leaves us clinging, for a time, to our protective bubbles, staring off into the void, until other friends rally to patch the communal leak.

The death of a friend reminds us that nonexistence is a cold and solitary place.

As I waited for Rona, I stood outside on the deck. I sipped my first beer of the evening, then lifted the bottle northward, in the direction of Tallahassee. A private toast. Stood thinking secret, reflective thoughts until Rona appeared. The lady wore black slacks and a silk blouse the color of wet pearls. She'd combed her black hair until it glistened, and added a touch of makeup to made her dark skin darker.

As I walked her to the marina, I told her she looked very elegant, and meant it. It surprised me that she flushed, embarrassed. "Thanks. I get so flustered when I hear something like that because I was such a gawky nerd for so many years. My body didn't start to fill out until I was in my thirties, so I'm not used to compliments. I'm just now starting to enjoy what it's like for men to be interested. Oh, and Doc" — she touched my arm; this was personal — "I'm so sorry about Mrs. Matthews. That I had to be the one to tell you."

I said, "She was a good woman. You told me I needed to see where she died for myself? I think I'll drive to Kissimmee tomorrow, and have a look around. Tonight, though, I think Frieda would want us to do what she did whenever she visited these islands. Have fun."

The party was reaching its cruising rhythm . . .

We'd missed sunset, but the earth's rotation continued to spill color over the horizon. Above a mangrove rim, the western sky was streaked with citreous mesas, bands of key lime and orange. Behind us, high shoals of cirrus clouds were a firestorm of lavender.

Mack had the dock lights wired to a timer, and they'd just come on: Pale pearl bands on a bay streaked with bronze. Added to the light show were the marina's Christmas decorations. Every houseboat, sailboat, cruiser, and sports fishing boat was trimmed with strings of holiday bulbs — red, green, or strobing white. Almost every mast or fly bridge sported a climbing plastic Santa, a lighted Christmas tree, a reindeer frozen in flight, a white cross or Star of David.

I paused outside the Red Pelican Gift Shop next to the bait tanks, my eyes taking it in, attempting to fix the scene, in memory: seeing the docks, the sky, the multicolored lights, the rows of boats. Seeing islanders mingling near picnic tables covered with platters of food; the marina's Christmas tree — actually, an Australian pine, twelve feet tall — decorated with fishing lures, and greeting cards from clients around the nation. Beneath the tree were stacked piles of presents, brightly wrapped and bowed.

Frieda had liked this place. She would

have enjoyed being here now.

Beside me, Rona said, "Gee, what a great little marina. It's kind of warm and old-timey, the way the shops are built next to the docks. Everything wooden, but like the wood has gotten way too much sun. And I love the Christmas decorations. I can see why so many people are here."

This edition of P'COT *had* attracted a big crowd, which was not unexpected. Dusk on the islands is a soft, sociable time of gathering. There are subtleties of color, scent, and sound that can only be appreciated outdoors, which is why almost everyone heads for the beach or the bay.

On this Friday evening, along with the couple of dozen marina inhabitants there were also several dozen guests. Everyone roamed the docks, drinks in hand, ricocheting from one convivial pod of souls to another, while Captain Buffett sang about gypsies in the castle, then the Beach Boys sang about St. Nick's sled of candy apple red, music blasting from speakers mounted atop the fly bridge of Dieter Rasmussen's Grand Banks trawler, *Das Stasi.*

Dieter is the resident shrink, a duly licensed psychiatrist, and an expert on all kinds of things related to the human brain. He and his stunning live-in Jamaican girlfriend, Mira, were sitting aft in swivel chairs. They waved. I pointed to my watch, telling them I'd stop by in a few minutes.

I searched the crowd, looking for the Internet guru. He was standing with a group of locals that included Laken. Lake was wearing shorts and an oversized Red Sox baseball jersey. Tomlinson was dressed in . . . a suit? Yep. One of the white silk suits he'd mentioned. Looked like a rock star. Or a homeless drunk who'd gotten lucky at some Salvation Army store.

The two of them had become buddies. It was easily read in their brotherly chiding, the private laughter. They did things together when they could: batting practice, sailing; a lot of time hanging out — which was worrisome until Lake took me aside and asked me to tell Tomlinson to knock off the antidrug sermons.

Straight-faced, I'd replied, "We're talking about the same Tomlinson?"

Yes, the same.

Tomlinson was worried about being a poor role model, so he'd been overcompensating, hammering out lectures on the dangers of cannabis and similar evils. It was getting tiresome, Lake informed me. He had no interest in the stuff to begin with, and asked me to tell Tomlinson to resume his own drug use — or whatever it was he did — because, lately, the man had been a pious, strung-out pain in the ass.

His new role as entrepreneur had something to do with it, too, I was sure.

But Tomlinson looked relaxed and at home on this night. His eyes had a contented, sedated glaze. He was barefooted; had a red hibiscus blossom tucked into his lapel of his white silk jacket. Both added to the impression of tropical élan.

I hadn't been in a mood to socialize but was now glad that I'd come. There was nothing I could do to change what happened to Frieda. Later, I'd give the e-mail documents a more thorough look. Maybe invite Tomlinson to focus his big brain on the puzzle. Lake, too, of course. He'd be flying back to Central America on Sunday, the same day I was leaving for Iowa. So I wanted to spend as much time with him as possible.

I suspect all parents enjoy secretly watching as their children interact socially. That's what I did now, taking pleasure in the easy way the boy handled himself; in the shape of his face, his mannerisms, the snatches of his laughter that filtered through the party din. I was so lost in thought that I couldn't help but stumble a little when I heard:

"I don't want to be nosy, but I've got to ask: Where's your girlfriend?"

I turned to look at Rona. She'd drifted off, but was back again. I stammered for a moment before managing to say, "Huh?"

"I'm asking about your girl. You're involved with someone; it shows. But here it is Friday night, and she's not around. She wasn't with you in Kissimmee, either. What's the deal?"

The lady investigator had recombed her wild surfer's hair to the side — different but interesting. I noticed that her eyes were a lucent amber in the late light.

"Her name's Dewey, and she's living in Iowa. We were good friends, then it became more than that. She's pregnant. My child. The baby's due mid-May."

Pregnant. That jarred her, but not for long. "An Iowa girl? You're not the kind of guy who preys on tourist ladies looking for a fling. They're plenty like that in Florida, but you're not one of them."

"Thanks."

"How'd you get together?"

"Dewey's not a tourist; she's local. Owns a house on Captiva, but Iowa is where she wants to be right now. It's a little farm; been in her family for generations. Nesting instinct?" I shrugged. "Tradition, maybe. I visit when I can. I leave Sunday to spend Christmas."

"She moved away?" I found the undertone of disapproval unsettling. "You two are having a child, but she's halfway across the country? That's an . . . interesting arrangement."

"She's got midwestern roots; sees Iowa as a healthier, safer place. There's nothing wrong with that."

"Safer. I see." Her flat tone said I was being stupid.

"Yes, *safer*."

"Whoa, whoa. Don't get pissed off, Doc. I saw that flash in your eyes. Holy cripes, like sparks. No offense intended."

"I'm not offended. Unusual people sometimes make unusual decisions. That's one of the reasons I like her."

Rona stared at me intensely for a moment with her Polynesian-colored eyes, her expression puzzled: What makes you tick?

"I don't know your girl. I've never been in her position. Don't go getting bigheaded, but it's hard to imagine being with a man who makes a woman feel safer than you. On Night's Landing, the way you handled yourself. Dealing with that shark. What you've just described between you and your girlfriend sounds more like a test than a relationship."

I glanced away as she added, "I've been tested a time or two. Personally, I don't think lovers give tests unless they secretly expect their partner to fail. Or want them to fail."

I found her quick assessment unfair, but I avoid debate when the subject's personal and private. I heard myself chuckle in the way men do when they want to dismiss the complicated subject of relationships by trivializing it. "I don't pretend to understand women. Especially pregnant women. I do whatever it takes to make her happy."

Rona replied cryptically, "When men say things like that, they think they're kidding. They're actually right. But only *half* right."

She looked toward the docks then and waved. "Hey, there's your friend Mack. I think I'll go join the party."

23

LOG
17 Dec. Friday 21:17
(addendum)
. . . The conjunction of visible planets confirms the existence of unseen planets, all fixed in orbit by gravity, a calculable force. Does a single force link Applebee, Frieda, assault/murder, African exotics, a 17-year-old prophecy, and water?

Standing behind me, looking over my shoulder as I sat at the computer, Tomlinson said, "Laken and I aren't going to be shocked if you admit you know something about cryptography. Scout's honor, no need to play innocent. Tell us the difference between secret code and a cipher. Or maybe they're the same thing."

It was nearly midnight. The party was still going strong. Only a few hundred feet of water separated us from music and loud laughter — Christmas carols in Spanish now. I could see silhouettes of people dancing on the docks, doing the salsa or merengue through the screened windows.

I'd left Rona chatting with Mack and the guides, men clustered around. She told me she had a hotel room, not to worry, she'd be just fine. I didn't doubt it. For a woman who claimed to have grown up gawky, she enjoyed being among men, and knew how to hold court.

Despite her prying questions, it didn't take long for us to get back on friendly terms, which was a relief. So, in good conscience, I'd returned home.

Tomlinson and Lake agreed to follow when they were ready.

When they joined me in the lab, I told them what had happened to Frieda, and Applebee. Tomlinson focused in when I mentioned Asperger's syndrome, which suggested he knew something about it. Then I opened the computer documents, including Frieda's note to me.

He'd met Frieda, and he'd seen Applebee's remarkable diorama, so Tomlinson was moved by what she'd written:

Hey, Doc. You're the only guy I know with the background to understand Jobe's files, attached here. Remember me telling you my brother used numbers as words? He also associated numbers with stuff like moods and emotions. Colors, too. Quite a few Aspie kids do this.

He told me 4 was the only true number because it had four letters. Numbers you could trust were 99 and 66, because they had value even upside down. 3, 6, and 13 were yellow numbers. 2 and 5 were red. 8 was blue.

He was a special brother, and I will miss him every day of my life. Maybe it's my twin's intuition, but I have a feeling that Jobe stumbled onto something bad that got him killed. It scared him enough to send his computer to me for safekeeping.

I've already set up some meetings with his clients, and started poking around. Nothing's going to stop me from finding out why someone would hurt such a gentle person.

He'd have wanted these files to go to you, Doc. Opposite sides of the same coin . . .

She'd signed it: See you soon!

I would not be seeing her soon. The lady was now sealed away in a refrigerated locker at the county medical examiner's office . . . or maybe already on a stainless steel table. She would soon be further diminished by a hole in a Tallahassee cemetery, or an urn, into which she would shrink and shrink and shrink in memory until she vanished into infinity.

Frieda Matthews was a good one. A fine person who was dear and bright and solid. I admired her intellect. I liked the sound of her laughter. I valued her as a person. The transition from animate to the inanimate occurs in a microsecond. It is the interval of a flame extinguished, but it is an eternal microsecond. I would never see her again.

I kept her message on the computer screen long enough to read twice. Then I opened the documents from a folder labeled: TROPICANE/EPOC.

At the top of the first page, first document, was written: DO NOT LET THEM FIND THIS!

A note from brother to sister.

Someone had been after his computer.

Otherwise, the pages consisted of nothing but numbers. Digits were sometimes separated by spaces, rarely punctuation. An occasional period or colon.

Studying the screen, Tomlinson and my son both reacted with the muted grunts and sentence fragments that signal confusion.

"That message at the top — *who* doesn't he want to have this?"

I said, "The people who were trying to beat information out of him the night I came along. The ones who also maybe killed his sister. I'm speculating."

Lake whistled softly. "Shouldn't the *federales* know? Or the police?"

The boy spoke English without accent, but he sometimes used Spanish words unconsciously. "The feds know. I'll forward these files to the FBI, but there's no reason for us not to try and decode them. Maybe we'll learn something."

Lake put his hand on my shoulder, as Tomlinson used a favorite phrase: "It is time for us to put on the ol' thinking caps, my brothers." Added: "Which means at least one of us will need beer. Several, in fact."

Tomlinson returned from the galley carrying a galvanized bucket heavy with ice and bottles. As he opened a beer and took a long gulp, I told them what I remembered about cryptography.

Tomlinson's guess was right. I've dealt

with various forms of secret writing. I've had to create methods of encrypting messages, and also tried to crack messages that had been encoded — too seldom successfully.

I shared the basics: Code substitutes groups of letters or figures for words or phrases. Shorthand is code. Police radio-speak is code — "10-4" means affirmative. In Morse code, SOS is three dots, three dashes, three dots.

A cipher, in contrast, is text in which every letter is assigned a substitute. Done well, the text is unreadable to all but those who possess the cipher's key.

I'd asked Frieda if there were any numbers larger than twenty-six, because the simplest form of cipher uses numbers in place of an alphabetical counterpart. If *A* is 1, *B* is 2, and *Z* becomes 26. The cipher's key can be shifted: If *A* is 25, *B* may be 24, and *Z* is 0.

A quick look told me this was more complicated. I touched the computer screen as I explained why. Many of the numbers were in blocks of four, set apart by spaces. There were also blocks of eight, though fewer.

I said, "A typical document doesn't contain that many four- or eight-letter words, but I still think it's a form of substitution cipher. Dr. Applebee knew it well enough to create long documents, which suggests that there's consistency in the substitution system. If there is, we'll figure it out."

A good cipher system cloaks repetition, I told them.

"That's why the Nazis' Enigma cipher was so tough for the Brits to crack. The Germans used a machine similar to a typewriter, but it had a series of wheels that changed the alphabetical sequence by one letter after every twenty-six keystrokes."

Otherwise, I said, patterns become obvious. Certain letters of the alphabet, specific combinations, are used more than others. The same is true of certain words; particularly short words.

"The most frequently used letters in English are *E, T, A, O* and *N*, in that order. The way I remember is to think of 'Estimated Time of Arrival, ON.' The next most commonly used letters are *I, R* and *S*, as in Internal Revenue. Easy. Beyond that, I've forgotten. I'll put it down on paper for you."

I described other decoding tricks: contact analysis; and also the most commonly used double letters.

"Keep in mind that Applebee created the system for himself, nobody else. The guy had Asperger's syndrome. What may've seemed sequential to him might seem unlikely to us. His sister told me their neuron pathways function differently."

Tomlinson surprised me, saying, "I may be able to relate to an Aspie better than you think. A month or so ago, Deet took me aside, and asked me a bunch of questions about what I was like as a kid. He kept me cornered for an hour or so."

"Deet" was Dieter Rasmussen, the German shrink with the beautiful boat.

"You didn't mention it."

"No. It would've sounded like I was blowing my horn. You know how some people talk about their flaws, but in a way that actually glorifies? A major turnoff, which I try to avoid. Deet told me he thought I have a touch of Asperger's syndrome."

"You're kidding."

"Some of the characteristics he described, I have to agree. Wired differently? No one's going to argue that one, compadre. When I was a kid, I preferred being alone to socializing. I transposed words, wrote my sevens backward — which is why I still cross sevens and my *g*s. And my interests tended to be, oh, shall we say, just to the right of lunatic obsessive."

He used both hands to shoo it away as if

unimportant. "The other stuff, though — lack of imagination, the temper tantrums — don't fit. But Dieter said symptoms vary. A touch of Asperger's can be a good thing. Thoreau, Thomas Edison, Isaac Newton, a bunch of others — they were undiagnosed Asperger's people. It's common in the arts and sciences."

I said, "If it helps you crack these files, I hope he's right. We don't have much time. Lake and I are both supposed to leave day after tomorrow."

My son said slowly, "Yeah, Doc, but we don't have to leave. Maybe *you* do, but I don't." He was looking at me, gauging my reaction. I got the impression he was testing to see if I'd risk upsetting Dewey by postponing my trip.

Interesting. He'd met the woman. They appeared to get along fine. Yet, he'd thrown this out to measure something, I felt sure. Maybe to find out how much independence I'd retained, how much I'd forfeited to the woman who would soon be the mother of his half-sibling.

There were complicated subissues involved. Children are no less complicated than adults — survival requires heightened awareness in primate young. I had to tread lightly.

I said, "Your mother isn't my biggest fan to begin with, and letting you stay longer wouldn't raise my stock. If you're not home by Sunday, she'll never let you come back. Let's not risk it."

Lake tilted his head — part shrug, part nod of concession — which told me that he was aware I'd dodged his deeper question.

Tomlinson, however, seemed oblivious to the subtext, because he plowed ahead. "The boy's right, Doc. It's no accident that the secret files of Jobe Applebee got dropped in our laps. We have a moral obligation to see this thing through — no matter what it reads on your plane tickets. We don't choose our evils; our evil chooses us."

I said nothing — Lake had to leave Sunday because what I'd said about his mother was true. She'd never let him return. Even so, I listened as Tomlinson asked, "What are the chances we'll crack these files within the next day or so?"

I said, "Zero. Even if we discover the cipher's key, we'd still have to create an algorithm that would convert it from numbers to letters. Either that or translate it one word at a time. Ransom probably knows enough about computers to do the programming, but we're still talking days. Maybe weeks."

Tomlinson had anticipated the answer. "Okay, then here's what we need to do." He nodded to me. "Let's drive to Kissimmee tomorrow and find where Frieda was killed. Take a look around, see what makes sense, what doesn't. If her death was accidental, then this deciphering gig is no longer a moral priority. You can both fly off as planned. But if we see something that tells us the lady was murdered, then that's our *dharma*. You can no more run off to Iowa than we can hear the sound of one hand clapping."

In reply to my son's puzzled expression, I shook my head quickly: Don't ask.

"Same's true for me," Tomlinson continued. "I've got to follow it through. How pissed off do you think your sister's going to be if I'm not here on Sunday for our live Webcast? She'll shit a brick. Or ice cubes, is more like it. What would that cost her in Good Karma offerings?"

I could see that he was inwardly pleased with the idea.

After they'd left, alone in my lab I continued the copepod procedure, hooked on the idea that a hybrid could be developed. During the waiting periods, I did some research on Florida's sugar industry — "Big

Sugar," it's commonly called — hoping for a clue to what Applebee might have hidden in his encrypted files. Internet search engines produced a pile of hits.

I'd forgotten how big Florida's sugar industry is, and how much political clout it has. I was also surprised at some of the environmental-friendly changes that had taken place in the last few years. Most of those changes had to do with the way the industry disposed of water.

More surprising was an entry in a Dutch newsletter that someone had translated into English and posted on an investment group's Web page. It claimed that Florida's sugar industry faced certain collapse. It predicted that much of its agricultural acreage would soon be for sale.

Could that be true?

I spent half an hour confirming it.

Something else I did was fret about Dewey. I'd left a message for her earlier. Around 1 a.m., I realized she hadn't returned my call.

I'd left the phone in the house, and so I walked across the breezeway and dialed Dewey's home phone. I got her voice mail again. Same when I tried her mobile.

I tried an hour later. Same results.

Odd.

It was only midnight, Iowa time, but it wasn't like her to stay out so late, even on a Friday. It also was unusual that she didn't answer her cell phone. The woman carried the thing everywhere.

I continued tinkering with Applebee's files, messing with different decoding keys, trying to get my mind off Dewey. Not easy.

I pace when I'm worried and I soon began to pace. I paced between the lab and the house, alternately willing the damn phone to ring, then willing Jobe's complicated cipher to give me a little break.

Neither cooperated.

We all have perverse, destructive components in our psychological makeup. I don't know why, but we do. Gradually, on some perverse level, I was pleased that Dewey hadn't answered, even though I was anxious to confirm that she was okay.

How many times had she criticized me for calling too late, or forgetting to call? Now here it was 2:30 a.m., Florida time, and she hadn't even bothered to tell me she'd be out of touch.

In the adolescent game of scorekeeping, leverage shifted a little bit my way. In the future, if I didn't feel like calling for a night or two the lapse was now acceptable. She'd set the precedent, not me. In fact, all future demonstrations of independence were now justified — satisfying because Lake had questioned whether I could still act independently.

I tried one more time at 2:45, standing outside on the porch above the shark pen, looking at stars, feeling a tropic wind on my face.

No answer, so I cloaked my indignation in a message saying that I was concerned, to please call no matter what time she got in. Added too sharply that I'd be driving to Kissimmee in the morning because of Frieda's death. I didn't need any additional worries.

Then I clomped down the steps to check my specimen tank a final time. Paused once for long seconds, listening, because I thought I heard the sound of footsteps on shells. Paused again, hearing something, or someone, moving through mangroves.

Got my rechargeable spotlight; shined it around from the top deck. I varied the search pattern, switching it off for minutes. Then switched it on, painting the shoreline yellow.

Raccoons.

I went to bed.

24

   From Dutch financial newsletter: "Florida's sugar industry anticipates its own collapse as confirmed by insiders who are quietly formulating plans to sell off fields as buildable real estate. These privately owned companies depend on federal subsidies and import limits for survival. Owners recognize that trade barriers are vanishing as U.S. transitions to a global free market.
   "The agricultural area consists of nearly a million acres located south of Disney World . . ."

Frieda had spent her last living moment on a stretch of isolated asphalt that linked State Route 60 with Canoe Creek Road, not far from where Lake Kissimmee once flowed as a river toward the Everglades but now runs straight, with dragline precision, through pastureland and citrus, partitioned by locks.

Rona wasn't with us. She'd gotten a case of island fever — "Sanibel Flush," it's called — and decided to spend the rest of the weekend on the beach and in the bars with Mack and her other new friends before returning to Kissimmee.

It happens. The causeway from the mainland is three miles of bridge and palm islands. Crossing it is a little like approaching Sanibel from the sea. It's on that first seaward approach that some are forever changed by what awaits — blue island beneath a sun-blue sky — and they are never again at ease on the mainland side of the bridge.

It happened to Rona. The flush is unmistakable, and I'd seen it in her. Which was fine, because she was an interesting, attractive lady who'd make a nice addition to the marina's orbiting, ancillary family of visitors.

The woman was eager to assist, however, and spent an hour with us Saturday morning drawing little maps, telling us what to look for and who to contact if we needed help. She also told me who not to contact.

"Stay away from Heller," she said, when I asked about Jimmy Heller, the squat little detective who hadn't impressed me or Frieda. "I've heard some rumors. There's something dirty about the guy. I'll write down names of cops you can trust."

Meeting with her helped take my mind off the fact that I still hadn't heard from my pregnant girlfriend.

Where are you, Dewey?

The question banged around in my head on the drive to inland Florida. I was alternately furious, then afraid that something bad had happened to her. What other explanation could there be?

Well . . . an equally plausible explanation was that she hadn't called because Dewey is Dewey. She's is a raging independent who, at times, can be touchingly considerate. In a different mood, though, she can become so tunneled that she ranks among the most thoughtless people I've ever met. It's not that she's cruel. Dewey spent childhood on her own, fending for herself, and so there are times when she slips back into a world in which she's the only person who exists.

Whenever I'm tempted to criticize her, I remind myself that there are times when I'm the same way.

Conversation stopped the obsessive worrying. I was glad I'd read up on the sugar industry, because our route took us along the edge of vast cane fields and it gave me something to talk about.

Lake was interested. Tomlinson, too, because the subject provided him opportunity to go off on one of his antisugar tirades.

He's not the only one who hates Big Sugar. Self-styled experts have blamed the industry for every environmental ill imaginable — often justly, sometimes absurdly. But Big Sugar has remained politically immune because it really is big. It's a multibillion-dollar business that provides thousands of jobs, and donates millions to both political parties. It's also big in terms of geographical area.

The state's sugarcane region, or Everglades Agricultural Area as it's named, consists of more than seven hundred thousand acres. Disney World is diminutive in comparison. The EAA's acreage partitions the Everglades from its own headwaters, including Lake Toho, and the two smaller lakes where guinea larvae had been found. Because the region had to be drained before it could be planted, it is now latticed with canals, levees, and dams, all linked to seven massive pumping stations.

Many billions of gallons of water are diverted to keep the EAA dry, all under the direction of the South Florida Water

Management District. Because fields are heavily fertilized, outflow contains high levels of phosphorus. Over many decades, the fertilizer has caused a cancerous spread of exotic plants. Cattails, melaleuca, and Brazilian pepper have obliterated ever-broadening hectares of the Everglades.

A few years back, legislators approved a plan to restore natural order. The plan may have teeth depending how courts and future legislators lean. The plan requires that forty-five-thousand acres of cane fields be transformed into treatment areas for phosphorus removal. Another sixty thousand acres must be used for water storage. At least one hundred thousand acres of Big Sugar's growing area must also be restored to its natural, pristine state.

From what I'd read, Big Sugar was now eager to clean up its own mess — but in its own way. It explained why Tropicane had hired an independent scientist like Applebee, and invited the environmental watchdog, EPOC, to monitor.

Most of this information was at least vaguely familiar to me. The article from the Dutch financial newsletter, however, was a shocker. Doubly so when I found a recent article in the *Palm Beach Post* that confirmed that Big Sugar was aware that it was doomed. It couldn't compete with the global market, and the cost of all the environmental mandates was killing it.

Owners were already considering options. Selling off a hundred thousand square miles of Florida's interior to developers was among them.

Driving along a horizon of golden sugarcane, I told Lake, "When there're billions of dollars involved, and the survival of a major industry's at risk, some people are capable of anything."

"Like murder," he said.

I told him, "Oh, that's just for starters."

Thanks to Rona's map, we had no trouble finding the spot where Frieda had been killed. Interpreting what we saw wasn't as easy.

Law enforcement had used blue spray paint to mark the impact point where vehicle and pedestrian met. The road ran north-south, and there was an X on the eastern edge of the road. Next to the X was an arrow that pointed north and a small blue circle.

They'd found one of her shoes at the point of impact, Rona had told us. The arrow indicated the direction the car was traveling when it hit her.

Thirty-three paces up the road, a few yards from a canal overgrown with cattails, they'd used white paint to mark where the woman's body had come to rest. It was a vague oval outline sprayed on sand and weeds, encircling a mottled black stain.

My friend's life had seeped away here among the sandspurs, bleached McDonald's wrappers, busted beer bottles, and other automotive jetsam — a clinical indignity that now coated the weeds. The oval seemed much too tiny to contain the enormity of what had occurred. To see it was to feel an existential jolt.

Disturbed, I looked at my son and said, "Are you okay? There's no need for you to deal with this."

Lake's face had paled in the morning sunlight. He cleared his throat over and over, eyes fixated on the death spot, yet he behaved as if he was surprised that I'd asked. "I'm fine. This is interesting. I've never tried to piece together something like this before."

Tomlinson and I exchanged looks before Tomlinson said, "Tragedy's always interesting. That's because it scares us so much. If you're upset, your reaction's healthy."

My friend gave me another look before adding, "Lake-meister, even if you're not upset would you mind going back to the van and starting the engine? We'll need your help later, but what I keep forgetting is that the little refrigerator shuts down when the engine stops. Unless I start the generator. We don't want all those delicious drinks getting warm now, do we? Plus, I've heard that mayonnaise can do strange, chemical things in the heat."

My son shrugged. "Sure, if you want. But this doesn't bother me, if that's what you're worried about."

"Oh, I can see that. What I'm worried about is my veggie burger and bad mayo. I'm not used to being nauseous this early in the day."

We watched Lake walk toward the van that Ransom had bought him, a Volkswagen Euro van camper. It was painted in paisley shades of pink, green, and blue, and there was a white peace sign on the door. Tomlinson had strapped two surfboards to the roof, including the refurbished Vector, just in case we had time.

At first, he'd called the van his "Pimpmobile." He later changed it to "Chimpmobile" because he said that's what he was doing, behaving like a trained monkey to make money.

I felt ridiculous riding in the thing.

When Lake was far enough away, I said, "Thanks. I shouldn't have brought him."

"Compadre, it's not your fault. It's mine. The conversation we had last night, my dumbass lecture about karma, was totally off the mark. Telling him he might be obligated to stay — idiotic! He wouldn't be here, if it wasn't for my big mouth. I realized it this morning when I sobered up."

I said, "We'll let him work on the Applebee code. He'll be good at that. But from Central America. He flies back tomorrow no matter what."

"I agree. I've been doing that more and more, lately — saying dumbass, stupid things. What I need is that shock collar I mentioned. Give myself a little zap every time I do something dumb."

I was looking at the stained weeds. "I know the feeling."

Tomlinson watched Lake slide the van's door open. "Let's finish up and get the hell out of here. This place gives me the willies. There's the stink of something dark here. Evil."

I told him, "I don't smell anything but the canal and hot asphalt. What you just did, though, was confirm your own bias. Which could be useful. Let's walk through it again, but, this time, you take the side opposite your bias. Point out anything that suggests Frieda's death was accidental. Try to convince yourself — that'll make you think it through. I'll argue the other way — that it's murder. We give it our best shot and see where it takes us."

Frieda had been hit on an open stretch of road, in good weather, so Tomlinson said the driver had to be impaired — poor eyesight, old age, alcohol or drugs. Also, the car had to be traveling so fast that Frieda didn't have time to jump out of the way.

Combine those elements, he said, and her death was accidental.

We'd returned to the blue X at the point of impact. Waited until Lake had rejoined us to talk it through.

"Dr. Matthews was on the asphalt when she was hit. The sand's soft here, so there'd be tire marks if the car drifted onto the shoulder and clipped her. She went flying. So did everything she had with her — cell phone, and the missing laptop. Was she carrying her purse, too?"

I said, "I don't know. I'll ask Rona. I should have thought of that."

Tomlinson was silent for a moment, eyes panning the area, visualizing what might have happened. "Okay. There had to be a heck of a lot of speed to knock her more than a hundred feet. She landed near the canal. The stuff she was carrying was lighter than her body, so it traveled farther. If the death was accidental, her phone and the computer went into the water, or got buried in the cattails. A less likely possibility is that someone arrived on scene before the cops and robbed her."

He began walking toward where the body had come to rest. "The fact that there're no skid marks before the point of impact supports my idea that the driver was either half-blind or very screwed up. But why aren't there skid marks *after* the point of impact? Even if a person's old and senile, that kind of collision would have to make a terrible noise. Don't most drivers jam on the breaks automatically when they're scared or surprised?"

I said nothing, waiting for him to draw his own conclusions.

"So that narrows it down to a driver who was so crazy drunk he didn't know he hit something. Probably didn't remember it the next morning, either. A guy on a binge. Which we might be able to prove."

He had a map, and showed me where the road deadened a few miles away at the Kissimmee Canal.

"There should be a bunch of dead soldiers on the ground there — crushed beer cans or an empty liquor bottle or two. A dead-end road that overlooks water is every drunk's friend."

"Smart," I said. "Let's go have a look."

We loaded into the van. I slid in behind the wheel because Tomlinson drives like a man who really does believe in life after death. He combines the wandering inattention of a child with a teenager's love of speed. Terrifying.

He no longer argues with me about who drives.

After slightly more than four miles, the road ended at a littered turnaround near the water's edge. It was a quiet place where the canal was wide and straight, and where people sometimes fished, judging from paths cut along the bank.

Among the scrub was the trashy spoor of lowlifes who'd used it as a handy garbage dump: rusted washing machines, stained bedding, sodden magazines. On asphalt and sand, there was also a glitter of broken bottles and squashed cans — but no fresh beer or liquor bottles.

We searched for ten minutes or so before Tomlinson said, "Okay, so maybe they had a bottle of vodka; a jug so big they couldn't finish it. Or they tossed them in the water.

My scenario is still workable. It could've been accidental. Let's hear you convince us that it wasn't. That it was murder."

The case I made wasn't any stronger than Tomlinson's. My argument was based on the absence of evidence, not the presence of evidence. I listed what those absences implied:

There were no skid marks before or after impact. Someone *wanted* to hit her.

On a fast, narrow road like this, Frieda would have walked facing traffic. If she'd heard a car coming, she would have turned to look as it swerved toward her.

"She would've jumped for cover," I said. "Not stand there on the road waiting to get hit."

This was the only open stretch where her killers would be able to spot traffic approaching from a mile or two in either direction — the perfect place to wait as an accomplice drove by at speed, before giving her a push.

"The reason her cell phone and the laptop are missing," I said, "is because she was abducted from her car. After the killers futzed with her battery. They have the laptop, but they probably dumped the cell phone at the first place handy."

Lake asked, "Why?"

I said, "Because cell phones are risky. You can hit the redial button accidentally, or accept an incoming call. Plus, they can be tracked electronically. That's a biggie.

"My guess is, they'd have dumped the phone first thing. Tossed it into the closest water, someplace murky, near where she was parked. I think we should go look."

My son said, "Just like Tomlinson's empty beer bottles, if we find it."

"Uh-huh. Except for what it would prove. It means they took the woman off and killed her in cold blood."

25

We'd already located the dirt service road where Frieda's car was found. We'd passed it on our way to look for empty beer cans. It was a rutted lane that followed a power line swath bordered by oaks, poison ivy, and swamp maples. I drove with my window open. High-voltage wires hummed overhead.

After half a mile or so of bouncing along, I braked to a stop, surprised to see another vehicle parked near a section of canal: a white pickup truck, recent model. According to our map, this was the approximate spot where they'd found Frieda's disabled SUV.

As we got closer, I could see that the truck was empty. There were words stenciled on the door in black letters:

TROPICANE INC.
ENVIRONMENTAL ENGINEERING
VEHICLE 5

"I rest my case," Tomlinson said. "Providence and God are steering us. You said you need to talk to the Tropicane people? Here they are. It's very fortuitous that the Big Sugar goons are here waiting."

I didn't bother telling him that, in a long-term study, sample sites are standardized for consistency. With both Jobe and Frieda dead, the job would fall to the agencies that had commissioned the tests. I would've been more surprised if this vehicle wasn't from Tropicane.

Instead, I said, "You're in charge of providence and God. But leave everything else to me, okay? Oh . . . and Tomlinson? If we meet the people who belong to that truck, please don't go into one of your anti–big business, antisugar rants. We're here to collect information, not dish it out."

He said primly, "Okay, okay, for you I'll go easy. But they've been bleeding the Everglades to death for decades, and we all know it. I'm surprised a certain biologist pal of mine doesn't consider it his duty to inform the dupes on their payroll."

I replied, "According to the latest literature, the industry's exceeding federal environmental mandates. Their own decision. So cut them some slack. Plus, with your new understanding of profit sharing, I'd expect you to be more tolerant. You're both money machines in your way."

He made a puffing noise. "That hurts. Money, sure, I've been corrupted. Yes, the almighty dollar and I have been making the creature with two backs. But destroying the environment for profit — that I would not do."

As I parked beside the Tropicane truck, I touched my finger to my lips — Enough — and got out.

The accepted method of alerting unseen strangers is to slam car doors.

We did.

A minute later, a skinny college-aged guy with John Lennon glasses and a ponytail came walking over the canal bank wearing hip boots, and an inquisitive expression, and carrying a rack of test tubes.

His expression softened when he saw us — men accompanied by an adolescent boy are an unlikely threat. He waved, calling, "If you're here to fish, don't worry about me. I was just leaving."

I said, "There's no rush. We're not fishing. In fact, maybe you can help us."

"Me? Sure, if I can —" He created a partition, the way he said it. Wary of strangers asking favors. But then he suddenly grinned

— he'd noticed the Volkswagen van. "Ohhh . . . *man.* You guys came in that? Is it for real?"

"Too real," I said. "Most people can't look at it without sunglasses."

"Not me, man. I love it. How wild. That is the coolest camper I've ever seen. It's like . . . it's like the perfect little Magic Bus." He stared for a couple more seconds before repeating himself: "Just too cool. The paint job is living *history.* Is it yours, sir? No . . . it can't be."

His gaze swiveled from me, to Lake, then settled on Tomlinson. "It's yours, man. *Gotta* be. Classic VW love wagon . . . but it's *new.* I didn't know they made them anymore. So you had it done custom, huh?"

Tomlinson said, "Magic Bus?," stuck on the name, considering it, tasting the words.

"As in the song. You know, by The Who? Man, I am so jealous." He indicated the white truck. "I'm driving a company cookie cutter."

"You . . . that's your *company* truck? This's gotta be one of those evil flashbacks they promised us."

The kid's grin broadened. "You're too much, man. You're the real deal, aren't you? I love the whole look. Your hair — are those Samurai shocks? — the peace sign, the flowers. Who *are* you guys?"

He came off as unpretentious as a child. Tomlinson, however, was flummoxed. He'd anticipated meeting some Big Sugar corporate drone, but was now struggling to reevaluate a guy who could have been a shorter, younger version of himself.

He said, "*You* work for Big Sugar? How can someone who works for a giant like Tropicane get off on the Chimpmobile — the Magic Bus, I mean?"

The kid — he looked like a kid with his peach-fuzz goatee and sideburns — said, "Yeah man, I work for Tropicane. I'm a biologist, the environmental department. Two years, and they're already moving me up the corporate ladder. I like it okay. It's a *job*, know what I mean? But it's not who I am. Your generation — the whole hipster scene — that's what I was born for. It's my generation, too. Only I got transferred to planet Earth just a little late."

Tomlinson remained baffled. "You believe that? You're one of the brethren?" He was studying the man's gaunt face, the Jesus hair, the wire glasses. The tie-dyed T-shirt he wore wasn't clearly visible because of the chest-high waders, but there it was.

The kid said, "Man, I've read tons of books on the subject. It started out like a hobby, when I was little. But then it became my life. San Francisco; the Haight; Jimi Hendrix, the *White Album*. The whole philosophy. Immersion, man. Do you know how something just *feels* right? That feeling of coming home to a place you've never been?"

Tomlinson replied, "Well . . . of course. In astral projection, any kind of soul travel, that's our only anchor. It's the feeling that keeps us from spinning off. A kind of knowing."

"*Knowing*. Exactly. I share an old chicken farm; rent with a dozen other people — like a commune? In the family, we've got Ravers, Wiccans, Punks, a Pagan, and a Christian. But professionals. Work for Daddy Tropicane."

Tomlinson managed to follow that. "You're a Raver. Definitely not a Punk. And the whole Wiccan deal is just too witchy-woman."

The kid was nodding; the two of them connected. "Very intuitive, brother. Yes, I'd be considered a Raver, but I'm not into the whole *today* scene. A generation ago, that was my time. You ought to come see the classic posters I've got on the wall. Our whole family's into it. Across the country, all over the world, the movement's growing.

'EX-sters' — that's what we call ourselves. As in Hipsters? We still play *vinyl*, man. Not that CD crap. *Revolver* — that's my all-time favorite Beatles album."

"Okay, okay. I'm starting to get a fix on where you're coming from. You and your friends are on your own personal vision quest. A little old, a little new. But, man! How can you work for the big-money screwheads?"

The kid, who turned out to be Jason Reynolds, Ph.D., was walking toward the paisley-painted Volkswagen in a sort of trance. "It's biologists like yours truly who keep the old corporate leeches on the straight and narrow. But the younger suits, dude, the guys with the ties and stock options, they're starting to get it. Mother Earth *matters*.

"I talk to them," he said. "I get into their heads by preaching to their wallets. These days, they want to save the environment *plus* make a profit. Which is very cool. Money's cool, man. Those're two things I've learned: You've gotta join a tribe before you can change a tribe. And making money is very cool."

Suddenly sounding more like a student than a teacher, Tomlinson asked, "*Really?* How do you figure?"

"Because it's the only ticket to the party, man. The power structure is where it's happening. If you want to change things, you've got to be part of it. My motto? Money doesn't count — it *rules*. Hey, mind if I open the door and have a look?"

Tomlinson was following along behind him. "Ticket into the tribe, huh? Interesting that we should meet. I've been experimenting with that whole mind-set. Money. Materialism. Greed as a form of spirituality. You seem to have a handle on the big picture. I'd love to get together sometime, see how deep the roots go. Knock back a few, or burn something interesting — your call."

Reynolds was inside the van, exploring, opening compartments, touching this and that. "Sure. In return, you could maybe tell us some stories from the old days. I'm a historian. I've got photo albums; a whole archive of taped interviews with people who lived it. This one dude I talked to, he's met Timothy Leary, Janis Joplin, Edward Abbey, Hunter S. Thompson, a bunch of the icons."

"Tim and Dr. Gonzo," Tomlinson said fondly. "The Monkey Wrench Gang and poor Janis. Such beautiful spirits."

"You *knew* them?"

His reaction — a slight dip of the head —

said friendship is a personal matter made vulnerable by public declaration. "During those sweet years, if you hung out at the Hotel Jerome in Aspen, or rode a Harley in San Francisco, you met all forms of enlightened souls."

"Edward Abbey. The *man*."

"Ed did have a thorny side."

"Oh, dude, we have *got* to sit down and talk. But to change the subject, this thing?" — Reynolds was in the van, preoccupied with what he was seeing, squinting through his glasses — "is this a refrigerator?"

"Uh-huh. Holds a couple cases of beer. Food, if you need it. I've got the deluxe Swiss Alps touring package. Special telescopic shocks, electric-start generator, and an automatic pop-top. Check it out: a ten-speaker Levenson sound system that'll pulverize kidney stones if you crank it. All the options. Hey" — Tomlinson was chuckling, showing he understood the wealth angle — "it's only money, right?"

Maybe he saw Lake and me exchange looks, because he dropped the façade seconds later, his expression sobering. "Which, to tell the truth, is something I just can't make myself give a damn about. Money, I mean."

"That's too bad, man. If you want to

change the system, you gotta have it. Remember: If you're not part of the solution, you're part of the problem."

Tomlinson rallied. "When you put it that way, yeah, I totally dig where you're coming from." Lake and I exchanged looks again, as he added, "The fridge is loaded with beverages. Coldies. Take it from an experienced member of the family: Here in the tropics, it's very important to rehydrate."

The biologist, who was squatting next to the refrigerator, opened the door, and looked at rows of bottles for a moment. *"Sweet."*

When Tomlinson took me aside and asked if it was okay if he told Reynolds why we were here and what we were looking for, I told him, sure, tell the man everything. I wanted Tropicane headquarters to know that I had copies of Applebee's files. I was in the area because I suspected foul play. Retracing Frieda's footsteps.

I wanted everyone to know.

Same with the Environmental Protection and Oversight Conservancy. I'd already spoken to a secretary by phone, told her I was on the job, and asked for an appointment with one of the head people.

Her reply had been frosty, noncommittal.

I'd spelled my name for her, to make sure she had it.

"F-O-R-D. Like the car."

There were at least two predators out there: the Russian couple. There also had to be some directing force. I wanted fresh scent in the water. I hoped to lure them near.

"There's something I'd like you to ask your new best friend, too. Did you catch his reaction to Edward Abbey? Ask him if he read the *Rolling Stone* article. He could be one of the copycat weirdoes. Maybe even a murderer."

Tomlinson's reply was frosty. "Give my instincts some credit. This dude's no murderer. I like him better *because* he's a fan of the Monkey Wrench Gang. Got a very decent spirit. I bet he offers to help us search for the phone."

"At least ask, okay?"

"Okay!"

I didn't accept Tomlinson's quick endorsement. I'm dubious of people who choose to evade the realities of their own era. Reynolds seemed as misplaced as his fantasy about the idyllic days of hippiedom. Plus, anyone who'd worked with Jobe Applebee was a subject of suspicion. The two *had* worked together. Reynolds had already told us. It was only for an afternoon, he said, and months ago.

He also told me that he'd read my paper on nutrient pollution in Florida Bay. "Interesting," he said. "Liked it."

He left it at that, a small mark in his favor.

Tomlinson was right. The biologist offered his help.

"For one thing, it's Saturday; just getting in some extra work. I was officially off duty the moment I opened this beer. Besides, I've already got my waders on.

"I didn't know Dr. Applebee's sister, and I can't say I knew Dr. Applebee — he was on a whole different trip. Quiet, you know. *Intense.* But if finding that phone gets you closer to the truth, I'll go in and hunt around with my feet."

We'd already talked about the possibility that guinea worm larvae were here, so that's how we'd have to do it: wade around and search with our feet. He had a box of disposable surgical masks, he said. No sense risking the ingestion of contaminated water.

He knew about the parasites. On Tuesday, he'd been contacted by an epidemiologist from the Florida Department of Health. A woman physician, not Dr. Clark.

"She was notifying all the environmental

agencies, anyone who works with water," Reynolds said. "Christ, I read about those worms when I was in school. Disgusting."

On Thursday, the woman called again to tell him that water samples from lakes near Disney World had tested positive for *Dracunculiasis*. She asked his department to test water in the Tropicane system, and e-mailed lab photos to help in identification.

"I wouldn't know what to look for if she hadn't done that," Reynolds told us. "It's not the sort of thing I'm expected to do."

"Have you tested here?"

"Yesterday. All tests negative. I took samples from a bunch of areas. Lots of copepods, but no guinea larvae. So it's probably safe. I came back today just to be certain."

A thorough guy. Another mark in his favor.

As he worked his way down the canal bank toward the water, Reynolds listed the standard evaluations that Applebee had been doing for Tropicane: gas chromatograph test, for volatile organic analysis; and pesticide analysis. Spectrophotometer scans for inorganic analysis and organic compound identifica-tion — phosphorus flowing into the Everglades was still the big concern, he said.

"We do miscellaneous membrane filtration. What we're looking for is fertilizer overload, or coliform bacteria — pathogenic stuff that indicates degraded water quality. Not water fleas with parasitic larvae inside them." He swung his head toward the truck where he'd left the rack of water samples. "I have some disposable 115-milliliter filter flasks in my kit. But no microscope, or we could take a look now."

I watched as he paused at the water's edge, then took a long careful look before he stepped in. I could guess why. This was gator country. The big ones had been grabbing people lately. Their dinosaur coding makes no differentiation between modern primates and primates with prehensile tails. This was cottonmouth country, too.

"This section isn't too deep," he called to us. "Only a couple of places it might be up to our necks."

Back in the 1960s, when the Corps of Engineers gutted the Kissimmee River to make a canal, they'd dredged it a hundred yards wide and thirty feet deep, then abandoned the name for the more sterile designation of "Canal 38."

Fitting.

This section of water, though, was a drainage link to the main canal. It was a shady spur, fifty or sixty feet wide, and not deep, judging from the cattails. The water was clear but stained amber with humic acid, and dense moss grew on the bottom.

According to our map, they'd found Frieda's SUV not far from the water. It was a good, private place to jettison incriminating evidence . . . or to introduce exotic parasites.

As Reynolds moved into deeper water, I stood atop the bank and found two rocks similar in weight to the cell phone in my pocket. I lobbed one rock southward. Waited until it made a satisfying *thwump* in the middle of the canal, then lobbed the second rock northward.

"That's our search area. Roughly. We can't spend a lot of time, but it's worth a shot."

I'd already told my son he couldn't get in the water; or even *near* it. No way, even if Reynolds's tests were negative. When the boy protested, I told him that, one day, I might describe what it's like to see a guinea worm exiting its host. But not now.

Something in my tone quieted him. So it was the three of us in the canal: the Tropicane biologist, Tomlinson, and myself.

While traveling, Tomlinson wears traditional clothing — traditional, anyway, compared to the robes and sarongs he prefers. I find the attention they draw distracting, which he's empathetic enough to understand. Today he wore baggy red shorts; a white, long-sleeved GATOR SPOON T-shirt; and the style of Birkenstocks that remind me of wooden shoes.

I'd brought shorts and running shoes in case I got a chance to work out. I had something to wear in the water. Tomlinson didn't. So, as I changed, he stripped down to violet boxer shorts decorated with . . . yes, red Santas and golden stars. He was humming one of his endless, tuneless melodies that sounded like *Oo-hummm. . . . Oo-hummm.*

"Tomlinson," I told him, "purple holiday underwear is acceptable, but you need to wear something on your feet. There'll be broken glass on the bottom, sharp metal, nails, and crap."

"I'll do the stingray shuffle," he replied. "Also, I'll do a special power med. It'll temporarily transfer all the auric vulnerability in my feet upward to other parts of my body. How's broken glass gonna deal with something like that?"

"Power med" was short for "power meditation," one of the man's new infatuations. When Reynolds asked about it, Tomlinson told him he'd developed a technique for brief but intense meditation that had many of the benefits of traditional meditation.

"It's on our Web page, man. Which you've got to check out."

"You have your own Web page?"

Tomlinson made the fluttering noise of a man who was powerless. "Fuckin' A."

"Shrewd," I told him. "Bulletproof feet. How's a doctor going to get a suture in when he tries to sew you up?"

I had my running shoes tied, and stepped into knee-deep water. I expected muck but found firm sand. Reynolds was to the south, slogging a slow zigzag route from bank to bank. He was squatting, letting the water support him, while his feet swept experimentally over the bottom.

A good technique. It made me lighter, more mobile when I tried it, and so I mimicked him, wading to the north, sliding the edge of my right shoe over the bottom, then my left, before transferring weight. There was moss, which quickly accumulated and had to be shaken loose. There were also sections of tree branches — easily identified by touch.

Behind me, I heard Tomlinson say, "Dr.

Jason? I'm getting some vibes here. I think you're working the right section of the ball-park. I'm coming your way."

I turned to see him entering the canal, arms extended at his sides for balance, as if he expected the water's surface to support his weight for a few moments before busting through. He looked like a naked scarecrow, rags and rope covered with skin.

I continued to search, sliding from bank to bank. When my foot found something that I couldn't identify — something solid but easy to move — I would sink until the water was chin deep, then reach to retrieve it.

There were lots of beer and liquor bottles — Tomlinson was correct about drunks loving roads that dead-ended near water. The first time my foot touched and moved a pint whiskey bottle, I got excited. It seemed the right size. I'd just retrieved my fifth or sixth pint bottle when, from the bank, I heard my own cell phone begin to ring.

Lake called, "Do you want me to get that, Doc?"

I was about to tell him yes — maybe it was Dewey returning my calls — but I was inter-rupted by a hoot from Tomlinson. "Hey! Lookee-lookee what I found! What'a you think, Dr. Jason? Everything's got its own magnetic aura, man. I followed a tractor beam straight to this one."

I turned to see that Tomlinson was about midway between Reynolds and myself. He was standing on one leg, arms extended for balance, as he slowly lifted his right foot from the water. He stood storklike, looking at his toes. Tomlinson has freakishly long toes — the guides kid him about being part monkey. Between his toes was a cellular phone.

The Tropicane biologist said, "I'll be damned! Is that the one?"

When we were in Kissimmee, I'd seen Frieda use her phone several times. It was a Nokia in a black leather case, one of the old models with an external antenna. This looked similar.

I felt a chill. *The sons of bitches murdered her.*

I said, "It's a hell of a coincidence if it's not Frieda's," before I told Tomlinson, "Careful of fingerprints. If you touch it, use two fingers on the antenna. Wait until I get there to take a look."

Grinning, very pleased with himself, Tomlinson touched his right foot to his left thigh, resting the phone there — a classic tai chi figure 4. "I can hold it like this for as long as you want. But it might be better if I use the two-fingered technique and meet you on the bank. It's time for me to offer some gold to the water gods."

Tomlinson-talk for "urinate."

"Bring the phone with you," I said. "That way, I won't have to stand here while the water level rises."

26

My son and I were listening to Jason Reynolds tell us that he'd worked for a branch of EPOC for two years as a college volunteer, then spent a year on the organization's payroll before getting hired by Tropicane.

"It wasn't the money. I felt I could do more good as a scientist with a company known as being antienvironment, than with a group of far-out environmentalists."

I said, " 'Far-out'?"

" 'Far-out,' as in good. EPOC is real conservative, starched-suit types who file lots of lawsuits. It drives state governments and big-business nuts, which is cool. But I worked for a branch organization that has a more holistic approach. The Albedo Society. More progressive. We accept the Gaia theory: the earth as a single organism. The guy who founded them both is a veteran hipster like your pal, but he's also made megabucks."

Desmond Stokes again. The vitamin empire recluse.

"You're a member of the Albedo Society? Tomlinson went to a rally they held a few months back in Coconut Grove."

Reynolds's grin said, I shoulda known. "I was there, man! A bunch of us EX-sters turned out. But, as I was saying, I didn't go with Big Sugar just for the cash. Although that's part of the Albedo philosophy, too: Wealth is power. The surest way to protect land is to own it —" Reynolds stopped abruptly, interrupted by Tomlinson, who was still in the water.

"What's wrong with him?"

Tomlinson had begun to hoot again — but this time, a harsh falsetto. The shrill sound of pain and shock.

"Ohhh . . . Hahhh! Whoa-a-a-a-a! *What the hell?*"

The three of us turned to see that he was on the other side of the canal where we'd left him. He had his back to us, but was now bent at the waste, jumping and thrashing, creating small shock waves in the hip-deep water.

"Holy cripes . . . Oh my God . . . Whoa, Mamma, that hurts!"

He swung his head toward us, turning, and I could see his wild eyes, and that he had both hands clamped over his genitals.

"Sheeeee-IT!"

Lake panicked. "Hey — he's hurt! What's wrong? *Tomlinson?*" As Reynolds yelled, "Jesus, what was he doing? Get out of there!"

No response from Tomlinson, who continued to jump and thrash, moaning.

Automatically, we were all three sliding down the incline. Before we got to the bank, I grabbed Lake, put a finger in his face, and yelled, "No! I'll get him," then lunged into the water, my brain searching for an explanation. Tomlinson had been peeing into a thicket of cattails and somehow managed to hurt himself. How? If he'd stepped on a broken bottle, why was he holding his genitals?

"Lordy, shitzkee! Doc! Get over here, Doc! *Marion!*"

"What's wrong?"

"*This* is what's wrong!" he screamed. He was slapping at his groin as if he were on fire. "Something's inside me. I saw it!" He looked down before yelling, "Come outta there, you little bastard. Goddamn it, I'll wring your neck. I'll drown you in cheap whiskey, if you don't come out!"

It sounded absurd — until I saw blood on his hands and legs, blood coming from his penis. There was too much blood, and too much pain, not to be serious.

I ran high-stepping through the shallows into deeper water. When I got to him, he let me support his body weight, though he continued to writhe in pain as I asked over and over, "What happened? Why are you bleeding?"

He repeated himself, groaning, "Ohhh . . . I got something up me, man. Came out of the water and swam up the tube. Holy hell, it hurts."

"*What?*"

"I've got something inside me! I saw it. Like a little eel, or fish, or something."

The young biologist came splashing up. Tomlinson was in so much distress, Reynolds spoke to me. "He's freaking, man. What's wrong? Did he say?"

"No. Something must've bit him. He's incoherent because of the pain." I was levering Tomlinson's arm over my shoulder, steering him toward shore.

Reynolds said, "Jesus, look at the blood. What happened to his shorts?"

I said, "I guess he pulled them off," as Tomlinson yelled. "I'm not incoherent. I *saw* the thing, damn it. I was taking a piss, and it swam right up my tallywhacker!"

I told Tomlinson, "Okay, okay, take it

easy, and we'll get you to the hospital." He was sweating, face pale. "I'm calling an ambulance."

"No — no sirens," he said quickly. "I hate sirens, too many bad memories. We go in the Magic Bus. I'll soak my nuts in ice water. Maybe the little son of a bitch will think it's time to migrate south."

Reynolds had Tomlinson's other arm, helping me guide him. "I've got a first aid kit in the truck, but I doubt if there's anything for pain." After a few more moments, he said, "The *phone*. What happened to the woman's cell phone? Did he give it to you?"

Tomlinson moaned, "Ohhh, what a *putz* I am. I dropped it when the fish attacked. Forgot all about it, Oh hell . . . let's go back and get it."

I said, "No. I'll call the sheriff's department. It's better if they recover it, anyway. I'll call from the road." I looked at Reynolds, interested in his reaction. "Do you mind if I give them your name and number? You could help."

"Sure," he replied. "You need to get him to the hospital."

Twice, on the fast drive to the Bartram County Hospital, I had to stop so Tomlinson could vomit. Pain can do that.

Most of the trip, he stayed balled up in a fetal position, moaning.

At one point, I said to him, "Would meditation help? To help block the pain, I mean."

"Oh-h-h-h . . . no way. Mr. Zamboni would never get the message. He and my brain stopped communicating years ago."

Zamboni and the Hat Trick Twins — the man's nickname for his private parts.

Because I was driving, Laken called Rona to tell her that we'd found what was probably Frieda's cell phone. I figured she'd get faster action out of the local sheriff's department. But the lady was still on Sanibel having fun. Didn't answer. Among the contact list she'd given us, though, was the name of a department captain. Lake dialed his number, then handed me the phone.

The man's name was Detective Ken Picking, special crimes division. I used Rona's name, then told him I'd been at Jobe Applebee's house the night he died, and that I was a friend of the man's sister — the woman who'd been found dead on Thursday, hit by a car.

A veteran state patrolman once told me that a cultivated sense of skepticism has saved the lives of more cops than body armor. It has also nailed more unlikely criminals than DNA testing. I expected Picking to be suspicious, and he was. It's not uncommon for perpetrators to try to find out how a case is progressing by presenting themselves as helpful citizens.

The detective's Cracker heritage was in his cow-hunter accent, his hard-ass manner. I listened to him say as if he were joking, "Okay, you knew the victims, and now you're calling me either to confess or to find out if we know you did it. Isn't that the drill? So tell me where you are and I'll come put the cuffs on."

His tone was breezy, but he wasn't humoring me. He'd thrown it out there to see if I got flustered. If I'd stammered, or laughed just a little too loudly, I had a feeling that Detective Picking would've dropped everything and come looking for me.

When I told him about finding the cell phone, though, his tone was anything but breezy. "Are you sure it was Dr. Matthews's phone?"

"It was the same type. It didn't look like it'd been in the water long. There's a good chance that it's hers."

"Mr. Ford, I don't know you from Adam. Now, if Rona gave you my cell number, you're probably okay. But do you know how dumb it is for amateurs to go around playing detective? Damn. Did you know we can still lift prints from an object that's been under-water?"

I told him I wasn't certain.

"Well, we sometimes can. Which you might have completely screwed up. Why the hell didn't you just call us an' tell us you had a bee up your butt, thinking the woman was killed not accidental-like. That maybe her phone was in that canal?"

I was tempted to tell him it was because his department *hadn't* thought of it.

Instead, I said, "You're right, the first thing I should've done was contact you. I guess I didn't expect to actually find it. A friend gets abducted and murdered? That's something that you only read about in the papers."

"What you did, Mr. Ford, could be called tampering with evidence."

I was appropriately contrite. "The faster you can get some people on-scene to re-cover the phone, the better we'll both feel."

When he asked me to meet him at the canal in half an hour, I told him that was im-possible because a pal was sick and I had to get him to the hospital. But I had the cel-lular number for Jason Reynolds, who was willing to help.

After I'd given him Reynolds's number, Picking said he'd have the dispatcher contact their water recovery team and meet them at the canal.

"But don't go leaving the county without telling me first. If we don't find it, we'll need you. If we *still* don't find it, there're a bunch more questions I want answered."

In the emergency room, the staff gave Tomlinson a shot of painkiller and did a manual examination for testicular torsion — a man's testicles can twist on the spermatic cord and shut off the flow of blood. It can be fatal if not treated quickly.

The results were negative.

During the examination, they also asked him if he'd ever had gonorrhea.

Groaning, Tomlinson told them no, but it wasn't through lack of activity.

Next they injected IVP dye and took X rays, looking for kidney stones.

Negative.

It was a good hospital with an energetic staff, and they were not immune to Tomlinson's charm. Determined to diagnose his mystery ailment, the ER boss, Dr. Mary McColgan, took the initiative and called in a urologist whose name was also Mary — Dr. Mary Ann Shepherd. Laken and I waited in the outpatient surgery wing while the physician used ocular tubing, a cystoscope, to take a look inside the man's urethra.

Dr. Shepherd came out, still wearing scrubs, smiling, shaking her head: unbelievable. She was an athletic-looking woman, square-jawed, very dark skin — an East Indian or American Indian — her expression telling us the mystery was solved.

The lady doctor's voice had an upbeat vigor — yes, she'd discovered something unexpected — as she said, "I've read about cases like this, but never in my wildest dreams thought I'd get to deal with it in my own practice. The cystoscope moved along just fine until about midway to the bladder. That's where I found the blockage. Ten years in this business, I thought I'd seen every weird object that can possibly fit inside the sprinkler system of an adult human male — golf tees, lipsticks, marbles. There's a whole book written by a urologist about strange stuff we've found. But I've never seen anything resembling to what's inside your friend."

It was a fish, she said. "Turns out that crazy story he's been telling isn't crazy after all. When I got the scope to the blockage, the first thing I recognized was a tail fin. I thought it must be some kind of artificial lure. That he'd stuck it up there himself. Guys do that sometimes, minus the hooks — if they're smart enough, and not too drunk. But then it moved. I *saw* it. The darn thing wiggled its way upstream as far as it could. It's still alive."

Even with a urologist standing there telling us it was true — even with the plague of exotics we'd been tracking — I still had trouble believing it. "I've worked all over the world with fish. I know there's a rare species of bloodsucking catfish in South America that supposedly swims into human orifices. But that's a myth. I *think* it's been proven to be a myth."

The physician looked to be in her mid-thirties, had a good face, and her Cherokee hair caught the light when she shook her head. She was shaking it now. "Just the opposite's been proven. I proved it myself today. Other doctors have documented it before me — but only within the last couple of years. That's *exactly* what the fish does. I just looked it up. The thing's called a 'candiru.' Kan-di-ru. I think that's how it's pronounced."

It wasn't the first time she'd read about it, she said.

"A year or so ago, a Brazilian physician —

I can't remember *his* name — published an article in the *American Journal of Urology*. He'd removed a candiru from the penis of a teenage boy. The article included ultrasonographic prints that showed the fish burrowed in the urethra, up near the prostate. There were photos of the thing after it was removed.

"The fish was a lot bigger than I would've believed — nearly six inches long, I think, and half an inch wide. That stuck with me because it indicated how tenacious that damn thing had to be to work its way up that far."

Dr. Shepherd said she'd read the entire piece, it was so unusual, but it'd been a while ago, so some of the details had faded. The boy had been wading in the Amazon and stopped to urinate. Candiru were attracted to the scent of uric acid because they are endoparasitic creatures — they feed from inside their hosts. Locating body openings would be key to their survival.

The boy was in thigh-deep water. He saw the fish leap out of the water into his urine stream. It clung to the penis opening for a moment, then burrowed up his urethral canal.

"I think the article said the kid actually grabbed the fish and tried to pull it out. But it was slippery, and candiru have gills or spines or something they stick up so they're impossible to remove."

In the Amazon, she added, indigenous people were the most common victims. No doctors for them, which is why we heard of it so rarely.

"There's some kind of herb they use to dissolve the fish, but the pain's so bad that males sometimes resort to self-inflicted penectomy. You can ask your friend about that."

Catfish have saw-edged spines, sharp as a hypodermic, and secrete a complicated protein poison. Thinking about it made me cringe.

She told me she'd bring a copy of the article when she came back that night to do the minor operation required to remove the candiru. She'd managed to get a catheter in Tomlinson; had the outpatient surgery reserved for 7:00 p.m. The phenomenon had so seldom been documented, she said, that she wanted to videotape the procedure. Other physicians were already asking to attend.

"But it's not serious. I want to stress that. Within two days, maybe three, he'll be completely recovered."

As she was leaving, I said aloud, "A parasitic catfish from the Amazon? Jesus, bizarre."

I was talking to Lake, but the woman stopped, laughing in a way that communicated congenial sarcasm. "Finding an illegal exotic species in *this* part of Florida? That *would* be shocking — if it wasn't an almost daily occurrence. All right, I'm exaggerating, but not much. The ER staff will tell you."

She said that, over the last week, the emergency room had treated five people who'd been bitten by nonnative spiders. Entomologists at the University of Florida had identified one as a Calcutta scorpion. She couldn't remember the name of the other spider. It was from Africa, and two of the patients nearly died.

"Crab spider? Maybe that was it."

I said, "A six-eyed crab spider? That's African — and dangerous. A lot more poisonous than a black widow, or brown recluse."

"*Yes*. That's the one. There were the spider bites and then, three days ago, a grade school janitor drives himself to the ER. He comes in, face white as a sheet, carrying a garbage bag that has a fifty-pound snake in it. The thing was more than eight feet long.

"He said he found it on the playground. The guy killed it when it came after him. One of those guys who carries a shotgun in his truck. His words: 'It charged me and struck.' It did sort of graze him, but no venom. Thank God, because we got a positive ID on that, too. African again. An illegal exotic. It was an African mamba, which they tell me is potentially lethal."

Something — the intensity of my expression, perhaps — had caused her to focus on me rather than on what she was saying, and so she spoke more slowly, almost by rote, as she finished, "The Disney World area's filled with exotics. Human and animal."

I said, "This has all been in the last week?"

"Seven, eight days, yes. That's why it hasn't made the national news yet. This county depends on tourism, so the local weeklies aren't going to put it in the headlines. But word's bound to leak out."

A South American fish, she added, was no surprise to her.

"Once I remove the candiru, I'll let you examine it," she said. "Get your professional opinion."

27

LOG
18 Dec. Saturday 18:04
Bartram County Hospital. . . . SMT
victim of escalating bio-sabotage. . . .
. . . updated Hal H. by phone. Asked
for background checks on J. Reynolds
& D. Stokes. H. said he's surprised I'm
no longer his reluctant operative. Accurate. Now in SMT's room trying to decipher why I'm willing to go back in service, piecing together a premise . . .

It was an hour before his surgery, and
Tomlinson was his abnormal, cheery self.
Cheerier. He sat in his private room, bed
cranked up like a lounge chair, wearing a
gown that tied at the back. There was a big,
familiar grin on his face. A drunken grin.

The PCA system to which he was attached had everything to do with his good
mood. PCA as in "patient-controlled anal-

gesia." It allows the patient to administer his own pain medication.

When they told him about it, Tomlinson stopped groaning long enough to say, "If the gadget works, I'll have one installed on my boat. I've got *money*."

The nurses set up an intravenous morphine sulfate drip overhead, found a vein, inserted a needle, and taped it to his arm. Within easy reach, they placed a button connected to the PCA system. As long as he didn't breach the preset lockout parameters, Tomlinson could get additional morphine by pushing the button.

During the first hour, he'd drummed on the thing like it was the flipper of a pinball machine. Now, though, with the pain finally masked, he sat happily in his bed, grinning, flirting with nurses, using the phone whenever it came into his mind to call someone new.

That was often. Drunks get phone-happy in the early stages of a binge. Tomlinson is among the most phone-loving of drunks. In the right mood, he's also funny as hell. He plays the caricaturized role of the mind-zapped hipster so naturally that I'm never sure when he's acting or just being himself. The lines between the two are blurry.

Lake and I sat bedside as the man chatted

and laughed into his cellular phone. My son read a magazine while I sat thinking, making notes in my log, preoccupied with the string of poisonous exotics that Dr. Shepherd had listed. Spiders, scorpions, a snake, parasitic worms: all species from either Latin America or Africa.

Both regions house outlaw governments and violent extremists.

The exotics had other characteristics in common. With the exception of the snake, they all produce a prodigious number of eggs or larvae — life capsules so tiny that tens of thousands of each could be easily smuggled into the country. They wouldn't take up much more space than a paperback book. Once hatched, each species would also adapt to Florida's subtropical environment.

That was the most unsettling similarity. Multiply X thousands of breeding pairs, then multiply again by X hundreds of thousands of offspring. The population would grow exponentially.

Harrington was right. This wasn't biovandalism, this was a biological attack. The perpetrators had chosen well. A species that produces many thousands of offspring is an "evolutionary responder." It is a fecund, or reproductive, response to predators who've

386

adapted specialized feeding abilities — "phenotype characteristics" — that make the fecund species easy prey.

It's called "fecund selection."

But when a fecund-select species is introduced into a region where there are no predators, it is an environmental catastrophe. Historically, people responsible for these catastrophes have not been terrorists. They've been well-intended government officials, or private importers of plants and animals.

I'm a scientific journal junkie. I know that four or five thousand exotic plant species have already established themselves in the United States, along with a couple of thousand exotic animals, all reproducing. I'd read that, annually, these exotics cost us millions a year, because we must assume the aggressive role of artificial predator.

Devastating examples of fecund-select exotics came to mind:

The gypsy moth was brought to the U.S. from France by an entomologist who hoped to cross them with indigenous moths and create better silk. A few gypsy moths escaped, multiplied, multiplied again. They were soon an unchecked cloud that defoliated entire forests throughout New England.

In the 1950s, government biologists turned calamity into cataclysm when they began spraying DDT to kill the moths. It took much too long for officials to admit that DDT also decimated our native insect and bird populations. Several species were poisoned to the brink of extinction — eagles, brown pelicans, and osprey among them.

Dragonflies, which prey voraciously on mosquitoes, were among the earliest of DDT's casualties, so mosquitoes bred out of control — which required spraying heavier concentrations of the chemical.

DDT is a potent carcinogenic, readily absorbed through the cell walls of pasture grasses, ripening vegetables, and herbaceous fish. It also seeped into our water systems. A generation of children grew up drinking DDT-laced milk and water and eating DDT-contaminated food. Unknown thousands of that generation are still suffering the effects. All because of an exotic moth.

Water hyacinth, a South American floating plant, and kudzu vine, from Japan, were other examples. Kudzu vine arrived by ship in the late 1800s to shade porches of Southern mansions. In the 1940s, government agricultural agents decided it was the ideal answer to erosion because it grows rapidly — up to a foot a day. Within a few years, the vine was suffocating farmlands and forests. It now blankets millions of acres. Hyacinth clogs millions of acres of waterways.

In Florida and neighboring states, there are too many examples of noxious exotics that breed, travel, and destroy, unhampered by natural checks: the Cuban tree frog, the walking catfish, several species of tropical fish, and, recently, the Indo-Pacific species of lionfish — dangerous because its spines are lethal.

Brazilian fire ants are some of the most vicious little bastards on Earth, and among the most ecologically destructive. The ant, named for its fiery bite, entered via ship through Mobile, Alabama, in the 1930s — the beginning of a long, slow nightmare. Fire ants sprout wings during their breeding cycle, can travel miles during mating flights, and hatch copious numbers of eggs.

The ant was soon killing local populations of native insects, whole colonies of ground-nesting birds, and infant mammals, as they ate their way into neighboring states. Ironically — and sadly — I've yet to hear of an environmental group that has aimed its financial or political guns at this biological cancer. Annually, fire ants destroy more indigenous species than the most heartless of developers.

I've done enough reading to know that plague and pestilence are not just words entombed in an ancient book. On the largest of scales, a balance between predator and prey is requisite if a biota is to function as a whole, because the health of the macrocosm is dependent on the health of all its living parts.

It is a fragile symbiosis. Predation is one of the few checks that prohibits one species from dominating, then destroying all others.

The only exotic on Dr. Shepherd's list that didn't seem an efficient choice as a bioweapon was the mamba. The species is too dangerous to handle, and snakes lay too few eggs to have much impact on a sizeable geographic area.

But then I gave it some thought. Decided maybe I was wrong.

In the African bush, only once had I seen a green mamba. Along with the taipan of Australia, it's the scariest snake I've encountered. Confronting a mamba? Chilling.

The snake grows more than fourteen feet long. Over ground, some claim, it crawls faster than an Olympic sprinter can run — unlikely, but illustrative of the fear it creates. The grade school janitor said that the snake he killed had charged him. The janitor was lucky. He had a shotgun. I'd heard accounts of pissed-off mambas running down men from behind and biting them in the back. Maybe apocryphal, but the animal's physical abilities are well documented.

The snake I'd encountered was face-to-face, and once was enough. When agitated, a mamba stands erect, a third of its body off the ground, so it's at eye level. You and the snake, staring at each other, its face and jaws not much smaller than your own. Just before it strikes, a mamba shakes its head violently, flattening cobralike. It opens its mouth wide to show the black interior. The snake is olive gray to green, not black. The name comes from this attack display.

If a mamba wet-strikes a healthy adult, death is statistically certain if the victim doesn't receive antivenom within half an hour. It is not a Hollywood death. Because of the megadose of neurotoxin, the victim dies slowly, clearheaded, but as a suffocating paraplegic. Its venom reserve is so massive that there are accounts of a single African mamba dropping through the roof of a house and killing as many as twelve inhabitants before crawling away.

So maybe it *was* a good choice as a bioweapon. Release a small number of mambas at places chosen to create the greatest possible public outrage: the Mall of the Americas; public schools. The terror factor would be enormous.

"Diabolical" — the right word.

The green mamba I'd encountered had behaved like an irritable, hyperactive teen. "Probably had a nest in the area," one of the locals told me later. "Makes them fierce. Deadly mean." The snake's head swayed like a metronome, but its eyes never broke contact with mine. The eyes were convex scales on an organism covered with scales. They were a lucent gray-blue, as dead looking as keratin plates, yet they implied the irrelevance of all knowledge because they reflected all that could be genetically known: If it touched its mouth to me, my beating mammalian heart would stop.

An African mamba is among the few creatures on earth instinctually certain of its ascendancy. I hoped I'd never face another.

It crossed my mind that the people doing this were another form of exotic. There is nothing sinister about snakes, or sharks, or spiders. They are what they are, beautifully coded, the trophies of adaptation. But these people were purposeful; seditious exotics, no less poisonous than the creatures they'd smuggled into the U.S. So far, they'd operated without being discovered. Like the fecund-select creatures they were using, there was no predator to track them and intercede.

Until now.

I'd been given the assignment. My options included whatever extreme action I deemed appropriate. *Eternalize.*

My license had been reissued.

I thought of Jobe Applebee, the little man who'd experienced too much chaos during his life. I thought of a good lady who once placed the imperatives of scientific method only after the love she had for her son, and husband. I thought of Tomlinson's pain . . . remembered the disgusting vision of guinea worm on the move.

Sitting in that hospital room, I sent a silent message to the perpetrators: *You are being tracked now.*

LOG
18 Dec. Saturday 18:43
(addendum from a reluctant operative)
    Bartram County Hospital.
    Premise: Predation is a necessary

393

check that prohibits one species from destroying all others. A society whose moral ideals inhibit its own defense is a society doomed to destruction by those predators it defines as immoral.

. . . all primate units struggle for ascendance, the weaknesses of many sheltered by the strength of a few. Conventional human conduct — trappings of respect, ceremony, alliance, and ritual — are added later to maintain the comforting illusion of a sentimental, civilized world . . .

— MDF

I sat thinking dark thoughts, writing in my log, as I listened to Tomlinson, the cheerful drunk, hold court on the phone. He'd already called several island fishing guides — Jeth, Alex, Neville, Doug Fisher, and Dave Case among them. Next he dialed my cousin, Ransom.

When she answered, Laken and I listened to what was by now a familiar, one-sided conversation: "Guess who's got a fish stuck up his willy. Yeah, it's me. Who else? Nope. My *penis*. I'm not kidding. Seriously . . . a *fish*. The little fiend went for a swim up the Sunshine Skyway. I'm in the hospital right now.

"No, I'm not drunk. I'm doing mainline morphine, which is like visiting an ol' war buddy. Makes the wounds seem fun. They've got this special machine I plan to buy and keep aboard *No Mas* . . ."

I watched Tomlinson tilt his head, listening to Ransom for what seemed like a long time, before he became insistent. "Yes . . . I told you. They're gonna do surgery in about half an hour. Listen to me closely: I . . . HAVE . . . A . . . FISH . . . UP . . . MY . . . DICK. Which means no live broadcast tomorrow. Sorry, no can do. In fact, I've gone to work with Doc on a special government project. Top secret; can't say. I'm his researcher and personal assistant. So we may have to tell our Zen students it's recess time. Go play alone in their own heads for a few months . . ."

He listened for several moments before raising his voice. "Lady, I'm surprised someone hasn't dropped a house on you. They don't make ruby slippers in size twelve?" He looked at me and wagged his eyebrows, enjoying himself. "I didn't mention my new seafood special. If I wrap Zamboni in a bun, cover 'im with tartar sauce, is there a chance you might get a case of the Tomlinson munchies again? Just for old times' sake? Doctor says he'll be standing tall, right as rain, within a couple of days."

I watched him grimace, then hold the phone away from his ear.

"Here," he said, "your sister wants to talk to you."

I took the phone. Waited quietly as Ransom added an epilogue to her heated rant. When she was done, I said, "Some of those words, I'm surprised you know. Some of them, *I* don't even know."

In her singsong, Bahamian lilt, Ransom replied, "Oh. It's you, my brother. Thought I was still talkin' to that idiot business partner of mine. His Holiness, Mr. Two-Timing Tomlinson. Is what he said true? Does he really have a fish in his thingee?"

I told her, yes, he apparently had a fish in his thingee. "The doctor used a special scope to take a look. She thinks it's a fish called a 'candiru.' "

" 'Candy-roo'? With that skinny boy, I'm surprised it ain't a damn moray. He say he doan want me to come up there, but I'm bringing my video guys anyway. We got our live broadcast tomorrow. I don't care what that ganja bum say. Our students will be tuned in, all over the world. He not gonna cost me twenty, thirty thousand just 'cause he caught a fish."

I said, "That's between you two. As of now, Lake and I plan on driving the Volkswagen back to Sanibel tonight. But just in case the surgery doesn't go the way it's supposed to, I've got a taxi on standby. A limo service —" I smiled at my son. "He thinks it's cool. No matter what happens here, Lake's flying out tomorrow."

Ransom said that was fine. If I didn't stay the night, she could bring Tomlinson home whenever he was discharged. "I thought you was leaving tomorrow, too. Going to Iowa. Does your sweetie pie, the pregnant jock, know you standin' her up again?"

There's an antagonism between Ransom and Dewey that I don't understand. Never will.

I told her that I'd probably leave Monday. "But if there're complications here, it'll be okay. Dewey'll understand."

"Will she, now?"

"Of course."

"You big, dumb, sweet boy. Do you realize every time that woman in trouble, she come running to you? When there ain't no more trouble, she's like a hermit crab — leaves you behind like an old shell."

"This time," I said, "it's different."

I wondered if it were true.

As I handed the phone to Tomlinson, I

felt my son looking at me, eyes assessing. When I'd told him about the limo, he'd shrugged, his expression tolerant. "Not a stretch limo?" His voice said he hoped it was.

"No. Just a car."

We were alone in the hallway at the time. He'd given me a quick, private hug.

"I'll get on the plane. Promise. You're right — mom wouldn't let me come back."

Turned out it was okay for me to arrive in Iowa a day or two late. Or a week late. Or a month late. Whatever I wanted.

Sort of.

After orderlies had wheeled Tomlinson into surgery, I walked outside and dialed Dewey's number. I'd had so much trouble reaching her by phone lately, I was taken aback when she answered.

"Hello, Doc. How're all the little fishes doing?"

Chilly. The undercurrent of sarcasm telling me, once again, I paid too much attention to my work, not enough to her.

I said, "It's good to hear your voice. It's been a hell of a couple of days. The nightmare variety."

I told her about Frieda, and what had happened to Tomlinson. The icy tone warmed. But there was still an unmistakable reserve. I got the impression someone was with her, listening.

"That's so sad! I met Frieda. I liked her. But what you say about Tomlinson can't be —"

"It's true," I said. "He's in surgery right now. Nothing serious — just uncommon. A parasitic fish from South America. His main worry was that he couldn't perform. The urologist is a woman, really first-rate. She told him he'd get so much sympathy from the ladies that his tool would not only work, it'd have to work overtime."

I expected to hear her laugh. Instead, she said, "I guess that's to be expected. Tomlinson, yeah. Maybe most other guys I know, too. Doc?" — long pause — "He's your pal. You need to be with him, so don't worry about busting ass to fly up here."

In a way, I was hurt. In a way, I was relieved.

I was in the hospital parking lot, security lights showing gray cars, black tires, a few empty spaces reserved for physicians, moths casting frantic shadows on asphalt. Stars up there beyond the glare, an ellipse of planets in line. Or would be in just three days. The winter solstice.

I began to pace.

"I'm not worried about it. I *want* to be there. I miss you. But I have to make sure Tomlinson's okay, then —"

"I understand. Friends are important. You take it seriously — it's one of the things people like about you. Marion Ford, the neighborhood rock. That's why I'm saying, if you don't make it for Christmas it's okay."

In the background, I heard a woman's voice say something that sounded like "Why don't you just tell him —" before it was muffled, probably by Dewey's hand.

Just those few words, I recognized who it was. I felt my stomach tighten, a sickening adrenaline flutter. It was a territorial response. Jealousy.

Speaking softly, I asked, "How long has Bets been there?"

Irritated, she replied, "Bets? Not that it's any of your business, but what makes you think she's here with — ?"

I interrupted. "Dewey. Please don't."

Bets, as in Walda Bzantovski — Bets to her friends. I'd once counted myself among them. She was Romanian, an internationally known tennis icon who'd retired a while back but still traveled the world doing clinics, making public appearances — a jet-setter name and face familiar to people who watch TV and read sports magazines.

I'd met the woman years ago when Dewey was still her live-in lover and partner. They would break up, then make up. Happened three times. Between each split, I'd played the role of understudy-pal, and, sometimes, lover.

This time, though, with a child coming, I'd thought Bzantovski was out of the picture.

The phone was still muffled. I heard Dewey say something, then Bets say something, not angry but emotional — the dominate partner — before Dewey said to me, "Okay. You're right. It's not like it's a big deal or anything. She's here. So what?"

"Tell her I said hello."

Silence. I waited, seeing Bets in my mind: a woman with tendons and muscles; long arms and longer legs; brown hair brushed back like some old rock singer; lean, European face with dark, aggressive eyes beneath heavy brows.

"Dewey. Are you still there?"

"Yeah."

"Why didn't you tell me?"

"Last Sunday, I *tried* to tell you. She was doing a clinic in Chicago; called from New York and said she might drop by to say hello. A last-minute deal. But you never gave me the chance."

I cleared my throat, putting some space between my anger and my intellect. I fought the urge to point out we'd talked several times during the week. She'd had plenty of chances to tell me any damn thing she wanted. That included informing me that her old lover was going to drive a couple hundred miles, Chicago to eastern Iowa, so they could stay together on her isolated farm.

Instead, I said gently, "Good. I'm glad you're not alone. During the holidays, it's important for old friends to be together."

"Are you sure, Doc? I've been worried." Finally, a hint of warmth.

I felt like crawling through the phone. Felt like slamming my fist against the wall — something I've never done, never will. I told her, "I'm sure. Winter in Iowa, for Christ's sake." I heard myself laugh. "You need company."

Silence.

"Will she be staying long?"

"I'm not sure. We haven't talked about it."

"Sounds like she'll still be there when I arrive."

"Stop it! How'm I supposed to know what her schedule is?"

Infuriating.

More silence. Spaced between barrier islands and winter cornfields, satellite towers created a hollow echo.

"Dew . . . ? How's the baby?"

"She's fine. She's happy here."

"She?"

"My last appointment, I decided to ask so we can get the room decorated. A little girl."

We.

"Doctor says she should arrive right on time."

"Punctual, huh? She gets that from me."

Dewey released a subtle, concessional breath. The sound of nostalgia. "I can't argue that one."

"If Tomlinson's surgery goes okay, I could be there Monday, Wednesday at the latest. That's three days before Christmas — if you still want me to come."

She thought about it before saying slowly, "I've met some friends here. A nurse and an EMT. A couple. They're taking us pheasant hunting Wednesday. They've got the shotguns, a dog. I'm kind of excited" — I again heard Bzantovski's voice in the background, quickly muffled — "so Wednesday's not good."

I said, "You with a shotgun, blasting birds out of the sky. That's hard to picture."

Dewey's tone became severe. "That's because you don't know anything about guns, Doc. I knew you'd be pissy if I told you. But my friends have lots of experience. With them, it's safe."

I could hardly trust myself to speak. "I'd like to meet them. Maybe they can give me a pointer or two. On shooting."

"Maybe. If they have time, but they're kinda fussy about their guns." Another long pause. "If you still want to fly up, sure. After Wednesday, come if you want. There's plenty of room. If . . . you don't mind dealing with the snow. And being so far from the ocean."

Plenty of room? The meaning of that seemed evident.

My phone was beeping — another call. I overcame the perverse urge to hang up; end it with some quick, cutting remark. A couple of years back, Dewey had surprised Bzantovski at a Madrid hotel. Charmed a key from the desk clerk and walked in to find the Romanian in bed with one of the young stars on the circuit, a French girl named Wengo.

A couple of parting shots flashed through my mind: *You and Bets will always have Paris. Plus, how many other European capitals?*

Instead, I said, "I guess this isn't a good

time to talk. Maybe tomorrow'll be better. If that's okay."

"Sure, Doc. If you want."

I tried to catch the other call but too late.

I checked the number. It was Jason Reynolds.

He'd left a voice message. I listened to it as I returned to the waiting room.

The cops couldn't find Frieda's phone, he said. Maybe I should return to the canal and help the search . . .

I looked at my watch: 7:23 p.m. I pictured crime scene lights mounted on tripods; water recovery jocks in wet suits, arms locked, wading a search grid.

If what Reynolds had said was true — which I doubted.

I'd find out soon enough.

28

An hour after she had pushed Dr. Frieda Matthews into the path of the SUV rental, Dasha padlocked the door of the storage garage, then removed the surgical gloves she was wearing.

Aleski's cousin, Broz, had been waiting for them when they arrived. He'd raised his eyebrows when he saw the SUV's bumper and windshield. Said in Russian, "What a fat cow you must have hit!"

A clever joke for that slow-witted fool.

Broz was driving one of the numbered Tropicane trucks, which infuriated Dasha, though she said nothing.

Sloppy. Unprofessional. He's even stupider than Aleski!

Amazing that he'd learned to operate a plane.

The time would come, she suspected, when she would have to kill them both. With Broz, she would make it last. If he wasn't so damn ugly, maybe even find a way to get some pleasure out of it.

Aleski, though, he'd die quickly, painlessly. The man was her partner, after all. A fellow professional. He deserved respect.

It would happen. Maybe sooner than later.

Dasha had reviewed her mental checklist: wiped the rental vehicle clean of prints, dumped a bottle of Clorox over the interior and exterior. Used Clorox-soaked towels to clog the garage's vents and airspaces.

Vultures sitting outside a storage garage invite attention. The car would soon begin to stink.

Dasha had decided the woman's body was too badly damaged to load into the back of the SUV. It would've been too time-consuming, searching through the weeds next to the canal, collecting all that needed to be collected. What a mess. A car, she decided, was an interesting way of killing, but not a good way, because it was impossible to manipulate the crime scene afterward.

Unprofessional, like Broz.

Should've used the hypodermic loaded with Versed. To hell with Aleski and his recreational games.

Still . . . Dasha had to admit to herself that her last moments with Frieda Matthews had been stimulating in an unexpected way. She replayed it in her mind, as she slid in behind the wheel of the Tropicane vehicle, started the engine, and accelerated away. . . .

She could see herself helping the confused woman to her feet after she had tumbled at speed from the back of the SUV. Knew from an Army medic's course that Matthews had compound fractures, right femur, right wrist, nearly one side of her body skinned raw, blouse torn off.

Sickening if you weren't hardened to that sort of thing. In shock. A concussion, too.

"What's happening? *Help* me. Will you help me?" Adults in shock sometimes revert to the speech patterns of childhood.

"Of course. Put your arm over my shoulder. We will take you to hospital."

. . . Then the two of them, waiting in weeds at the side of the road where Aleski had dropped them — a straightaway where she could see vehicles approaching from a mile in either direction. Matthews babbling, and crying about some child she missed so badly, starting to feel pain for the first time, the adrenaline mask fading.

Supporting the woman's body, Dasha had let her hands explore around. Done it unthinkingly, at first, then with specific interest, finding Matthews to be bustier than she looked, skin soft to the touch, her abdomen firm, silky. A woman who used clothes to cover herself, not reveal.

It was arousing, Dasha had to admit it. Standing, holding the warmth of damaged flesh, aware of another human's absolute vulnerability, hands cupping a woman's breasts for the first time in her life, Dasha watched the SUV bearing down on them, Aleski going way too fast because he was furious.

Frieda Matthews had nearly gouged out the man's right eye; used her teeth to mangle his ear. Aleski was bleeding from the groin — he wouldn't explain why.

Another middle-aged woman who refused to be humiliated by life, by a man, by anything.

In that instant, Dasha had felt something resembling fondness for Matthews. Pulled her closer, watching the SUV growing huge as it flew toward them, wanting to time it right and cause this strong woman the least amount of pain. Touched her lips tenderly to Frieda's cheek . . . then pushed her away gently — a steering sort of push — and watched Matthews wobble groggily out onto the road.

The woman's back was to the vehicle when it hit her. An explosion touched

Dasha's own cheek as a vaporous sprinkle. Warm, like soft rain.

The Russian dabbed at the moisture with fingertips. Red.

Yes, fondness. That's what Dasha had felt. Arousal, too.

Both unexpected.

She wondered if she'd get the chance to experience those confusing feelings again one day.

Mr. Earl was waiting for them at the Tropicane Ranch. Sat on the porch of the plush, two-story minimansion that was reserved for major stockholders and dignitaries, but used almost exclusively by the tall Lincoln-looking man with the big white teeth.

Mr. Earl the Black Pearl was king shit around the Tropicane staff. Most didn't know Mr. Sweet existed.

Mr. Earl was showing his teeth now, a huge smile. He was dressed very stylishly in a white linen suit, with a white cane and panama strawhat within easy reach, as Dasha approached carrying the laptop computer in both hands, like an offering.

"Is it Applebee's?"

Ten feet away, Dasha could smell the lavender lotion he used. Saw that his red bow tie was crooked — which might mean Mr. Earl was already a little drunk. He drank *mojito*s in public, vodka in private.

"This is his computer. But you told me not to open it, that you wanted to get the first look. So I can't confirm it."

Mr. Earl stood, took the computer as he fitted spectacles on his nose — the lenses were dime-sized.

"Go! Get food, drink, go for a swim, whatever you want." The man was excited. He might have been accepting gold, not a laptop. "I'll meet you here later for cocktails. Eightish is cool."

Dasha had hoped to fly back to the island that night with Aleski and Broz, but she answered, "As you wish."

At her staff apartment, Dasha shaved her legs. Chose white satin slacks, no underwear, a gauzy blue blouse, no bra, just in case the tall man wanted something special in trade for closing the deal. Her read, though she had nothing to prove it: Mr. Earl dressed like a homosexual but wasn't. Not full-time, anyway.

Disgusting, if he insisted, but necessary.

That was Dasha's impression. The two of them were about to agree on a way of leveraging Mr. Sweet. Wealthy people sometimes have accidents; disappear — there's nothing suspicious about that if their assets are undisturbed. Creating an independent cash flow after a wealthy person vanishes, though, required unusual opportunity, plus planning.

She had her theory about how Stokes hoped to profit from introducing exotic parasites into Florida. Mr. Earl maybe knew. Or had a theory of his own.

An important meeting. It required giving thought to appropriate dress.

When Dasha returned to the little mansion, minus Aleski and his idiot cousin, she got a surprise. Mr. Earl was no longer smiling. He was on the porch, pacing beneath the yellow light, smoking a cigarette in an ivory holder.

Mr. Sweet didn't allow tobacco on his islands. Smoking was a Florida indulgence.

"The good news?" Mr. Earl told her before she got seated, even before asking her if she wanted a drink. "You got the right computer. There's no doubt about who the software's licensed to. I also checked the applications system, and you told me the truth. You didn't take a secret little peek at his files. Like I would have bet you would."

Dasha stood comfortably, pleased with her own professionalism, but curious about where he was going with this. She hadn't opened the computer because she'd guessed the man had a way to check. He was shrewd, always a step ahead of everyone. The first time she'd realized for certain how smart Mr. Earl was the first time Dasha suspected she might have an ally. Someone to help her displace Mr. Sweet.

"The bad news?" Mr. Earl's tone was a mix of irritation and amusement. "The bad news is, that lil' fool who went and hung himself, wasn't a retard like our boss man claims. Applebee was a damn genius, far as I can tell. Let's go sit inside, have a look at the computer. I'll show you what I'm saying."

There was only one folder on the computer's desktop. Labeled EPOC/ TROPICANE.

Mr. Earl said, "Watch this." He opened the folder. One by one, he opened the files within.

"Numbers," he said. "The little man didn't write with letters. He wrote with numbers. Jesus Christ, it had to take him forever to learn how to write this way. His own language."

During intelligence training evolutions in the Russian Army, Dasha had gone through a three-week school on encryption and secret writing. It had mostly dealt with computers, how to hide and recover data.

A portion of the evolution had been called "Forensic Computer Analysis."

"Is that code? Or cipher?" She was looking over Mr. Earl's shoulder at columns of numbers, seeing his face in the screen's reflection, her eyes two dark spaces next to his left ear. She didn't think he'd have a clue.

He pushed himself away from the desk. "You tell me. You're head of security." The man leaned, lighted a cigarette, smiling — playing a game with her, giving a test. Blew a cloud of smoke into her hair; touched his fingernail to her back and traced a horizontal line typically covered by her bra strap.

That was something else unexpected. More than two years they'd worked together, and this was the first indication the man was interested in having fun.

Dasha sat, rebooted the computer with system extensions off. She checked the software's kernel version, the boot volume, and the amount of memory available.

They all told her something. There was a lot more data stored on this computer than was visible on the desktop, or hard drive.

She restarted the computer, then went to system preferences and opened security options, feeling Mr. Earl out there next to the porch window, watching her, smoking, expecting her to fail.

Security vault activated. Master password required.

One after another, Dasha typed in default passwords. She'd memorized several during training. All declined.

Yebat!

She looked at the laptop's cover as if to remind herself. This was a Mac, a system she'd never used. Russian Intelligence — its three-week encryption school had dealt only with PCs. All IBM clones that used Windows. Never a word about Macs.

Typical. Myopic bureaucrats still ran the government. Mother Russia. A gigantic country inhabited by small losers.

Outside, Mr. Earl lit another cigarette. She could hear his throaty chuckle.

Dasha called, "We need an expert to look at this."

Mr. Earl opened the door. "You want a third person involved?" His tone asked if she wanted a third person to share the score.

No doubt now. The man was on the make. Maybe he knew about Applebee's guinea worm study, or had a theory similar to her own — lots of money at stake.

"How else are we going to find out what's on the computer?"

Mr. Earl held up a skinny index finger, then leaned over the computer's keyboard, the odor of lavender and tobacco potent. He typed for several seconds, then said, "Look."

On the screen appeared rows of blue folders, each labeled with words, not numbers. Many dozens of folders, some with interesting tags. Several had to do with Autism: Autism/mercury.doc;Autism/panic.

Some strange, angry ones that referenced Disney World: Dis/conspiracy.doc; Satanic mouse.

There was a long list of topics that indicated the quiet little man had had a busy, busy world going on inside his head.

Another folder was labeled: DR.D.STOKES/PRIVATEFILES.DOC.

Interesting.

Dasha hesitated, not sure she should risk it, before saying, "There they are, Stokes's private files. Applebee copied them — I had my doubts. What do you think's in there?"

Mr. Earl looked at her frankly. "I just finished going through it. It's written in plain English, not numbers. You're in there, I'll tell you that much. All that the cops need to put you away for murder. Or me — for something I did a long time ago."

Dasha widened her eyes, telling him she'd like to know more. For personal reasons.

Big grin. "Years back, I was what they called a 'political subversive.' What I was into, though, was drugs. Money. Dropped acid, screwed teenyboppers, hung out with LSD freaks. They made crazy predictions that, at the time, got a lot of press. They're still getting press, thanks to yours truly and Dr. Stokes. Makin' us even more money. Understand? Which is very, very cool."

Dasha knew he'd been busted for more than that, because he added, "The Bahamian police, the FBI, Interpol. If any of them get a copy of this file, we're both gone. When the time's right, maybe I'll let you have a look."

She was impressed that Mr. Earl had beaten the computer's security system so quickly but was also suspicious. Why was the man sharing the information with her?

Mr. Earl let her think about that for a moment before he said, "May I tell you something in confidence? Between us. Only us."

"Of course. You trust me; I'll trust you. Partnerships sometimes start in strange ways."

His mean, judgmental eyes stared at her from above a broadening smile. "I have special software. It's illegal for anyone not in law enforcement. It recovers keystrokes made *prior* to installation. Anything typed on the keyboard during the hard drive's history, I can recover. It downloads automatically on any computer that signs on from the island. That's how I got Applebee's passwords."

His confession was also an implied warning: The man had her private files, and files from every other computer on the island.

The Russian waited, not expecting him to offer anything else, but he did.

"Six-six-four. Cardinal numbers, spelled out. That's one of Applebee's passwords. The man's little joke."

"What do you mean?"

"What's the number mean? No idea. But the joke I can show you." Mr. Earl moved the cursor to a file labeled: Dracunculus Eminences. "Do what know what this is?"

"I wouldn't want to try to pronounce it. Something to do with Dracula?" Dasha thought for a moment. "I've seen it written someplace before."

"It's the Latin name for the guinea worm

parasite." The man clicked on the file and several more file icons appeared. One was labeled: Eradicating Dracunculus Infestation.

He opened it, and six icons remained, all studies related to guinea worm parasites. Dasha was getting excited.

According to the dates, the three most recently created files were labeled: Raising Copepod/Hybrids, Eradication-Plan/Florida, Post-Dracunculus Africa.

"I'll be damned, the man did it. Applebee discovered a cure." The woman pointed at the screen. "Africa after the parasite's all gone. What else could it mean?"

"A cure?" Mr. Earl sounded surprised, or maybe tried to sound it. "Oh — I see what you're saying. Yes, I think he did. Solved a problem no one bothered to mess with. But here's the joke I mentioned."

He opened one of the files. Numbers again.

"Passwords and labels, he used letters. Funny. *Ha-ha!* Teasing anyone who tried to break into his system. Everything else Applebee wrote is in code."

Dasha felt his frustration now. "There's got to be a key. It's probably hidden somewhere in the hard drive."

"If it is, it's all numbers."

"Then we'll figure it out ourselves."

"That's where we're screwed. Unless you've got some special training in the area, we're not going to have time to crack this before Stokes expects us back on the island."

Dasha hoped she hadn't misinterpreted his meaning. She had to be very careful here. "Why's it so important that we translate it before we give the computer to Dr. Stokes?"

Mr. Earl was on the keyboard again, typing. "I didn't say we had to translate it. I said we have to find the key before *he* finds it. Here — read this."

A e-mail appeared on the screen. It was addressed to someone named Doc at Sanibel Biological Supply, sent from F.matthews.

Frieda Matthews.

Hey, Doc, you're the only guy I know with the background to understand Jobe's files, attached here. Remember me telling you my brother used numbers as words . . . ?

Mr. Earl said, "I did an Internet search. Sanibel Biological is owned by a biologist named Marion Ford. Dr. Ford. *Doc*. Does the name sound familiar?"

Dasha thought, *Jesus Christ, the crazy idiot who almost killed me with his boat.*

One of Stokes's stooges had gotten the name, had told them that the same guy, Ford, had been with Frieda when she'd toured her brother's house. A close friend of the family.

Detective Jimmy Heller, the stooge.

Heller had also said Applebee's body was infested with the worms. The dates that the last computer files were created — "Dracunculus Solved" — told Dasha that he'd discovered the solution too late.

Mr. Earl said, "We find Ford, maybe we find the key. Getting information out of people who don't want to cooperate — your specialty."

That's why he needs me.

Still playing it safe, Dasha said, "Then we give the information to Dr. Stokes?"

The dried-up man, all bones and face, was shaking his head, looking at her with his mean dark eyes. "No, we go ahead and spread the parasites in Florida. Stick with the plan, woman. The only difference is, we got Applebee's formula. Stokes don't. Buy the land cheap, then sell to all those developers waiting in line. *Millions.*"

Dasha was right with him. *Millions.*

She let her hand slide over and touch the man's thigh.

A little before midnight, Thursday, sitting at a computer inside Mr. Earl's minimansion, Dasha did an Internet search and found two photos of Marion Ford, Ph.D. It took a while. There was very little information on the guy; no background data at all.

Weird.

Or not.

She'd tried to wade through a couple of his scientific papers, titles like "Difficulties Spawning *Megalops atlanticus* in Captivity," before almost saying, screw it, the man was an egghead scientist who must have been whiskey-brave the night of the boat chase.

Then she got lucky. Went to the Web page of a weekly newspaper, the *Sanibel Shoppers Guide*, and there he was with a story about a place called "Dinkin's Bay Marina."

"Doc Ford and Tomlinson, Two Colorful Locals" was the cutline. A pair of photos, the first posed: Broad-shoulder man, hair wind mussed, eyes staring out through thick glasses, his expression neutral, standing beside a bony-faced hippie,

Jesus hair, with a friendly grin, glazed eyes.

One man stoned. The other man stone.

Her first impression: Ford was a nerdy scientist, just as the articles he'd written suggested. Right at home with the other loser in the picture, two tropical bums who found opposite ways to underachieve.

But then she reminded herself that she was looking at a man who, on a black night, had launched a boat over a ski ramp while Aleski fired at him — and still had the balls and skill to time it so perfect he'd damn near crushed them.

The second photo was more suggestive. The photographer had caught Ford by surprise. Face was the same, but the eyes were very, very different. His head was turned toward the camera, expression intense.

Reassessment time.

Dasha was in no hurry, sitting there in the minimansion's computer room and library. A good place to burn time while Mr. Earl snored a fifth of vodka away in the master bedroom upstairs.

A couple hours earlier, he'd said to her, "Your security system, those redundancy cells, I thought it was such a good idea. I finally realized, you can use it like a rope around my neck. You hired nothing but Russians. I can't make a move without your permission."

Dasha had anticipated this. She handed him an order she'd already signed. It excluded him from all security "impositions."

She let him read the paper before handing him a second packet, then pointed to Mr. Earl's name, and the line where he was supposed to sign. Watched him smile. The paper was already notarized.

"This judge in Nassau, did you bribe her with money? Or slip her some skin?" Watched the man tilt his head back, laughing. "You'll never get Stokes to sign this. But me? Sure, I'll sign — if you agree to a little celebration afterward. I don't want any money. What you probably gave the judge, that would be cool."

Disgusting old leech. A predator, really. The man screwed like he was double-parked, or might turn into a pumpkin. Probably thirty-five years older than her — plus he was drunk. He had to use an index finger to stuff his pecker inside, like a magician hiding a scarf in a fist.

Next time, I'll make the nasty thing disappear. My turn to fuck Mr. Earl.

Saying she had to do research was a good excuse to escape the stink of lavender and Mr. Earl's dried-up fingertips. A relief . . . until she used the computer's toolbar to have a closer look at this second photo of Ford.

Zoomed in on eyes looking out through wire glasses. Thick glasses. Eyes that seemed dark even though they reflected pale light, the man's expression showing that he'd been startled by the photographer, the eyes chilly, expectant; expectant in the way of someone who sits back and accesses before making a move.

Surprise a carnivore in tall grass, you'd get the same reaction.

The eyes reminded her of something. The image of Solaris came into Dasha's mind — Solaris and the newly hatched snake that killed him.

A death adder.

A reptile that, from birth, knew instinctively to wait, calculate, before striking.

Efficient. That was another way of saying it.

Ford's eyes were similar. Vague and dusty. Something dark inside there coiled.

In Vegas, when Mr. Earl had interviewed her, there'd been all those *Soldier of Fortune* types strutting around. Fakes, skinheads, Hollywood dreamers. Out of all those pretenders, she'd seen two, maybe three people who'd earned the look. People who'd been places; done some jobs.

If you serve in the Russian military, the Chechen border, hustling both sides, you learned to recognize the real ones at a glance. Or died.

He used a ski ramp to attack. At night. While taking fire.

Marion D. Ford, Ph.D.

Looking at the man's photo, Dasha felt a stimulating awareness, the preface to fury, but also the preface to arousal. In her, the two emotions were nearly the same.

Biologist, my ass.

The woman still had connections in Russia; former KGB people, black ops specialists. She looked at her watch — a little after 8:00 a.m. in Moscow. Just for the hell of it, she wrote an e-mail asking if anyone had additional information on Ford. She sent it to several addresses, not expecting much.

Surprise.

An hour later, after showering yet again, Dasha checked her e-mail before heading for bed in the guest room. She'd already received three responses.

Two wrote that there was no data available — "suggestive," one noted, in a typically understated Russian way.

The third reply was written in Chechen.

Excellent intel; better than she'd hoped.

. . . only match for Marion D. Ford is from compromised Mossad files, data not verifiable. Tropics; Biologist; Born South Florida — suspected nightshift operator, never confirmed. Assets: Unknown. Affiliated agency: Unknown; possibly illegal deep-cover black ops group. Designation: W.

MDF's geo-transects are too numerous to be coincidental with the deaths or disappearances listed here in reverse order: Islamic cleric Hada Salharra, Detroit; Ricardo Palmera (aka Simon Trinidad), FARC leader, Colombia; Omar Muhammad, head of Abul Nidal. . . .

Dasha was smiling, energized. The targets, the organizations — in the world of covert operations, this was big-time. It took the breath out of her. She had Ford's photo enlarged on the screen as she skipped ahead; she wanted to see how the man got started.

. . . while in secondary school, MDF was suspect in the disappearance and presumed murder of a man rumored to have had an affair with subject's mother just prior to her own death. According to sealed records, a juvenile court judge (and friend of subject's Masonic uncle) strongly suggested MDF leave Florida and enlist in the military . . .

The final paragraph read:

. . . subject was employed by a CIA front corporation, Air America, during operations Phoenix and Blue Light. MDF is also suspected of infiltrating political activist organizations on U.S. college campuses, Colorado, Wisconsin, Berkeley, and Harvard, in operations called Purple Haze and Bad Moon Rising. Several deaths and disappearances associated with same . . .

"Nightshift." KGB slang.

This man was a professional, like herself. An operator.

With someone like this, she'd have to be very, very careful.

The woman was imagining various scenarios. Letting it play out in her head.

Her guess was right: *A killer.*

A man like Ford she might be able to use . . .

29

The phone message Jason Reynolds left on my cell phone bothered me, set off warning gongs.

"Dr. Ford, it might be smart if you drive back to the canal, win yourself some points. The cops can't find the damn phone for some reason, and they're sorta freaked-out suspicious. Either way, give me a call from the hospital, and tell me how our friend's doing."

I saved the message as I stepped through the *whoosh* of automatic doors, into the hospital.

His voice sounded strained, the sentences rehearsed. Too many oddities.

I checked my watch again: 7:31 p.m.

If the sheriff's department couldn't find the phone, why hadn't they contacted me? The detective from the special crimes division had my number. He had already threatened to come looking for me if I'd given him bad info.

Instead, I hear it first from some imitation hipster?

Something else: There were only two plausible reasons why they hadn't found the phone. They were searching the wrong place, or someone had removed it before they got there.

. . . *drive back to the canal, win some points . . .*

A deserted road. Only one way in or out. A perfect little ambush point if someone wanted to get me alone and ask about Applebee's computer files — files that several people now knew I possessed.

My boat shoes squeaked on sterile hallway floors, medical staff in scrubs streaming past, as I listened to the message a second time.

. . . *give me a call from the hospital . . .*

How did Reynolds know we were still at the hospital?

He was either guessing, or someone was doing drive-bys, keeping an eye on the Magic Bus, which I'd parked in the rear lot, near the ER entrance.

The waiting room was separated from the main hall by hydraulic double doors, shatterproof glass. Lake was inside with a magazine — it looked like *Scientific American* — slumped in the plastic chair, bored but dealing with it. I stood and stared for a moment, feeling pleasure in the shape of his face, wanting the image to stick with me, enjoying an awareness of heritable bonds.

When I stepped through the doorway, he looked up, grinned, raised an index finger — his characteristic greeting.

"Any word on Tomlinson?"

"Naw. Doctor said it'd be about an hour. She's funny. I like her. We had a pretty good talk."

"In her business, I guess a sense of humor's required."

I noticed that when the boy grinned, his eyes glittered, familiar as my own. "Know what she told me? She said, 'When adults tell you that adolescence is the best time of your life, they're full of shit.' " He lost it for a moment, chest bouncing as he laughed. *Hilarious.* "Said she didn't really start feeling comfortable, having fun, until she was in her late twenties. Hated her teens."

"A smart woman; she's right. I was a little older. Early thirties."

"No shit?" Lake had been experimenting with profanity. I had to force myself not to smile.

"I shit you not. Early thirties."

There was something else on his mind. A sly look. He was about to share a secret.

"Dr. Shepherd told me she's single, made a point of it. The only reason I can think of, she wants you to know."

I said, "Really? I must have missed something."

My son said, "I'm the same way with girls. I can't ever tell, either. She asked me some questions about you, then told me she'd lived alone since doing her residency. I think she's really pretty for a woman her age."

"Very attractive. She's got character — it's in her eyes." A passing observation said without real interest. The conversation with Dewey had congealed as a knot in my chest. I felt it there now; pain that would last.

The leather-bound log book Lake had given me was on the table next to his backpack — he carried the thing everywhere — and near to the keys to the van.

I sat, opened the log, noted date and time, as I told my son where I was going and why. I added, "I don't have a choice," as I wrote:

Tomlinson, I'm driving your van to the canal where you found Frieda's phone. If I'm not back by morning, call a guy named Hal Harrington at the number below. Tell him to have your new pal, Jason Reynolds, questioned. Here are other names he should check . . .

"You seem to enjoy that. Keeping a journal."

Still writing, I said, "Yeah, my memory's getting so bad, it helps."

"I know better."

"The book's from you. There's the main reason I like it."

That made the kid smile. Nice.

. . . there's a fireproof locker under my bed. You'll find an envelope addressed to you. It contains information that'll keep you safe for a long, long time. If I don't make it back, keep a weather eye on Lake . . .

My son asked, "You think there's a chance you'll get down to Central America after the holidays? Tomlinson says the surfing on the Pacific Coast of Panama is unbelievable."

My turn to smile. "I'll make a point of it. Lake Nicaragua — you need to see that place. We'll go together."

I tore the page out, folded it. I'd leave it for Tomlinson with the receptionist on the way out. I told Lake, "I called the limo guy. He's underway. You'll be back on Sanibel by ten-thirty. Still time to get something to eat, then pack. Jeth'll take you to the airport tomorrow."

I hate good-byes. I saw that my son was no different; both of us not eager to part but eager to get this process over with. He stood facing me, holding the magazine.

"In the lab, I printed out a couple of sample pages from Dr. Applebee's documents. Six pages, paper-clipped, next to the computer. Take them to Central America, work on the code. But do *not* copy the files. And don't tell anyone you have those pages. Understand?"

Lake nodded.

"I'll talk to the hospital security people. They'll let you know when the car's here. I'll make sure they check out the driver."

"You don't have to do that, Dad. I can take care of myself."

"I know. But you're valuable property." He stuck out his hand but I pushed it aside. Gave him a hug; my cheek tight against his head. "Crack the code, son, and I'll buy you something very cool. You're one of the few people smart enough to figure it out."

As I picked up the keys, Lake said, "You don't have to buy me anything. I'll do it because it's what you want me to do."

★ ★ ★

I exited at the front of the hospital, not the ER entrance, which was closer to where I'd left the Magic Bus. I walked through the parking lot to a side street, then began to jog, using tree shadows as cover when I had the chance.

An adult male walking alone at night, or sprinting, draws attention. But joggers are part of the landscape — local jocks who own the street no matter the time of day or night.

My fishing shorts and T-shirt weren't a perfect disguise, but close enough.

I circled the hospital, crossing the street to avoid the brighter lights of a strip mall, then crossed again to a sidewalk that fronted low-income ranch houses in a subdivision that was once middle class. Ficus and oak trees, probably planted in the fifties, had outgrown their domino lots. They hung dense over concrete that was in slow upheaval because of the roots beneath.

There was an ambulance sitting at the ER entrance, lighted sign above — EMERGENCY ONLY — and I began to slow in the gloom of trees, scanning the parking lot. I spotted a wedge of the Magic Bus beneath security lights. Could see its camper top, plus surfboards, above nearby cars. Could see its VW logo on the blunt front end, a peace sign painted there; white paint that became strawberry in the sodium haze.

The parking lot was half full, but felt deserted because of the absence of activity. There were EMTs in their blue coverall uniforms busy at the back of the ambulance, floodlights there, three people in scrubs watching, but no other movement. No security people in gold carts, which was unexpected.

I stopped, keys to the VW in my hand. I stood alert to anomalies — a car parked on a nearby side street, an inhabited vehicle, people waiting in shadows. Maybe Reynolds's Tropicane truck, but that was unlikely. If this was a setup, he wouldn't be that obvious. Or stupid.

A block away, a car turned the corner, lights panning. I knelt to tie my shoes, hiding my face until it'd passed.

A white sedan with black antenna, dorsallike, on the trunk.

An unmarked squad car? It had that look.

I waited, feeling the quarter moon brighten, then sail behind clouds. Waited until the car turned in the distance, and I began to jog again.

I made one more lap around the block. Stopped briefly near the hospital's front entrance and watched two security guards escort my son to a black Lincoln Town Car. I felt an uncharacteristic surge of emotion as one of the guards held the rear door open for Lake. The other chatted with the driver while also inspecting what I assumed to be his chauffeur's license.

Good men. It explained the absence of security in the rear parking lot.

My son was getting his ride in a limo. A small surprise from his father. A parting gift.

At a faster pace, I jogged past the strip mall a final time, cut through the parking lot, and approached the Magic Bus from behind. Curtains covered the side windows of the VW, so I peeked in the rear. It was impossible to be certain, but it looked empty.

I touched fingertips to metal, sensitive to any slight movement, a shifting of weight.

Nothing.

Nearby cars also looked empty. I decided that if this was a setup, the X spot — where they'd hit me — would be somewhere on the dirt road that led to the canal.

More likely, though, I'd over-analyzed Reynolds's phone message. I'd probably find the cops still searching for the cell phone, suspicious of my motives, just like he'd said.

I unlocked the driver's-side door, then started to slide in behind the wheel when I realized the dome light had not come on.

Uh-oh.

In the same instant, I heard a car start a few spaces to my left, and was simultaneously aware of someone running — light-footed, on asphalt — before the car's engine grew louder, audibly thumping into gear.

Trouble.

I turned to see the silhouette of a woman closing on me, as a pale-colored car appeared, lights off. It was timed to let the woman pass before the car pulled in tight behind the Volkswagen, shielding my view of the EMTs at the ER entrance, and also any chance of anyone seeing what was happening to me.

Professionals . . .

It was the Russian woman charging me. The one who'd taken such pleasure in torturing Jobe Applebee. I got a flickering look at the short blond hair, the feral eyes, her skin glazed orange with industrial light. She had something in her hand. An aluminum flashlight?

It made no sense. Even if it were a gun, she couldn't be planning to take me down all by herself.

Where's her partner?

The driver's-side window of the blocker car was tinted; I could see a vague male shape at the wheel as the woman stopped abruptly a couple of yards away. As she lifted her hand toward me — *maybe it's a weapon* — I reached for my cell phone, feeling for the keypad, hoping to hit the redial button, any number would do. I wanted there to be some record of what was happening here.

I tensed, expecting to hear a gunshot. Instead, a laser-bright light blinded me momentarily. From behind, two huge, hairy hands grabbed me from inside the van, one of them locked around my windpipe. I didn't have a chance to bury my chin against my chest but managed to wedge a couple of fingers between my Adam's apple and the man's hand, hearing the woman whisper something harsh in Russian.

An instant later, my back muscles spasmed as if voltage charged when I felt a sickening, hypodermic pain — a needle had been driven deep into the side of my throat. I felt the gagging pain for several long seconds before the needle was removed.

More whispered Russian as I coughed and heaved reflexively, feeling woozy-headed, eyes blurring . . . I was aware of a flooding weariness as my brain struggled to translate the grotesque images that gradually appeared before me.

The Russian woman, with her feral eyes, now had the skeletal face of a screaming death's-head. Her partner appeared briefly, walking upright, then was liquefied and reassembled as an animal from a cartoon vision. He dropped to all fours, his body as thick and hairy as a lion, but with the leering, hairy head of a jackal.

"Walk, you clumsy idiot. If you make us carry you, we'll let you die here."

The screaming death's-head spoke a whispered English, heavily accented.

I then stood for a moment, teetering on the edge of an expanding abyss — the trunk of a car was opening next to me, I realized. A third figure was now involved. A man with a plaid jacket, a Bronx accent, eyes smoldering with the stink of cigars.

I tried to say his name — Jimmy Heller — but the words exited my numb face as the blubbering sound of an invalid weeping.

"Tough guy," I heard the squatty little detective say. "The way he handles himself — like his shit doesn't stink. Listen to 'im now, crying like a baby."

I watched, beginning to tilt earthward, as the checkered jacket became an animal's spotted pelt, and smoldering eyes centered themselves on Heller's pointed, yellow face — the face of a hyena. Then I was falling . . . falling toward a dark concavity that had been the trunk of a car but was now a spinning coffin.

Felt the air go out of me. Felt an acidic welling that signals the need to vomit as the coffin lid slammed shut . . .

30

Marion D. Ford — if the man really is an operator, what's the best way to take him down . . . ?

Dasha had been thinking about it Friday morning when she'd found the address of Sanibel Biological Supply on the Internet, and used MapQuest to print directions. She was still excited; couldn't wait to meet the man face-to-face.

She'd also printed Ford's photograph. *Those eyes* . . . thinking of the way he'd used a boat as a weapon added to the anticipation.

She had Broz drop them at Orlando International, where she used a counterfeit credit card to get another rental, a green Pontiac midsize, nondescript.

Aleski was with her, of course. Aleski, whose right eye was now swollen closed, ear blood-clotted beneath antibiotic salve.

Irritating. She'd have much preferred to make the trip alone, she and Ford, two operators meeting — that's the way she pictured it — but there was no escaping Aleski. Like a dog, the way he followed her around. Lately, though, it was more like a guard dog.

Four hours later, they were driving over a causeway bridge onto Sanibel Island, mica-bright water beneath, the molten fire of a western sky familiar in a misplaced way.

An image formed in Dasha's mind: the Foundry furnaces of Volstak blazing, doors wide, ghost men swinging shovels . . .

One of them probably my idiot father.

Her mother had worked the factories at lunchtime. To Dasha, the heat from the furnaces felt like heaven. Her mother said they were doors that opened to hell.

"This is a pretty island. I like the way coconuts trees look at sunset."

Aleski's first combination of sentences since they'd left Orlando. He sat there, his face looking as if he'd been beaten with a hammer, now suddenly the insightful romantic.

The images of furnaces and ghost men lingered. "Shut your stupid mouth. Concentrate on the job. I told you — this man, Ford, isn't some typical American amateur.

You can't even defend yourself from a woman. And you're wasting your time thinking about fruit trees?"

"Sorry, Dasha." Aleski sniffed, obviously irritated, but still not done with it. Finally, he asked, "Coconuts are fruit?"

"Oh God . . ."

"I didn't know that. But, if they are a fruit, why are they called 'nuts'?"

"Enough!"

"I'm tired of you speaking to me as if I'm stupid! Fruit is *soft* on the outside. Nuts are *hard*."

Dasha couldn't wait to park the car, get away from Aleski. Find a private room, take a long, sudsy shower. The stink of Mr. Earl seemed to cling — it had to be her imagination. But work came first.

The woman drove straight to Dinkin's Bay because that was the professional thing to do. Check out the place; fix landmarks in her mind.

The first of several disappointments that night.

Following the map, Dasha turned right onto Tarpon Bay Road. Narrow shell lane, mangroves. Rounded a slow curve . . . then braked to a stop when they were confronted unexpectedly by a man in the process of locking the marina gate.

"Sorry, folks! Friday nights, we always close at sunset. Unless you got an invitation."

A wide-bodied older man, white plantation hat, smoking a cigar.

Dasha had been so worried he'd get a close look at their faces, she had nearly skidded into the swamp in her rush to get away.

"It must be a very exclusive marina if customers are required to have invitations," Aleski said as tires spun, shells flying. "Have you ever been on such a wealthy island?"

Fool. "Shut up!"

Dasha didn't get her shower, or a hotel. On west Gulf Drive, they'd stopped at Tradewinds, then Island Inn. Both desk clerks said the same: It was December 17, a week before Christmas, and every room on the island was booked.

Fuming, the woman parked the rental a few blocks from Dinkin's Bay at a little shopping center — Bailey's General Store, Island Cinema. Then she and Aleski walked to the marina gate, as if they were a couple out for an evening stroll.

All she wanted to do was eyeball Marion Ford's home and lab; have a plan. Maybe get a look at the man himself. Decide if it was plausible to break in later, stick him with 10 ccs of Versed, and snatch him.

The Mossad profile was alluring in itself, but the photo had really hooked her.

A carnivore surprised in tall grass.

Yes. Exactly the same. But had the photo lied? Photos often did.

There was a secret place within her where she hoped the photo was accurate.

Now, though, there was loud music playing beyond the marina gate, people dancing on docks silhouetted by holiday lights. Big party going on.

Dasha and Aleski returned an hour later. Then three hours later. Then at midnight.

Music was still booming.

Impossible.

Finally, nearly 3:00 a.m., Sanibel traffic had thinned enough for them to attempt to wrestle their way through the mangrove swamp that bypassed the fence and gate. Mosquitoes screamed in their ears; muck sucked at their shoes. The bay stank of rotting eggs. Awful.

"Duck! Stay down."

Off to the right, there was an abrupt detonation of light. It transformed the mangrove leaves overhead from black to beige, erased stars. Blinding.

Dasha tensed as the light became a focused yellow conduit that panned along the mangrove fringe. It nearly found them once, swept away, but then returned quickly and found them again.

"Don't move."

The light came from a house previously unseen, a structure built on stilts over water. The bright conduit swept back and forth, the timing unpredictable. It went off for seconds, sometimes minutes, before the blazing column began to probe again.

A lone figure up there on the porch, wide-shouldered, who knew how a search was done.

The unpredictable rhythm kept the Russians pinned for more than half an hour while mosquitoes drank their blood in the sulfur stink, and dropping December chill.

Back in the car, Aleski said, "I feel like I'm going to be sick. My eye's infected, my ear's infected. I don't mind that rotten egg odor so much. But something in this car smells worse. What's that terrible perfume old women wear? *Lavender.*"

"Shut up! You *fool.* Shut your filthy mouth!"

Late the next morning, though, their luck changed. One of Dr. Stokes's stooges tipped off Mr. Earl.

It was Hartman, the stooge, vice president in charge of environmental oversight.

Dr. Marion Ford was on his way to Kissimmee. He had called for an appointment; was returning to ask questions about Frieda Matthews's death. It sounded like he planned to retrace the woman's steps, Hartman said, and he claimed he had Applebee's computer files.

"An interesting opportunity to introduce yourself to the man you were supposed to interview last night," Mr. Earl told her, his contempt undisguised. "If you can manage to get back in time."

At a little after 5:00 p.m., Saturday afternoon, when they were near Kissimmee, and only a few miles from the Bartram county line, Mr. Earl called again, his voice oddly formal. "Dr. Ford is on his way to the county hospital. I don't know for certain, but a friend of his may be the victim of an unusual parasitic fish."

"You're not serious. A candiru?" Dasha's vicious mood was instantly lightened. "Those fish were my idea. Wonderful! Did it actually climb into this man's —"

"Yes," Mr. Earl interrupted, "we're trying to shed light on the matter now."

He was in a room, people listening. Obvious.

Dasha thought he was joking about the

fish, working some kind of angle, until he added, "One of our employees insists it's true, and he doesn't find it humorous. He came to me and demanded that I notify law enforcement. I'm sitting here with him right now. Dr. Jason Reynolds, Department of Environmental Oversight. And a detective from the sheriff's department who just finished taking his statement."

Dasha could guess the cop's name: Jimmy Heller.

She was already driving faster, phone to her ear.

"Dr. Reynolds told Detective Heller some very disturbing things. About company employees taking part in a conspiracy to pollute the Everglades with exotic animals. Worms. Parasites? Snakes, too — but he's only guessing about snakes.

"We may have a terrible scandal on our hands if we don't take immediate steps. But Detective Heller and his department can only do so much." Long pause. "That's why we need our head of company security. The detective has agreed to turn the investigation over to our internal affairs department once you get here. Hopefully, that'll be very soon."

The woman understood. "You're at the ranch? Twenty minutes."

Mr. Earl said, "I'm so very glad you're taking this seriously. If what Dr. Reynolds says is true, he's going to need all our help and protection. Unfortunately, Dr. Reynolds has also confessed to taking part in the conspiracy, so we'll need to assign him one of our corporate attorneys."

Another message there: They had leverage on Reynolds if needed.

Located on the Tropicane acreage, several miles from the mansion, was a place known as the "Chicken Farm." A dozen employees lived there — "multiple executive housing" was the classification, because the company couldn't acknowledge that it was actually a commune. There was an organic garden, goats for milk, hens for eggs, a spring-fed pond where residents could swim naked, smoke dope, baptize themselves during sacred satanic rituals — Dasha didn't know or care.

More than a year ago, she'd done a "security/safety assessment" at Mr. Earl's insistence. It had to do with singling out problems that might cause Tropicane legal headaches down the road. She spent an afternoon at the Chicken Farm, the only time she visited the place.

She came back and said to Mr. Earl, "You

got a bunch of overeducated American brats playing dress-up games, every one of them a lawsuit waiting to happen. My advice? Pour gasoline around the doors, wait until they're stoned, then strike a match. Mass suicide — cult groups do that sometimes."

That won Mr. Earl's broadest grin. "I hear what you're telling me. *Fire* them. Woman, you don't need to tell me about spoiled white kids."

They both had a good laugh. The man could be funny on occasion.

Her advice didn't seem so extreme now, sitting alone in a locked room with Jason Reynolds, one of the overeducated American brats. *Doctor* Reynolds, he reminded her, when he got tired of playing his flaky, nice-guy role. Scraggly-haired with a goatee, wearing a silly tie-dyed T-shirt, sitting there with his scrawny arms telling her he was concerned for the environment, doing his humanitarian duty, that's all. And didn't appreciate being interrogated by a company security hack.

It was in his attitude. Dasha, with her accent, her spotty grammar, irritated him.

"I've already talked to the official fuzz. Why do I have to answer the same questions from you?"

He'd said that several times, several ways.

"Fuzz," he explained to her, rolling his eyes, was another word for "cop."

Dasha knew that. She'd asked just to piss the kid off. Giving him rope.

She'd given him plenty.

On the table between them was a little silver tape recorder. The same one she'd used when she'd try to get information out of Jobe Applebee.

"Remember how that one went," Mr. Earl reminded her before she took Reynolds into the room. "Come up with a secondary plan in case he won't cooperate."

She already had: In exchange for not prosecuting, she'd tell the kid he had an hour to collect his things, kiss his commune family good-bye, and they'd escort him off the property.

Actually, she'd stick him with the knockout drug, have Aleski load his body and belongings into a plane. Then dump everything halfway between the Florida Keys and Cuba from nine thousand feet.

"Very workable," Mr. Earl told her, adding that he'd decided to fly back in the DC-3 earlier than planned. He'd be waiting in the Bahamas, interested to see what she decided.

Washing his hands of the matter, in other words.

"No," Dasha told him. "We leave together. We're partners now. Am I correct? Besides, the DC-3's bigger. We may be taking two extra people back to the island. Ford and that idiot kid."

She put it out there experimentally, not expecting him to go along with it. But Mr. Earl did. Seemed almost meek.

Signing those orders, then fucking the old man — a very smart thing to do.

Now Mr. Earl was somewhere upstairs, stirring up a fresh pitcher of martinis, probably, while Dasha sat across the table from Jason Reynolds. She had the recorder, and also a notebook, but only pretended to write in it.

On the floor beside her was a canvas purse that contained four vials of Versed, a box of disposable hypodermics, duct tape, and a rolled-up copy of the *Tampa Tribune*.

She used her toe to nudge the bag closer as she listened to Jason Reynolds say, "How many times do I have to tell you this? Look, sister, *yes*, I released guinea larvae into water systems that connect to Disney. Several thousand catfish hatchlings, too. Candiru. But I never really believed the fish would attack a human being. It's just too far-out, man — scientifically speaking.

"Even so, I stand by my decision. It was the right thing to do. It's not ecoterrorism. We call it 'ecotage' — 'ecosalvage' — another term to describe a proactive way to help save a planet that's being gutted and poisoned."

In her flat cop's voice, Dasha said, "You were aware that you were breaking the law?"

The kid sighed. "Like a broken record, you keep asking the same shit."

"You were aware that it's a felony? A federal crime."

Bigger sigh. "Yes! Sister, do you have any idea how much destruction that damn theme park has caused this state? Any idea how many more housing units they'll build in the Everglades if the sugar companies sell their land to developers?"

Dasha was briefly interested. "How much money you think that land's worth? Millions?"

"Millions?" Reynolds snorted. "Construction conglomerates have already run the figures. *Billions.* That's why we . . . why people like me are taking action. Doing things like releasing parasites into the water system. Earth's natural guardians — what do you think mosquitoes are? Scare the hell out of potential buyers, make the land worthless as a commodity. But for a reason

— create a haven for wildlife."

Billions. Dasha felt her abdomen flutter. The kid seemed to know what he was talking about. She really *was* going to be rich.

"The activist group you mentioned, the Albedo Society, has a few hundred thousand members. How many of them have been doing this sort of crap —"

"Whoa, sister, I won't talk about anyone's involvement but my own. Nationwide, though? Good people, righteous organizations, are finally standing up, taking an activist approach." The kid had his martyr's speech down. He sounded like Mr. Sweet — only this kid actually believed.

"Putting worms in the water that eat through people's skin — you see that as a good thing."

"The parasites are a total gross-out, I agree. But they don't take lives. They don't cause any more misery than overdevelopment has caused our environment. That's why I went to Mr. Hartman — I've never said he's not just as guilty as I am, remember. Dig what I'm telling you? *I'm* the one who insisted on talking to police."

Dasha said, "More of your sabotage — to give Tropicane a bad name."

"No. Just like I told the detective: I don't

participate in activities that kill people. Someone murdered Dr. Matthews. Probably Dr. Applebee, too. Someone who works for Tropicane, I think. Secretly, I'd been wondering about it. There are a couple of dudes here on the Chicken Farm who're wrapped too tight. Wiccans, a Pagan — I have my own ideas, but that's all I'm going to say.

"Today, though, I saw proof that the woman was murdered. And I saw a very good man — a spiritual man — in terrible pain that I'm partially responsible for." The kid threw his hands up. "No more. I'm done with it. Inflicting pain is very negative karma."

He'd said that before, too.

The Russian looked at the desk clock: 6:20 p.m. Time to invite some negative karma of her own.

"A couple times, I've asked you to telephone the man you mentioned. Ford? Asked you to tell me details about him. Each time, you refuse to do me this small favor."

"Dr. Ford is a fairly well-known biologist — although I personally find his papers middle-of-the-road. He refuses to take an advocacy position in his work. You want me to lie to him — that's why I won't call. I don't kill, and I won't lie!" Reynolds's superior tone was infuriating.

"Not a lie. Tell the man to drive to the canal where you found the phone. Detective Heller says the police are still searching."

"No, they're not, and you know it. I *got* the phone; gave it to Heller myself. I panicked, thinking I might be implicated in Dr. Matthews's murder. That's why I went back and fished the thing out. The cops have no reason to keep searching."

"Maybe they're trying to find something else."

"Bullshit."

Dasha had the rolled-up newspaper in her hand. She didn't think she'd have any trouble beating this little idiot into submission, but Aleski was outside the door just in case. Unless he'd snuck off to drink vodka with Mr. Earl. He'd been doing that more and more lately.

She stood; walked around the desk toward Reynolds. "Take your clothes off."

"What?"

"You heard me. Strip down. Pants first, then your shirt." She had no interest in Reynolds, but making a prisoner strip was the first procedural step in a hostile interrogation. The beginning of the dehumanization process.

"Screw you, lady! I'm walking out of here. I'm calling an attorney." Reynolds was standing, chin out — *You can't intimidate me* — didn't flinch when she drew her arm back because he didn't believe she'd hit him.

She did. Hit him with the newspaper across the face so hard that he dropped to the floor, butt-first.

"You asshole! That hurt!"

On his cheek, a feverish red welt was beginning to swell. His lips were trembling. Jason Reynolds had never been hit in the face before. It was obvious.

"I want you to make a telephone call. I want you to tell Dr. Ford to get in his car and drive to the canal."

Reynolds was still touching his face. "Don't hit me again, Okay. Please? I'm not into the violence scene."

"I *am* into the violence scene."

"Please . . . please don't."

Dasha thought, *This won't take long.*

It didn't.

A little more than an hour later, Dasha got her first look at Ford. He'd surprised her, jogging out of the shadows from the front of the Bartram County Hospital, not from the ER entrance, which was closer to the weird-looking Volkswagen camper that

Reynolds had pointed out and said belonged to Ford's friend.

Reynolds — the kid had started bawling, he was so happy, when Dasha told him she didn't need his help anymore. Time for him to go back to the ranch, gather his belongings, tell his doper pals good-bye. Leave Tropicane property and never come back.

He'd just finished making the phone call to Ford. Was in the back of a company van, Broz at the wheel.

"Go with this man, do what he tells you to do, and we won't prosecute."

"I will. I promise I will! I don't want to cause the company any more problems."

Dasha had nodded her head at Broz. He'd nodded in return. Broz wasn't bright, but at least he knew what the woman was telling him to do.

"You'll never see me, or hear from me, again — I swear."

Dasha said, "That's something I would bet on," and slid the van's door closed.

A short time later, Aleski was crouched in the back of the Volkswagen, Dasha was in the Pontiac rental only two spaces down from the VW. Jimmy Heller was in his unmarked squad car, assigned to pull in tight behind the van.

Bait, trap, and blocker ready.

"I pull behind the camper, you got sixty seconds, no more, then I'm outta here. It'd better be clean — no noise, no blood — or I'm gone before that."

A New York hustler with a badge. Dasha was ducked down in the Pontiac, thinking how much fun it would be to work on Heller with a rolled-up newspaper. That's when Ford suddenly appeared in the rearview mirror. Surprising as hell.

The woman became a statue, waiting. She felt his shadow cross the window.

Had he seen her?

No . . . the man continued running at an easy pace through the parking lot, then out onto the street again.

He's scouting the perimeter. Suspicious.

Finally seeing the man in person, arms swinging, calves flexing, Dasha felt an abdominal rush. He was bigger than expected. A nerd with muscles. An operator born with the perfect disguise.

A few minutes later, when Ford appeared again, Dasha was ready. She had her head down, watching him in the mirror, one hand on the door handle, the other on the button that opened the trunk. Watched him slow to a walk, approaching the camper cautiously, head swiveling. Watched the man touch his fingers to the van, testing for movement.

A pro. Competent.

Watched him freeze as he opened the driver's door, instantly aware something was wrong . . . then Dasha had her feet on the pavement, running, the sound of the unmarked car's engine roaring, its headlights panning across the VW, everything happening at once as the trap slammed closed.

In the microsecond before Aleski grabbed the biologist from behind, Dasha saw Ford's face clearly, his expression fierce. There it was, the intensity she'd hoped would be there.

A carnivore surprised in tall grass. Like that.

The photo hadn't lied.

With Ford unconscious in the trunk, the pleasure she felt changed incrementally to anxiety as she drove from the parking lot, Aleski beside her, the hairy man breathing heavily, damaged ear bleeding again.

"Big sonuvabitch. First time I saw him run by, I knew. Strong as a horse. Didn't think he'd ever go out."

Dasha tensed. "But you only gave him ten ccs of Versed, correct? Like I told you: no more than that."

"Yeah, I'm pretty sure. Maybe just a drop or two extra. First time he ran by, I knew he'd be a tough one."

Shit. Aleski was lying. "You idiot! How much was in the needle?"

The woman accelerated through the shadowed neighborhood, turned right into an alley behind what looked to be a warehouse, green garbage Dumpsters in the shadows. She had already switched off the lights and punched the trunk open before she braked to a stop, threw her door open.

Marion D. Ford lay on his back, knees and shoulders wedged grotesquely, blood coagulating on his windpipe, skin waxen as his body cooled, both eyes wide beneath crooked glasses, two blue voids reflecting light.

The man wasn't breathing.

"Idiot, you gave him too much. He's in respiratory arrest!"

Aleski snapped, "Kill him now, kill him later, what's the fucking difference?" The insubordination was out of character, but Dasha didn't stop to deal with it.

The woman's medical training took over. She touched Ford's neck, then wrist, checking for a pulse: None. Tilted the big man's head back as she used her fingers to open his mouth, feeling chin stubble, the chill of his skin, as she checked for a clear airway.

Heard the soft percussion of a last warm

breath leaving the man's body.

A death rattle. Dasha had heard the sound enough to know.

He's gone.

She yelled, "If you've hurt him, I'll kill you. *Idiot!,*" as she gave Marion Ford five pounding chest compressions.

Dasha then leaned into the trunk, touched her lips to Ford's, and blew air into his lungs, thinking that they had to get him to the plane.

There was oxygen, a full medical kit, on the DC-3 . . .

31

At 8:37 p.m. Tomlinson surprised Dr. Mary Ann Shepherd, her assistant, a nurse anesthetist, and three physician observers by sitting up abruptly during his surgery, saying, "Marion Ford's dead. My friend just died. I need a quick psychic patch, a chemical booster rocket. There's not a second to waste."

When no one reacted, he clapped his hands together twice. "This is *serious*. Work with me, people!"

His voice was energized with dread, he would say later. The nightmare variety.

The physician's assistant tried to pull Tomlinson back onto the table, as the anesthetist looked at Dr. Shepherd, his expression saying, Don't blame me.

"The patient requested sevoflurane gas. I wanted to do a spinal, but he insisted on sevoflurane. I've pumped nearly a liter into him, plus a full dose of Diprivan. That combination would put a normal person down until noon tomorrow. Hey — !" The anesthetist turned to Tomlinson, who'd yanked out his Diprivan IV. He was now sitting naked on the table, reaching for the yellow canister of liquid anesthetic labeled: $C_2HBrClF_3$. "— Get your hands off that. Leave it alone!"

Tomlinson had the gas mask and was fitting it over his nose and mouth. "Only a liter? I don't mean to be critical, but a liter of sevoflurane is barely recreational. Two liters? Happy hour at Cypress House, Key West, is a better buzz. But urethral surgery? Jesus Christ, next time just gag me with rum, and give me a bullet to bite."

He'd shrugged off the assistant, then the nurse, and was inhaling deeply through the mask as his bony fingers opened the valve wide. Voice muffled, he said something indistinguishable.

Dr. Shepherd said, "What?," thinking she should humor him until . . . what? Call security? Give him a chance to anesthetize himself, sucking on that gas? "I didn't understand what you said."

Tomlinson removed the mask. She was surprised to see that his eyes weren't crazed, as she expected. He was frightened, urgent, but focused.

Does sevoflurane cause violent hallucinations? — the doctor was scanning among rational explanations for why this was happening. She was also picturing the man's face — Marion Ford — interested because he'd had an unusual physical presence. Attractive in an unconventional way. She'd even pulled the schoolgirl stunt of pumping his son for information. Unheard of.

The woman felt a chill when Tomlinson said it again, "My friend died. Just a few seconds ago. *Shit.*" He took several more deep whiffs of gas, inhaling rhythmically — he might have been smoking a joint — the entire medical team standing and watching, immobilized by the bizarre circumstances, and the man's self-assurance.

It was impossible, but he seemed to know exactly what he was doing.

"Personally, I'm not ready for a world without Doc Ford. There's already too much chaos and darkness." Tomlinson held the mask to his face, filled his lungs, then inhaled again. "Fortunately, I'm in the business of seeking light. I still have some pull in high places. A rendezvous — it's worth a shot. Dr. Shepherd?"

The physician had settled into humor-him mode. "Give us the gas mask, Mr.

Tomlinson. Then lay down on the table. As a personal favor, okay?"

Deep breath. "Are you done with the surgery?"

"Just finishing up."

"Did the fish make it?" Deeper breath.

"I had to remove the parasite in sections. I'll let you have a look — if you cooperate."

"Damn, I was hoping to put it in an aquarium, watch it grow. Every year, my story would get better." A huge gulp, chest inflating.

"Sorry. Mr. Tomlinson, please — no more gas."

Three deep breaths in succession. "Put the pieces in a freezer. I live aboard a boat at a marina. I'll either have it mounted, or give it to the guides for bait."

As the anesthesiologist took a step toward him, saying, "You're going to kill yourself if you take much more —" Tomlinson held up a warning palm. "That's what I was about to tell you. For the next two or three minutes, ignore the heart monitor, the blood pressure gauge. Do not — repeat, *do not* — overreact and try anything crazy like open-chest heart massage. I have enough scars. Autopsy? Put the nix on that one, too. The electric paddles — save those for later. A little R and R, sure, good for a few yuks when we have some time. Otherwise, ignore all life support monitors."

Dr. Shepherd was exchanging looks with the three other physicians.

Sure we will.

"Anything you want, Mr. Tomlinson. Lay back, give us the mask. *Please.*"

The room relaxed when the man settled himself on the table, hands folded over his abdomen, eyes closed, face showing a soft, sad smile as his lips moved, whispering something over and over. Garbled syllables that sounded like *"Omni Padi Hum-m-m-m,"* but then changed to something else.

Words formed but unheard, repeated as a mantra:

Come back, Doc.
Come back, Doc.
Come back, Doc.

. . . I fell toward the car's open trunk, and into a dream. I was in a vast black sleep, afloat in a chilled and enormous space. A gathering of molecules, of watery salt, a loose cohesion of cells, my nucleus dissipating . . .

Fragments of thoughts flared briefly, sparks of electrical discharge.

Wind. Rock. Black morning sea.

Physics: sun-heavy liquid, gas constrained by stars, gravity below, nothing between. A man's voice booming from waves: "Come back, Doc . . . Come back . . . Come back . . ."

Driftwood fire. A mangrove shore.

Smoke, lichens, scent of an autumn-shaded voice, a woman.

"I knew we'd arrive again on the same small island. My dear love. *Finally,* you are coming back to me . . ."

Black waves booming: "Come back, Doc. Come back. Doc, come back, Doc . . ."

Moon-haired girl, my beloved in a golden locket. Lighted portions of chin and cheek, strong nose creating shadow, perceptive heart indifferent to her own beauty. Small precise breasts, eyes not scarred by uncertainty.

The face of Dewey Nye appeared . . . faded.

Was not the face of my girl.

Heard Dewey's long-ago voice saying, "It took me forever to admit but I'm in love with a woman. Always have been; always will . . ."

Dewey, with her deer stride, aside a dark-haired Romanian, their backs to me, walking among spring corn, tassel-haired child between.

Tropic rain. Banana leaves fauceting water.

Village fire, a dog's howls sparking starward.

Faces of men transected by a rifle's cross-hairs. Faces of men vaporized, a misting of red. Buoyancy of midnight water; words of a valued friend: "The only safe haven for guys like us, the only home we'll ever know, is in the dead of night."

Pencil on rice paper: *In any conflict, the boundaries of behavior are defined by the party that values morality least . . .*

Heredity. Blood. Tribe.

. . . All primate units struggle for ascendance, the weaknesses of many sheltered by the strength of a few . . .

Rolling waves. Black water, white-cresting: ". . . coming back to me. Come back . . . Come back . . . Doc, come back to me . . ."

I felt the urge to linger, to take the soft hand extended, to float away with dissipating molecules and vanish into delicious nonexistence.

Then I was aware of a woman's touch. Warm lips on a numb vacancy. Warm wind funneling into a sealed space.

My lungs inflating, deflating.

BOOM-BOOM-BOOM. Pounding on a door, someone demanding entrance through my chest.

A kiss: Inflate . . . deflate.

Another: Inflate . . . . deflate.

The woman's warm breath becoming cold, fueling slow light in a dark place. Dying embers flared by a breeze.

Male voice. A guttural raging. Then a woman.

"Idiot, speak English. You know my rules when Mr. Earl's around."

"I said this guy, he's so goddamn heavy, Broz should be here to help."

"To hell with Broz, we're leaving without him."

"Even if the man's breathing, his brain's dead by now. Why bother? And I'm getting *very* tired of your orders!"

"Get him in the *plane*. Behind the cargo curtain. And don't drop the oxygen cylinder, you idiot!"

Sound of a woman walking away. Silence. Footfall of a man approaching. Stink of lavender, a burning cigarette.

"Stay cool, Aleski. Keep it together until we get to the islands. They're expecting us. I just got off the phone."

"She makes me so mad. I hate her."

"Just be cool. We've got business to discuss, you and me. I suddenly don't like that bitch as much as I thought."

"She treats this guy like treasure, but treats me like shit — and he almost killed us one night with a boat."

I felt a withering spinal compression, simultaneously a hollow melon thud.

"Don't kick him. If you want, give him another shot before she comes back — that way, no surprises during the flight. If he tells us something useful, afterward, you can do whatever you want."

Bee-sting burning in my arm.

"I'd like that. And what about Dasha? Can I . . . ?"

"Whatever you want. You're the new head of security. You make the rules."

"Me? *Really?*"

"Really. I just got real bad news about Dr. Stokes. The medic says our boss has a problem. Parasites. We probably all do. Me, I'm such a genius. I put the bitch in charge of our water supply."

Engines synching, torque of propellers, a robotic turn. G-force stomach of Earth falling away.

Vibration. Cargo plane hydraulics. Familiar.

Thermal pockets in darkness; straining for altitude . . . then a deeper, cozier darkness. Air becoming sea. I was on my pretty new surfboard, slow lifting waves, riding deeper, deeper into a drug-gauzy sleep.

Dreaming again . . .

Warm air flooding a sealed space. Inflate, deflate, chest rising.

A kiss: Inhale. Exhale.

Another: Inhale. Exhale.

A woman's eyes, shampoo scent of hair, whispered words above propeller rumble.

"Nice, your lips. I found a photo of you. I've wanted to try this."

A kiss. Another. Inhale, exhale. Inhale, exhale.

"Do you like? There was a fairy tale when I was a girl. Awakening a prince with a kiss. You're probably the closest I'll ever come. You almost killed me — *you bad, bad boy.*"

Lips joined, two bodies breathing. Touch of fingertips on chest, unbuttoning, moving downward, skin touching skin, fingers spreading, flexing. Cat paws searching.

"This isn't right . . . the drug shouldn't . . . unless that idiot gave you another shot. Can you hear me? I straightened your glasses. Open your eyes. Try. I'm here."

Fuzzy image of a woman's face, short blond hair, Slavic cheeks, sharp chin. Attractive, in a feral way. Familiar . . . a memory just beyond reach.

"Doctor Ford. *Marion.* Wake up. We don't have much time."

Kissing again, breathing as one, the

woman suddenly naked, pushing her pear-curved breasts to my lips, hips seeking. The sound of a zipper, fingers slowing, touching experimentally as they find me. Tracing, lifting, positioning.

"Hello, my *yieldak*. *Yes.* Keep me company while your large friend sleeps."

Pleasure dream; unreality becoming reality . . .

"I have something here. You might feel a little sting. Nothing serious. It's not dangerous."

Blurry image of the naked woman standing over me, something in her hand, legs wide as she squatted. "For now, though, you're doing just what Dasha needs you to do . . ."

32

I awoke in a yellow shard of sunlight, eyes squinting, head pounding, groaning in pain. My chest and throat felt as if I'd swallowed glass. For a confused few seconds, I thought I had the all-time worst hangover. A taste in my mouth. Metallic, disgusting.

Then a jumble of dreams came tumbling back. My sluggish brain struggled to separate what was real, what wasn't.

Hospital parking lot, Tomlinson hurt. Big hands grabbing me from behind, a stabbing stiletto pain. The irksome realization that I'd stepped into a trap, that the fatal error was mine, no one else to blame.

The only friend you don't take care of is yourself — the only friend I think you're capable of hurting.

Tomlinson's warning words.

I touched my neck. Swollen, crusted with blood.

There was the memory of drowning

panic, of suffocating, a chemical dispersal — dying.

Bad judgment — a variety of suicide?

Then . . . what? I was on a plane.

Yes.

Flown where?

I tried to roll to my feet; collapsed. Had to lean against the wall to keep from falling, I was so dizzy. I was in a small room made of coral rock, morning sunlight streaming through the only window. Bars on the window. Two metal doors. Box-sized cages stacked floor to ceiling, a scamper-tittering from within. Stink of urine and dust.

My eyes were open but not focusing. I realized my glasses were tied around my neck with fishing line, as usual. Fitted them over my ears. One lens was shattered, yet the world sharpened. I saw that cages were filled with rats, white mice, grain and turds scattered across the floor.

There was a spiderweb in the corner, a skeleton of a bird suspended within above a sprinkling of feathers.

I checked myself — saw that I was naked. Filthy. Grass and sand in coated chest hair; arms bruised, backs of my heels raw.

I'd been dragged.

I stumbled to the window, looked out.

A rain forest mountainside. Silver beach,

turquoise bay. Scent of frangipani and diesel. Low cliffs on the opposite shore, roofs of buildings showing red tile through foliage. A narrow cut, quarter mile wide, where current boiled in gelatinous whirlpools, waves breaking outside the reef.

Beyond, water darkened where it deepened. A crowded boat was outward bound: stacks of furniture, strawhats and bright umbrellas, brown faces suspended above the deep.

People fleeing.

I was in the tropics, possibly the Caribbean. An island. In a room made of rock slabs with bars — something from pirate days.

There were sheds nearby, tin, rock, and wood. A portion of open field that might have been part of a landing strip, a small harbor where a barge was also churning water, struggling against heavy current, its high bow pointed seaward. There was something hidden beneath camouflaged netting on the vessel's cargo deck.

I saw four distinct rotors. Wedges of red metal above aircraft tires.

Helicopters . . . ?

Four helicopters, drone-sized, incongruous in this Third World setting. One man in the elevated wheelhouse, two deckhands coiling lines astern.

Who? *Why?*

The vessel was headed north, morning sun to starboard.

"I've been waiting for you to wake up."

I jumped, surprised by a woman's voice behind me.

"You're in the Bahamas, only thirty miles from Cuba. We've got to get out of here. They're coming to kill us both."

I turned to see a long-legged blond woman curled in the corner. She was dressed in a khaki-colored blouse and shorts, pressed and pleated. A uniform. It looked as if she'd been dozing. It had to be uncomfortable with her hands tied behind her back, ankles bound with duct tape.

Not tied — handcuffed. I saw the cuffs when she rolled to her side, tried to stretch.

"Even if you tell them everything, they're going to kill you. They'll *make* you tell them. No matter how tough you think you are. Soon as they find out you're alive, they'll go to work. We've got to move now."

Russian accent, a face linked to a specific memory. A dream? Possibly. But also something real. It took a moment.

The woman who was torturing Jobe Applebee.

I tried to speak. Gagged with pain. Tried again. Coughed and grabbed my neck.

"An animal named Aleski stabbed you in the throat with a needle. He drugged you, but I saved your life. Did CPR for an hour. Hurry — get this tape off my ankles."

CPR? I'd had a strange, unsettling dream. *Mouth-to-mouth. Erotic images* . . . Could that explain it?

"You helped me?"

"Only because there's a chance you can help me. Now I'm glad I did."

"Where . . . are . . . ?"

"Your clothes are in the corner. What they left you. Over there."

Canvas shorts, that was all — shirt, shoes, wallet, cell phone, and keys missing. I pulled them on. Turned my back before zipping, a pointless modesty.

"I managed to hide your shoes. Under that crate. They didn't want you to have shoes."

My running shoes. I knelt to tie them as my tongue found moisture. Swallowed, swallowed again, words beginning to form. Started to speak, but was interrupted by a strange, distant wailing. The sound had a primal resonance, a shriek of terror, the scream of nightmares.

Perhaps a monkey suffering out there in

the rain forest, dying. A primate being devoured.

A question exited my mouth as a constricted whisper. "What is *that?*"

The woman had begun to crawl toward me, inching over tile like a caterpillar. "A crazy man named Dr. Stokes. He's infected with a parasite. African worms. Every man on the island will have parasites, but Stokes has a phobia. The fear, I guess, it's driven him crazy. Last night, I was trying to help him when his brain finally snapped. Nothing I could do. They locked him in a room, hoping he'll —"

She stopped. That terrible sound again: a falsetto howl rising, then falling, a werewolf's scream. I turned my head slightly, attempting to decipher something human at its source. An anguish of torn vocal cords, a creature dangling above flames. Torment.

In South America, there's a giant cockroach that screams when thrown into a fire. Similar.

No. Not human.

The woman finished, "They locked him in a room, hoping Stokes will kill himself. The way Bahamian law's set up, a person who commits suicide abandons all possessions. Laws of marine salvage — a ship that hits a reef. It's like that. Strangers can take what they want."

"*Who* locked him in a room?"

"Men who are stealing what he has." Her impatient tone asked, *Who else?* She used her chin to indicate what lay beyond the window. "They want these islands, housing. His money, everything. Not all rats are caged here. Everyone's running except the men coming to kill us."

The woman continued to crawl toward me. I realized I was backing away. I'd once seen a different expression on her face: the pleasure of inflicting pain.

"Why are you handcuffed?"

"Because of them. Stokes and his partners."

"Desmond Stokes? The environmentalist."

"Him?" The woman's chuckle had an acid edge. "Stokes is an environmentalist the same way a pedophile is a priest. I worked for him. I found out he's been breaking laws, smuggling. That's *why* they locked me here. They figured out a way to spread the parasites by air and get rich — I can explain later. Hurry! Get this tape off my legs —" She stopped abruptly; strained to listen. "A boat. Was that a boat? *Shit.* They're coming!"

Her eyes scanned the cages, rats watching us from inside. "Maybe it's feeding time."

I asked, "For what?," preoccupied. Returned to the window, listening to her say, "Snakes, monkeys. Research animals, but also garbage they've been smuggling into the States."

I saw that the barge carrying the drone helicopters was now moving away at speed, plowing a white wake.

Drones that were used to spray pesticides?

"They figured out a way to spread the parasites by air . . ."

I turned from the window, looked at the woman, then stared out again.

"What do they want from me?"

"They think you know Dr. Applebee's formula for destroying the parasites."

"Formula? There's no formula . . ." I was looking at the barge.

Drone crop dusters. Waterborne parasites. The connection was immediate. So was my self-recrimination.

You should have anticipated this, Ford. Another screwup.

I watched a huge man stumble off a boat. He was several hundred yards away, where the cut narrowed. The man helped the struggling pilot push the boat away again — it was too dangerous to leave it grounded among rocks. The heavy tide spun the vessel like a leaf, pushed it seaward, until the outboard's propeller gained purchase.

I recognized him: Ox-man, from Night's Landing. The black hair and muscle, workman's rough clothes — probably the guy shooting at me the night of the boat chase, firing as the woman drove.

The man was carrying a gun in the crook of his arm, walking toward me. At first glance, the weapon looked to be a Kalashnikov, the classic AK-47 automatic rifle, judging from the folding wire stock, the scimitar shape of the magazine. Then I wasn't so sure: the magazine looked too boxy, its barrel too short. Difficult to tell from that distance. Whatever the weapon was, the man was comfortable with it, no rush. He'd had some training.

The woman was now near my feet. Recognizing the two Russians catalyzed a rush of images: the bulging eyes of a man hanging in a closet. The eyes of a friend, Frieda Matthews, widening as a speeding car bore down.

"Who is in the boat? Can you see? Is it a big man who has hair like a bear?"

My voice was hoarse, but stronger. "Your partner, you mean? Yes."

She touched her face to my ankle, a pathetic gesture. "Dear God, you've got to help me. You don't know what Aleski does to women. *Please* don't make me go through that. He rapes them, tortures them. I've seen him with women —"

Something stopped her. Maybe the expression on my face.

I moved my leg out of her reach. "Is that what he did to Dr. Matthews?"

"*Yes.*"

"You helped him."

She hesitated, her eyes not just looking at me, but also accessing. She showed no fear until I leaned, grabbed her blouse in both hands. I lifted the woman off the ground, as she said quickly, "Yes. I *helped.* I'm not going to lie. It was my job, but I didn't want to hurt the woman. I had . . . feelings. I wanted it painless. But not him. That's not Aleski's way."

I held her there, face so close to mine that I felt the warmth of her breath, as she added, "I tried to help your friend. Just like I helped you. Marion Ford — I know who you are. I was with Russian Intelligence, the *Federalnaya. Listen* to me. Weren't you ever ordered to do something you didn't want to do?"

My conscience translated her question accurately: Haven't you killed a person you didn't want to kill?

A woman with pale, iceberg eyes. She wasn't afraid now. Not of me. The man coming for us, yes. She feared him. But she'd evaluated me efficiently, used the knowledge like a weapon. She was trying to force a bond between us. Her expression wasn't easily read, but there was a hint of triumph. Inexplicably, there was also disappointment. *I've got you.*

Or so she thought.

I lifted her higher, so that her face was above mine. "You killed Frieda. Who'd you get to kill Applebee?"

"No one! I was surprised when I heard. He . . . he was a strange man. I think he fell a little in love, but knew I'd never go with him. He blamed the men here, what they were doing."

"Your smuggling operation."

"Yes."

"How many people are involved?"

"Many! All over the states. At Tropicane Sugar, several. But only three behind it all: Dr. Stokes, Aleski, and a man named Luther Earl — he looks like a black Abraham Lincoln. They supply exotics to environmental idiots, anyone who'll buy. The big plans, though — real biological sabotage — it's just them. *And they're all still here.*"

When I didn't respond, her glistening eyes narrowed. "Kill them if you want. I'll help!"

Her tone said, Don't miss this opportunity.

I lowered the woman to the ground, then let her drop. She managed to stay on her feet for a few seconds — a good athlete even with ankles taped. She did several quick ballerina steps on tiptoes before falling hard on tile.

Her expression changed: surprise, a flash of anger. Her inexplicable disappointment had vanished.

"Is everyone on the island armed?" I was watching Ox-man. Listened to her correct me: two islands, not one, a treacherous cut between. The man was a hundred yards away, head scanning. He appeared nervous now, holding his weapon at combat ready.

"I kept all the guns locked in a safe, but then I stupidly gave Luther Earl permission" — she choked up, emotional — "I stupidly lost *control*. They're armed. I'm sure they are. But Mr. Earl and Aleski, they're the only ones you have to worry about. Maybe one other. Aleski's cousin, Broz."

I stepped to the door that opened toward the bay. *Locked.* Hurried toward the opposite door.

"Don't open that!"

I froze with my hand on the door's handle.

"That opens into a pit where they dug coral. It's where we keep the snakes, the monkeys. I mentioned feeding time? Last night, when the place started going crazy, some idiot opened all the cages. That's why the staff's running away. You'd have to be insane to go out there without a weapon."

Her voice began to crack again — panic. "*Please*, help me get my legs free. Don't leave me alone with Aleski. We can overpower him, then take his boat. No one can get across to the other island without a boat because of the current —"

She stopped talking as I turned the handle and began to open the door slowly. "Lady, I'll take my chances with the snakes."

"Why? I *helped* you."

"Because you're right — I'm a pro. I think you're a bad actress with an angle. I think you taped your own legs. And if I'm wrong —"

I pushed the door wider, looked out: a rock pit that was gymnasium-sized, mossy coral walls, panes of shattered Plexiglas, retainer screening above ripped away.

"— Lady, if I'm wrong, I hope you have better luck than Frieda. Or Jobe Applebee."

I took a moment to confirm that the door's lock was not the sort that latched automatically. Then stepped into the pit.

33

The quarry floor was coral chips and ferns. Banana thickets and birds-of-paradise created scattered domes of shade. Otherwise, it was a rock crater with walls fifteen to twenty feet high, open to the sky now that the overhead screen had been torn away.

The walls were vertical. There were calcium remains of limpets, brain corals, sea fans, vertebrates — evolution etched in limestone. They'd mined the stuff in blocks, so the walls were scarred with ridges where seeds of ficus and fern had rooted. There were cascading vines with umbrella-sized leaves.

Along the wall to my left were shelves of wooden cages of varying size, some as big as small rooms. Each had a door or lid, usually Plexiglas. Most of the doors were open.

Nearby was an enclosed cement circle, and a laboratory table, not unlike the table in my lab. Beneath a roof of corrugated plastic was an industrial-grade incubator, heating tubes suspended above.

This was a place to hatch crawling creatures. A safe place to extract venom.

A serpentarium.

There were also larger enclosures made of wood and wire mesh. Tire swings hanging from chains; rotting banana peels on rock floor.

Monkeys. They'd been freed, too.

The woman hadn't lied, as I'd suspected. I'd ignored her warning, and now I'd have to deal with it. It gave me a sick feeling in my stomach.

The incubator was operational. A light was blinking near a row of gauges. I got close enough to see that, beneath the incubator's opaque cover, were hundreds of eggs in open cartons.

Some reptiles are protective of their nest. They use their tongues to wind-track eggs if they've been moved. This was not a place to linger.

I walked to my right. Vines grew sunward on pitted rock. They looked strong enough to hold a man's weight, and there were crevices for feet and fingers. I had to find a way out of the quarry, or soon face Ox-man, the Russian. Him and his rifle. Maybe him, his rifle, and the woman, too.

Or worse.

I reached, grabbed a vine, feeling its triangular edges, and began to pull myself up the wall, hand over hand. Got a few feet off the ground when the vine snapped. I landed butt-hard on gravel, dust and leaves raining down.

Got to my feet, all senses firing. Stepped toward a neighboring vine. I was reaching to get a grip when I noticed a shadow moving through the high foliage. Stood for a moment, then backed away.

Something alive was up there. It appeared as a descending darkness, thick as a man's wrist, augering downward at a speed that created a barber-pole illusion. A wall of elephant's ear leaves, from quarry lip to floor, rustled incrementally, synchronized with the shadow's slow uncoiling. The expanse of trembling leaves suggested the shadow's size. Twice as long as I am tall. Longer.

In a pool of sunlight, I got a glimpse: green scales flexing as muscle undulated. A single black eye in a head the size of my fist.

I became a statue, temples thumping.

Ahead and to my left, there was unrelated activity. A second shadow, rustling. Ferns in the area were knee-high. I watched ferns parting in a pattern of serpentine switchbacks as something vectored toward me, ground level.

For an instant, an image of the woman came to mind. Crawling after me over tile.

I began retreating, eyes shifting from vines to moving ferns, until I reached the metal door. Searched blindly. Finally touched its handle. Tested. Felt the door begin to open. Second option, confirmed.

My choices: snakes at feeding time, Russian with a gun.

I'd shifted into crisis mode; began projecting, then rejecting, a rapid list of alternatives. My eyes drifted to the incubator. Paused. Remembered the words of an African friend: "They get aggressive. Deadly mean, if you're near their nest."

I touched the door again. Not much of an escape route. But all I had.

I hurried passed the cages to the incubator. Opened the lid . . . then froze.

Shit.

A few paces away, a cobra sprouted from the ferns, skull ribs flattening its head like a mummy's cowling, black eyes lasering. It leaned toward me, unhinged its mouth wide, and exhaled. There was a stink of rodents. *Hiss* does not describe the sound.

The snake's swaying head was chest-high. Ten or twelve feet of reptile. A king cobra.

It was aware of me; unimpressed.

In the banana thickets, other reptiles were

stirring. On the quarry's far wall, I noticed snakes exiting crevices. Beyond the swaying cobra, ferns had become animated.

My body remained motionless as my hand moved. It reached without looking and found a carton of eggs. Felt to make certain the carton was full, took it. I began to back away, slowly at first, then turned to run . . . but stopped. Froze once again.

To my right, shadow had touched earth. A hatchet-sized head lifted off gravel, tongue-testing the molecular content of air, a yard of its lichen-colored body visible. It was an African mamba, the genetic model of ascendency. I looked up. Saw its tail twitching twelve feet above among vines on the quarry wall.

The snake's head turreted in slow assessment. Swept past me. Paused. Turreted back. Paused once again, tongue probing for specifics. Head lifted another few inches, dusty eyes vague above zombie-stitched lips.

A mammalian heart was beating.

Mine.

Behind me, near the top of the quarry, I heard a sudden thrashing among leaves; heard the gunshot crack of a tree limb breaking, then a shriek. I looked up in time to see a dark shape falling toward me. I thought it was a man, at first, because of the flailing arms.

The Russian?

I jumped and ducked, covering my head. Jumped again when it landed face-first a few yards away. The sound of a primate's body impacting on earth is distinctive. A cavity containing lungs is percussive.

A gorilla?

The animal was the size of a teenager, big-shouldered, covered with hair. It groaned, stirred. Struggled to get to its knees. Collapsed and rolled, eyes open. It had a black elongated face, and golden, human eyes.

A chimpanzee.

Its left arm, I noted, was grotesquely swollen. I looked up and saw a gray snake in the tree canopy. A black mamba. Not large.

The chimp groaned once again, head turning as glazed eyes found me. Seemed to focus in recognition — a great sadness to be shared. Lifted its right arm, muscles beginning to spasm, and reached its hand out to me, index finger pointing.

I've never felt such a combination of shock and fear. Unconsciously, I leaned toward the chimp, hand extended. Our fingers touched for a moment. Its skin was leathery, warm as my own. The hand fell as the chimpanzee shuddered, grunted, made a rattling sound of exhaustion. I watched its eyes dim, then close.

Dead.

I forced myself to step away, aware that a few more seconds of inattention could be fatal.

The cobra had disappeared among ferns. Where?

The head of the giant mamba was still visible. The rest of its body had arrived at ground level. The snake was moving in my direction.

I pivoted, sprinted, lunged into the doorway.

The woman was sitting, watching as I hurried to the window. She didn't seem surprised that I'd returned.

Ox-man was life-sized now; he would be opening the door within the next minute. He still held the weapon at combat ready — not an AK-47 but similar. The man was spooked; I could see that, too.

Someone had let the animals out. He was aware.

The woman kept her voice low. "Take the tape off my ankles and we'll overpower him. Together."

I'd put the carton of eggs on the floor, was leaning over her. I began to rip away duct tape. Her lean calves were fuzzed with hair; thighs muscled. She didn't flinch.

When the tape was gone, the woman flexed her legs; stretched. "Help me up."

I shook my head. "Roll on your side and step through those handcuffs."

"*What?*" As if she had no idea what I meant.

"Drop the act, lady. I don't think you want to go out there with your hands behind your back." I was pushing her legs into a fetal position, trying to position the cuffs. "You never jumped rope? Same concept, only the rope's shorter."

She contracted into a ball and extended her arms. I helped her work one foot through, then the other. Lifted her by the elbow and she came to her feet, hands cuffed in front now. Tall woman, dark tan, body of an athlete.

"My name's Dasha. Not 'lady.' "

I said, "Then you'll understand why I don't shake hands," as I took her by the shoulders and spun her body away.

"*Idiot.* What are you doing? Aleski will kill —"

I clamped my hand over her mouth, pulled her close. Held her in a bear hug until she stopped struggling. Took my hand away, and said into her ear. "I think you and your partner are setting me up. I'll find out soon enough."

She turned, pale eyes searching for something. "No. I swear it. You can trust me."

I'd saved a section of tape. Turned her again, saying, "No, I can't," as I pressed the tape over her mouth and did a quick wrap. Put my lips close to her ear again. "If you don't do what I tell you, we're *all* going to die."

Outside, there was the scuff of footsteps on gravel.

I picked up the carton of reptile eggs and steered the woman toward the quarry door. Took a deep breath, then stepped out, pulling her along behind.

The giant mamba had found the chimp. Even though it was too big for a meal, the snake was preoccupied with inspection. Its tongue stabbed the air, its head flattening cobralike, as it raised six feet of its body off the ground.

The tape didn't stop the woman from talking, only muffled her voice. She said something that sounded like, "Jesus Christ, are you crazy? Don't make me do this."

She wasn't acting now. She was hyperventilating, her eyes locked on the mamba only a few dozen yards away. I'd backed her against the bank of snake cages, which was to the left as you exited the door. She was the first thing Ox-man would see if he peeked out.

I was tempted to say that I'd be crazier to let her, and her partner, go to work on me. Instead, I whispered, "Stick with the plan and you'll be fine." Then I hurried to the other side of the doorway. Flattened my back against the coral wall.

The instructions I'd given her weren't complicated, but I didn't expect her to follow them. If she did, we both had a good chance of surviving this hell hole. If she didn't, I had a plan for that, too.

I could hear Ox-man inside the room. He was kicking rat cages, making sure we weren't hidden among them. Yelling words in Russian that had the rhythm of profanity.

Then silence.

I'd stationed the woman at an angle a few yards from the door so that I had an unobstructed view of her. Hands cuffed, mouth taped, ankles crossed as if bound, she looked convincing — a comrade in distress. Her terrified fixation on the snake added to the effect.

I pressed harder against the wall when I saw the door handle move. I watched the door open an inch . . . another inch. Could see the wire stock of the man's weapon through the hinges. He saw the woman. I heard him speak — an exclamation of surprise, but also anger. I got the impression that he had a reason to be surprised — something in her expression, not only his tone.

For an instant, Dasha looked at me, then looked away.

I had the carton of reptile eggs palmed in my right hand. Had my left hand up and ready as the door opened wider. I expected the woman to pull the tape away and yell a warning to her partner. Nod in my direction, or at least use her eyes to tell the man that he was walking into a trap.

Instead, the woman surprised me. Again.

"PANILA?"
Ox-man's voice grew louder. He was shouting questions. Hopefully, an obvious question: Where's the American? In response, I watched the woman motion to the incubator, and gesture vigorously with her head: He's behind that box, hiding.

Exactly what I'd told her to do.

The door pressed against me as Ox-man took a careful step into the quarry. The barrel of his weapon preceded him. I waited a beat, then grabbed the barrel with my left hand; jerked it skyward, expecting him to fire.

BOOM.

A shotgun's discharge.

In the same motion, I mustered all the torque my legs could produce as I lunged around the door and knocked his head backward with the heel of my open palm. A potentially lethal blow not softened by the plastic carton I held.

"Govnosos!"

He roared the word. Nearly went down but caught himself. Then he used his left hand to paw at the mess of yolk, and shell that was blinding him; used the other to wrestle for control of the gun.

I had a good grip on his right wrist, my thumb buried deep in the soft flesh beneath tendon. To move him away from the open door, I kneed him hard in the thigh. Moved him a few more steps from safety, then clamped my arm over his right elbow. I adjusted to get effective leverage, then let my legs collapse beneath me.

When a hinge joint breaks, it makes a sickening sound. That sound was simultaneous with Ox-man's bawling scream of pain.

The shotgun was on the ground and I gave it a kick — accidentally lofted it in the woman's direction. A mistake.

Ox-man wasn't done. I was. I wanted to send him crashing into the incubator. All those eggs in a pit inhabited by nesting reptiles. The scent of the invader was already dripping down his face. A horrible end for a man who'd done something horrible to a friend.

But even with a broken arm, he was too big and strong to pursue a determined finesse.

I got behind him and levered his left wrist up between his shoulder blades. Pivoted him to face the incubator. Tried to drive him toward it but couldn't get any momentum. He outweighed me by seventy, maybe a hundred, pounds. His heels dug just as hard in opposition.

As we wrestled, I glanced over my shoulder. The giant mamba was giving us her full attention. She was flushed with color, head flattened for attack, the zombie-stitched mouth wide as she shook her head. A striking display. It reminded me of the rattle on a rattlesnake's tail.

She'd already covered half the distance between the dead chimp and us.

I gave Ox-man a last shove. When I felt his legs drive backward in response, I swung him in the opposite direction, and used his momentum to give him a final thrust. An old game: crack-the-whip. I watched him go running, stumbling toward what he thought was freedom.

I continued to watch as I retreated to the door.

Saw Ox-man slow, then stop, when he noticed the snake. They were separated by a few yards, the mamba at eye level. Two creatures with heads of similar size, each studying the other in this unexpected encounter.

Ox-man turned to look at Dasha without moving his body. His face was white, paled by a mix of the inevitable and terror. He tried to cry out but could only whisper, a pleading phrase in Russian. He backed a few steps, then he began to run. Legs churning, left arm pumping. Big man, adrenaline-charged.

The snake lunged after him. Ox-man looked over his shoulder and howled something. I've read that, according to black boxes recovered after plane crashes, the most common last words of doomed pilots are: *"Momma! Momma!"* His words had that childlike quality.

The snake was gaining.

I was only a few strides from the doorway. Glanced to see that the woman had picked up the gun. She held it awkwardly because of the handcuffs, but she was studying her grip, trying to get it into a workable firing position. As I started toward her, she swung the barrel in my direction.

"Drop it!"

I saw her startled reaction when she looked up. She hadn't realized I was sprinting in her direction.

She thrust the weapon out. "Here, take this! Shoot!"

As I took it from her hands, I heard Oxman scream, then scream again. Looked to see that he was down on one knee; the mamba's head a blur as it struck him near the neck once . . . twice . . . a third time.

"Shoot him! Hurry!"

"Shoot *who?*" I thought she meant the snake. The snake was doing what it was born to do. Destroy a creature so highly evolved?

I leaned away as she reached to reclaim the shotgun. I finally understood when she said, "Shoot *Aleski!* He was my partner. A quick death among professionals — he deserves that much."

I saw the snake bury its fangs in the man once again, lingering this time, head sawing for maximum dispersal. Like a fire ant hunkering to inject venom.

Aleski was on the ground, the mamba over him. The king cobra had also now appeared — broad head moving, adjusting its unfocused eyes by varying the distance, perhaps wind-scenting objects as pheromone-distinctive as her own eggs.

As I opened the door, I told Dasha, "Doing favors for your partner wasn't part of our deal."

What I was thinking, though, was *Frieda*.

34

"Do you hear it? That sound. The screaming — he's stopped. The silence, it took a while to register."

The woman asked, "Mr. Sweet?"

"*Who?*"

"Dr. Stokes. Yes, he's stopped screaming. He must be dead. Or Mr. Earl could've knocked him unconscious. That would be his way. That man is very smart, and very sneaky. Him, you cannot trust."

We were standing on a cement bulkhead near the point of land where Ox-man had come ashore. I now understood why the boat couldn't wait. Outside the cut separating the islands, trade winds stacked great volumes of water, compressing it through the narrows like water sprayed from a nozzle. A precept of physics, the "venturi effect": When a liquid or gas is constrained by space, velocity increases.

"Now you can see for yourself why we

have to go by boat. If you swim here, the sea will take you."

I sat on the bulkhead's edge, seeing tropical fish among corals, water clear, a fathom deep. Flashes of red, iridescent gold. "The sea's taken me before. I'm used to it. Keeps me on my toes."

Dasha was to my right, looking absurdly prayerful because of the handcuffs. She'd told me the key was in Stokes's office, didn't know where.

"But I want to go with you. I can call Broz on the intercom, tell him to come for me, then trick him. Or there's a little open boat we could use at the other end of the island. Only a quarter mile away."

I was familiarizing myself with the weapon I'd taken from Ox-man. It wasn't an AK-47, although the appearance was similar. I had to read the stamping on the barrel to refresh my memory. It was a Russian-made combat shotgun. A Saiga-12, with folding stock, stubby full-choke barrel, and a box magazine that held . . . ?

I popped the magazine to check. Counted seven sausage-sized rounds, plus one in the chamber. The ammunition was military issue. Red plastic cartridges produced by Sabot. Waterproof.

I have the same interest in guns that I

have in carpentry tools: zero. I don't use either for pleasure, but there are times when I have no choice. So I keep up on the technology. I knew that these cartridges contained dozens of razor-tipped needles, not pellets. There was a name for them I couldn't remember. Better range and accuracy, more killing power.

I was very glad Ox-man hadn't gotten a clean shot at me.

"Please. We take the boat."

"Nope. What's the point of arriving unannounced if the neighbors know you're coming?" I tapped the magazine on my knee, then locked it into the weapon. The selection lever had three settings: safety, semiautomatic, and automatic three-round bursts. Lethal.

"Why are you being such an *idiot* about this? I want to help you!"

"Because I can't figure out what you have to gain by helping me. You and your pals are going to jail, lady."

"You still don't trust me."

"No."

Her eyes became pale glass. Furious. "But you can't leave me here with all those damn snakes!"

Fitting the shotgun's sling over head and shoulder, I said, "The snakes will just have to fend for themselves until I get back."

I rolled into the water.

The current was racing from southeast to northwest, and I allowed it sweep me along, using my feet and hands like sails to steer.

The main island was to the west: A mansion-sized two-story surrounded by poinciana trees in red bloom, three cottages nearby that I guessed would be staff housing. They looked as if they were made of coral rock. There was also a wide clearing, grass neatly mown, and a helicopter landing pad. I could see that the orange wind sock was fully inflated on its pole — strong northeasterly trade wind. "Christmas wind," it's called by sailors in the Caribbean.

Fitting. I had to think for a moment before deciding that it was the nineteenth of December, a Sunday. Five days before the holiday.

My son would be on his way home. Members of the little floating village that is Dinkin's Bay would be finishing their shopping, then rushing back to the docks in time for sunset. Dewey and Walda would be out among the corn stubble and snow, blasting fast red birds from the sky.

Iowa, Florida, Central America. Dissimilar lives, dissimilar regions, yet all intimate, connected within me.

I kept my eyes on the shoreline as I drifted. I expected to see armed men searching — Dasha had mentioned an intercom system. The water was salt-heavy; warm. I occasionally had to swim sidestroke to adjust my course. I wanted to land at the island's northernmost point. No buildings there. A lonely-looking place of rock, and the bonsai silhouettes of mangrove trees.

The crossing took me less than twenty minutes. I waded ashore over rock and sand, eyes searching a grove of coconut palms for movement. I held the shotgun at waist level, the selector switch on semi-automatic. Or so I thought.

If Dasha had tipped off her pals, I guessed they'd be waiting inside the window of one of the coral structures near the main house. Good protection, excellent field of fire.

I didn't expect to surprise a man who was hidden in the shadows of palms, smoking a cigarette. A big guy, nearly as large as Oxman, with similar Slavic features, and the same bearish black hair.

The woman had mentioned someone named Broz, part of the smuggling ring. One noxious exotic trafficking other noxious exotics.

From his guilty reaction, I got the impression he wasn't supposed to be smoking. But then he realized who I was; recognized the weapon I was carrying — his eyes widening as his brain put it together.

The man then surprised me by producing a pistol, a short-barreled revolver, heavy caliber, nickel plated, with some weight. He brought it up from the shadows and pointed at me so fast, yelling something in Russian, that I reacted without thinking. As I'd been trained to do.

I fired from the waist. A single squeeze of the trigger. I wasn't prepared for a three-round burst, nor the recoil that nearly jarred the shotgun out of my hands.

Broz wasn't prepared, either. No man could be. The blast lifted him off the ground and flung him backward.

I stepped into the smoke and drifting detritus, close enough to see what three direct hits from combat munitions can do to the human body.

Razor-tipped needles. *Arrows.*

Efficient.

I could hear Dasha saying, "A quick death among professionals."

The man had certainly been granted that.

I checked the weapon's selector switch. Saw that I'd accidentally moved it to automatic.

Five rounds left.

I stepped into the gloom of palms and began to jog toward the main house.

A distinguished-looking man told me, "Dr. Stokes, he took his own life. It's very sad. You can see the body, if you want. I can't make you *prove* you have some affiliation with the police. But it's not a nice thing to see."

I'd gone from cottage to cottage. In one of them, I'd found three women and a little boy cowering in a corner, terrified. Otherwise, the cottages were empty.

I'd spent too much time taking the best tactical route to the main house, only to be greeted by this: the bizarre sight of this man sitting on the porch in a rocker. He was wearing a white linen suit, a white panama hat. He had a drink in his hand and a frosty pitcher on the table beside him. A cigarette in an ivory holder.

It looked like he was enjoying Derby Day in the shade of his Lexington mansion.

Very civilized. An articulate gentleman who didn't get upset. *Don't worry, be happy*.

His skin was dusty black. He had a gaunt Abe Lincoln face.

Mr. Luther Earl, Dasha had called him. "He's very mean and sneaky."

There was a quality she'd left out: The man had balls.

When I'd pivoted around the edge of the porch and leaned the shotgun into his face, he'd reacted as if I were a neighbor arriving for cocktails. Not a flicker of fear. The way he handled it told me the guy was used to dealing with cops and bag guys.

Big smile. "Oh . . . hello! Would you like a *mojito?* Mint and rum, with lots of ice. It's what we drink down here on the islands. They're very refreshing, Dr. Ford."

"Dr. Ford, huh? You know my name."

"Those thugs that Dr. Stokes made the mistake of hiring, a woman and her partners. Russian Mafia. They told me they caught you trying to steal some kind of formula from us and had to lock you up. But I'm smart" — that smile again — "I snuck a look at your billfold. You got the credit cards, the cash. You're a Ph.D.! It's those damn Russians working some kind of con, again. Dr. Stokes was going to fire them all."

The man surprised me by removing my cell phone and billfold from the inside pocket of his jacket. He leaned and place them on the porch railing. The impression was that he'd been sitting, waiting on me.

"My credit cards are here, but the cash is missing. I had a gold Krugerrand in the inside pocket. That's gone, too."

Mr. Earl appeared saddened. "It's a dangerous world, Dr. Ford. I warned you about them Russians. Very typical."

Innocent. I spent a moment calculating how much he had stolen from me, then stepped onto the porch and positioned myself in the doorway to his right and slightly behind him, weapon at belt level. I kept an eye on the stairway inside the house, a nearby line of avocado trees to the south, and the boat landing, which was beyond the helipad, at the water's edge.

Rounding the point of the island where I'd left Dasha, I could see two cutter-sized boats coming fast. They were military green, .50 caliber machine guns on the bow, radar antennas scanning. I also saw an open boat that looked like a Boston whaler, a blond female at the wheel.

When Mr. Earl noticed the cutters, his mood brightened. "That's the Bahamian Coast Guard finally getting here," he said. "I called them more than an hour ago. Asked for helicopters, but that's what they send. We got a serious problem here that needs taken care of."

Those damn Russians needed to be arrested, he told me, because Dr. Desmond Stokes was dead.

"What they done to him caused it," he said. "That bitch of a woman. She got me, too. Here, see for yourself."

I watched the man stand, find his balance, and walk toward me. I realized he was very drunk. As he neared, I smelled the overpowering odor of lavender. It touched one of the memory synapses. Last night, when they'd kidnapped me — the stink of lavender. Luther Earl was there.

"Looka this." He was pulling up his sleeve. "Want to see what that split-tail's done to every man on the islands?"

There was a bandage on his forearm. I knew what would be there before he lifted the gauze: the pointed white scolex, or head, of a guinea worm struggling to exit.

"I got two more coming out of my leg. Can you imagine doing something so awful to people? It was a *woman*."

I said, "I met her. You locked us in the same cell — or maybe you forgot. We had an interesting talk this morning."

For an instant, the cheery façade vanished, and I got a snapshot of the real Mr. Earl. Mr. Nasty. "You *know* where that bitch is? We never locked her up, but, man oh man, I'd sure like to. Last night, she got in the room with Dr. Stokes, then run away and let all our research animals loose.

Which was smart, I've got to admit, 'cause then no one would go look for her. Staff was so scared, we won't be able to get them back here for a month."

The man was a superb liar — my guess. But I didn't think he was lying now.

He'd recognized the shotgun immediately. Played it cool, though. Waited until this moment to gesture to it. "Looks like you met Aleski, too. Better be careful if he comes back here. The man's a bad one."

His question was implicit. I decided to answer.

"Aleski was busy playing fetch with the local pets the last time I saw him."

"You don't say?" Mr. Earl liked that. "Wouldn't bother me at all to find out him and the woman was both dead. Whoever did it, I'd think the man deserves a reward. Privatelike." The guy was drunk but managed to underline the offer with innuendo. "I heard that you knew Dr. Applebee. That you might know something about a cure he invented for these damn worms. Could be, there's all kinds a money I'd be happy to pay you. If you're a businessman, the smart kind interested in making a deal."

I replied, "Seems like everyone on the islands wants to make a deal. It makes a stranger feel important. We can talk." I

515

glanced to my right: the Coast Guard cutters were closing in. I didn't want to be here when they arrived. "But first, I need to confirm that Stokes is dead."

"That's the sort of thing a cop says. Confirm so-and-so's done this or that."

"Being sleepy makes me rude. We didn't leave Florida until — what? — after midnight?"

Mr. Earl was shaking his head tolerantly. Said, "No, we left hours before —," then caught himself. His mean eyes acknowledged his slip. *Okay, you caught me. So what?*

"That's something else a cop does. Tricks innocent people for no reason."

I didn't respond.

That's when the man told me I could see the body if I wanted.

"I've got to ask you not to touch anything," he said, leading the way into the house. "Desmond Stokes was my dearest friend. He *appreciated* what I did for him. That's why he left the place to me. People been stealing from this island all morning, even though I keep telling them: I own everything you see."

35

Desmond Stokes was sitting sprawled behind a desk in an office that had been ransacked, his head back, eyes open, mouth stretched wide in the pantomime of a scream. One hand was visible. On it was a cotton glove stained black with his own blood. His forearm and face were gray. Wasp nest gray. Dry.

His body had been drained of fluid.

"See? Here's what I told you. The man took his own life, but it was murder, the way the woman done it. Take a look for your own self. You'll understand what I'm saying."

I looked at Earl, and motioned once again: *Stay where I can see you.* I walked to the desk.

Stokes had worn green surgical scrubs, but was now naked below the waist. It took me a moment to confirm that his pants had been tossed into the corner. The chair was pushed away from the desk so that his legs and feet were visible.

The gentleman in white linen was correct. Not nice.

Stokes had scrawny legs, no muscle tone. His skin was the same bloodless color of his face, but the flesh of both legs was alive with animated, parasitic activity. For a man who was a phobic neurotic, it would have been the ultimate horror.

Perhaps that's why someone had used duct tape to lash the doctor's wrists to the chair's armrests, to protect the patient from self-inflicted injury.

Possibly, though, they'd done it to add to his torment.

But, somehow, Stokes had wrestled his right hand free, and found a surgical scalpel . . .

I paused to think about that. No . . . it wasn't plausible. Even crazed with adrenaline, this man didn't have the strength.

I squatted beside the chair for a closer look. Saw that the tape had been cut cleanly. Looked beneath the desk — nothing sharp, or saw-edged. It told me that someone had used the scalpel to cut the tape. Then they'd handed the instrument to the hysterical Dr. Stokes. A ruthless irony.

The scalpel was similar to one of many I

keep in my lab — a German-manufactured, one-inch blade. It was now buried into the dead man's thigh. The last of many dozens of stab wounds between ankles and groin. His legs were a checkerwork of contusions. They'd drained the life out of him.

Earl was correct. Murder, in its way.

"The doctor hated germs. Been fighting them all his life. When he couldn't take it no more, I guess he used that little knife and went to war with them one more time, trying kill them as they come out."

"Who taped his arms to the chair?"

"I did. We were going through some paperwork last night when the man lost it. I was afraid he'd hurt himself. I went off to take a leak, and that's when that Russian bitch locked herself in the room with him." Mr. Earl had theatrical sensibilities. He knew how to communicate both sorrow and anger with a single sigh.

I stood. As with Jobe Applebee's body, I chose not to linger on detail. I crossed the room to a wall lined with books, a microscope, jars of things that must be preserved in formaldehyde. Personal libraries have themes, usually unrealized by owners. This was the library of a physician who specialized in nutrition, real estate, and investment finance. He also had a researcher's interest in the chemical properties of animal venoms. More telling, though, were rows of books on abnormal psychology, deviant behavior, chemical imbalances of the human brain, sexual dysfunction.

The physician knew he was sick, but that hadn't altered his behavior.

I began to leaf through a stack of magazines. Luther Earl stood blocking an open window. I moved slightly to get a better view of the water. Coast Guard cutters were slowing as they neared the boat landing. Dasha had already docked the Boston whaler and was nearly to the porch. She was no longer handcuffed, I noticed.

Not a surprise.

I placed the shotgun on a nearby table, barrel pointed at the open door where the woman would soon appear, then tilted my head listening to an approaching rumble. The sound of a helicopter?

Yes.

It wasn't a Huey. Didn't sound like Coast Guard.

Very soon, I'd have to disappear. Mr. Earl seemed to sense it. He began to show signs of nerves for the first time.

"Do you understand what I'm telling you? The woman poisoned our water with these damn worms, then she gave the doctor a knife, knowing he'd gone crazy enough to use it. She's a *murderer*. Going to fucking jail in Nassau. Which is why the person you need to be discussing the formula with is me. Not her."

My remark about making deals had stuck. I said, "What formula?"

"The one that was on Applebee's computer! He figured out how to get rid of these parasites in Florida, Africa. Name it, man! You really don't know."

"Do you have the computer? I'll have a look."

No. I could read it in his face. He didn't have the computer. Presumably, Dasha had gotten away with that, too.

"Doesn't matter if I have it or not, because the man used numbers instead of letters when he wrote. But I saw the file labels. There were words he used over and over. 'Eradicate.' 'Cope-ee-pods'?"

I smiled, secretly pleased. Was it possible that Applebee and I had come up with the same solution independently?

" 'Copepods,' " I said. "In that case, I do know the formula."

That pleased him. His eyes glittered.

On a shelf, I'd found a box of copies of a recent *Rolling Stone* article — familiar, thanks to Tomlinson — and several old counterculture magazines. Each had an inside page marked with a paper clip. I opened one. Found nothing obvious. Opened another, and smiled again. Looked at it for a moment before saying to Luther Earl, "Nice picture of you. Twenty years ago, maybe? Love the ammo belts. You haven't changed much. Except for your hair. And your name."

Mr. Earl said, "Sometimes it's good for a man to change his name. Gives you a real free and clean feeling. Down the road, you may want to consider it."

I read silently for a moment. "Sounds like you changed your ethics, too. Unless you were just as full of bullshit back then. What the hell's 'Aquarian numerology,' and how do you become an expert on it?"

The tall man beamed. "It *was* bullshit, man. But it's the fool crap people want to believe. Can't miss. Just like the deal I'm offering you." He took a step from the window, hands out, big smile telling me that I'd be joining a winner. "I'll form a limited liability corporation, give you forty percent of the stock. Forty-*five* percent. In trade, you share Applebee's formula. Tell me this" — his hands moved as if to create a stage — "how much will real estate in the Disney

World area be worth when owners start finding these fucking worms eating their skin? If we've got an exclusive on the formula, and we buy the land for nothing —"

He stopped. We'd both heard a noise in the hallway. I still had the shotgun leveled at the open door. Now I reached, checked the selector switch — semiauto — then touched my finger to the trigger. Waited for Dasha to appear.

A moment later, I heard a soft mewing coming from outside the window. Then a whispered "Mr. Earl?"

th-WHAP.

The rim-shot blast of a heavy-caliber handgun is definitive. My brain identified the noise as I ducked away from the doorway, the pepper odor of gunpowder blooming, both hands on the shotgun, aware that Earl's head had disintegrated in the same instant that his body collapsed beneath it.

Where the hell was she?

To my left, Dasha's voice yelled: "Ford! Toss your weapon toward the door. A *long* way away. Don't be an idiot."

She sounded calm. She appeared at the window in a classic combat stance, both hands holding a revolver that was pointed at my chest.

I hesitated . . . no options. I pushed the shotgun away, cringing reflexively as the weapon hit the floor, wondering how she'd created the noise in the hallway. Was there another open window? Toss a rock, then sprint? She had the speed.

"Lock your fingers behind your head and drop to your knees. Do it!"

I felt sick. Stupid.

From my knees, I watched her step through the window into the room. I thought the revolver might waver for a moment. It didn't. She wore the same khaki shorts and blouse, but now carried a canvas purse over her shoulder. She also wore surgical gloves.

She took a quick look at Earl. Shot in the head at close range, there was no doubt he was dead. Then she scrambled to the shotgun. "Did you fire this? I heard a burst."

I said nothing.

"Goddamn it, I'm trying to help. Did you kill Broz?"

I said, "Somebody killed somebody. I saw a body."

She translated. "Good. You got two of them. I don't think I could have taken all three myself. Aleski — he was the most dangerous. He knew my moves."

I could hear myself earlier telling the woman that she had nothing to gain in helping me — *wrong*. Now I understood. She'd needed muscle. I'd provided it.

Luther Earl had told me the truth. She'd freed the snakes to keep searchers at bay, then hid in my cell.

"The key to the handcuffs. Where'd you keep it?"

She replied, "In my mouth. I was afraid you'd catch on and frisk me."

I watched her take a cloth and begin to scrub the shotgun's exterior, erasing my fingerprints.

"Instead of going to all that trouble, why didn't you just tell me what you wanted?"

She paused to glare at me. "Would you have done it?"

Of course not. A pointless question.

She added, "Unless you make it seem like their idea, most men are too stupid to understand anything. When Aleski showed up, though, I thought we were both dead."

I watched her stand, step to the window, and toss the shotgun into the bushes. With no wasted motion, she knelt beside the body of Luther Earl and squeezed the revolver into his left hand.

I started to speak but she cut me off. "He

was left-handed. Do you take me for a fool?"

She gave the scene a last, critical sweep as she snapped off the surgical gloves. Would authorities read it as she intended? Mr. Earl's dear friend, Dr. Stokes, had died horribly, so he'd committed suicide out of grief — and, perhaps, guilt.

"Follow me. Keep your mouth shut and they probably won't question you. But Bahamian feds can be assholes no matter how much bribe money they're paid."

I stood, feeling ridiculous. But was also relieved. I'd assumed she was going to kill me. Sphincter muscles are barometers of the elemental. Mine began to relax. Tentatively.

I followed her through the hallway, toward the main entrance. I was shirtless, bruised, and filthy. The *whopa-whopa-whopa* of a helicopter was shaking the house. I had to raise my voice to ask, "When the Coast Guard starts asking questions, what's my role? How are we going to work it?"

Dasha stopped, turned. From the canvas bag, she took a sheaf of papers and held them up for inspection. "The only role you have here is to do what I tell you. Dr. Stokes signed title of his property over to me in exchange for Applebee's computer files. Which I gave him. I cut the tape on his arm and handed him a pen. The doctor . . . seemed very eager to trade."

"You handed him a pen, and . . . what else?"

"I gave him what he asked for."

Did she mean the scalpel?

The woman continued toward the door. My instincts told me to bolt in the opposite direction, but she dragged me along as if caught in a weird force field. "These papers are witnessed by Dr. Stokes's *late* administrative assistant, and notarized by a Nassau judge. A good woman; respected. The Bahamian cops aren't going to ask many questions once they find out I'm the new owner. They depend on landowners for bribes. But, Ford?"

Dasha was stepping onto the porch into the sun, the green of tropic foliage melding with the jade of Caribbean Sea beyond. A mild smile changed the feral contours of her cheeks, as iceberg eyes took in all that heat and light. "If you ever do want to play a role? Come back and stay a few days." She faced me. "Last night, on the plane? Maybe you had an interesting dream. *Fun*. Between professionals. It could be like that."

I was grateful for the noise of the helicopter hovering above us because I was afraid to answer. The woman scared me. I focused on the aircraft, as if I hadn't heard.

The copter wasn't local Coast Guard. It was a U.S. special ops chopper used to ferry commandos into tight spots, a "Little Bird." The cockpit was a Plexiglas bubble attached to a fuselage bristling with miniguns, rocket tubes, antennas, and infrared sensors.

Withering firepower, plus speed.

The craft displayed no markings, which I found odd. It had to be American.

Dasha stood her ground, as ropes were deployed, and four men wearing body armor and masks fast-roped down, weapons already shouldered: two submachine guns aimed at her, two .50 caliber machine guns covering the cutters. The helicopter then rotated a few degrees so that its rocket tubes communicated an unmistakable message to the Bahamians: Interfere, we'll open fire.

The chopper ascended, touched earth tentatively, then settled. It was then I realized why the aircraft was operating clean, no ID. In the doorway, Hal Harrington appeared looking like a corporate executive, in gray suit, gray tie.

How the hell did he know I was on the island?

The intelligence chief swung out of the fuselage, a black SIG-Sauer held vertical to his leg, concealing it. He stayed low, taking long strides, then stood. At the same time, he pointed the handgun at Dasha.

The Little Bird was maintaining rpms. Harrington had to yell over the noise. "Ford! You okay?"

I nodded, aware that he was assessing my condition. Not good.

"Do you have more business here?" Harrington was looking at Dasha, weapon still aimed. The two had locked eyes. I got the impression the woman saw something in the man that scared her. Her cheek, I noticed, had begun to twitch. She *was* capable of emotion.

I yelled, "I'm clear. Let's load up and move. Get our feet wet." Meaning, let's get over the water.

When we were airborne, I'd tell him about the barge carrying the drone helicopters. Harrington's decision. Order Little Bird to sink them or let the FBI deal with it.

I walked toward the chopper, but stopped when I realized Harrington wasn't following me. The fire team wasn't going to budge until their boss was safely aboard.

"Hal? Do we have a problem?"

He still had the weapon aimed at the blonde. "Who is this woman? Are you sure you don't need more ground time?" The man had great instincts. And he probably already knew who she was.

I said, "It's the woman who owns this island, Hal. We're leaving. My call."

Slowly, the man lowered the SIG-Sauer. Turned, gave me a bitter glance — *You owe me, pal* — and ducked toward the chopper, done with her.

Dasha moved her eyes to mine. I shrugged: *We have a deal.* Then climbed aboard, determined not to look back.

The troop seating in the Little Bird helicopter was cramped, the interior dark except for red tactical lighting, and the green sweep of radar screens. I slid into the nearest seat, aware of an odd odor among the familiar smells of diesel, graphite, and webbing.

Patchouli?

The four members of the fire team were boarding, and I heard one of them mutter, "I swear to God, skipper, I'd rather stay here with the bandits. That fucking hippie's perfume makes me gag."

A familiar, indignant voice replied, "For your information, officer, it's not perfume. It's *fragrance*. I'd explain the difference, but

I'm not allowed to speak."

"*Officer?* The guy still thinks we're fucking cops. What planet's he from?"

The familiar voice said, "*Exactly.* There's an interesting topic for the flight home. Regression to previous lives — don't let your hostile cop natures fool you. It's *waiting* out there."

My eyes were still adjusting, which is why I recognized the voice before I recognized the familiar man across from me: goatee, stringy surfer's hair, and still wearing hospital scrubs.

We both banged our heads on the low ceiling when we stood. "*Tomlinson?* What the hell are you doing here?" "With Harrington," I didn't add.

He replied, "Sorry, can't answer. Your friends have rebuked me, Marion. On the flight over, Hal told me I wasn't allowed to talk until we got back to Florida." Laughing, we pounded each other on the back, then I listened to a rushed explanation: The note I'd left at hospital reception said to call Harrington if I didn't return. Jason Reynolds, the Tropicane biologist, had escaped his kidnapper, telephoned Tomlinson, and provided key information — a hero. The fish died . . .

"And so did you, Doc. Your heart

stopped. Dead for ten or twenty minutes. Ask that pretty Indian doctor! I had to take a brief leave of absence myself. Did a deep space intercept — which is a damn dangerous thing to do when you're all screwed up on sevoflurane. Morphine, on the other hand, is the drug of choice under those circumstances. I'm perfectly capable of operating at full capacity with a snoot full of morphine —"

"Enough! Not another word!" The helicopter's shocks adjusted to Harrington's weight as he slid into the copilot's seat, then closed the door. "Ford, I am holding you personally responsible. I just did you a favor, damn it. Now it's your turn."

He glanced over his shoulder to make certain he had my attention. "You hired this man, I'll pay him. I'll even read his product, if you think it's good. But, commander, if he begins another talking jag about soul travel, or the earth as a single-celled organism, or a catfish he says swam up his penis, I swear to Christ I will open the door, jump out of this helicopter, and take that irritating son of a bitch with me."

I'd never heard Harrington so flummoxed.

"The only time he wouldn't talk is when he refused to tell me your location. Not unless he could tag along. So that's why he's here. But never again, Ford. Never again."

Harrington fixed me with a fierce look.

"Don't think this changes anything."

I didn't.

The helicopter lifted skyward, rotated, then banked. Tomlinson looked at me, grinning. Closed his lips tight, locked them with an imaginary key, and threw the key away. He didn't realize it, but he had no reason to be happy.

I'd accepted a truce that was only temporary. Maybe I could leverage it into something. A bargain with Harrington down the road. Maybe . . .

I looked through the window. Below, the Russian woman grew smaller, as her islands filled the glass, green mountain peaks anchored in deep ocean.

I expected her to wave farewell. Told myself I would ignore her if she did.

She didn't.

epilogue

On a balmy, tropic-scented January evening, fifty miles off the coast of Cuba, aboard the *Queen Mary 2* — the world's fastest, most luxurious ocean liner, according to its own literature — I hugged the woman as she entered our stateroom, and kissed her cocoa brown cheek.

I said to her, "You gave him the message?" I was wearing a white tuxedo; had been fitted that morning by the ship's tailor. It was the first tux I'd ever owned. Maybe the first tux I'd ever worn. I wondered about that as I used a full-length mirror to straighten my red bow tie.

She laced her arm through mine affectionately. "He's below on second deck, gambling. Playing blackjack at the hundred-dollar-minimum table. A big crowd."

"He's winning tonight?"

She answered, "Yeah. But he hasn't met you yet."

I smiled.

"Does he cheat?"

The woman had told me she knew what to watch for.

"At cards, *probably* — if security wasn't so good. Does he cheat on his mistress? Definitely. He said he'd meet me on the promenade deck. Forward, where the ship's superstructure will provide some cover. At the outboard railing."

Just as I'd instructed.

The woman was dressed in gold: a glittering, full-length gown that clung to incremental curves, long legs, narrow waist, breasts. The gown accented her height, and her beauty. Added a regal countenance.

The *QM2* does that. Its own regal history elevates passengers through association.

Prior to the voyage, I'd only seen the woman in the common informal dress of the tropics. I realized that she was stunning.

I said, "My guess is, he'll show."

She began unbuttoning her gown. I turned my back as a courtesy, even though she'd already told me it wasn't necessary. Ten days spent island-hopping, Lauderdale to Panama, is a long time to preserve modesty, even if we were sharing a plush suite. "That man's the touchy-feely type. Fingers on my butt, feeling for my bra strap, letting me know he knows where things are. Sweet talker. He told me every woman in the islands should look like me. He'll be there. Midnight sharp."

I checked my watch: 11:25 p.m.

I nodded, looking into her unusual eyes. "Things seem to be going as planned. Thanks to you."

She stepped closer, and rested both hands on my shoulders. "Be careful; come back quick. I know you're good at what you do, but he's big. Got that nasty 'screw you' look about him." Something was hidden in her hand, and she pressed it into mine.

A gold coin.

I looked at it. Looked at her, amused by her craftiness.

"For luck," the woman said.

I went out the door.

I felt nervous. I'd done this sort of thing once before, but never aboard a ship as well appointed as the *Queen Mary 2*. She is the length of three football fields, as tall as a Lauderdale condo, and packed with every high-tech amenity — including electronic surveillance on each deck.

If that wasn't sufficiently daunting, I'd learned at the Captain's Ball (by personal invitation only) that ship's security was maintained by the *Queen*'s own Gurkhas —

Nepalese mercenaries who are among the most feared commandos on Earth.

It was not an exaggeration, as I knew. I'd worked with them long ago in Southeast Asia, Hong Kong, and Belize. Small, dark men who never unsheathe their oddly shaped knives — kukris — without drawing blood. If Great Britain ever withdraws the Gurkhas from Belize, Guatemala will take control of that marijuana-dazed country within a week.

Yes, daunting. Which is why I'd spent the previous three days doing reconnaissance of my own, scouting for the right spot, calculating the right time.

I was now as ready as I would ever be. Thanks to the woman. But also nervous.

I had half an hour to burn. I considered going below to watch the man gamble, but decided it was unnecessarily risky to let security video capture me in the same room with him so close to midnight.

Instead, I jogged up a carpeted staircase a few decks to the ship's library. I walked among burled maple stacks, an articulate place for books, into a room appointed with brass and polished mahogany. I sat at a computer, signed onto the Internet.

Among the many e-mails was one from my son. The subject heading was: "You should have told me."

For the first time in days, I wasn't fixated on this midnight rendezvous.

I opened Lake's letter. Leaned and scanned it for what I'd been waiting to receive: the results of the paternity test he'd ordered. I read the letter again, then a third time much more slowly. It touched on two important topics, including the test results.

The first few graphs explained a document that was attached. My son had cracked Jobe Applebee's code. It wasn't difficult, he said, once he deciphered the pattern Applebee used to avoid repetition.

"Number 4 is the key," Lake wrote. "His documents were a confusing pain in the butt until I remembered Dr. Matthews's e-mail. She said Dr. Applebee considered 4 to be the only true number because it has four letters. That was a start. I tried shifting the numbers 1 through 26 four letters to the right of the alphabet. 1 was *D*, 2 became *E*. It worked! But only for the first paragraph — and every fourth paragraph after that."

Lake soon figured out that after each paragraph, Applebee shifted the numerical key four more letters. After four paragraphs, though, he returned to the original pattern: 1 represented *D*, 2 became *E*.

One of the attachments was labeled: "Selecting Copepod Hybrids to Control Guinea Worms."

I could hear the voice of my much-missed friend, Frieda Matthews, telling me that her brother and I had more in common than I realized.

An amazing little man. I regretted never meeting him.

As interesting as that was, though, I was far more concerned with what Lake had written about the paternity test.

I lingered on his last few sentences.

You could have told me, even though I probably wouldn't have listened. Only a compulsive freak for accuracy would order this test when two great guys like you and Tomlinson are the men in question. A compulsive accuracy freak — someone like you.

I'm sure you recognized the genetic traits. I should've. But now we know for sure. I'm a pretty happy guy, Dad. No offense to Tomlinson . . .

I had a great big grin on my face as I read it over and over.

The news from Lake was especially welcome because I'd spent Christmas in Iowa. The visit could have gone worse, but not much worse.

Three adults in a two-bedroom farmhouse, snowdrifts, wind and freezing weather outside. The first night, huddled near the fire, Dewey's Romanian girlfriend, Bets, had made it clear that they'd renewed their relationship, and that she planned to be at the bedside when Dewey's child was born.

"Our child," I'd corrected her, looking to my old friend, workout partner, and former lover for reassurance.

It wasn't offered.

Bets was in a mood to argue. I didn't press it.

Anyone who invites emotional meltdowns is a fool. The same is true of a man or woman who burns a bridge and forever separates from the partner they once treasured.

I assumed a role: supportive friend of two old friends who were embarking on a new, exciting chapter in their lives. Each afternoon near sunset, I found relief from the tension that filled the house by walking along the Mississippi River. Frozen paths, black trees.

I was envious of the direction that water flowed beneath its mask of ice.

"You'll always be the girl's father," Dewey told me before I drove away in my rental. Walda had nodded her head in agreement. I gave each woman a hug, and touched my fingers to Dewey's belly, wondering if I would ever see any of them again.

Thinking of Christmas changed my mood.

I checked my watch: 11:51 p.m.

At midnight, I was standing on the promenade deck, in shadows near the bow, my tuxedo jacket flapping in gale winds created by a ship traveling at thirty-plus miles an hour through Caribbean darkness.

I was on the starboard side, looking west. Cuba was on the horizon, not many miles away. The last of the Bahamas, too. Cay Sal Bank. Ragged Cays. Islands adrift beneath a husk of copper moon, and six star-bright planets evenly spaced among a riot of stars.

Seven planets, not six, I decided, if I counted the ship.

I did.

Isolated lights marked isolated islands, some joined by darkness, others set apart. The woman, and her islands, came to mind. Dasha had somehow found my Internet address and sent me a note that was troubling, and suggestive. But it also contained a satisfying revelation. She'd been doing some reading. She didn't realize it took guinea worms a year to hatch, and it had only been seven months since "someone" had contaminated their water supply.

"Applebee must have had the same idea months before. He did it first. Never piss off an autistic, I guess."

Snakes, she added, continued to be a problem. She hinted that she wouldn't mind a break from her own isolation.

"Snakes are always a problem," I'd replied.

True.

A sentence fragment came to mind. Words of a respected friend.

There's only one safe haven for guys like us. Only one home we will ever know . . .

The same good man, who, on a rainy jungle night, helped me craft a precept that began: "In any conflict, the boundaries of behavior are defined by those who value morality least . . ."

It was something to think about until I heard: "Excuse me!"

A man's voice startled me from the shadows of the bow. A large man with an accent. He brushed by, his shoulder touching mine, even though there was plenty of room to pass. An aggressive signal.

He took a place at the railing, also too close. Checked his watch as I checked mine.

12:14 a.m.

I moved away a few feet, conceding the space. He obviously wanted me to disappear.

The man was wearing a white tux that was as well tailored as my own. His black hair was groomed back, oiled to a sheen. He wore a diver's watch on a heavy silver bracelet, a single ring on his pinkie finger.

In a cheery, midwestern voice, I said, "Nice night, huh? Have you tried one of them rum punches? Really *good.*"

The man turned his head away. Didn't bother to grunt.

I gave it a few seconds. "You waiting for somebody?"

He looked at me. Used his eyes to communicate contempt. Looked away.

I checked the promenade deck. Empty, both directions. Leaned to get a look at decks beneath, water flowing by seven stories below.

A few people visible, but it couldn't be helped.

Moved a half step closer to him as I said, "Me, I'm waiting on a woman. Beautiful woman, wore a gold evening gown tonight. She told me to meet her here. But she's late."

Abu Sayyaf, the Islamic disciple who'd help plan a train bombing in Madrid, and who was now developing a plan to bomb school buses, turned slowly to face me. "A woman in gold? With very dark skin?"

I'd taken the gold coin from my pocket. Flipped it into the air, caught it. Flipped it again. "That's right! How'd you know?"

Sayyaf could also use laughter to communicate contempt. He was laughing now. "You must be the jealous husband she mentioned. Were you spying on her? Of course, why else would you be here?" He waved his hand, dismissing me. "Tell your wife she had her chance but blew it." Once again his eyes followed the coin as I flipped it into the air.

As if shocked, I said to him, "*Wife?* That's not my wife, mister. I'd trust that woman with my life, but we're not married —"

I flipped the coin a last time. Flipped it so that it spun high, but too far out over the water for me to reach. Sayyaf had quick hands but bad instincts. He threw both hands outboard and leaned to snag it.

I'd already dropped to one knee for maximum leverage. I locked my arms around his thighs, buried the side of my head into his short ribs, using neck muscles to turn his back to the sea. Battled briefly for hand control, as Sayyaf hyperventilated, slowed by the shock of what was happening. Remained stiff, almost resigned, as I squat-lifted his weight off the deck and vaulted him over the railing. Only then did he become animated, hands clawing at darkness to impede his fall, his body shrinking as he descended toward black water, falling at the same speed as the golden coin — a voodoo charm the lady had handed me for luck.

I stood, waited for a moment, then walked calmly to the ship's port side, sensitive to reverse thrust of engines, or security alarms, comforted by the knowledge that a black ops helicopter was shadowing us in case, I, too, had to vanish into the safety of midnight water.

Nothing.

I straightened my white tuxedo jacket, looked at my watch — 12:33 a.m. — then headed downstairs toward the champagne bar to meet my much-trusted cabinmate for a drink. Ransom Gatrell, an island woman who was gorgeous in gold, said that she'd be expecting me. . . .

About the Author

Randy Wayne White is the author of eleven previous Doc Ford novels — *The Heat Islands, Sanibel Flats, The Man Who Invented Florida, Captiva, North of Havana, The Mangrove Coast, Ten Thousand Islands, Shark River, Twelve Mile Limit, Everglades*, and the *New York Times*–bestselling *Tampa Burn* — and of the non-fiction collections *Batfishing in the Rainforest, The Sharks of Lake Nicaragua, Last Flight Out*, and *An American Traveler*. A veteran fishing guide, he lives in an old house on an Indian mound in Pineland, Florida. White can be found on the Internet at www.docford.com

The employees of Thorndike Press hope you have enjoyed this Large Print book. All our Thorndike and Wheeler Large Print titles are designed for easy reading, and all our books are made to last. Other Thorndike Press Large Print books are available at your library, through selected bookstores, or directly from us.

For information about titles, please call:

(800) 223-1244

or visit our Web site at:

www.gale.com/thorndike
www.gale.com/wheeler

To share your comments, please write:

Publisher
Thorndike Press
295 Kennedy Memorial Drive
Waterville, ME   04901